PENGUIN BOOKS

A HOME AT THE END OF THE WORLD

Michael Cunningham's novels include *Golden States*, *Flesh and Blood*, *Specimen Days* and *The Hours*. *The Hours* won the 1999 Pen/Faulkner Award and the 1999 Pulitzer Prize, and in 2002 was made into an acclaimed film. Michael Cunningham's most recent novel is *By Nightfall*. He lives in New York.

SWANSEA LIBRARIES

6000253581

Michael Cunningham

A Home at the End of the World

PENGUIN BOOKS

PENGUIN BOOKS

Published by the Penguin Group
Penguin Books Ltd, 80 Strand, London WC2R ORL, England
Penguin Group (USA) Inc., 375 Hudson Street, New York, New York 10014, USA
Penguin Group (Canada), 90 Eglinton Avenue East, Suite 700, Toronto, Ontario, Canada M4P 2Y3
(a division of Pearson Penguin Canada Inc.)
Penguin Ireland, 25 St Stephen's Green, Dublin 2, Ireland (a division of Penguin Books Ltd)
Penguin Group (Australia), 250 Camberwell Road,
Camberwell, Victoria 3124, Australia (a division of Pearson Australia Group Pty Ltd)
Penguin Books India Pvt Ltd, 11 Community Centre,
Panchsheel Park, New Delhi – 110 017, India
Penguin Group (NZ), 67 Apollo Drive, Rosedale, Auckland 0632, New Zealand
(a division of Pearson New Zealand Ltd)
Penguin Books (South Africa) (Pty) Ltd, 24 Sturdee Avenue,
Rosebank, Johannesburg 2196, South Africa

Penguin Books Ltd, Registered Offices: 80 Strand, London WC2R ORL, England

www.penguin.com

First published in the USA by Farrar, Straus & Giroux, New York 1990
First published in Penguin Books 1991
Reissued in this edition 2012

003

Copyright © Michael Cunningham, 1990
All rights reserved

The moral right of the author has been asserted

Two chapters of this book appeared in earlier form in the *New Yorker*

Acknowledgements for permission to reprint previously published material appear on page 344,
which constitutes an extension of this copyright page

Printed in England by Clays Ltd, St Ives plc

Except in the United States of America, this book is sold subject
to the condition that it shall not, by way of trade or otherwise, be lent,
re-sold, hired out, or otherwise circulated without the publisher's
prior consent in any form of binding or cover other than that in
which it is published and without a similar condition including this
condition being imposed on the subsequent purchaser

ISBN: 978-0-241-95453-9

www.greenpenguin.co.uk

Penguin Books is committed to a sustainable
future for our business, our readers and our planet.
This book is made from Forest Stewardship
Council™ certified paper.

This book is for Ken Corbett

The Poem That Took
the Place of a Mountain

There it was, word for word,
The poem that took the place of a mountain.

He breathed in its oxygen,
Even when the book lay turned in the dust of his table.

It reminded him how he had needed
A place to go to in his own direction,

How he had recomposed the pines,
Shifted the rocks and picked his way among clouds,

For the outlook that would be right,
Where he would be complete in an unexplained completion:

The exact rock where his inexactnesses
Would discover, at last, the view toward which they had edged,

Where he could lie and, gazing down at the sea,
Recognize his unique and solitary home.

—WALLACE STEVENS

A Home at the End of the World was started during hard times. By the date of its completion – nearly six years later – things had eased somewhat. For those more comfortable circumstances I thank the National Endowment for the Arts and the *New Yorker*.

I must reserve the bulk of my gratitude, though, for several friends whose generosity literally rescued this book during its early phases, when encouragement, shelter, and even a working typewriter were sometimes hard to find. Thanks, with love, to Judith E. Turtz, Donna Lee, Cristina Thorson, and Rob and Dale Cole.

Also of immeasurable help were Jonathan Galassi, Gail Hochman, Sarah Metcalf, Anne Rumsey, Avery Russell, Lore Segal, Roger Straus, the Yaddo Corporation and, as always, my family.

PART I

PART I

BOBBY

ONCE our father bought a convertible. Don't ask me. I was five. He bought it and drove it home as casually as he'd bring a gallon of rocky road. Picture our mother's surprise. She kept rubber bands on the doorknobs. She washed old plastic bags and hung them on the line to dry, a string of thrifty tame jellyfish floating in the sun. Imagine her scrubbing the cheese smell out of a plastic bag on its third or fourth go-round when our father pulls up in a Chevy convertible, used but nevertheless—a moving metal landscape, chrome bumpers and what looks like acres of molded silver car-flesh. He saw it parked downtown with a For Sale sign and decided to be the kind of man who buys a car on a whim. We can see as he pulls up that the manic joy has started to fade for him. The car is already an embarrassment. He cruises into the driveway with a frozen smile that matches the Chevy's grille.

Of course the car has to go. Our mother never sets foot. My older brother Carlton and I get taken for one drive. Carlton is ecstatic. I am skeptical. If our father would buy a car on a street corner, what else might he do? Who does this make him?

He takes us to the country. Roadside stands overflow with apples. Pumpkins shed their light on farmhouse lawns. Carlton, wild with excitement, stands up on the front seat and has to be pulled back down. I help. Our father grabs Carlton's beaded cowboy

3

belt on one side and I on the other. I enjoy this. I feel useful, helping to pull Carlton down.

We pass a big farm. Its outbuildings are anchored on a sea of swaying wheat, its white clapboard is molten in the late, hazy light. All three of us, even Carlton, keep quiet as we pass. There is something familiar about this place. Cows graze, autumn trees cast their long shade. I tell myself we are farmers, and also somehow rich enough to drive a convertible. The world is gaudy with possibilities. When I ride in a car at night, I believe the moon is following me.

"We're home," I shout as we pass the farm. I don't know what I am saying. It's the combined effects of wind and speed on my brain. But neither Carlton nor our father questions me. We pass through a living silence. I am certain at that moment that we share the same dream. I look up to see that the moon, white and socketed in a gas-blue sky, is in fact following us. It isn't long before Carlton is standing up again, screaming into the rush of air, and our father and I are pulling him down, back into the sanctuary of that big car.

JONATHAN

W E GATHERED at dusk on the darkening green. I was five. The air smelled of newly cut grass, and the sand traps were luminous. My father carried me on his shoulders. I was both pilot and captive of his enormity. My bare legs thrilled to the sandpaper of his cheeks, and I held on to his ears, great soft shells that buzzed minutely with hair.

My mother's red lipstick and fingernails looked black in the dusk. She was pregnant, just beginning to show, and the crowd parted for her. We made our small camp on the second fairway, with two folding aluminum chairs. Multitudes had turned out for the celebration. Smoke from their portable barbecues sharpened the air. I settled myself on my father's lap, and was given a sip of beer. My mother sat fanning herself with the Sunday funnies. Mosquitoes circled above us in the violet ether.

That Fourth of July the city of Cleveland had hired two famous Mexican brothers to set off fireworks over the municipal golf course. These brothers put on shows all over the world, at state and religious affairs. They came from deep in Mexico, where bread was baked in the shape of skulls and virgins, and fireworks were considered to be man's highest form of artistic expression.

The show started before the first star announced itself. It began unspectacularly. The brothers were playing their audience, throwing out some easy ones: standard double and triple blossomings, spiral rockets, colored sprays that left drab orchids of colored smoke. Ordinary stuff. Then, following a pause, they began in earnest. A rocket shot straight up, pulling a thread of silver light in its wake, and at the top of its arc it bloomed purple, a blazing five-pronged lily, each petal of which burst out with a blossom of its own. The crowd cooed its appreciation. My father cupped my belly with one enormous brown hand, and asked if I was enjoying the show. I nodded. Below his throat, an outcropping of dark blond hairs struggled to escape through the collar of his madras shirt.

More of the lilies exploded, red yellow and mauve, their silver stems lingering beneath them. Then came the snakes, hissing orange fire, a dozen at a time, great lolloping curves that met, intertwined, and diverged, sizzling all the while. They were followed by huge soundless snowflakes, crystalline bodies of purest white, and those by a constellation in the shape of Miss Liberty, with blue eyes and ruby lips. Thousands gasped and applauded. I remember my father's throat, speckled with dried blood, the stubbly skin loosely covering a huge knobbed mechanism that swallowed beer. When I whimpered at the occasional loud bang, or at a scattering of colored embers that seemed to be dropping directly onto our heads, he assured me we had nothing to fear. I could feel the rumble of his voice in my stomach and my legs. His lean arms, each lazily bisected by a single vein, held me firmly in place.

I want to talk about my father's beauty. I know it's not a usual subject for a man—when we talk about our fathers we are far more likely to tell tales of courage or titanic rage, even of tenderness. But I want to talk about my father's frank, unadulterated beauty: the potent symmetry of his arms, blond and lithely muscled as if they'd been carved of raw ash; the easy, measured grace of his stride. He was a compact, physically dignified man; a dark-eyed theater owner quietly in love with the movies. My mother suffered headaches and fits of irony, but my father was always cheerful, always on his way somewhere, always certain that things would turn out all right.

6

When my father was away at work my mother and I were alone together. She invented indoor games for us to play, or enlisted my help in baking cookies. She disliked going out, especially in winter, because the cold gave her headaches. She was a New Orleans girl, small-boned and precise in her movements. She had married young. Sometimes she prevailed upon me to sit by the window with her, looking at the street, waiting for a moment when the frozen landscape might resolve itself into something ordinary she could trust as placidly as did the solid, rollicking Ohio mothers who piloted enormous cars loaded with groceries, babies, elderly relations. Station wagons rumbled down our street like decorated tanks celebrating victory in foreign wars.

"Jonathan," she whispered. "Hey, boy-o. What are you thinking about?"

It was a favorite question of hers. "I don't know," I said.

"Tell me anything," she said. "Tell me a story."

I was aware of the need to speak. "Those boys are taking their sled to the river," I told her, as two older neighborhood boys in plaid caps—boys I adored and feared—passed our house pulling a battered Flexible Flyer. "They're going to slide it on the ice. But they have to be careful about holes. A little boy fell in and drowned."

It wasn't much of a story. It was the best I could manage on short notice.

"How did you know about that?" she asked.

I shrugged. I had thought I'd made it up. It was sometimes difficult to distinguish what had occurred from what might have occurred.

"Does that story scare you?" she said.

"No," I told her. I imagined myself skimming over a vast expanse of ice, deftly avoiding the jagged holes into which other boys fell with sad, defeated little splashes.

"You're safe here," she said, stroking my hair. "Don't you worry about a thing. We're both perfectly safe and sound right here."

I nodded, though I could hear the uncertainty in her voice. Her heavy-jawed, small-nosed face cupped the raw winter light that

7

shot up off the icy street and ricocheted from room to room of our house, nicking the silver in the cabinet, setting the little prismed lamp abuzz.

"How about a *funny* story?" she said. "We could probably use one just about now."

"Okay," I said, though I knew no funny stories. Humor was a mystery to me—I could only narrate what I saw. Outside our window, Miss Heidegger, the old woman who lived next door, emerged from her house, dressed in a coat that appeared to be made of mouse pelts. She picked up a leaf of newspaper that had blown into her yard, and hobbled back inside. I knew from my parents' private comments that Miss Heidegger was funny. She was funny in her insistence that her property be kept immaculate, and in her convictions about the Communists who operated the schools, the telephone company, and the Lutheran church. My father liked to say, in a warbling voice, "Those Communists have sent us another electric bill. Mark my words, they're trying to force us out of our homes." When he said something like that my mother always laughed, even at bill-paying time, when the fear was most plainly etched around her mouth and eyes.

That day, sitting by the window, I tried doing Miss Heidegger myself. In a high, quivering voice not wholly different from my actual voice I said, "Oh, those bad Communists have blown this newspaper right into my yard." I got up and walked stiff-legged to the middle of the living room, where I picked up a copy of *Time* magazine from the coffee table and waggled it over my head.

"You Communists," I croaked. "You stay away now. Stop trying to force us out of our homes."

My mother laughed delightedly. "You are *wick*ed," she said.

I went to her, and she scratched my head affectionately. The light from the street brightened the gauze curtains, filled the deep blue candy dish on the side table. We were safe.

My father worked all day, came home for dinner, and went back to the theater at night. I do not to this day know what he did all those hours—as far as I can tell, the operation of a single, unprosperous movie theater does not require the owner's presence

8

from early morning until late at night. My father worked those hours, though, and neither my mother nor I questioned it. He was earning money, maintaining the house that protected us from the Cleveland winters. That was all we needed to know.

When my father came home for dinner, a frosty smell clung to his coat. He was big and inevitable as a tree. When he took off his coat, the fine hair on his forearms stood up electrically in the soft, warm air of the house.

My mother served the dinner she had made. My father patted her belly, which was by then round and solid as a basketball.

"Triplets," he said. "We're going to need a bigger house. Two bedrooms won't do it, not by a long shot."

"Let's just worry about the oil bill," she said.

"Another year," he said. "A year from now, and we'll be in a position to look at real estate."

My father frequently alluded to a change in our position. If we arranged ourselves a certain way, the right things would happen. We had to be careful about how we stood, what we thought.

"We'll see," my mother said in a quiet tone.

He got up from the table and rubbed her shoulders. His hands covered her shoulders entirely. He could nearly have circled her neck with his thumb and middle finger.

"You just concentrate on the kid," he said. "Just keep yourself healthy. I'll take care of the rest."

My mother submitted to his caresses, but took no pleasure in them. I could see it on her face. When my father was home she wore the same cautious look she brought to our surveys of the street. His presence made her nervous, as if some part of the outside had forced its way in.

My father waited for her to speak, to carry us along in the continuing conversation of our family life. She sat silent at the table, her shoulders tense under his ministrations.

"Well, I guess it's time for me to get back to work," he said at length. "So long, sport. Take care of the house."

"Okay," I said. He patted my back, and kissed me roughly on the cheek. My mother got up and started to wash the dishes. I sat watching my father as he hid his muscled arms in his coat sleeves and returned to the outside.

Later that night, after I'd been put to bed, while my mother sat downstairs watching television, I snuck into her room and tried her lipstick on my own lips. Even in the dark, I could tell that the effect was more clownish than alluring. Still, it revised my appearance. I made red spots on my cheeks with her rouge, and penciled black brows over my own pale blond ones.

I walked light-footed into the bathroom. Laughter and tinkling music drifted up through the stairwell. I put the bathroom stool in the place where my father stood shaving in the mornings, and got up on it so I could see myself in the mirror. The lips I had drawn were huge and shapeless, the spots of crimson rouge off-center. I was not beautiful, but I believed I had the possibility of beauty in me. I would have to be careful about how I stood, what I thought. Slowly, mindful of the creaky hinge, I opened the medicine cabinet and took out my father's striped can of Barbasol. I knew just what to do: shake the can with an impatient snapping motion, spray a mound of white lather onto my left palm, and apply it incautiously, in profligate smears, to my jaw and neck. Applying makeup required all the deliberation one might bring to defusing a bomb; shaving was a hasty and imprecise act that produced scarlet pinpoints of blood and left little gobbets of hair—dead as snakeskin—behind in the sink.

When I had lathered my face I looked long into the mirror, considering the effect. My blackened eyes glittered like spiders above the lush white froth. I was not ladylike, nor was I manly. I was something else altogether. There were so many different ways to be a beauty.

My mother grew bigger and bigger. On a shopping trip I demanded and got a pink vinyl baby doll with thin magenta lips and cobalt eyes that closed, when the doll was laid flat, with the definitive click of miniature window frames. I suspect my parents discussed the doll. I suspect they decided it would help me cope with my feelings of exclusion. My mother taught me how to diaper it, and to bathe it in the kitchen sink. Even my father professed interest in the doll's well-being. "How's the kid?" he asked one evening just before dinner, as I lifted it stiff-limbed from its bath.

"Okay," I said. Water leaked out of its joints. Its sulfur-colored hair, which sprouted from a grid of holes punched into its scalp, had taken on the smell of a wet sweater.

"Good baby," my father said, and patted its firm rubber cheek with one big finger. I was thrilled. He loved the baby so.

"Yes," I said, holding the lifeless thing in a thick white towel.

My father hunkered down on his huge hams, expelling a breeze spiced with his scent. "Jonathan?" he said.

"Uh-huh."

"You know boys don't usually play with dolls, don't you?"

"Well. Yes."

"This is your baby," he said, "and that's fine for here at home. But if you show it to other boys they may not understand. So you'd better just play with it here. All right?"

"Okay."

"Good." He patted my arm. "Okay? Only play with it in the house, right?"

"Okay," I answered. Standing small before him, holding the swaddled doll, I felt my first true humiliation. I recognized a deep inadequacy in myself, a foolishness. Of course I knew the baby was just a toy, and a slightly embarrassing one. A wrongful toy. How had I let myself drift into believing otherwise?

"Are you all right?" he asked.

"Uh-huh."

"Good. Listen, I've got to go. You take care of the house."

"Daddy?"

"Yeah?"

"Mommy doesn't want to have a baby," I said.

"Sure she does."

"No. She told me."

"Jonathan, honey, Mommy and Daddy are both very happy about the baby. Aren't you happy, too?"

"Mommy hates having this baby," I said. "She told me. She said you want to have it, but she doesn't want to."

I looked into his gigantic face, and could see that I had made

some sort of contact. His eyes brightened, and the delta of capillaries that spread over his nose and cheeks stood out in sharper,
redder relief against his pale skin.

"It's not true, sport," he said. "Mommy sometimes says things
she doesn't mean. Believe me, she's as happy about having the
baby as you and I are."

I said nothing.

"Hey, I'm late," he said. "Trust me. You'll have a little sister
or brother, and we're all going to be crazy about her. Or him.
You'll be a big brother. Everything'll be great."

After a moment he added, "Take care of things while I'm gone,
okay?" He stroked my cheek with one spatulate thumb, and left.

That night I awoke to the sound of a whispered fight being
conducted behind the door of their bedroom at the end of the hall.
Their voices hissed. I lay waiting for—what? Soon I had fallen
asleep again, and do not know to this day whether or not I dreamed
the sound of the fight. It is still sometimes difficult to distinguish
what happened from what might have happened.

When my mother delivered one evening in December I was left
behind with Miss Heidegger, the neighbor woman. She was a
milky-eyed, suspicious old soul who had worried her hair to a
sparse gray frazzle through which the pink curve of her skull could
be seen.

As I watched my parents drive away together Miss Heidegger
stood behind me, smelling mildly of wilted rose perfume. When
the car was out of sight I told her, "Mommy's not really going
to have the baby."

"No?" she said pleasantly, having no idea how to talk to children
when they began speaking strangely.

"She doesn't want to," I said.

"Oh, now, you'll love the baby, dear," Miss Heidegger said.
"Just you wait. When Momma and Poppa bring it home, you'll
see. It'll be the sweetest little thing you can imagine."

"She doesn't like having a baby," I said. "We don't want it."

At this poor Miss Heidegger's remaining blood rushed to her
face, and she went with a sound like rustling tissue to the kitchen

to see about dinner. She put together something limp and boiled, which I with my child's devotion to bland food liked enormously.

My father telephoned from the hospital after midnight. Miss Heidegger and I reached the phone at the same moment. She answered and stood erect in her blue bathrobe, nodding her withered head. I could tell something was wrong from her eyes, which took on a thinness and brilliance like that of river ice just before it melts, when it is no more than the memory of ice lingering another moment or two over bright brown water.

The baby would be described to me as a canceled ticket, a cake taken too soon from the oven. Only as an adult would I piece together the true story of the snarled cord and ripped flesh. My mother had died for nearly a minute, and miraculously come back. Most of her womb had had to be scooped out. The baby, a girl, had lived long enough to bleat once at the fluorescent ceiling of the delivery room.

I suppose my father was in no condition to talk to me. He left that to Miss Heidegger, who put the telephone down and stood before me with an expression of terrified confusion like that with which I imagine we must greet death itself. I knew something dreadful had happened.

She said in a whisper, "Oh, those poor, poor people. Oh, you poor little boy."

Although I did not know exactly what had happened, I knew this to be an occasion for grief. I tried feeling inconsolable, but in fact I was enlivened and rather pleased by the chance to act well in a bad situation.

"Now, don't you worry, dear," Miss Heidegger said. There was true horror in her voice, a moist gargling undertone. I tried leading her to a chair, and found to my astonishment that she obeyed me. I ran to the kitchen and got her a glass of water, which was what I believed one offered somebody in a state of emotional agitation.

"Don't you worry, I'll stay with you," she said as I got a coaster for the glass and set it on the end table. She tried pulling me onto her lap but I had no interest in sitting there. I remained standing at her feet. She petted my hair and I stroked the thin, complicated bones of her flannel-covered knee.

She said helplessly, almost questioningly, "Oh, she was so healthy. She just looked perfectly fine."

Emboldened, I took one of her brittle, powdery old hands in mine.

"Oh, you poor thing," she said. "Don't you worry now, I'm here."

I continued standing at her feet, holding the bones of her hand. She smiled at me. Was there some aspect of pleasure in her smile? Probably not; I suspect I imagined it. I gently kneaded her hand. We stayed that way for quite a while, bowed and steadfast and vaguely satisfied, like a pair of spinsters who have learned to find solace in the world's unfathomable grief.

My mother came back over a week later, reserved and rather shy. Both she and my father looked around the house as if it were new to them, as if they had been promised something grander. In my mother's absence Miss Heidegger had instituted a smell of her own, compounded of that watery rose perfume and the odor of unfamiliar cooking. She squeezed my parents' hands and left discreetly, hurriedly. She might have been told privately that at any moment the house would catch fire.

After she had gone my mother and father both kneeled down and held me. They surrounded me, all but buried me, with their flesh and their brisk, known smells.

My father wept. He had never before shed a single tear in my presence and now he cried extravagantly, great phlegmy sobs that caught in his throat with the clotted sound of a stopped pipe. Experimentally, I placed my hand on his forearm. He did not brush it off, or reprimand me. His pale hairs sprouted up raucously between my fingers.

"It's okay," I whispered, though I don't believe he heard me over his keening. "It's okay," I said again, in full voice. He did not derive any visible comfort from my reassurances.

I glanced at my mother. She was not crying. Her face was drained not only of color but of expression as well. She might have been a vacant body, waiting dumbfounded to be infused with a human soul. But when she felt my eyes on her she managed, in a strong-limbed, somnambulistic fashion, to draw me to her breast. Her embrace caught me off guard, and I lost my hold on my father's forearm. As my mother crushed my face into the folds of her coat I lost track of my father entirely. I felt myself being pulled down into the depths of my mother's coat. It filled my nose and ears. The sound of my father's laments grew muffled and remote as I was impelled deeper into my mother's clothes, through the outer layer of cold toward the scented, familiar-smelling core. I resisted a moment, tried to return to my father, but she was too strong. I disappeared. I left my father, and gave myself over to my mother's more ravenous sorrow.

Afterward she was more reluctant than ever to go outdoors. Sometimes in the mornings she took me into bed with her and kept me there, reading or watching television, until mid-afternoon. We played games, told stories. I believed I knew what we were doing together during those long, housebound days. We were practicing for a time when my father would no longer be with us; when it would be just we two.

To make my mother laugh I did imitations, although I no longer felt inclined to imitate Miss Heidegger. I settled into doing my mother herself, which sometimes made her screech with laughter. I would put on her scarves and hats, speak in my own version of her New Orleans accent, which I made half Southern and half Bronx. "What are you thinking?" I'd drawl. "Honey, tell me a story."

She always laughed until her eyes shone with tears. "Sweetheart," she would say, "you're a natural. What do you say we put you on the stage, you can support your old mama in her dotage?"

When finally we got up she dressed hurriedly, and set about cooking and cleaning with the relentlessness of an artist.

My father no longer massaged her shoulders when he came home at night. He did not plant exaggerated, smacking kisses on her forehead or the tip of her nose. He couldn't. A force field had grown up around her, transparent and solid as glass. I could see it go up when he came home, with the rampant smells of the outside world clinging to his coat. When the field was up my mother looked no different—her face remained clever and slightly feverish, her movements exact as a surgeon's as she laid out the perfect dinner she had made—but she could not be touched. We knew it, both my father and I, with a visceral certainty that was all the more real for its inexplicability. My mother had powers. We ate our dinner (her cooking got better and better, she hit ever more elaborate heights), talked of usual things, and my father kissed the air in our vicinity as he readied himself to return to the outside.

One night in late spring, I was awakened by the sound of a proper fight. My parents were downstairs. Even in rage they kept their voices down, so that only an occasional word or phrase worked its way up to my room. The effect was like that of two people screaming inside a heavy sack. I heard my father say, "*pun*ishment," and, nearly a full minute later, my mother answer, "what *you* want . . . something . . . *self*ish."

I lay in the dark, listening. Presently I heard footsteps—my father's—mounting the stairs. I believed he would come into my room, and I feigned elaborate, angelic sleep, my head centered on the pillow and my lips slightly parted. But my father did not come to me. He went instead to the room he shared with my mother. I heard him go in, and heard nothing more.

Minutes passed. My mother did not follow him. The house was silent, filled with a gelid, wintery hush even as lilac and dogwood leaves brushed darkly against the windowpanes. I lay carefully in my own bed, uncertain of what was expected and what allowed on a night like this. I thought I would just go back to sleep, but that refused to happen.

Finally, I got out of bed and walked down the hall to my parents' room. The door stood ajar. Light from their bedside lamp—a pink-gold light tinted by the parchment shade—hung with a certain weight in the semidarkness of the hall. From the kitchen my mother could be heard shelling pecans, a series of sharp, musical cracks.

My father lay diagonally across the double bed, in an attitude of refined, almost demure, abandon. His face was turned toward the wall on which a blue-and-green Paris street, unpeopled, hung in a silver frame. One of his arms was draped over the edge of the mattress, the large fingers dangling extravagantly. His rib cage rose and fell with the steady rhythm of sleep.

I stood in the doorway for a while, contemplating my position. I had expected him to hear me, to look up and commence worrying over the fact that I had been disturbed. When he maintained his posture on the bed I stepped quietly into the room. It was time for me to speak but I could not think of what to say. I had thought my simple presence would cause a next thing to happen. I looked around the room. There were the twin bureaus, with my mother's makeup and perfumes arranged on a mother-of-pearl tray. There was the oak-framed mirror, displaying a rectangle of flowered wallpaper from the opposite wall. Empty-handed, without an offering, I crept to the bed and cautiously touched my father's elbow.

He lifted his head and looked at me as if he didn't recognize me; as if we had met once, long ago, and now he was trying to summon up my name. His face nearly stopped my heart. For a moment it seemed he had left us after all; his fatherly aspect had withdrawn and in its place was only a man, big as a car but blank and unscrupled as an infant, capable of anything. I stood in the sudden glare of his new strangeness, shyly smiling in yellow pajamas.

Then he brought himself back. He reoccupied his face and laid a gentle hand on my shoulder. "Hey," he whispered. "What are you doing up?"

I shrugged. Even today, as an adult, I can't remember a time when I did not pause and consider before telling the truth.

He could have picked me up and taken me onto the bed with him. That gesture might have rescued us both, at least for the time being. I ached for it. I'd have given everything I imagined owning, in my greediest fantasies, to have been pulled into bed with him and held, as he'd held me while the sky exploded over our heads on the Fourth of July. But he must have been embarrassed at having been caught fighting. Now he was a man who had awakened his child by yelling at his wife, and had then flung himself across the bed like a heartbroken teenage girl. He could become other things, but he would always be that as well.

"Go back to sleep," he said, in a voice gruffer than he may have intended it to be. I believe he hoped the situation could still be undone. If he acted forcefully enough, we could jump back in time and restitch the fabric of my sleep. I would wake in the morning with nothing more than dimly recollected dreams.

I refused. I would settle for nothing less than consoling him. My father ordered me back to bed and I grew balky and petulant. I hovered at the edge of tears, which strained his patience. I wanted him to require my presence. I needed to know that by my kindness and perseverance I was victorious in the long contest for his love.

"Jonathan," he said. "Jonathan, come on."

I let myself be taken back to my room. I had no options. He picked me up and for the first time I did not exult in his touch or his spicy smell, the broad curving shine of his forehead. At that moment I came to know my mother's reticence, her delicate-boned sense of remove. I had practiced imitating her and now, in a rush, I could do nothing else. If my father rubbed my weary shoulders I would tense up; if he stomped in from the snow I would think nervously of the collapse of my spinach soufflé.

He put me into bed tenderly enough. He pulled the covers over me, told me to get some shut-eye. He did not act badly. Still, in a fury, I slipped out of bed and ran across the room to my toy chest. Unfamiliar feelings racketed in my ears, made me light-headed. "Jonathan," my father said sharply. He started after me, but I was too quick for him. I dug to the bottom of the chest, knowing just where to reach. I pulled the doll out by her slick rubber leg and held her roughly in my arms.

He hesitated, half standing over my miniature bed. On my headboard, a cartoon rabbit danced ecstatically on a field of four-petaled pink flowers.

"This is mine," I said, in a nearly hysterical tone of insistence. The floor of my bedroom felt unsteady beneath my feet, and I clung to the doll as if it alone could keep me from losing my balance and slipping away.

My father shook his head. For the single time in my recollection, his kindness failed. He had wanted so much, and the world was shrinking. His wife shunned him, his business was not a success, and his only son—there would be no others—loved dolls and quiet indoor games.

"Jesus Christ, Jonathan," he hollered. "Jesus H. Christ. What in the hell is the matter with you? *What*?"

I stood dumb. I had no answer to that question, although I knew one was expected.

"This is mine" was all I could offer by way of an answer. I held the doll so close to my chest her stiff eyelashes gouged me through my pajamas.

"Fine," he said more quietly, in a defeated tone. "Fine. It's yours." And he left.

I heard him go downstairs, get his jacket from the hall closet. I heard my mother fail to speak from the kitchen. I heard him close the front door, with a caution and deliberateness that implied finality.

He would return in the morning, having slept on the couch in his office at the theater. After an awkward period we would resume our normal family life, find our cheerfulness again. My father and mother would invent a cordial, joking relationship that involved neither kisses nor fights. They would commence living together with the easy, chaste familiarity of grown siblings. He would ask me no more unanswerable questions, though his singular question would continue crackling in the back of my head like a faulty electrical connection. My mother's cooking would become renowned. In 1968, our family would be photographed for the Sunday supplement of the Cleveland *Post*: my mother cutting into a shrimp casserole while my father and I looked on, proud, expectant, and perfectly dressed.

BOBBY

WE LIVED then in Cleveland, in the middle of everything. It was the sixties—our radios sang out love all day long. This of course is history. It happened before the city of Cleveland went broke, before its river caught fire. We were four. My mother and father, Carlton, and me. Carlton turned sixteen the year I turned nine. Between us were several brothers and sisters, weak flames quenched in our mother's womb. We are not a fruitful or many-branched line. Our family name is Morrow.

Our father was a high school music teacher. Our mother taught children called "exceptional," which meant that some could name the day Christmas would fall in the year 2000 but couldn't remember to drop their pants when they peed. We lived in a tract called Woodlawn—neat one- and two-story houses painted optimistic colors. Our tract bordered a cemetery. Behind our back yard was a gully choked with brush, and beyond that, the field of smooth, polished stones. I grew up with the cemetery, and didn't mind it. It could be beautiful. A single stone angel, small-breasted and determined, rose amid the more conservative markers close to our house. Farther away, in a richer section, miniature mosques and Parthenons spoke silently to Cleveland of man's enduring accomplishments. Carlton and I played in the cemetery as children and, with a little more age, smoked joints and drank

Southern Comfort there. I was, thanks to Carlton, the most criminally advanced nine-year-old in my fourth-grade class. I was going places. I made no move without his counsel.

Here is Carlton several months before his death, in an hour so alive with snow that earth and sky are identically white. He labors among the markers and I run after, stung by snow, following the light of his red knitted cap. Carlton's hair is pulled back into a ponytail, neat and economical, a perfect pinecone of hair. He is thrifty, in his way.

We have taken hits of acid with our breakfast juice. Or rather, Carlton has taken a hit and I, considering my youth, have been allowed half. This acid is called windowpane. It is for clarity of vision, as Vicks is for decongestion of the nose. Our parents are at work, earning the daily bread. We have come out into the cold so that the house, when we reenter it, will shock us with its warmth and righteousness. Carlton believes in shocks.

"I think I'm coming on to it," I call out. Carlton has on his buckskin jacket, which is worn down to the shine. On the back, across his shoulder blades, his girlfriend has stitched an electric-blue eye. As we walk I speak into the eye. "I think I feel something," I say.

"Too soon," Carlton calls back. "Stay loose, Frisco. You'll know when the time comes."

I am excited and terrified. We are into serious stuff. Carlton has done acid half a dozen times before, but I am new at it. We slipped the tabs into our mouths at breakfast, while our mother paused over the bacon. Carlton likes taking risks.

Snow collects in the engraved letters on the headstones. I lean into the wind, trying to decide whether everything around me seems strange because of the drug, or just because everything truly is strange. Three weeks earlier, a family across town had been sitting at home, watching television, when a single-engine plane fell on them. Snow swirls around us, seeming to fall up as well as down.

Carlton leads the way to our spot, the pillared entrance to a society tomb. This tomb is a palace. Stone cupids cluster on the peaked roof, with stunted, frozen wings and matrons' faces. Under the roof is a veranda, backed by cast-iron doors that lead to the house of the dead proper. In summer this veranda is cool. In winter it blocks the wind. We keep a bottle of Southern Comfort there.

Carlton finds the bottle, unscrews the cap, and takes a good, long draw. He is studded with snowflakes. He hands me the bottle and I take a more conservative drink. Even in winter, the tomb smells mossy as a well. Dead leaves and a yellow M & M's wrapper, worried by the wind, scrape on the marble floor.

"Are you scared?" Carlton asks me.

I nod. I never think of lying to him.

"Don't be, man," he says. "Fear will screw you right up. Drugs can't hurt you if you feel no fear."

I nod. We stand sheltered, passing the bottle. I lean into Carlton's certainty as if it gave off heat.

"We can do acid all the time at Woodstock," I say.

"Right on. Woodstock Nation. Yow."

"Do people really *live* there?" I ask.

"Man, you've got to stop asking that. The concert's over, but people are still there. It's the new nation. Have faith."

I nod again, satisfied. There is a different country for us to live in. I am already a new person, renamed Frisco. My old name was Robert.

"We'll do acid all the time," I say.

"You better believe we will." Carlton's face, surrounded by snow and marble, is lit. His eyes are bright as neon. Something in them tells me he can see the future, a ghost that hovers over everybody's head. In Carlton's future we all get released from our jobs and schooling. Awaiting us all, and soon, is a bright, perfect simplicity. A life among the trees by the river.

"How are you feeling, man?" he asks me.

"Great," I tell him, and it is purely the truth. Doves clatter up out of a bare tree and turn at the same instant, transforming themselves from steel to silver in the snow-blown light. I know at that moment that the drug is working. Everything before me has become suddenly, radiantly itself. How could Carlton have known this was about to happen? "Oh," I whisper. His hand settles on my shoulder.

"Stay loose, Frisco," he says. "There's not a thing in this pretty world to be afraid of. I'm here."

I am not afraid. I am astonished. I had not realized until this moment how real everything is. A twig lies on the marble at my feet, bearing a cluster of hard brown berries. The broken-off end is raw, white, fleshly. Trees are alive.

"I'm here," Carlton says again, and he is.

Hours later, we are sprawled on the sofa in front of the television, ordinary as Wally and the Beav. Our mother makes dinner in the kitchen. A pot lid clangs. We are undercover agents. I am trying to conceal my amazement.

Our father is building a grandfather clock from a kit. He wants to have something to leave us, something for us to pass along. We can hear him in the basement, sawing and pounding. I know what is laid out on his sawhorses—a long raw wooden box, onto which he glues fancy moldings. A single pearl of sweat meanders down his forehead as he works. Tonight I have discovered my ability to see every room of the house at once, to know every single thing that goes on. A mouse nibbles inside the wall. Electrical wires curl behind the plaster, hidden and patient as snakes.

"Shhh," I say to Carlton, who has not said anything. He is watching television through his splayed fingers. Gunshots ping. Bullets raise chalk dust on a concrete wall. I have no idea what we are watching.

"Boys?" our mother calls from the kitchen. I can, with my new ears, hear her slap hamburger into patties. "Set the table like good citizens," she calls.

"Okay, Ma," Carlton replies, in a gorgeous imitation of normality. Our father hammers in the basement. I can feel Carlton's heart ticking. He pats my hand, to assure me that everything's perfect.

We set the table, spoon fork knife, paper napkins triangled to one side. We know the moves cold. After we are done I pause to notice the dining-room wallpaper: a golden farm, backed by mountains. Cows graze, autumn trees cast golden shade. This scene repeats itself three times, on three walls.

"Zap," Carlton whispers. "Zzzzzoom."

"Did we do it right?" I ask him.

"We did everything perfect, little son. How are you doing in there, anyway?" He raps lightly on my head.

"Perfect, I guess." I am staring at the wallpaper as if I were thinking of stepping into it.

"You guess. You guess? You and I are going to other planets, man. Come over here."

"Where?"

"Here. Come here." He leads me to the window. Outside the snow skitters, nervous and silver, under streetlamps. Ranch-style houses hoard their warmth, bleed light into the gathering snow. It is a street in Cleveland. It is our street.

"You and I are going to fly, man," Carlton whispers, close to my ear. He opens the window. Snow blows in, sparking on the carpet. "Fly," he says, and we do. For a moment we strain up and out, the black night wind blowing in our faces—we raise ourselves up off the cocoa-colored deep-pile wool-and-polyester carpet by a sliver of an inch. Sweet glory. The secret of flight is this—you have to do it immediately, before your body realizes it is defying the laws. I swear it to this day.

We both know we have taken momentary leave of the earth. It does not strike either of us as remarkable, any more than does the fact that airplanes sometimes fall from the sky, or that we have always lived in these rooms and will soon leave them. We settle back down. Carlton touches my shoulder.

"You wait, Frisco," he says. "Miracles are happening. Fucking miracles."

I nod. He pulls down the window, which reseals itself with a sucking sound. Our own faces look back at us from the cold, dark glass. Behind us, our mother drops the hamburgers sizzling into the skillet. Our father bends to his work under a hooded lightbulb, preparing the long box into which he will lay clockworks, pendulum, a face. A plane drones by overhead, invisible in the clouds. I glance nervously at Carlton. He smiles his assurance and squeezes the back of my neck.

24

March. After the thaw. I am walking through the cemetery, thinking about my endless life. One of the beauties of living in Cleveland is that any direction feels like progress. I've memorized the map. We are by my calculations three hundred and fifty miles shy of Woodstock, New York. On this raw new day I am walking east, to the place where Carlton and I keep our bottle. I am going to have an early nip, to celebrate my bright future.

When I get to our spot I hear low moans coming from behind the tomb. I freeze, considering my choices. The sound is a long-drawn-out agony with a whip at the end, a final high C, something like "ooooooOw." A wolf's cry run backward. What decides me on investigation rather than flight is the need to make a story. In the stories my brother likes best, people always do the foolish, risky thing. I find I can reach decisions this way, by thinking of myself as a character in a story told by Carlton.

I creep around the side of the monument, cautious as a badger, pressed up close to the marble. I peer over a cherub's girlish shoulder. What I find is Carlton on the ground with his girlfriend, in an uncertain jumble of clothes and bare flesh. Carlton's jacket, the one with the embroidered eye, is draped over the stone, keeping watch.

I hunch behind the statue. I can see the girl's naked arms, and the familiar bones of Carlton's spine. The two of them moan together in the dry winter grass. Though I can't make out the girl's expression, Carlton's face is twisted and grimacing, the cords of his neck pulled tight. I had never thought the experience might be painful. I watch, trying to learn. I hold on to the cherub's cold wings.

It isn't long before Carlton catches sight of me. His eyes rove briefly, ecstatically skyward, and what do they light on but his brother's small head, sticking up next to a cherub's. We lock eyes and spend a moment in mutual decision. The girl keeps on clutching at Carlton's skinny back. He decides to smile at me. He decides to wink.

I am out of there so fast I tear up divots. I dodge among the stones, jump the gully, clear the fence into the swing-set-and-

25

picnic-table sanctity of the back yard. Something about that wink. My heart beats fast as a sparrow's.

I go into the kitchen and find our mother washing fruit. She asks what's going on. I tell her nothing is. Nothing at all.

She sighs over an apple's imperfection. The curtains sport blue teapots. Our mother works the apple with a scrub brush. She believes they come coated with poison.

"Where's Carlton?" she asks.

"Don't know," I tell her.

"Bobby?"

"Huh?"

"What exactly is going on?"

"Nothing," I say. My heart works itself up to a humingbird's rate, more buzz than beat.

"I think something is. Will you answer a question?"

"Okay."

"Is your brother taking drugs?"

I relax a bit. It is only drugs. I know why she's asking. Lately police cars have been browsing our house like sharks. They pause, take note, glide on. Some neighborhood crackdown. Carlton is famous in these parts.

"No," I tell her.

She faces me with the brush in one hand, an apple in the other. "You wouldn't lie to me, would you?" She knows something is up. Her nerves run through this house. She can feel dust settling on the tabletops, milk starting to turn in the refrigerator.

"No," I say.

"Something's going on," she sighs. She is a small, efficient woman who looks at things as if they give off a painful light. She grew up on a farm in Wisconsin and spent her girlhood tying up bean rows, worrying over the sun and rain. She is still trying to overcome her habit of modest expectations.

I leave the kitchen, pretending sudden interest in the cat. Our mother follows, holding her brush. She means to scrub the truth out of me. I follow the cat, his erect black tail and pink anus.

"Don't walk away when I'm talking to you," our mother says.

I keep walking, to see how far I'll get, calling, "Kittykittykitty." In the front hall, our father's homemade clock chimes the half hour. I make for the clock. I get as far as the rubber plant before she collars me.

"I told you not to walk away," she says, and cuffs me a good one with the brush. She catches me on the ear and sets it ringing. The cat is out of there quick as a quarter note.

I stand for a minute, to let her know I've received the message. Then I resume walking. She hits me again, this time on the back of the head, hard enough to make me see colors. "Will you *stop*?" she screams. Still, I keep walking. Our house runs west to east. With every step I get closer to Yasgur's farm.

Carlton comes home whistling. Our mother treats him like a guest who's overstayed. He doesn't care. He is lost in optimism. He pats her cheek and calls her "Professor." He treats her as if she were harmless, and so she is.

She never hits Carlton. She suffers him the way farm girls suffer a thieving crow, with a grudge so old and endless it borders on reverence. She gives him a scrubbed apple, and tells him what she'll do if he tracks mud on the carpet.

I am waiting in our room. He brings the smell of the cemetery with him, its old snow and wet pine needles. He rolls his eyes at me, takes a crunch of his apple. "What's happening, Frisco?" he says.

I have arranged myself loosely on my bed, trying to pull a Dylan riff out of my harmonica. I have always figured I can bluff my way into wisdom. I offer Carlton a dignified nod.

He drops onto his own bed. I can see a crushed crocus, the first of the year, stuck to the black rubber sole of his boot.

"Well, Frisco," he says. "Today you are a man."

I nod again. Is that all there is to it?

"*Yow*," Carlton says. He laughs, pleased with himself and the world. "That was so perfect."

I pick out what I can of "Blowin' in the Wind."

Carlton says, "Man, when I saw you out there spying on us I thought to myself, *yes*. Now *I'm* really here. You know what I'm saying?" He waves his apple core.

"Uh-huh," I say.

27

"Frisco, that was the first time her and I ever did it. I mean, we'd talked. But when we finally got down to it, there you were. My brother. Like you *knew*."

I nod, and this time for real. What happened was an adventure we had together. All right. The story is beginning to make sense.

"Aw, Frisco," Carlton says. "I'm gonna find you a girl, too. You're nine. You been a virgin too long."

"Really?" I say.

"*Man*. We'll find you a woman from the sixth grade, somebody with a little experience. We'll get stoned and all make out under the trees in the boneyard. I want to be present at your deflowering, man. You're gonna need a brother there."

I am about to ask, as casually as I can manage, about the relationship between love and bodily pain, when our mother's voice cuts into the room. "You did it," she screams. "You tracked mud all over the rug."

A family entanglement follows. Our mother brings our father, who comes and stands in the doorway with her, taking in evidence. He is a formerly handsome man. His face has been worn down by too much patience. He has lately taken up some sporty touches—a goatee, a pair of calfskin boots.

Our mother points out the trail of muddy half-moons that lead from the door to Carlton's bed. Dangling over the foot of the bed are the culprits themselves, voluptuously muddy, with Carlton's criminal feet still in them.

"You see?" she says. "You see what he thinks of me?"

Our father, a reasonable man, suggests that Carlton clean it up. Our mother finds that too small a gesture. She wants Carlton not to have done it in the first place. "I don't ask for much," she says. "I don't ask where he goes. I don't ask why the police are suddenly so interested in our house. I ask that he not track mud all over the floor. That's all." She squints in the glare of her own outrage.

"Better clean it right up," our father says to Carlton.

"And that's it?" our mother says. "He cleans up the mess, and all's forgiven?"

"Well, what do you want him to do? Lick it up?"

"I want some consideration," she says, turning helplessly to me. "That's what I want."

I shrug, at a loss. I sympathize with our mother, but am not on her team.

"All right," she says. "I just won't bother cleaning the house anymore. I'll let you men handle it. I'll sit and watch television and throw my candy wrappers on the floor."

She starts out, cutting the air like a blade. On her way she picks up a jar of pencils, looks at it and tosses the pencils on the floor. They fall like fortune-telling sticks, in pairs and crisscrosses.

Our father goes after her, calling her name. Her name is Isabel. We can hear them making their way across the house, our father calling, "Isabel, Isabel, Isabel," while our mother, pleased with the way the pencils had looked, dumps more things onto the floor.

"I hope she doesn't break the TV," I say.

"She'll do what she needs to do," Carlton tells me.

"I hate her," I say. I am not certain about that. I want to test the sound of it, to see if it's true.

"She's got more balls than any of us, Frisco," he says. "Better watch what you say about her."

I keep quiet. Soon I get up and start gathering pencils, because I prefer that to lying around trying to follow the shifting lines of allegiance. Carlton goes for a sponge and starts in on the mud.

"You get shit on the carpet, you clean it up," he says. "Simple."

The time for all my questions about love has passed, and I am not so unhip as to force a subject. I know it will come up again. I make a neat bouquet of pencils. Our mother rages through the house.

Later, after she has thrown enough and we three have picked it all up, I lie on my bed thinking things over. Carlton is on the phone to his girlfriend, talking low. Our mother, becalmed but still dangerous, cooks dinner. She sings as she cooks, some slow forties number that must have been all over the jukes when her first husband's plane went down in the Pacific. Our father plays his clarinet in the basement. That is where he goes to practice, down among his woodworking tools, the neatly hung hammers and awls that throw oversized shadows in the light of the single bulb. If I put my ear to the floor I can hear him, pulling a long low tomcat moan out of that horn. There is some strange comfort

29

in pressing my ear to the carpet and hearing our father's music leaking up through the floorboards. Lying down, with my ear to the floor, I join in on my harmonica.

That spring our parents have a party to celebrate the sun's return. It has been a long, bitter winter and now the first wild daisies are poking up on the lawns and among the graves.

Our parents' parties are mannerly affairs. Their friends, school-teachers all, bring wine jugs and guitars. They are Ohio hip. Though they hold jobs and meet mortgages, they think of themselves as independent spirits on a spying mission. They have agreed to impersonate teachers until they write their novels, finish their dissertations, or just save up enough money to set themselves free.

Carlton and I are the lackeys. We take coats, fetch drinks. We have done this at every party since we were small, trading on our precocity, doing a brother act. We know the moves. A big, lip-sticked woman who has devoted her maidenhood to ninth-grade math calls me Mr. Right. An assistant vice principal in a Russian fur hat asks us both whether we expect to vote Democratic or Socialist. By sneaking sips I manage to get myself semi-crocked.

The reliability of the evening is derailed halfway through, however, by a half dozen of Carlton's friends. They rap on the door and I go for it, anxious as a carnival sharp to see who will step up next and swallow the illusion that I'm a kindly, sober nine-year-old child. I'm expecting callow adults and who do I find but a pack of young outlaws, big-booted and wild-haired. Carlton's girlfriend stands in front, in an outfit made up almost entirely of fringe.

"Hi, Bobby," she says confidently. She comes from New York, and is more than just locally smart.

"Hi," I say. I let them all in despite a retrograde urge to lock the door and phone the police. Three are girls, four boys. They pass me in a cloud of dope smoke and sly-eyed greeting.

What they do is invade the party. Carlton is standing on the far side of the rumpus room, picking the next album, and his girl cuts straight through the crowd to his side. She has the bones and the loose, liquid moves some people consider beautiful. She walks through that room as if she'd been sent to teach the whole party a lesson.

Carlton's face tips me off that this was planned. Our mother demands to know what's going on here. She is wearing a long dark-red dress that doesn't interfere with her shoulders. When she dresses up you can see what it is about her, or what it was. She is responsible for Carlton's beauty. I have our father's face.

Carlton does some quick talking. Though it's against our mother's better judgment, the invaders are suffered to stay. One of them, an Eddie Haskell for all his leather and hair, tells her she is looking good. She is willing to hear it.

So the outlaws, house-sanctioned, start to mingle. I work my way over to Carlton's side, the side unoccupied by his girlfriend. I would like to say something ironic and wised-up, something that will band Carlton and me against every other person in the room. I can feel the shape of the comment I have in mind but, being a tipsy nine-year-old, can't get my mouth around it. What I say is, "Shit, man."

Carlton's girl laughs at me. She considers it amusing that a little boy says "shit." I would like to tell her what I have figured out about her, but I am nine, and three-quarters gone on Tom Collinses. Even sober, I can only imagine a sharp-tongued wit.

"Hang on, Frisco," Carlton tells me. "This could turn into a real party."

I can see by the light in his eyes what is going down. He has arranged a blind date between our parents' friends and his own. It's a Woodstock move—he is plotting a future in which young and old have business together. I agree to hang on, and go to the kitchen, hoping to sneak a few knocks of gin.

There I find our father leaning up against the refrigerator. A line of butterfly-shaped magnets hovers around his head. "Are you enjoying this party?" he asks, touching his goatee. He is still getting used to being a man with a beard.

"Uh-huh."

"I am, too," he says sadly. He never meant to be a high school music teacher. The money question caught up with him.

"What do you think of this music?" he asks. Carlton has put the Stones on the turntable. Mick Jagger sings "19th Nervous

Breakdown." Our father gestures in an openhanded way that takes in the room, the party, the whole house—everything the music touches.

"I like it," I say.

"So do I." He stirs his drink with his finger, and sucks on the finger.

"I *love* it," I say, too loud. Something about our father leads me to raise my voice. I want to grab handfuls of music out of the air and stuff them into my mouth.

"I'm not sure I could say I love it," he says. "I'm not sure if I could say that, no. I would say I'm friendly to its intentions. I would say that if this is the direction music is going in, I won't stand in its way."

"Uh-huh," I say. I am already anxious to get back to the party, but don't want to hurt his feelings. If he senses he's being avoided he can fall into fits of apology more terrifying than our mother's rages.

"I think I may have been too rigid with my students," our father says. "Maybe over the summer you boys could teach me a few things about the music people are listening to these days."

"Sure," I say, loudly. We spend a minute waiting for the next thing to say.

"You boys are happy, aren't you?" he asks. "Are you enjoying this party?"

"We're having a great time," I say.

"I thought you were. I am, too."

I have by this time gotten myself to within jumping distance of the door. I call out, "Well, goodbye," and dive back into the party.

Something has happened in my small absence. The party has started to roll. Call it an accident of history and the weather. Carlton's friends are on decent behavior, and our parents' friends have decided to give up some of their wine-and-folk-song propriety to see what they can learn. Carlton is dancing with a vice principal's wife. Carlton's friend Frank, with his ancient-child face and IQ in the low sixties, dances with our mother. I see that our father has followed me out of the kitchen. He positions himself at the party's edge; I jump into its center. I invite the fuchsia-lipped math teacher to dance. She is only too happy. She is big and graceful as a parade float, and I steer her effortlessly out into the middle of everything. My mother, who is known around school for Sicilian discipline, dances freely, which is news to everybody. There is no getting around her beauty.

The night rises higher and higher. A wildness sets in. Carlton throws new music on the turntable—Janis Joplin, the Doors, the Dead. The future shines for everyone, rich with the possibility of more nights exactly like this. Even our father is pressed into dancing, which he does like a flightless bird, all flapping arms and potbelly. Still, he dances. Our mother has a kiss for him.

Finally I nod out on the sofa, blissful under the drinks. I am dreaming of flight when our mother comes and touches my shoulder. I smile up into her flushed, smiling face.

"It's hours past your bedtime," she says, all velvet motherliness. I nod. I can't dispute the fact.

She keeps on nudging my shoulder. I am a moment or two apprehending the fact that she actually wants me to leave the party and go to bed. "No," I tell her.

"Yes," she smiles.

"No," I say cordially, experimentally. This new mother can dance, and flirt. Who knows what else she might allow?

"Yes." The velvet motherliness leaves her voice. She means business, business of the usual kind. I get myself out of there and no excuses this time. I am exactly nine and running from my bedtime as I'd run from death.

I run to Carlton for protection. He is laughing with his girl, a sweaty question mark of hair plastered to his forehead. I plow into him so hard he nearly goes over.

"Whoa, Frisco," he says. He takes me up under the arms and swings me a half-turn. Our mother plucks me out of his hands and sets me down, with a good farm-style hold on the back of my neck.

"Say good night, Bobby," she says. She adds, for the benefit of Carlton's girl, "He should have been in bed before this party started."

"*No*," I holler. I try to twist loose, but our mother has a grip that could crack walnuts.

Carlton's girl tosses her hair and says, "Good night, baby." She smiles a victor's smile. She smooths the stray hair off Carlton's forehead.

"*No*," I scream again. Something about the way she touches his hair. Our mother calls our father, who comes and scoops me up and starts out of the room with me, holding me like the live bomb I am. Before I go I lock eyes with Carlton. He shrugs and says, "Night, man." Our father hustles me out. I do not take it bravely. I leave flailing, too furious to cry, dribbling a slimy thread of horrible-child's spittle.

Later I lie alone on my narrow bed, feeling the music hum in the coiled springs. Life is cracking open right there in our house. People are changing. By tomorrow, no one will be quite the same. How can they let me miss it? I dream up revenge against our parents, and worse for Carlton. He is the one who could have saved me. He could have banded with me against them. What I can't forgive is his shrug, his mild-eyed "Night, man." He has joined the adults. He has made himself bigger, and taken size from me. As the Doors thump "Strange Days," I hope something awful happens to him. I say so to myself.

Around midnight, dim-witted Frank announces he has seen a flying saucer hovering over the back yard. I can hear his deep, excited voice all the way in my room. He says it's like a blinking, luminous cloud. I hear half the party struggling out through the sliding glass door in a disorganized, whooping knot. By that time everyone is so delirious a flying saucer would be just what was expected. That much celebration would logically attract an answering happiness from across the stars.

I get out of bed and sneak down the hall. I will not miss alien visitors for anyone, not even at the cost of our mother's wrath or our father's disappointment. I stop at the end of the hallway, though, embarrassed to be in pajamas. If there really are aliens, they will think I'm the lowest member of the house. While I hesitate over whether to go back to my room to change, people start coming back inside, talking about a trick of the mist and an airplane. People resume their dancing.

Carlton must have jumped the back fence. He must have wanted to be there alone, singular, in case they decided to take somebody with them. A few nights later I will go out and stand where he would have been standing. On the far side of the gully, now a river swollen with melted snow, the cemetery will gleam like a lost city. The moon will be full. I will hang around just as Carlton must have, hypnotized by the silver light on the stones, the white angel raising her arms up across the river.

According to our parents the mystery is why he ran back to the house full tilt. Something in the graveyard may have scared him, he may have needed to break its spell, but I think it's more likely that when he came back to himself he just couldn't wait to get back to the music and the people, the noisy disorder of continuing life.

Somebody has shut the sliding glass door. Carlton's girlfriend looks lazily out, touching base with her own reflection. I look, too. Carlton is running toward the house. I hesitate. Then I figure he can bump his nose. It will be a good joke on him. I let him keep coming. His girlfriend sees him through her own reflection, starts to scream a warning just as Carlton hits the glass.

It is an explosion. Triangles of glass fly brightly through the room. I think for him it must be more surprising than painful, like hitting water from a great height. He stands blinking for a moment. The whole party stops, stares, getting its bearings. Bob Dylan sings "Just Like a Woman." Carlton reaches up curiously to take out the shard of glass that is stuck in his neck, and that is when the blood starts. It shoots out of him. Our mother screams. Carlton steps forward into his girlfriend's arms and the two of them fall together. Our mother throws herself down on top of him and the girl. People shout their accident wisdom. Don't lift him. Call an ambulance. I watch from the hallway. Carlton's blood spurts, soaking into the carpet, spattering people's clothes. Our mother and father both try to plug the wound with their hands, but the blood just shoots between their fingers. Carlton looks more puzzled than anything, as if he can't quite follow this turn of events. "It's all right," our father tells him, trying to stop the blood. "It's all right, just don't move, it's all right." Carlton nods, and holds our father's hand. His eyes take on an astonished light. Our mother screams, "Is anybody *doing* anything?" What comes out of Carlton grows darker, almost black. I watch. Our father

35

tries to get a hold on Carlton's neck while Carlton keeps trying to take his hand. Our mother's hair is matted with blood. It runs down her face. Carlton's girl holds him to her breasts, touches his hair, whispers in his ear.

He is gone by the time the ambulance gets there. You can see the life drain out of him. When his face goes slack our mother wails. A part of her flies wailing through the house, where it will wail and rage forever. I feel our mother pass through me on her way out. She covers Carlton's body with her own.

He is buried in the cemetery out back. Years have passed—we are living in the future, and it's turned out differently from what we'd planned. Our mother has established her life of separateness behind the guest-room door. Our father mutters his greetings to the door as he passes.

One April night, almost a year to the day after Carlton's accident, I hear cautious footsteps shuffling across the living-room floor after midnight. I run out eagerly, thinking of ghosts, but find only our father in moth-colored pajamas. He looks unsteadily at the dark air in front of him.

"Hi, Dad," I say from the doorway.

He looks in my direction. "Yes?"

"It's me. Bobby."

"Oh, Bobby," he says. "What are you doing up, young man?"

"Nothing," I tell him. "Dad?"

"Yes, son."

"Maybe you better come back to bed. Okay?"

"Maybe I had," he says. "I just came out here for a drink of water, but I seem to have gotten turned around in the darkness. Yes, maybe I better had."

I take his hand and lead him down the hall to his room. The grandfather clock chimes the quarter hour.

"Sorry," our father says.

I get him into bed. "There," I say. "Okay?"

"Perfect. Could not be better."

"Okay. Good night."

"Good night. Bobby?"

"Uh-huh?"

"Why don't you stay a minute?" he says. "We could have ourselves a talk, you and me. How would that be?"

"Okay," I say. I sit on the edge of his mattress. His bedside clock ticks off the minutes.

I can hear the low rasp of his breathing. Around our house, the Ohio night chirps and buzzes. The small gray finger of Carlton's stone pokes up among the others, within sight of the angel's blank white eyes. Above us, airplanes and satellites sparkle. People are flying even now toward New York or California, to take up lives of risk and invention.

I stay until our father has worked his way into a muttering sleep.

Carlton's girlfriend moved to Denver with her family a month before. I never learned what it was she'd whispered to him. Though she'd kept her head admirably during the accident, she lost her head afterward. She cried so hard at the funeral that she had to be taken away by her mother—an older, redder-haired version of her. She started seeing a psychiatrist three times a week. Everyone, including my parents, talked about how hard it was for her, to have held a dying boy in her arms at that age. I'm grateful to her for holding my brother while he died, but I never once heard her mention the fact that though she had been through something terrible, at least she was still alive and going places. At least she had protected herself by trying to warn him. I can appreciate the intricacies of her pain. But as long as she was in Cleveland, I could never look her straight in the face. I couldn't talk about the wounds she suffered. I can't even write her name.

37

JONATHAN

OUR seventh-grade class had been moved that September from scattered elementary schools to a single centralized junior high, a colossal blond brick building with its name suspended over its main entrance in three-foot aluminum letters spare and stern as my own deepest misgivings about the life conducted within. I had heard the rumors: four hours of homework a night, certain classes held entirely in French, razor fights in the bathrooms. It was childhood's end.

The first day at lunch, a boy with dark hair hanging almost to his shoulders stood behind my friend Adam and me in the cafeteria line. The boy was ragged and wild-looking: an emanation from the dangerous heart of the school itself.

"Hey," he said.

I could not be certain whether he was speaking to me, to Adam, or to someone else in the vicinity. His eyes, which were pink and watery, appeared to focus on something mildly surprising that hovered near our feet.

I nodded. It seemed a decent balance between my fear of looking snobbish and my dread of seeming overeager. I had made certain resolutions regarding a new life. Adam, a businesslike barrel-shaped boy I had known since second grade, dabbed at an invisible spot on his starched plaid shirt. He was the son of a taxidermist, and possessed a precocious mistrust of the unfamiliar.

We slowly advanced in the line, holding yellow plastic trays.

"Some joint, huh?" the boy said. "I mean, like, how long you guys in for?"

This was definitely addressed to us, though his gaze had not yet meandered up to address our eyes. Now I was justified in looking at him. He had a broad handsome face with a thin nose slightly cleft at the tip, and a jaw heavy enough to suggest Indian blood. There were aureoles of blond stubble at his lips and chin.

"Life," I said.

He nodded contemplatively, as if I had said something ambiguous and thought-provoking.

A moment passed. Adam would have gotten through the conversation by feigning well-mannered deafness. I struggled to be cool. The silence caught and held—one of those amicable, protracted silences that open up in casual conversations with strangers and allow all members to return, unharmed, to the familiarity of their own lives. Adam visibly turned his attention toward the front of the line, as if something delightful and unprecedented was taking place there.

But then, forgetting my resolution, I fell into a habit from my old life, one of the personal deficiencies I had vowed to leave behind.

I started talking.

"I mean, this is it, don't you think?" I said. "Up till now everything's been sort of easy, I mean we were *kids*. I don't know what school you came from, but at Fillmore we had recess, I mean we had *snack* periods, and now, well, there are guys here who could fit my head in the palm of their hand. I haven't been to the bathroom yet, I hear there are eighth-graders waiting in there for seventh-graders to come in and if one does they pick him up by his feet and stick his head in the toilet. Did you hear that?"

Adam impatiently plucked a speck of lint from his collar. My ears heated up.

"Naw, man," the stranger said after a moment. "I didn't hear anything like that. I smoked a joint in the head before third period, and I didn't have any problems."

His voice carried no mocking undertone. By then we had

reached the steam table, where a red-faced woman parceled out macaroni casserole with an ice-cream scoop.

"Well, maybe it's not true," I said. "But you know, this is a rough place. A kid was murdered here last year."

Adam looked at me impatiently, as if I were a new stain that had somehow appeared on his shirtfront. I had abandoned my second resolution. I was not only babbling, I was starting to tell lies.

"Oh yeah?" the boy said. He appeared to find the assertion interesting but unexceptional. He wore a washed-out blue work shirt and a brown leather jacket that dribbled dirty fringe from its sleeves.

"Yeah," I said. "A new kid, a seventh-grader. It was in all the papers. He was, well, sort of fat. And a little retarded. He carried a briefcase, and he kept his glasses on with one of those black elastic bands. Anyway, he showed up here and a whole gang of eighth-graders started teasing him. At first it was just, you know, regular teasing, and they would probably have gotten tired of it and left him alone if he'd been smart enough to keep his mouth shut. But he had a bad temper, this kid. And the more they teased him, the madder he got."

We worked our way down the line, accumulating small bowls filled with corn kernels, waxed cartons of milk, and squares of pale yellow cake with yellow icing. We sat together without having formally decided to, simply because the story of the murdered boy wasn't finished yet. I stretched it out over most of the lunch period. I omitted no detail of the gang's escalating tortures—the stolen glasses, the cherry bomb dropped in the locker, the dead cat slipped into the victim's briefcase—or of the hapless boy's mounting, impotent rage. Adam alternated between listening to me and staring at the people sitting at other tables, with the unabashed directness of one who believes his own unimportance renders him invisible. We had finished our macaroni and corn and had started on our cake before the victim took his revenge, in the form of a wire stretched all but invisibly, at neck's height, across the trail where the older boys rode their dirt bikes. We were through with our dessert by the time he botched the job—he had not secured the wire tightly enough to the tree trunks—and were on our way to our next classes before the police found him floating in the reservoir, his new glasses still held in place by their elastic band.

We walked together, we three, to Adam's and my math class. He and I had planned to share as many classes as possible. I finished the story at the door.

"Hey, man," the stranger said. He shook his head, and said nothing more.

"My name is Jonathan Glover," I said.

"I'm, um, Bobby Morrow."

After a moment, Adam said, "Adam Bialo?" as if uncertain whether such a name would be believed. It was the first time he had spoken.

"Well, see you later," I said.

"Yeah. Yeah, man, I'll see you later."

It was not until he walked away that I saw the faded blue eye stitched to the back of his jacket.

"Weird," Adam said.

"Uh-huh."

"I thought you weren't going to tell any more lies," he said. "I thought you took an oath."

In fact, we had traded oaths. I was to abandon my storytelling, and he to cease inspecting his clothes for imperfections.

"That was a tall tale. It's different from a lie."

"Weird," he said. "You're about as weird as he is."

"Well," I answered, with a certain satisfaction. "I guess maybe I am."

"I believe it," he said. "I have no doubt."

We stood for a moment, watching the stranger's embroidered eye recede down the biscuit-colored hall. "*Weird*," Adam said once again, and there was true indignation in his voice, a staunch insistence on the world's continuing responsibility to observe the rules of cleanliness and modesty. One of Adam's attractions had always been his exasperated—but ultimately willing—sidekick quality. His shuffling, uncurious ways made me look more exotic than I was; in his company I could be the daring one. As I chronicled our mild adventures in my own mind, I cast Adam as a hybrid of Becky Thatcher and Sancho Panza, while I was Huck,

Tom, and Nancy Drew all mixed together. Adam considered a nude swim or a stolen candy bar to be broaching the limits, limits I was only too happy to exceed. He helped me realize my own romantic ideal, though lately I'd begun to suspect that our criminal escapades were pathetically small-time, and that Adam would not accompany me into waters much deeper than these.

Bobby was waiting for us at lunch the following day. Or, rather, he managed to turn up next to us in line again. He had a particular talent for investing his actions with the quality of randomness—his life, viewed from a distance, would have appeared to be little more than a series of coincidences. He exerted no visible will. And yet, by some vague-eyed trick, he was there with us in line again.

"Hey," he said. Today his eyes were even redder, more rheumily unfocused.

"Hey," I said. Adam bent over to pull a loose thread from the cuff of his corduroys.

"Day number two, man," Bobby said. "Only a thousand five hundred to go. Yow."

"Have we really got one thousand five hundred days of school left?" I asked. "I mean, is that an actual count?"

"Uh-huh," he said. "Like, give or take a few."

"They add up, don't they? Two years here, four in high school, and four in college. Man. A thousand five hundred days."

"I wasn't counting *col*lege, man." He smiled, as if the idea of college was grandiose and slightly absurd—a colonial's vision of silver tea sets gleaming in the jungle.

"Right, man," I said.

Again, the silence opened. Again, in defiance of Adam's fierce concentration on the front of the line—where the red-faced woman ladled up some sort of brown triangles in brown sauce—I started in on a story. Today I told of a new, experimental kind of college that taught students the things they would need to know for survival in the world: how to travel inexpensively, how to play blues piano and recognize true love. It wasn't much of a story—I was only an adequate liar, not a brilliant one. My fabricating technique had more to do with persistence than with inspiration. I told lies the way Groucho Marx told jokes, piling one atop another in the hope that my simple endurance would throw a certain light of credibility onto the whole.

Bobby listened with uncritical absorption. He did not insist on the difference between the believable and the absurd. Something in his manner suggested that all earthly manifestations—from the cafeteria peach halves floating in their individual pools of syrup to my story of a university that required its students to live for a week in New York City with no money at all—were equally bizarre and amusing. I did not at that time fully appreciate the effects of smoking more than four joints a day.

All he did was listen, smile vaguely, and offer an occasional "Yeah" or "Wow."

Again, he sat and ate with us. Again, he walked us to our math class.

When he had gone, Adam said, "I was wrong yesterday. You're *weirder* than he is."

Adam and I took less than a month to realize that our friendship was already a childhood memory. We made certain attempts to haul it into the future with us, because we had, in our slightly peevish, mutually disapproving way, genuinely loved one another. We had told secrets; we had traded vows. Still, it was time for us to put one another aside. When I suggested one afternoon that we steal the new Neil Young album from the record store, he looked at me with a tax accountant's contempt, based not so much on my immediate dishonesty as on the whole random, disorderly life I would make for myself. "You've never even *listened* to Neil Young," he said. "Man," I said, and left the sphere of his cautious, alphabetizing habits to stand near a group of long-haired high school students who were talking about Jimi Hendrix, of whom I had never heard. I stole *Electric Ladyland* after Adam, with a sigh of exhausted virtue, had walked out of the store.

We did not accomplish the split without rancor or recriminations. I had an immediate new friend and he didn't. Our final conversation took place at the bus stop before school on a warm October morning. Autumn light fell from a vaulted powder-blue

43

sky that offered, here and there, a cloud so fat and dense-looking it might have been full of milk. I motioned Adam away from the knot of other kids waiting for the bus and showed him what I'd brought: two pale yellow pills stolen from my mother's medicine cabinet.

"What *are* they?" he asked.

"The bottle said Valium."

"What's that?"

"I don't know," I said. "A tranquilizer, I guess. Here. Let's take one and see what they do."

He looked at me uncomprehendingly. "Take one of these pills?" he said. "Now?"

"Hey, man," I whispered. "Keep your voice down."

"Take one and go to *school*?" he asked, in a louder voice.

"Yep," I said. "Come on."

"We don't even know what they'll *do* to us."

"This is one way to find out. Come on. My mom takes 'em, how bad can they be?"

"Your mom is *sick*," he said.

"She's no sicker than most people," I told him. The pills, yellow disks the size of nailheads, sat in my palm, reflecting the suburban light. To end the discussion, I snatched one up and swallowed it.

"Weird," Adam said sorrowfully. "*Weird.*" He turned from me and went to stand with the others waiting for the bus. We had our next conversation twelve years later, when he appeared with his wife out of the red semidarkness of a hotel bar in New York and told me of his cleaning business, which specialized in the most difficult jobs: wedding gowns, ancient lace, rugs that had all but married themselves to the dust of ten decades. He seemed, in truth, to be quite content.

I slipped the second pill back into my pocket, and spent the morning in a drowsy bliss that matched the weather. When I saw Bobby at lunch, we smiled and said, "Hey, man," to one another. I gave Adam's pill to him. He accepted it, slipping it into his mouth with simple gratitude and no questions. That day I did not tell any stories; I hardly spoke at all. I learned that Bobby found sitting silently beside me just as amusing as he did listening to me talk.

* * *

"I like those boots," I said as he sat for the first time on the floor of my bedroom, rolling a joint. "Where did you get them? Or, wait a minute, that's the kind of question you're not supposed to ask, isn't it? Anyway, I think those boots of yours are great."

"Thanks," he said, expertly sealing the joint with a flick of his tongue. I had never smoked marijuana before, though I claimed to have been doing it regularly since I was eleven.

"That looks like good stuff," I said of the plastic bag full of green-gold marijuana he had produced from his jacket pocket.

"Well, it's—you know—all right," he said, lighting up. There was no scorn in his stunted sentences, just a numbness and puzzlement. He had about him the hesitant quality of an amnesiac struggling to remember.

"I like the smell," I said. "I guess I'd better open the window. In case my mother comes by."

I naturally assumed we needed common enemies in the forms of the United States government, our school, my parents.

"She's nice," he said. "Your mother."

"She's all right."

He passed the joint over to me. Of course I tried to handle it in a polished, professional manner. Of course on my first toke I gagged so hard I nearly vomited.

"It's pretty strong," he said. He took the joint back, sucked in a graceful nip of smoke, and returned it to me without further comment. I choked again, and after I'd recovered was given the joint a third time, as if I was every bit as practiced as I pretended to be. The third time I did a little better.

And so, without acknowledging my inexperience, Bobby set about teaching me the habits of the age.

We spent every day together. It was the kind of reckless overnight friendship particular to those who are young, lonely, and ambitious. Gradually, item by item, Bobby brought over his records, his posters, his clothes. We spent just enough time at his house for me to know what he was escaping from: a stale sour smell of soiled laundry and old food, a father who crept with

45

drunken caution from room to room. Bobby slept in a sleeping bag on my floor. In the dark, I lay listening to the sound of his breath. He moaned sometimes in his dreams.

When he awoke in the mornings, he'd look around with a startled expression, realize where he was, and smile. The light slanting in through my window turned the medallion of hair on his chest from gold to copper.

I bought myself a pair of boots like his. I started growing my hair.

With time, he began to talk more fluently. "I like this house," he said one winter evening as we sat idly in my room, smoking dope and listening to The Doors. Snowflakes tapped against the glass, whirled down into the empty, silent street. The Doors sang "L.A. Woman."

"How much would a house like this cost?" he said.

"Can't be too much," I said. "We're not rich."

"I want a house like this someday," he said, passing me the joint.

"No you don't," I told him. I had other things in mind for us.

"Yeah," he said. "I do. I like this place."

"You don't really," I said. "You just think you do because you're stoned."

He sucked on the joint. He had a cultivated, almost feminine way of handling his dope, pinching a joint precisely between thumb and middle finger. "So I'll stay stoned all the time," he said on his exhale. "Then I'll always like this house and Cleveland and everything, just the way it is now."

"Well, that would be one way to live," I answered.

"Don't you like it?" he said. "You should like it. You don't know what you got here."

"What I've got here," I said, "is a mother who asks me first thing in the morning what I think I'd like to have for dinner that night, and a father who hardly ever leaves his movie theater."

"Yeah, man," he grinned.

His forearm, thick-wristed, golden-haired, rested casually on his knee. It just rested there, as if it was nothing special.

46

* * *

I believe I know the moment my interest turned to love. One night in early spring Bobby and I were sitting together in my room, listening to the Grateful Dead. It was an ordinary night in my altered life. Bobby passed me the joint, and after I'd accepted it, he withdrew his hand and glanced at a liver-colored mole on the underside of his left wrist. His face registered mild incredulity—in the thirteen years he had known his own body, he had apparently not taken stock of that particular mole, though I had noticed it on any number of occasions, a slightly off-center discoloration riding the fork in a vein. The mole surprised him. I suspect it frightened him a little, to see his own flesh made strange. He touched the mole, curiously, with his right index finger, and his face was nakedly fretful as a baby's. As he worried over that small imperfection, I saw that he inhabited his own flesh as fully and with the same mix of wonder and confusion that I brought to my own. Until then I had believed—though I would never have confessed it, not even to myself—that all others were slightly less real than I; that their lives were a dream composed of scenes and emotions that resembled snapshots: discrete and unambiguous, self-evident, flat. He touched the mole on his wrist with tenderness, and with a certain dread. It was a minute gesture. Seeing it was no more dramatic than seeing somebody check his watch and register surprise at the time. But in that moment Bobby cracked open. I could see him—he was *in* there. He moved through the world in a chaos of self, fearful and astonished to be here, right here, alive in a pine-paneled bedroom.

Then the moment passed and I was on the other side of something. After that night—a Tuesday—I could not have returned, even if I'd desired it, to a state that did not involve thinking and dreaming of Bobby. I could not help investing his every quality with a heightened sense of the real, nor could I quit wondering, from moment to moment, exactly what it was like to be inside his skin.

Night after night we roamed the streets like spies. We befriended a bum named Louis, who lived in a piano crate and bought us bottles of red wine in exchange for food we stole from my mother's

47

kitchen. We climbed up fire escapes onto downtown roofs for the strangeness of standing in a high place. We dropped acid and wandered for hours through a junkyard that sparkled like a diamond mine, rife with caverns and peculiar glitterings and plateaus that glowed with a bleached, lunar light I tried to scoop up with my hands. We hitchhiked to Cincinnati to see if we could get there and back before my parents realized we were missing.

Once, on a Thursday night, Bobby took me to the cemetery where his brother and mother were buried. We sat on their graves, passing a joint.

"Man," he said, "I'm not afraid of graveyards. The dead are just, you know, people who wanted the same things you and I want."

"What do we want?" I asked blurrily.

"Aw, man, you know," he said. "We just want, well, the same things these people here wanted."

"What was that?"

He shrugged. "To live, I guess," he said.

He ran his fingers over the grass. He handed me the joint, which was wet with our mingled saliva, and I blew a stream of white smoke up into the sky, where the Seven Sisters quivered and sparked. Cleveland sent up its own small lights—television and shaded lamps. A passing car left a few bars of "Helter Skelter" behind on the cold night air.

April came. It was not swimming weather yet, but I insisted that we go to the quarry as soon as the last scabs of old snow had disappeared from the shadows. I knew we'd go swimming naked. I was rushing the season.

It was one of those spring days that emerge scoured from the long, long freeze, with a sky clear as melted snow. The first hardy, thick-stemmed flowers had poked out of the ground. The quarry, which lay three miles out of town, reflected sky on a surface dark and unmoving as obsidian. Except for a lone caramel-colored cow that had wandered down from a pasture to drink in the shallows, Bobby and I were the only living things there. We might have hiked to a glaciated lake high in the Himalayas.

48

"Beautiful," he said. We were passing a joint. A blue jay rose, with a single questioning shrill, from an ash tree still in bud.

"We have to swim," I said. "We have to."

"Still too cold," he said. "That water'd be freezing, man."

"We have to, anyway. Come on. It's the first official swim of summer. If we don't swim today, it'll start snowing again tomorrow."

"Who told you that?"

"Everybody knows it. Come *on*."

"Maybe," he said. "Awful cold, though."

By then we had reached the gravel bed that passed for a beach, where the cow, who stood primly at the water's edge, stared at us with coal-black eyes. This quarry had a rough horseshoe shape, with limestone cliffs that rose in a jagged half circle and then fell back again to the beach.

"It's not the least bit cold," I said to Bobby. "It's like Bermuda by this time of year. Watch me."

Spurred by my fear that we would do no more that day than smoke a joint, fully clothed, beside a circle of dark water, I started up the shale-strewn slope that led to the clifftop. The nearer cliffs were less than twenty feet high, and in summer the more courageous swimmers dove from there into the deep water. I had never even thought of diving off the cliff before. I was nothing like brave. But that day I scrambled in my cowboy boots, which still pinched, up the slope to the cracked limestone platform that sprouted, here and there, a lurid yellow crocus.

"It's summer up here," I shouted back to Bobby, who stood alone on the beach, cupping the joint. "Come on," I shouted. "Don't test the water with your fingers, just come up here and we'll dive in. We've got to."

"Naw, Jon," he called. "Come back."

With that, I began taking off my clothes in a state of humming, high-blown exhilaration. This was a more confident, daring Jonathan standing high on a sun-warmed rock, stripping naked before the puzzled gaze of a drinking cow.

"Jon," Bobby called, more urgently.

As I pulled off my shirt and then my boots and socks, I knew a raw abandon I had never felt before. The sensation grew as each

49

new patch of skin touched the light and the cool, brilliant air. I could feel myself growing lighter, taking on possibility, with every stitch I removed. I got ungracefully out of my jeans and boxer shorts, and stood for a moment, scrawny, naked, and wild, touched by the cold sun.

"This is it," I hollered.

Bobby, far below, said, "Hey, man, no—"

And for the sake of Bobby, for the sake of my new life, I dove.

A thin sheet of ice still floated on the water, no more than a membrane, invisible until I broke through it. I heard the small crackling, felt the ice splinter around me, and then I was plunged into unthinkable cold, a cold that stopped my breath and seemed, for a long moment, to have stopped my heart as well. My flesh itself shrank, clung in animal panic to the bone, and I thought with perfect clarity, I'm dead. This is what it's like.

Then I was on the surface, breaking through the ice a second time. My consciousness actually slipped out of my body, floated up, and in retrospect I have a distinct impression of watching myself swim to shore, gasping, lungs clenched like fists, the ice splintering with every stroke, sending diamond slivers up into the air.

Bobby waded in to his thighs to help pull me out. I remember the sight of his wet jeans, clinging darkly to his legs. I remember thinking his boots would be ruined.

It took another moment for my head to clear sufficiently to realize he was screaming at me, even as he helped me out of the water.

"Goddamn it," he yelled, and his mouth was very close to my ear. "Oh, goddamn you. God*damn*."

I was too occupied with my own breathing to respond. He got us well up onto the gravel before letting go of me and launching into a full-scale rant. The best I could do was stand, breathing and shivering, as he shouted.

At first he strode back and forth in a rigid pattern, as if touching two invisible goals ten feet apart, screaming "You motherfucker, you stupid motherfucker." As he shouted, his circuit between the two goals grew shorter and shorter, until he was striding in tight little circles, following the pattern of a coiled spring. His face was magenta. Finally he stopped walking, but still he turned completely around, three times, as if the spring were continuing to coil inside him. All the while he screamed. He stopped calling me a motherfucker and began making sounds I could not understand, a stream of infuriated babble that seemed directed not at me but at the sky and the cliffs, the mute trees.

I watched dumbly. I had never seen wrath like that before; I had not known it occurred in everyday life. There was nothing for me to do but wait, and hope it ended.

After some time, without saying what he was going to do, Bobby ran off to retrieve my clothes from the clifftop. Though his fury had quieted somewhat, it was by no means spent. I stood nude on the gravel, waiting for him. When he came back with my clothes and boots he dumped them in a pile at my feet, saying, "Put 'em on fast," in a tone of deep reproach. I did as I was told.

When I had dressed he draped his jacket around me, over my own. "No, you need it," I said. "Your pants are all wet . . ."

"Shut up," he told me, and I did.

We started back to the highway, where we would hitch a ride to town. On the way Bobby put his arm around my shoulders and held me close to him. "Stupid fucker," he muttered. "Stupid, stupid. *Stupid*." He continued holding me as we stood with our thumbs out by the roadside, and continued holding me in the back seat of the Volkswagen driven by the two Oberlin students who picked us up. He kept his arm around me all the way home, muttering.

Back at my house, he ran a scalding-hot shower. He all but undressed me, and ordered me in. Only after I was finished, and wrapped in towels, did he take off his own wet clothes and get in the shower himself. His bare skin was bright pink in the steamy bathroom. When he emerged, glistening, studded with droplets, the medallion of pale hair was plastered to his chest.

We went to my room, put on Jimi Hendrix, and rolled a joint. We sat in our towels, smoking. "Stupid," he whispered. "You could have killed yourself. You know how I'd have felt if you'd done that?"

"No," I said.

"I'd have felt like, I don't know."

And then he looked at me with such sorrow. I put the joint down in the ashtray and, in an act of courage that far outstripped jumping off a cliff into icy water—that exceeded all my brave acts put together—I reached out and laid my hand on his forearm. There it was, his arm, sinewy and golden-haired, under my fingers. I looked at the floor—the braided rug and pumpkin-colored planks. Bobby did not pull his arm away.

A minute passed. Either nothing or something had to happen. In terror, with my pulse jumping at my neck, I began to stroke his arm with the tip of my index finger. Now, I thought, he will see what I'm after. Now he'll bolt in horror and disgust. Still I kept on with that single miniature gesture, in a state of fear so potent it was indistinguishable from desire. He did not recoil, nor did he respond.

Finally I managed to look at his face. His eyes were bright and unblinking as an animal's, his mouth slack. I could tell he was frightened too, and it was his fear that enabled me to move my hand to his bare shoulder. His skin prickled with gooseflesh over the smooth broad curve of his scapula. I could feel the subtle rise and fall of his breathing.

Quickly, because I lacked the nerve for deliberation, I moved my hand to his thigh. He twitched and grimaced, but did not retreat. I burrowed my hand in under the towel he wore. I watched expressions of fear and pleasure skate across his eyes. Because I had no idea what to do, I replicated the strokes I'd used on myself. When he stiffened in my hand it seemed like a gesture of forgiveness.

Then he put out a hand and, with surprising delicacy, touched me, too. We did not kiss. We did not embrace. Jimi sang "Purple Haze." The furnace rumbled from deep in the house. Steam hissed through the pipes.

We mopped up with Kleenexes afterward, and dressed in silence. Once we were dressed, however, Bobby relit the joint and began talking in his usual voice about usual things: the Dead's next concert tour, our plan to get jobs and buy a car together. We passed the joint and sat on the floor of my room like any two American teenagers, in an ordinary house surrounded by the boredom and struggling green of an Ohio spring. Here was another lesson in my continuing education: like other illegal practices, love between boys was best treated as a commonplace. Courtesy demanded that one's fumbling, awkward performance be no occasion for remark, as if in fact one had acted with the calm expertise of a born criminal.

ALICE

O UR SON Jonathan brought him home. They were both thirteen then. He looked hungry as a stray dog, and just that sly and dangerous. He sat at our table, wolfing roast chicken.

"Bobby," I asked, "have you been in town long?"

His hair was an electrified nest. He wore boots, and a leather jacket decorated with a human eye worked in faded cobalt thread.

"All my life," he answered, gnawing on a legbone. "It's just that I've been invisible. I only lately decided to let myself be seen."

I wondered if his parents fed him. He kept glancing around the dining room with such appetite that I felt for a moment like the witch in *Hansel and Gretel*. As a child in New Orleans, I had watched termites browsing the wooden scrollwork under our parlor window, and found that the intricate carving broke away in my hands like sugar.

"Well, welcome to the material world," I said.

"Thank you, ma'am."

He did not smile. He bit down on that bone hard enough to crack it.

After he'd gone I said to Jonathan, "He's a character, isn't he? Where did you find him?"

"He found *me*," Jonathan said with the exaggerated patience that was a particular feature of his adolescence. Although his skin was still smooth and his voice sweet, he had devised a brusque knowingness by way of entry into manhood.

"And how did he find you?" I asked mildly. I could still work Southern innocence to my advantage, even after all those years in Ohio.

"He came up to me the first day of school and just started hanging around."

"Well, I think he's peculiar," I said. "He gives me the creeps just a little, to tell you the truth."

"I think he's cool," Jonathan said with finality. "He had an older brother who was murdered."

In New Orleans we'd had a term for people like Bobby, unprosperous-looking people whose relations were more than usually prone to violent ends. Still, I allowed as how he was quite evidently a cool customer.

"What would you say to a game of hearts before bed?" I asked.

"No, Mom. I'm tired of playing cards."

"Just one game," I said. "You've got to give me a chance to recoup my losses."

"Well, okay. One game."

We cleared the table, and I dealt the cards. I played badly, though. My mind kept straying to that boy. He had looked at our house with such open, avid greed. Jonathan took trick after trick. I went upstairs for a sweater and still could not seem to get warm.

Jonathan shot the moon. "Look out," he said. "I'm hot to-night."

He took such simple, boyish delight in winning that he forgot about his new peevishness. I could not imagine why he wasn't more popular at school. He was clever, and better-looking than most of the boys I saw around town. Perhaps my Southern influence had rendered him too gentle and articulate, too little the brute for that hard Midwestern city. But of course I was no judge. What mother isn't a bit in love with her own son?

* * *

55

Ned got home late, after midnight. I was upstairs reading when I heard his key in the door. I resisted an urge to snap out the bedside light and feign sleep. Soon I would turn thirty-five. I had made some promises to myself regarding our marriage.

I could hear his breathing as he mounted the stairs. I sat up a bit straighter on the pillow, adjusted the strap of my nightgown. He stood in the bedroom doorway, a man of forty-three, still handsome by ordinary standards. His hair was going gray at the sides, in movie-star fashion.

"You're still up," he said. Was he pleased or annoyed?

"I'm a slave to this," I said, gesturing at the book. No, wrong already. *I waited up for you.* That was the proper response. Still, the book had in fact been what kept me awake. I liked to think you could change your life without abandoning the simple daily truths.

He came into the room, unbuttoning his shirt. A V of chest appeared, the dark hair flecked with gray. "Looks like *Deliverance* is a little too strong for Cleveland," he said. "Three sets of parents called to complain tonight."

"I don't know why you booked it," I said.

He peeled off his shirt and wadded it into the clothes hamper. Sweat glistened under his arms. When he turned I could see the hair, like a symmetrical map of Africa, that had sprouted on his back.

No. Focus on his kindness, his gentle humor. Focus on the shape of his flanks, still lean, in his gabardine slacks.

"I'm lucky to have it," he said. "It'll be a hit. The seven o'clock was three-quarters full."

"Good," I said. I put my book down on the night table. It made a soft but surprisingly audible sound against the wood.

He took his slacks off. If I'd been a different sort of person I could have said, humorously, "Sweetheart, take your socks off first. If there's one thing I can't abide, it's the sight of a man in nothing but his Jockey shorts and a pair of black socks."

I wasn't that sort of person. Ned hung his pants up neatly and stood for a moment in the lamplight, wearing briefs and the slick dark socks he insisted on buying. They had rubbed the hair off his shins. When he removed them, they would leave the imprint of their weave on the hairless flesh.

He put his pajama bottoms on over his shorts, then sat on the bed to remove his socks. Outside of the shower, Ned was rarely stark naked.

"Whew," he said. "I'm beat."

I reached over to stroke his back, which was moist with perspiration. He startled.

"Don't you worry," I said. "I mean you no harm."

He smiled. "Nervous Nellie," he said.

"Jonathan had a new friend over tonight. You should see him."

"Worse than Adam?" he asked.

"Oh, much. Of a different order entirely. This one's a little, well, frightening."

"How so?"

"Grubby," I said. "Silent. Sort of hungry-looking."

Ned shook his head. "Leave it to Jonny," he said. "He can pick 'em."

I felt a twinge of annoyance. Ned was away so much of the time. Whatever took place in his absence became a domestic comedy of sorts; a pleasant little movie playing to a sparse house across town. I continued stroking his back.

"But this boy seems frightening in a more *adult* way," I said. "Adam and the others were children. I feel like this boy could steal, he could be up to all kinds of things. And it got me thinking. Jonathan himself is changing, there'll be girls and cars and lord knows what-all."

"Sure there will be, Grandmaw," Ned said, and got good-naturedly under the bedcovers. I knew how he pictured it: a teen-age comedy, harmlessly entertaining, replete with first dates and hippie friends. Perhaps he was right. But I couldn't see it as a movie, myself. I couldn't tell him how different it feels when it's your hour-to-hour experience. I knew that if I tried to, I'd end up sounding just like the mother in the movie: a bird-like, overly dramatic character; the one who doesn't get the jokes.

"Okay with you if I douse the lights?" he said. "Or are you going to flail away at that book a little longer?"

"No. Turn out the light."

We settled ourselves and lay side by side, breathing in the darkness. It seemed there should be so much for us to talk about. Perhaps the biggest surprise of married life was its continuing formality, even as you came to know the other's flesh and habits better than you knew your own. For all that familiarity, we could still seem like two people on a date that was not going particularly well.

"I made the chicken with tarragon tonight," I said. "You should have seen him gobble it up. You'd have thought he hadn't eaten in a week."

"The friend?" Ned said.

"Yes."

"What's his name?"

"Bobby."

Outside, one of the neighbor's cats yowled. Since Miss Heidegger died, her house had been rented to a succession of three different families, all of whom were prone to noisy, underfed pets and sudden departures. The neighborhood was going down.

"Ned?" I said.

"Mm-hm?"

"Do I look much older to you?"

"You look about sixteen," he said.

"Well, I'm far from sixteen. Thirty-four used to seem so old. Now it doesn't seem like anything. But I've got a son who's going to be shaving soon. Who's going to be keeping secrets and driving away in the car."

I didn't know how to tell him in a way he'd understand: I felt myself ceasing to be a main character. I couldn't say it in just those words. They would not pass through the domestic air of our bedroom.

"Thirty-four is nothing, kiddo," he said. "Look who you're talking to. I can hardly *remember* being thirty-four."

"I know. I'm just vain and foolish."

I reached over, under the blanket, and stroked his chest. Again, his skin prickled under my hand. He was not accustomed to these attentions from me.

"You look great," he said. "You're in the prime of your life."

58

"Ned?"

"Uh-huh?"

"I do love you, you know. Lord, how long has it been since I've said that?"

"Oh, sweetheart. I love you, too."

I worked my fingers down along his bicep, petted his forearm. "I'm being mawkish tonight," I said. "I'm departing from my old stiff-backed ways."

"You're not stiff-backed," he said.

"Not tonight," I said in an even voice. It was not seductive, but neither was it dry or matronly.

He wrapped his fingers over mine. I'd imagined marriage in one of two ways: either you loved a man and coupled with him happily, or you didn't. I'd never considered the possibility of loving someone without an accompanying inclination of the flesh.

He cleared his throat. I leaned over to kiss him, and he let himself be kissed with a passivity that was virginal, almost girlish. That touched me, even as his beard stubble scraped against my skin.

"Not tonight," I said again, and this time I was able to make my voice low and breathy. It seemed a good imitation of lust, one I might catch up with and take as my own if he caressed me as shyly as he permitted my kiss.

"Mmm," he said, a low growl that rumbled up from deep in his throat. I felt a lightness in the pit of my stomach, a sense of expanding possibility I had not known with him in some time. It could still happen.

Then he kissed me back, raising his head off the pillow and pressing his mouth against mine. I felt the pressure of his teeth. The lightness collapsed inside me, but I did not give up. I answered his kiss, took his bare shoulder in the palm of my hand. It was moist with sweat. I could feel the coarse corkscrew hairs on the palm of my hand. His teeth, only thinly cushioned by his upper lip, bit urgently into my mouth.

And I knew I couldn't make it. Not that night. I fell out of the scene. My attention left my body and stepped to the far side of the room, where it watched disapprovingly as a man of forty-three roughly kissed his wife, ran moist hands over her aging back and sides. I could have gone through the motions but it would have been only that and nothing more. I'd have suffered through it with the smoldering anger that lies bring.

I disengaged my mouth, planted a series of small kisses along his neck. "Honey," I whispered, "just hold me a minute. Okay?"

"Sure," he said easily. "Sure." To be honest, I think he was relieved.

We lay embracing for a while, until Ned kissed my scalp affectionately and turned away for sleep. We did not sleep in one another's arms; never had. Soon he was breathing rhythmically. Sleep came easily to Ned. Almost everything did. He had a talent for adjusting his expectations to meet his circumstances.

Perhaps tonight had been a start. Perhaps, the following night, I would manage a little more.

I didn't want to be the monster of the house—the fretting mother, the ungenerous wife. I made the promises to myself once again, and hardly slept until the windows were blue with the first light.

Jonathan persisted in his fascination with Bobby, who became a fixture at our table. Ned tolerated him, because it was Ned's nature to go along. He kept a layer of neutral air between his person and the world, so that whatever reached him had been filtered and rarefied.

It was I who kept the accounts.

Bobby seemed to have no other plans. He was perennially available. He never invited Jonathan to his house, which sat all right with me, but still I began to wonder. One night I asked him, "Bobby, what does your father do?"

We were eating dinner, he sopping up the last of his *beurre blanc* with his third piece of homemade bread seemingly before Jonathan or Ned or I had started to eat.

"He's a teacher" was the answer. "Not our school. Over at Roosevelt."

"And your mother?"

"She died. About a year ago."

He stuffed the bread into his mouth and reached for another piece.

"I'm so sorry," I said.

"You shouldn't be sorry," he told me. "You didn't even know her."

"I meant it in a more general way. I meant I'm sorry about your loss."

Gorging, he looked at me as if I had just spoken in Sanskrit. After a moment he said, "How do you make this sauce?"

"Butter and vinegar," I said. "Lemon, a little vermouth. Nothing to it, really."

"I never had sauce like this," he said. "You made this bread?"

"Bread's a hobby of mine," I said. "I just about do it in my sleep."

"Yow," he said. Shaking his head in astonishment, he reached for his fourth slice.

After dinner the boys went up to Jonathan's room. In a moment we heard the stereo, an unfamiliar drumbeat that thumped through the floorboards. Bobby had brought some of his records over.

Ned said, "My God, the kid's an orphan."

"He's not an orphan," I said. "His father is alive."

"You know what I mean. That kid's in a bad way."

I got up to clear the dishes. When I was a girl there had been parts of town we never went near. They were dark spots, blank areas on the map. I said, "Yes, and that's why Jonathan is so taken with him. If he were lame on top of it, we'd have him here every night instead of every other."

"Whoa there," Ned said. "This doesn't sound like you."

I stacked Bobby's empty plate on top of Jonathan's. Jonathan had artfully distributed his food around the edges of his plate, so it would appear to have been consumed. He was so thin you could just about see through him in a strong light. Bobby's plate was spotless, as if he had scoured it with his tongue. Nary a crumb was left on the cloth where he'd sat.

"I know it doesn't," I said. "I'm sorry about all that's happened to him, I really am. But something about that boy frightens me."

"He's wild, is what he is. He's a boy with no one but a father, growing up half wild. We have resources enough to give some shelter to a wild boy, don't you think?"

"Of course we do."

61

I carried the plates into the kitchen. I was sullen, bone-hard Alice, married to Ned the Good.

He followed, bringing dishes. "Don't worry," he said from behind me. "Every kid brings home a few wild friends. Jonathan will grow up fine, regardless."

"But I do worry about him," I said, running water. "He's thirteen. This is like—oh, I don't know. It's almost like seeing some hidden quality of Jonathan's come suddenly to light. Something he's been harboring all along that we never knew about."

"You're overplaying the scene."

"Am I?"

"Yes. If I had the time I'd tell you all about Robby Cole. He was my best friend in grade school. I was devoted to him because he could set off caps with his teeth. Among other things."

"And look how you turned out."

"Well, I married you," he said.

"A laudable accomplishment. Perhaps less than a life's purpose, though."

"I married you and I run the best movie theater in Greater Cleveland. And I've got to go."

"Goodbye."

He put his hands around my waist, kissed me loudly on the neck. I was visited briefly by his smell, the particular odor of his skin mingled with citrus after-shave. It was like entering his sphere of inhabited air, and as long as I stood within that sphere I could share his belief that bad things passed away of their own accord, that the world conspired toward good outcomes. I turned and lightly kissed his rough cheek.

"Worry less," he said.

I promised to try. While he was in the house, it seemed possible. But as soon as he left, the possibility receded like light from a lantern he carried. I watched him through the kitchen window. Perhaps Ned's most remarkable feature was his ability to walk serenely in this city of gray stone and yellow brick, where the wind off the lake could shrink people's hearts to pins.

I took down the new cookbook I had just bought, full of recipes from the French countryside, and began planning tomorrow's meal.

Bobby stayed until well after ten, until I'd called out, "Boys, it's a school night." Even then, after thirteen years of it, I was surprised at how much like somebody's mother I could sound.

I was reading the paper when Bobby came downstairs. "Good night," he said.

His way of speaking, his whole manner, was like that of a foreigner learning the customs of the country. He resembled more than anything a refugee from some distant place, underfed and desperate to please. His delivery of the words "good night" had precisely matched my own.

"Bobby?" I said. I had no next statement, really. It was just that he stood so expectantly.

"Uh-huh?"

"I truly am sorry about your mother," I said. "I hope I didn't sound just polite at the dinner table."

"It's okay."

"Do you and your father manage all right? Does dinner get cooked, and the house cleaned up every now and then?"

"Uh-huh. A woman comes once a week."

I said, "Why don't you bring your father for dinner one night? Maybe early next week?"

He looked at me darkly and questioningly, as if I had violated some taboo from his country; as if he could not immediately know whether I had meant to insult him or whether the rules were just that different over here.

"I don't know," he said.

"Well, maybe I'll give him a call. You'd better get along now, it's late."

"Okay."

I believe he'd have just continued standing in front of me until I told him to go.

"Good night," I said again, and had the sentiment returned to me in a young male version of my own voice.

After he'd gone I went upstairs and knocked on Jonathan's door.

"Uh-huh?" he said.

"Only me. May I come in?"

"Uh-huh."

He lay on his bed. A nasal male voice, accompanied by acoustic

63

guitar, rasped through the speakers. The window stood open though it was early November, and frosty. I believed I detected a smell, something sweet and smoky which the chill air had not quite dissipated.

I said, "Did you have a good evening?"

"Sure."

"Bobby's had a hard time of it, hasn't he?" I said.

"You shouldn't pity him."

"Did you know before that his mother was dead?"

"Uh-huh," Jonathan said.

"Do you know how she died?"

"Sort of. I mean, she took too many sleeping pills. But she had a prescription, she'd been taking them for years. I guess she'd started complaining they weren't working anymore. So it could have been an accident."

"Bobby had a brother who died, too?"

Jonathan nodded. "That was definitely an accident. It wasn't a murder after all. That's when the mother started in on sleeping pills."

He delivered these facts with a certain pride, as if they represented Bobby's worldly accomplishments.

"Lord. The things that happen to people."

I went and shut the window. It was almost cold enough to steam your breath in that room.

"And nothing's ever happened to us," Jonathan said. "Nothing bad."

"We're very lucky."

As I turned from the window I saw Bobby's leather jacket, draped over the chair. The embroidered eye, cyclopean, iris big as a hockey puck, stared from the worn cowhide.

"Bobby forgot his jacket," I said.

"He's loaning it to me," Jonathan said. "It used to be his brother's. I loaned him mine at school today."

"Your good windbreaker? You traded it for that?"

"Uh-huh. Bobby talks about his brother a lot. I mean, it sounds like he was pretty cool. When he died, it just about blew their whole family apart."

"Do you know what that windbreaker cost?" I asked.

He looked at me in the new way, his jaw set challengingly and his eyes gone hard.

I decided to let it go. I thought I'd give him the leeway to work it through his system.

"What would you think about veal stew for dinner tomorrow night?" I said. "There's a recipe I'd like to try, veal with mushrooms and pearl onions. How does that sound?"

"I don't care." He shrugged.

I held my arms close over my chest. It was freezing in that room.

"How about a quick game of hearts before bed?" I asked. "I'm in disgrace, you know. I lost so badly the last couple of times, I can barely hold my head up."

"No. I'm beat."

"One short game?"

"*No*, Mom."

"All right."

I stood for a moment, though it was clearly time to leave him alone. The light from his bedside lamp, which I had bought ten years ago, shone on his pale hair and precise, sculpted features. He took after me, but in an idealized way. My own looks, which any mirror told me were rather too severe, had come up softened in him.

"Good night," he said.

"Good night. Sleep well."

Still I lingered. I could not leave off looking at him, even if he resented me for it. If I'd had the courage I'd have said to him, "Don't do it. Please don't start hating me. You can have the world without shutting me out of your life."

I walked quietly from the room, as full of him as I had been when I was pregnant.

I invited Bobby and his father for dinner the following Tuesday. They arrived half an hour late, with two bottles of wine. "Sorry," the father said. "We had to drive all over town looking for a decent Chardonnay. I hope you like Chardonnay."

I told him we loved it.

He wore a goat's beard, and a mustard-colored jacket with bright brass buttons. His florid face was a riot of broken capillaries. He looked like an older, drunken Bobby.

The father's name was Burton. He scarcely touched his food when we sat down to eat. He drank wine, smoked Pall Malls, and paused occasionally in these activities to fork up a bit of my poached sole, hold it aloft for a moment or two, and insert it into his mouth with no more notice than a carpenter gives a tenpenny nail.

Ned asked him, "How do you find the kids over at Roosevelt?"

Burt Morrow looked at him uncomprehendingly. I recognized the expression.

"They can be difficult," he said in a measured voice. "They are not bad kids by and large but they can be difficult."

After a moment, Ned nodded. "I see."

"We try to get along," Burt said. "I try to get along with them. I try not to offend them, and am mostly successful, I believe." He turned to Bobby and asked, "Would you say that I'm mostly successful?"

"Yeah, Dad," Bobby said. He looked at his father with an expression neither loving nor disdainful. They shared a certain stunned quality, a way of responding to a question as if it had been posed by some disembodied voice whispering from the ether. They might have been the kindly, dim-witted older brothers in a fairy tale—the ones on whom the charms and enchantments are wasted. Jonathan sat between them, his blue eyes snapping with intelligence.

"That's all I try to do myself," I said. "Just stay out of Jonathan's way and let him experience life. Lord, I wouldn't know how to discipline. I sometimes still feel like a child myself."

Both Bobby and his father looked at me with numbly astonished faces.

"I married young, you know," I said. "I wasn't but a few years older than these boys are now, and I certainly hadn't planned on falling in love with a Northerner named Ned Glover, nor on getting myself moved to Ohio, with that Canadian wind blowing sleet up off the lake. Brr. Not that I'd do things any differently."

Ned winked and said, "I call her Helen of Louisiana. I'm still waiting for a bunch of Southerners to leave a wooden horse on the front lawn."

Burt lit another cigarette. He let the smoke drift out of his open mouth, and watched it snake its way over the table. "I might do some things differently," he said. "I think you'd have to say that I would. Yes."

I was not ignorant of psychology. I knew Jonathan needed to escape from his father and me, to sever the bonds: to murder us, in a sense, and then resurrect us later, when he was a grown man with a life of his own and we had faded into elderly inconsequentiality. I wasn't blind, or foolish.

Still, it seemed too soon, and Bobby seemed the wrong vehicle. At thirteen we have so many choices to make, with no idea about how consequences can rattle through the decades. When I was thirteen I had consciously decided to be talkative and a little wild, to ensure that my own parents' silent dinners and their long, bookish evenings—marked only by the chimes of the clock— would have no lasting effect on me. I had been barely seventeen when I met Ned Glover, a handsome, humorous man in his twenties, owner of a Chrysler convertible, full of stories from the North.

That night in bed I said to him, "Well, at least now we know how Bobby comes by it."

"Comes by what?"

"Everything. His whole personality. Or the mysterious lack thereof."

"You really can't stand that kid, can you?" Ned said.

"I don't bear him any particular malice," I said. "I just, well, this is an important time in Jonathan's life. I'm not sure he should be hanging around with a character like that. Do you think Bobby might be a little retarded?"

"Sweetie, the infatuation will wear off. Trust your own kid a little more. We've been raising him for thirteen years, we must've taught him a thing or two."

I didn't speak. What I wanted to say was "I've taught him a thing or two; you've been holed up in that theater." But I kept quiet. We lay waiting for sleep. There would be no sexual congress that night. I was miles from the possibility. Still, I thought we had time.

Perhaps I struggled too hard to remain Jonathan's friend. Perhaps I ought to have distanced myself more. I simply could not believe that the boy with whom I'd played and shared secrets— the achingly vulnerable child who told me every story that entered his head—needed suddenly to be treated with the polite firmness one might apply to a lodger.

Our ongoing game of hearts came to an end, as did our Saturday shopping trips. Bobby continued wearing Jonathan's blue windbreaker, and started turning up in Jonathan's shirts as well. When he stayed overnight, he slept in Jonathan's room on the folding cot. He was consistently cordial to me, in his rehearsed, immigrant's fashion.

One morning in March I was slicing a grapefruit for breakfast. Jonathan sat alone at the kitchen table, it being one of the mornings Bobby was not with us.

I said, "Looks like a lovely day if you like ducks."

A moment passed. Jonathan said, "Yes, if yew lack ducks."

He was mocking my voice, my Southern accent.

I ought to have let the insult pass. I ought simply to have ignored him and served the grapefruit. But instead I turned and asked pleasantly, "What did you say?"

He just smiled as if unutterably pleased with himself.

I asked again, "What did you say, darling? I'm not sure if I heard correctly."

He stood up and left the house, saying, "Believe I'll skip break-fuss this mornin', dahling." As he walked away that eye stared at me from the back of the jacket.

It happened again in the evening, while we were watching television. That night we did have Bobby. Ned was at the theater, and we were watching a *Star Trek* rerun, the boys and I. I said, "Mr. Spock might not be much fun at parties, but I love him best of all."

Jonathan said, "He's on a five-year mission in deep space. If you were married to him, you'd need a dozen sons to keep you company."

I might have laughed along like a true sport but I was still too surprised by this new, outright meanness. "I rather thought we kept one another company," I said.

"That's right," he said. "Boys like nothing better than to shop and cook."

Bobby sat on the floor, as was his custom. He objected for some reason to furniture.

He said, "Quit, Jon."

"All in fun," Jonathan said.

"Yeah, but quit anyway."

And so Jonathan quit. He watched the program without further comment. His feet looked huge and rather weapon-like in the black cowboy boots he had insisted on buying.

Bobby had pared his fingernails, and forced a comb through his hair. He appeared to have abandoned boots in favor of simple black sneakers.

He was always polite to me. More than polite, really: he was courtly, in his way. He inquired after the particulars of the dinners I made, and asked me how my day had gone. Answering wasn't always easy, because I was never quite sure to whom I spoke. He stubbornly retained his foreign quality, although with time he did a better job of simulating the clean-minded normality of a television character. He polished his act. He took to trimming his hair, and even turned up in some new clothes that had not originally belonged to Jonathan.

One night in May I was passing by Jonathan's room when I heard music less shrill and raucous than what the boys usually played. I had grown accustomed to the endless noise of their music, the way one does to a barking dog. Electric guitars and bass drums had become a new kind of silence for me, but this particular music—a single, sweet female voice accompanied by a piano—was distinctly audible.

I hesitated outside Jonathan's door. Then I knocked, and was surprised by the timid little mouse-like sound my knuckles made

69

against the wood. He was my son, living in my house. I was entitled to knock on his bedroom door. I knocked again, louder.

"Yeah?" he called from within.

"Only me," I called back. "May I come in a minute?"

There was silence, filled with the tinkle of piano keys. After a moment, Bobby opened the door.

"Hey," he said. He stood smiling, looking rather peculiar—miscast—in a pin-striped dress shirt and jeans. I could see Jonathan within, sitting sulkily in his black boots and T-shirt.

"I didn't mean to bother you boys," I said, and was annoyed at the craven sound of my own voice. I might have been a poor relation, come for her annual duty dinner.

"It's okay," Bobby said. "It's fine."

"I just, well, I wondered what that music was. It sounded so . . . different."

"You like it?" Bobby asked.

It seemed a trick question. Would I open myself to ridicule? Then, brushing aside my own girlish fears, I answered like a woman of thirty-five. "It's lovely," I said. "Who is she?"

"Laura Nyro," Bobby said. "Yeah, she's good. It's an old one, you want to come in and hear it for a minute?"

I glanced at Jonathan. I should of course have said no. I should have gone about my offstage business, folding the towels and sheets. But I said, "All right, just for a minute," and stepped gratefully into the room to which I had previously enjoyed free access. During the past year, Jonathan had all but covered the walls with posters of scowling long-haired rock singers. The woman's voice, soaring and melancholy, filled the room rather tenuously, surrounded by all those hard masculine eyes.

Jonathan sat on the floor with his knees pulled up to his chest and his hands clasped over his shins. He had sat in just that way since the age of four—it was a sulking posture. I saw, perhaps for the first time, how the nascent man had always been folded up inside the boy. He would carry those same gestures with him right into adulthood. It surprised me a little, though it was the most ordinary of insights. I had rather imagined Jonathan transformed as an adult, appearing one day as a kind, solicitous stranger. I saw that I had been both right and wrong about that.

Bobby picked up the album cover and held it out to me, as if I had come to consider buying it. "This is it," he said. When I took it from him his face flushed, either with pride or with embarrassment.

The album cover was dark, a murky chocolate color. It depicted a rather plain-looking woman with a high, pale forehead and limp black hair parted in the middle. She might have been a poetic, unpopular student at a girls' school, more an object of pity than of ridicule. I'd known such girls well enough. I'd felt in danger of becoming one myself, and so had forced myself to change. To speak up and take risks, to date boys you couldn't take home to mother. Ned Glover had driven down from Michigan in an electric-blue convertible, a suave, humorous man far too old for me.

"Lovely," I said. "She has such a pretty voice."

It sounded exactly like the response of a prim middle-aged woman. I handed the album cover back quickly, as if it cost far more than I could afford.

"She quit singing," Bobby said. "She got married and, like, moved to Connecticut or something."

"I'm sorry," I said.

We stood there awkwardly, like strangers at a party. I could feel the force of Jonathan's desire impelling me from the room. It registered physically, a pressure on my forehead and shoulders.

"Well," I said. "Thanks for letting an old lady barge in."

"Sure," Bobby said. One song had ended and another begun, a faster number I thought I recognized. Yes. "Jimmy Mack," once sung by Martha and the Vandellas.

"I know this one," I said. "I mean, I've heard it before."

"Yeah?" Bobby said.

And then he did something peculiar. He started to dance.

I can only think that language ran out on him, and he resorted to what he knew. He did it automatically, as if it were a logical extension of the conversation. He started swaying his hips in rhythm, and shifting his feet. His sneakers squeaked on the floorboards.

"Yes, indeed," I said. "This is an ancient one."

I glanced at Jonathan, who looked startled. He returned my glance, and for a moment we found our old complicity again. We were united in our consternation over the habits of the local people. I half expected that once we were alone together, he might do an imitation of Bobby—dancing big-shouldered and dim-faced—just to make me laugh.

But then Bobby took my hand and pulled me gently forward. "Come on," he said.

"Oh, no. Absolutely not."

"Can't take no," he said cheerfully. He did not let go of my hand.

"*No*," I said again. But my refusal lacked force. Perhaps it was my Southern upbringing; my inbred determination to avoid social unpleasantness at any cost. I laughed a little as I said no, without quite having meant to.

He turned with me gently, moving in rhythm. He was a better dancer than his ordinary manner let on. I'd been quite a dancer myself as a girl—it was one of the resolutions I'd made, a salient feature of the person I'd meant to become—and I recognized the signs. There were boys you knew you could trust on the dance floor; you knew it almost instantly, more by feel than by appearance. Certain dancers imparted to the air itself a sense of confidence and inevitability. They had a generous grace that took you in; they told you just by the touch of their hands that you were incapable of making a wrong move. Bobby was that kind of dancer. I could not have been more surprised if he'd snapped a flock of live pigeons from under his pin-striped cuffs.

I responded. I took his other hand and danced with him as well as I could in that cramped room, under the disapproving eyes of my son and the sullen stares of the rock singers. Bobby smiled shyly. The woman's voice ran through the notes with sorrowful abandon, like somebody's gawky cousin set briefly, deliriously free.

After the song had ended I took back my hands and touched my hair. "Lord," I said. "Look what you drove an old lady to do."

"You're good," Bobby said. "You can dance."

"Used to. In the early Pleistocene."

"Naw," he said. "Come on."

I looked again at Jonathan, and saw what I expected: all sense of complicity was burned out of his face. He stared at me not so much with resentment as with nonrecognition, as if I were someone who only resembled his mother.

"Stroke of midnight," I said. "Love to stay, but I've got sheets to fold."

I got quickly out of the room. In less than a minute the melancholy woman had been replaced by a driving male voice and a cacophony of electric guitars.

Ned came home late that night, after I'd gone to sleep. I awoke and found him beside me, breathing deeply and frowning over a dream. I lay on my side watching him for a while. Ned had once been a boy. Perhaps the fact had never quite impressed itself on me, though of course I'd seen the pictures: little Ned grinning under an oversized bowler hat, Ned scrawny and big-footed in sandals at the beach. I had personally packed a carton of his iron cars and lead soldiers into the attic. Still, I'd never fully apprehended it. This man here was what grew from a boy. He had been twenty-six and I seventeen when we met; by my lights he'd been middle-aged even then. He might have been born an adult. Those pictures and toys might have been the artifacts of a boy who had died young, the former inhabitant of an old house who took his sense of limitless possibility out of the world with him when he went. What remained was china stored behind glass and the patience of African violets—an unhurried elderly life. But now, as if for the first time, lying beside Ned, I could see the boyish crook of his elbow under the pillow, the young muscles of a chest gone hairy and slack. Poor thing, I thought. Poor boy.

I reached over to stroke his shoulder. I might have kissed him. I might have let my hand stray down to the lush tangle of his chest. But my new sense of his innocent beauty was still too delicate. If he awoke and kissed me hard, if he mauled my ribs, it might collapse altogether. So I contented myself with watching him, and petting the soft, furred mound of his shoulder.

73

BOBBY

M Y FATHER has bought himself a new pair of glasses—avia-
tor style, with spindly pink-gold rims. He comes to my
bedroom door and poses there, one elbow crooked jauntily against
the frame.

"Bobby, what do you think?" he asks.

"Huh?" I say. I've been lying in the dark with the headphones
on, smoking a joint and listening to Jethro Tull. The music has
scooped out my thoughts and I need a few minutes to reenter the
world of cause and effect.

"Bobby, what do you think?" he asks again.

"I don't know," I answer eventually. He will have to give me
more time with the question.

My father points to his head. He is standing in light. Hundred-
watt rays stream around him, cut through the dusk of my room.

What do I think of his head? It is in fact an expansive question,
probably beyond my scope.

"Well," I say. I let the syllable hang.

"My glasses," he says. "Bobby, I got new glasses today."

A stitch of time passes. He says, "What do you think? Are they
a little young for me?"

"I don't know," I say. I can hear how foolish I sound; how
empty. But I am helpless before his questions. He might as well
be an angel, posing riddles.

He sighs, a slow punctured hissing sound. "Okay," he says. "I'll start dinner."

"Good, Dad," I say, in a voice I hope comes out cheerful and cooperative. I check with myself—is it his night or mine to make dinner? This is Tuesday. His. I have got that right.

Only after he's removed his shape from the doorway do I realize his questions were simple ones. He's traded in his tortoiseshells for a racier model, and wants reassurance. I should follow him to the kitchen, start the conversation over. But I don't do that. I collapse under the weight of my own self-interest, and permit myself a return to the music and the dark.

Sometime later, my father calls me to dinner. He has made chopped steak and squares of frozen hash browns. He sips Scotch from a glass decorated with pictures of orange slices round and evenly spoked as wagon wheels.

We eat for a while without talking. Once they've established themselves, our silences are hard to break. They are tough and seamless as shrink-wrap. Finally I say, "Those glasses look okay. I mean, I like them."

"I think they're probably a bit too young," he says. "I suspect a man my age probably looks a little foolish in glasses like these."

"Naw. All kinds of people wear that kind. They look fine."

"Do you honestly think so?"

"Uh-huh," I say.

"Well," he says. "I'm glad to hear that. I'm glad to have a younger person's opinion on the subject."

"They do. They look, you know, real nice."

"Good."

Silverware clicks against the plates. I can hear the action of my father's throat, swallowing.

For weeks now, he has been dyeing his hair. He is on a strand-by-strand agenda—every few days, he dyes a few more. In this way he hopes to present the change as natural, as if time had reversed itself against his personal will.

This is his solution—to age in big-collared shirts and leather vests, to try every combination of mustache, beard, and sideburns. I've seen him in the old courtship pictures, big-armed in T-shirts, a meandering, hard-drinking musician who bumped up against the limits of his own talent and fell in love with a farm woman, a widow who knew about seeds and harvest.

Then I remember. It comes to me: today is the anniversary. It is two years ago today.

He replenishes his drink from the Ballantine bottle and says, "Let me ask you another question."

"Okay."

"What would you think about a new car?"

"I don't know," I answer. "Isn't the one we've got okay?"

He sets his drink down hard enough to splash Scotch and a thumbnail-sized ice cube on the tabletop. "You're right," he says. "You're absolutely right. There is absolutely no need for change of any kind. I couldn't agree more."

The grandfather clock ticks. I say, "A new car would be okay, Dad."

"I was just thinking about something a little snazzier," he says. "Perhaps a foreign model, with a sunroof."

"Uh-huh. Good."

"Something that would let a little air in."

"Yeah."

We work our way through dinner. My father's face is remote and optimistic as he eats. He is taking the gray out, hair by hair. His eyes swim behind the oval lenses of his new glasses.

She left by slow degrees before making it official. She lived in the guest room, made rare silent appearances in a pale turquoise robe. Once, when she passed me in the hall on her way to the bathroom, she stopped long enough to stroke my hair. She didn't speak. She looked at me as if she was standing on a platform in a flat, dry country and I was pulling away on a train that traveled high into an alpine world.

After my father and I found her he made the calls and we sat together, he and I, in the empty living room. We left her alone —it seemed like the polite thing to do. We sat quietly, waiting for the police and the paramedics to arrive. We didn't speak.

In the dining room, the autumn farm scene hasn't changed. Cows still cast orange shadows, trees still sprout yellow leaves. My father nibbles demurely at his steak, doesn't touch the square potatoes. I finish my dinner, take my plate to the kitchen and add it to the pile. An enormous fly, iridescent, roams ecstatically over a quarter moon of yellowed lamb fat. The curtains still sport blue teapots.

Later, after my father has gone to bed, I get up and walk around. I took a hit of Dexedrine after school, thinking I might clean up the house, but I fell into music instead. Two joints haven't dulled the speed enough to allow anything like sleep, so once my father has killed the bottle and settled into bed, I take a walk through the rooms, my head crackling and blazing like a light bulb. Under the gathering disorder is a perfect replica of a house, like the period reproductions they put together in small-town museums. Here is their living room, a cherry-red sofa once considered brash, and an old copper washtub, where logs would be kept if fires were built in the hearth. Here is the front door, yellow oak with a single frosted-glass window through which strangers can be seen but not identified. And here is the rumpus room, paneled, with a rag rug like a bull's-eye on the brown linoleum floor.

After the accident, my father tried to sell the house. But in six months the single interested party offered slightly more than half the market value. This section of Cleveland was not a growth proposition.

Music plays inside my head. I walk down the hall to my father's door. My head is an illuminated radio—for a moment I believe the music will wake him up. I stand in front of his door, watching the grain of the wood. I open the door and creep inside.

My father breathes noisily. His digital clock flips the red seconds away. I stand, just stand, with time passing on the bedside table. My head plays "Aqualung." At that moment, I get the point of psycho killers. I could take his head in my hands, stroke his dead-black hair. I could punch him and feel his teeth break like sugar cubes, hear them scatter on the floor. I get it about the dark silence of the world, and your own crackling internal light and noise. I get the space-suit feeling.

I could have come to murder my father. Now, right now, I could sneak up and press a pillow over his face. He's too drunk to fight. I can see myself doing it. The movie plays inside my head, with Jethro Tull on the sound track. A snow-white pillow and my own body pinning his; a brief struggle and then the rapture of the drowned. *Aqualung my friend, don't you start away uneasy.*

Or I could plant a kiss on his worried head. He's drunk enough to sleep through that, too. I could crawl into bed with him and lose myself in the musky warmth, the smells of Scotch and underarm and British Sterling. I stand a minute beside his bed, considering the possibilities.

What I finally do is leave. I go out of my father's room, down the hall, and through the front door into the starry, streetlighted Cleveland night.

The Glovers live less than a mile away, in a house with diamond-pane windows. A white-wicker swing sways creakily on the front porch, crisp as frozen lace. I watch their house from among the irises. It is early June; flowers whisper around my knees. Careful as a thief I survey their property, keeping to the shadows. There is the light in Jonathan's window, a feeble ivory glow from the gooseneck lamp beside his bed. He is reading John Steinbeck for school, and will tell me the story afterward. I creep behind a mulberry tree. Kitchen light throws a long rectangle onto the grass as Alice dries the spoons and the measuring cups. I can't see her but I know her moves—she is fast and certain as science itself, though she cares more about perfection than she does about order. The cast-iron skillets are always oiled, but the Sunday paper still sits in the living room on a Wednesday night. The Glovers keep a nourishing, semi-clean house that has little to do with neatness. Things catch and hold here.

I wait breathing in the dark as she turns out the kitchen light and goes upstairs. Ned won't be home for another hour or more. I sneak around in time to see the light go on in her bedroom window. I watch her window and I watch the others, the ones that open onto empty rooms. Behind paired black windows is the gleaming darkness of the dining room, its silver tea service putting out an icy glitter. Behind a third, smaller window is the laundry room, with its scoured smell. Upstairs, Alice sends a brief shadow across the windowscreen.

I wait, watching, until Ned's car pulls up. I can see him walk from the garage to the front door, his white shirt brilliant in the porchlight, coins jingling in his pockets. Ned slicks his hair with Vitalis; he wears Sansabelt slacks. I hear the click of his key in the door—a perfect fit. He douses the light and goes upstairs. I can feel his tread. Alice is waiting for him, her hair pulled up off her neck. Jonathan still reads in his own room, taking in the story he'll tell me tomorrow.

I sit in the bushes until every light is out, until the house has settled itself for the night. Then I walk a slow circle around it, with stars and planets shining overhead. Above us, suns nova and collapse, punching holes in the galaxy, pulling their light after them into the next world. Here below, on an earth night humming with gnats and crickets, I orbit the Glovers' house.

ALICE

BOBBY rid his voice of its droning, metronomic quality and acquired a boyish lilt, finishing sentences on a high note, so that any statement sounded like an eager, tentative question. His electric hair, when submitted to a barber's shears, emerged as the ordinary, dryly windblown crop of a teenager prone to cowlicks. Once, as he stood grinning before our front door at noon, I saw that he had daubed his acne with a concealing flesh-colored ointment.

Still, he never managed the complete transition. He retained a subvert, slightly dangerous quality—something ravenous and watchful. It came out at dinner, as he scoured his plate, and it came out in his insistent, unfailing politeness. Only fugitives are capable of flawless courtesy from morning till night. And, besides, the boy Bobby was struggling to become could never have danced like he did.

He took to bringing over records he thought I'd like—a sweeter, more melodic music than the sort Jonathan favored. Every now and then he'd call down from Jonathan's room: "Mrs. Glover? If you're not too busy, come on up and listen to something?" I'd almost always go on up. How busy could I be, cooking and washing clothes?

I learned a collection of new names: Joni Mitchell, Neil Young, Boz Scaggs. Sometimes I just sat with the boys, listening. Sometimes, when an upbeat song came on, I accepted Bobby's invitation to dance.

His dancing was something to see. His sense of rhythm did not in any way derive from the granite cornices and box hedges of Cleveland. Dancing, he was an original—his hips swayed with a voluptuous certainty more graceful than lewd, and his arms and legs cut their own brisk, surprising pattern through the confined air of my son's room. Once the song ended he'd smile and shrug, as if dancing had been a slightly embarrassing failure of wit. He'd return by visible degrees to his continuing impression of the pallid suburban boys mothers are supposed to delight in.

Sometimes Jonathan grudgingly joined us dancing, sometimes he sulked with his knees drawn up to his chest. I wasn't a fool— I knew no fifteen-year-old boy would welcome his own mother's participation in his social life. But Bobby was so insistent. And, besides, Jonathan and I had always been good friends despite our blood bond. I decided that accepting Bobby's little gifts of music and dance would do no harm. I had been a bit wild myself, at Jonathan's age, not so very long ago.

Jonathan grew his hair nearly to his shoulders, in defiance of the school's dress code. He sewed bright patches on his jeans, and persisted in wearing Bobby's old leather jacket even after the elbows wore through. At home he was largely silent. Sometimes his silence was petulant, sometimes it was simply blank. Although he worked hard at it, Jonathan could not make himself a stranger to me. I knew him too well. His dancing was as hesitant and clumsy as his father's, and the flippant nastiness he affected had a shallow bottom. Caught off guard, he would slip into acquiescence automatically, without having meant to. He would smile before he remembered to scowl.

One night in January, Bobby called me up to listen to a new record by Van Morrison. I'd settled myself on the floor with the boys, nodding to the music. Bobby sat cross-legged and straight-backed to my immediate left, like a Yogi meditating. Jonathan sat farther away, sulkily hunched, his shoulders curved over his knees.

"This is nice," I said. "I like this Van Morrison."

"Van the Man?" Bobby grinned. Sometimes his meanings remained inscrutable, despite his careful intentions. I often just smiled and nodded, as I would to a foreigner speaking indecipherable but evidently friendly English.

At moments, even in his fits of eager incoherence, Bobby made sense to me. He was an outlander, striving to assimilate. Hadn't I myself been transplanted to a wintery place where most women of my age and station were overweight and undereducated? Years earlier, when I was still making an effort to fit in, the other women at the PTA and the church guild had offered me recipes for parfaits made with pudding and candy bars, and for frankfurters soaked in mustard and grape jelly. I couldn't begrudge Bobby his own difficulties with the local ways of making do.

"Van's all right," Jonathan said. "If you like this sort of thing."

"What sort of thing is he?" I asked.

"Well, folk-y. Moony. He's a good old boy singing about the love of a good woman."

"I don't know, Jon," Bobby said. "He's sort of, you know, better than that?"

"He's okay," Jonathan said. "Just a little wimpy. Mom, how about if I play you some real stuff?"

"This seems real enough," I said.

Jonathan looked at Bobby, whose smile had taken on a stiff, worried quality. "That's what you think," Jonathan said. He got up and took the needle off the record in the middle of a song, pulled another out of the collection that was stored in a series of orange crates lined up against the wall.

"This is Jimi Hendrix," he announced. "The world's greatest dead guitarist."

"Jon," Bobby said.

"You're going to love this, Mom. Really. I'm turning the volume up a little here, because you've got to listen to Jimi pretty loud."

"Jon," Bobby said, "I don't know if—"

Jonathan touched the needle to vinyl, and the room exploded with electric guitars. They squealed and shrieked like tortured animals. A thumping bass line started, so loud and insistent I could feel it up my spine. I had the impression that my hair was being disarranged.

"Nice, huh?" Jonathan shouted. "Jimi was the greatest."

Our eyes met through the storm of sound. Jonathan's face was flushed, his eyes brilliant. I knew what he wanted. He wanted to blow me out of the room, to send me tumbling downstairs into the familiar sanctity of dirty dishes and vacuuming. On the record, a male voice sang, "You know you're a cute little heartbreaker."

"The greatest," Jonathan hollered. "Much better than Van the Man."

I made a decision. I stood up and said, "Bobby, let's dance."

He joined me immediately. We danced together in the chaos of the music. It wasn't so bad, as long as you kept moving. It gave you the airy, buffeted sensation a sparrow must feel when caught in an updraft—a simultaneous sense of assault and liberation. You could scream into the face of this music. It all but lifted your arms into the air.

From the corner of my eye I could see that Jonathan was disappointed. His mother had not cowered before his hard-driving music. Once again, I could see the child contained in the burgeoning man—his expression at that moment recalled the times his checkers moves didn't work out, or no one fell for his April Fool's trick. If he'd permitted it, I would have reached over and pinched his cheek.

Presently, he started dancing, too. What else could he do? As we three swayed to the music, that small room seemed as densely packed as Times Square, and every bit as full of the weight of the moment. Jimi Hendrix growled "Foxy lady," and it struck me as a fair appellation. A smart older woman who didn't scare easily. Who wouldn't just retreat to her domestic chores, and start getting fat.

After that, I paid more regular visits. I abandoned my old rule about waiting to be invited. We seemed to have passed beyond that. When my ordinary errands took me upstairs I'd tap on the door and go in for a song or two. I never stayed long.

One night when I knocked on the door I detected a shuffling on the other side. Neither of them answered my knock. I thought I could hear them whispering. Then Jonathan called, "Come in, Mom."

I smelled it the moment I entered—that sweet smoky reek. The room was blue with it. Bobby stood in an attitude of frozen panic, and Jonathan sat in his accustomed place by the radiator. Bobby said, "Um, Mrs. Glover?"

Jonathan said, in a voice that was calm and almost suave, "Come on in, Mom. Have a hit."

He extended a smoldering, hand-rolled cigarette in my direction.

I stood uncertainly in the doorway. For a long moment I lost track of my own character and simply floated, ghost-like, watching dispassionately as my son extended a pathetic-looking gnarled cigarette, its ember glowing orange in the dim light of a baseball-shaped lamp I'd bought for him when he was seven years old.

I knew what I was supposed to do. I was supposed to express my shock and outrage or, at the very least, to speak gently but firmly to him about the limits of my tolerance. Either way, it would be the end of our familiar relations—our impromptu dance parties—and the beginning of a sterner, more formal period.

After the silence had stretched to its breaking point, Jonathan repeated his offer. "Give it a try, Mom," he said. "How else will you know what you're missing?"

"Your father would have a heart attack," I said evenly.

"He isn't here," Jonathan said.

"Mrs. Glover?" Bobby said helplessly.

It was his voice that decided me—his fearful intonation of my married name.

"I suppose you're right," I said. "How else will I know what I'm missing?"

I took three steps into the room, and accepted the sad little cigarette.

"Atta girl, Mom," Jonathan said. His voice was cheerful and opaque.

"How do you do this?" I asked. "I've never even smoked regular cigarettes, you know."

Bobby said, "Um, just pull the smoke, like, straight into your lungs. And hold it as long as you can?"

As I put the cigarette to my lips, I was aware of myself standing in a pale blue blouse and wraparound skirt in my son's bedroom, about to perform the first plainly illegal act of my life. I inhaled. The smoke was so harsh and bitter I nearly choked. My eyes teared, and I could not hold the smoke in my lungs as Bobby had told me to do. I immediately blew out a thick cloud that hung in the air, raggedly intact, for a full second before dissipating.

Nevertheless, the boys cheered. I handed the cigarette to Bobby. "You did it," he said. "You did it."

"Now I can say I've lived," I answered. My voice sounded cracked and strained.

Bobby pulled in a swift, effortless drag, pinching the cigarette between his thumb and first finger. The ember fired up. When he exhaled, only a thin translucent stream of smoke escaped into the air.

"See?" he said. "You have to, like, hold it in a little longer?"

He handed the cigarette back to me. "Again?" I asked.

He shrugged, grinning in his panicky, baffled way. "Yeah, Mom," Jonathan said. "You smoke the whole joint. One hit doesn't do much of anything."

Joint. It was called a joint, not a cigarette.

"Well, one more," I said. I tried again, and this time managed to hold the smoke in for a moment or two. Again, I dispelled a riot of smoke, very different from Bobby's gray-white, elegant jet trail.

I returned the joint to him. Jonathan said, "Hey, I'm here, too."

"Oops. Sorry." I handed it over. He took it greedily, as he had once accepted the little treats I brought home from shopping trips.

"What will this do, exactly?" I asked. "What should I prepare myself for?"

"It'll just make you laugh." Bobby said. "It'll just, you know, make you feel happy and a little foolish?"

"It's no big deal, Mom," Jonathan said. "The lamb chops won't start talking to you, or anything like that." He took a drag, with expert dispatch, and handed the joint along to Bobby. When Bobby passed it to me I shook my head.

"I think that's enough," I said. "Just do me one favor."

"Uh-huh?" Bobby said.

"Play me a Laura Nyro song, and then I'll get on about my business."

"Sure," he said.

He put the record on, and we three stood listening. I waited to start feeling whatever there was to feel. By the time the song was over, I realized that marijuana had no effect at all, beyond producing a dry scratchiness in the throat. I was both relieved and disappointed.

"Okay," I said. "Thanks for your hospitality, boys."

"Any time, Mom," Jonathan said. I could not read his voice. It might have been mocking, or swaggering, or simply friendly.

"Not a word to your father," I said. "Do you promise? Do you swear?" For a moment I thought the marijuana had affected me after all. But it was just the flush of my own guilt.

"I promise," he said. "I swear."

Bobby said, "Mrs. Glover? This is really cool. You are . . . I don't know. Really cool. Yow!"

"Oh, call me Alice, for God's sake," I told him. And then I left them alone.

A week or so later I tried dope again (it was called dope, not marijuana), and found that if you kept at it, it did have its effects. It made you giddy and pleasantly vague. It took the hard edge off your attention.

On a Wednesday afternoon in February, when a frigid white hush lay over the world, I sat with Jonathan and Bobby sharing a joint. It was the fourth of my career, and I had by then acquired a certain expertise. I held the smoke, feeling its heaviness and herbal warmth inside my lungs. On the stereo, Bob Dylan sang "Girl from the North Country." The lamp was lit against the afternoon dusk, and the paneled walls had taken on a rich, dark-honey color.

"You know," I said, "this should be legal. It's just utterly sweet and harmless, isn't it?"

"Uh-huh," Jonathan said.

"Well, it should be legal," I said. "If Nixon smoked a little, the world would be a better place."

Bobby laughed, and then looked at me self-consciously, to be sure I'd intended to make a joke. His expression was so hesitant —he agonized so elaborately over the simplest social transactions—that I started to laugh. My laughter inspired more laughter in him, and Jonathan joined in, laughing over some private joke of his own. This was one of the herb's best qualities: under its influence you could start laughing at any little thing and, once you'd started, feed it just by letting your eyes wander. Everything seemed absurd and funny—the Buddha-shaped incense burner standing next to a spring-driven hula girl on Jonathan's desktop; the domesticated, dog-like quality of Bobby's tan suede shoes.

Sometimes in those days I thought of Wendy from *Peter Pan*— an island mother to a troop of lost boys. I didn't make an outright fool of myself. I didn't buy gauzy skirts or Indian jewelry or sandals from Mexico. I didn't let my hair grow long and wild. But there was a different feeling now. I had a new secret, a better one. Previously, my only secrets had been the facts that I feared sex and could not summon any interest in getting to know our neighbors. I'd felt frail and thin to the point of translucence, an insubstantial figure who got headaches from the cold and sinus infections from the heat. But this new secret was buoying, exhilarating—I would be the scandal of the neighborhood if I was found out. The secret warmed me as I passed along the aisles of the supermarket. I was a mother who got stoned with her son. The local women—big women loading their wire carts with marshmallows and ice cream, with bright pink luncheon meats and sugared cereals—would have considered me unfit, scandalous, degenerate. I felt young and slender, full of devious promise. There would be a life after Cleveland.

And, perhaps best of all, I found that when I got stoned I could manage things with Ned. The dope loosened me, so that if he pressed his mouth onto mine or stroked me roughly I could go along with it in a lazy, liquid state that differed utterly from what

I had once meant by arousal. Sex had always produced a queasy inner tightening that turned quickly from pleasure to panic and from panic to pain, so that as Ned worked his sweaty way toward conclusion I lay nervous and angry beneath him, saying silently, "Finish, finish, finish." Now I could accommodate him with a languor that produced neither outright pleasure nor pain, but rather an unblemished ticklish sensation that struck me as slightly funny. Dope miniaturized sex; it reduced the act itself from a noisy obligation to a humorous, rather sweet little fleshly comedy. This was Ned, only Ned, bucking and groaning here; a boy grown big and ungainly. This was Ned and this was me, a woman capable of surprising herself.

It lasted into the spring. In my new life I was foxy and unorthodox, liberal-minded and sexually generous—I was the character I wanted to be. That character lived through the thaw and the first green into April, when the pear tree in the back yard exploded in white blossoms. On the Saturday night before Easter, after I had finished dressing the ham, I walked out to look at the tree. It was nearly midnight, and I was alone in the house. Ned had added a late show on Fridays and Saturdays, to compete with the theater complexes that were opening in the malls. Bobby and Jonathan were off somewhere.

I wore an old woolen shirt of Ned's over my sweater. The air smelled of wet, raw earth, and the pear tree stood in the middle of our small yard as splendid and strange as a wedding dress, its blossoms emitting a faint white light. I stood for a while on the kitchen steps. It was a moonless night, clear enough for the band of the Milky Way to show itself among the multitudes of stars. That night, even our modest back yard looked ripe with nascent possibilities. If the future was a nation, this would be its flag: a blooming tree on a field of stars.

I stepped onto the lawn, though my shoes were too thin for the weather. I wanted to feel the frosty crunch of the grass. I strolled under the tree's branches, past the beds where my tulips were already pushing their way up. By the time the tree had lost its flowers, the lilacs would be in bloom. Someday we would live in a house with a view of the water. I ran my fingers over the scaly bark of a low branch, shook a few loose blossoms onto my hair.

I'd been out there some time before I noticed that the boys were sitting in my car. It was parked in the graveled space between the garage and the house proper, shadowed by an aluminum over-hang, in a pocket of darkness so deep I could not have seen them at all if I hadn't stood in exactly the right position, so that their heads showed in silhouette between the rear and front windshields.

Their presence struck me as odd but marvelous. Perhaps they were playing at a cross-country trip. I was too enamored of the night to ask questions. The sight of them seemed, simply, a stroke of good fortune. We could smoke a joint together, and shake pear blossoms down onto our heads. I went without hesitation to the car. As I drew closer I could hear rock music playing on the radio. Derek and the Dominos, I thought. I skipped up to the driver's door, opened it, and said, "Hey, can I hitch a ride?"

We passed, all three of us, through a shocked silence filled with the clash of guitars. Sweet-smelling smoke drifted out of the car. Jonathan sat in the driver's seat. I saw his penis, pale and erect in the starlight.

"Oh," I said. Only that.

His eyes seemed to shift forward in their sockets, as if pressed from behind. Even at that moment I could perfectly remember him taking on the same expression at the age of two, when he was denied a bag of lurid pink candy in a supermarket aisle.

"Get out of here," he said in a tone of quivering control that cut through the music like a wire through fog. It was an entirely adult voice. "How dare you."

"Jon?" Bobby said. He pulled his jeans up, but before he did so I had seen his penis too, larger than Jonathan's, darker.

Jonathan waved the sound of his own name away. "Get out of here," he said. "Do you hear me? Do you understand?"

I was too surprised to argue. I simply closed the car door, and went back into the house. It was bright and warm inside. I stood in the foyer, breathing. I saw the empty living room with perfect

89

clarity: magazines fanned out on the coffee table, a throw pillow still bearing the dent made by someone's elbow. A fly walked a half circle across the celadon curve of my grandmother's vase.

I went upstairs and ran a hot bath. It was all I could think of to do. As I lowered myself into the water I felt a kind of relief. This was real and definite—water slightly too hot to bear. My feet burned as if stuck with pins. My thighs and buttocks and sex were scalded, but I held fast. I didn't rise up out of that steaming water.

It was not wholly a surprise. Not about Jonathan. I must have known. But I had never consciously thought, "My son won't marry." I had thought, "My son is gentler than other boys, kinder, more available to strong feelings." These were among his virtues. I knew the bite and meanness of boys was missing from his nature. I lowered myself deeper into the tub, so the hot water covered my shoulders and burned against my chin. When it started to cool, I opened the hot tap again.

How had I failed to notice the signs? Jonathan and Bobby were fifteen, yet they never talked of girls. They tacked no airbrushed nudes to the walls. Although I must have suspected, I had never in any part of my being imagined the fleshly implications of their love. To my mind Jonathan had been a perennial child; an innocent. What I could not accustom myself to was the sight of his small erection and Bobby's larger one, hidden away in the night.

How had I contributed? I knew too much of psychology, and yet I knew too little. Had I been the sort of mother who drives her son from women? Had I feminized him by insisting too obdurately on being his friend?

Jonathan came in hours later, after Ned had returned home and gone to sleep. I thought he might tap on my bedroom door but of course he couldn't, not with his father present. He went into his own room, producing his usual booted thump on the hall carpet. I wanted to go and comfort him, tell him it was all right. I wanted to go and pull his hair hard enough to draw blood.

It was Easter, and we went through the motions of the day. Ned, Bobby, and Jonathan invaded their baskets, exclaiming over the little prizes, filling their mouths with jelly beans and marshmallow chickens. Jonathan bit the ears off a chocolate rabbit with a gusto that sent an unexpected chill through me. Ned gave me a flat of delphiniums, which I was happy to have, and a silk scarf covered with the brilliant flowers sometimes favored by older women looking for a little flair when they go out to lunch.

Ned must have seen the dismay on my face as I pulled the bright, elderly scarf out of its tissue. He said softly, "What do I know about scarves? It came from Herman Brothers, you can take it back and get something else."

I kissed him. "It's fine," I said. "It's a lovely scarf."

I couldn't help thinking that Jonathan would have known what scarf to buy me.

We ate the dinner I'd made, talked of everyday things. After dinner, Ned left for the theater. On his way out the door, Jonathan said to him, "We'll come to the eight o'clock show, okay?"

"You bet," he answered, and winked enormously. After he was gone, the boys washed the dishes. I tried to help, but Jonathan shooed me out of the kitchen. From the living room, where I leafed through a magazine, I could hear the two of them speaking in low, undecipherable voices. Occasionally, they both laughed.

When they were through with the dishes, they went upstairs to Jonathan's room. "Great dinner, Mom," Jonathan said as they passed through the living room. Bobby added, "Yow! It was, like, the best?"

They did not invite me up. They did not put on any music. After an hour they came down again with their jackets on. They were out the door almost instantly.

"Night, Mom," Jonathan called from the lawn.

"Night, Mrs. Glover?" Bobby added.

I stood for a while watching them walk down the street, their hands in their jacket pockets. Bobby's stride was lithe and sure, Jonathan's slightly bowlegged in the way of adolescent boys who offer swagger in place of conviction. Behind me, the house was empty, the dishes dried and put away.

I waited to talk to Jonathan until we had a chance to be alone. It took almost a week. Finally he came home unaccompanied from his nocturnal rounds, and I caught him on his way upstairs. He could make such a racket with those boots.

"Jonathan?" I called. "Might I have a quick word?"

"Uh-huh." He stopped halfway up the stairs and leaned over the banister like a cowboy bellying up to a bar. His hair hung lankly over his face.

"Would you consider coming down?" I said. "I don't really feel like playing a balcony scene."

"Okay," he said with bland good cheer. He allowed himself to be taken into the living room, where we sat down.

"Well," I said. I did not quite know how to begin a difficult conversation with him. I had always spoken to him as effortlessly as if I were talking to myself.

"Uh-huh?" he said.

"Jonathan, honey, I know you care a great deal about Bobby." Wrong. The tone was sexless, schoolmarmish. I attempted a laugh but my laugh thinned out, went squeaky on me. "A great deal," I added.

Wrong again. Now my tone was too knowing, too suggestive. I was still his mother.

He nodded, looking at me with a blank, serene face.

"Well, honey," I said, "to be honest, I've been wondering if it's good for you to see so much of Bobby. Don't you think you should have some other friends, too?"

"No," he said.

I laughed again, more successfully. "At least you're open-minded on the subject," I said.

He shrugged, and wrapped a hank of hair around a finger.

"I remember when I was your age, we ran around in a big gang," I said. "We were all more or less in love with one another, and there were seven or eight of us. Girls and boys alike. I mean, I think I know what it's like to so desperately love a friend."

"Uh-huh," he said, in what seemed a less impenetrable, good-boy's voice. I suspected—I *knew*—his love for Bobby must have frightened him. It might in fact have been the true cause of this manly posturing, these clomping seven-league boots.

"Listen, now," I said. "I'm your friend. I think I understand about Bobby. He can be very—compelling. But I have to tell you. Don't hem yourself in too much. Not so early in life."

He looked at me from under his ragged shelf of hair, and I saw in his face a lick of my old Jonathan, plagued by doubts and almost ostentatiously available to harm. For a moment it seemed we had broken through.

"Oh, sweetheart," I said. "I know how you feel. Honestly, I do. So trust me. The day will come when Bobby will just seem like somebody you used to know."

His face shut down. It was a visible process, like shutters slammed over a lighted window.

He said, "You don't know how I feel. And you don't know Bobby. I'm the one who knows him. Stop trying to take over my life."

"I'm *not*."

"Yes you are. I can't stand it. You use up all the air in here. Even the plants keep dying."

I stared at him disbelievingly. "Your life is your own," I said. "I'm only trying to tell you I'm on your side."

"Well, honey, there jest ain't no room on ma side for nobody but me."

I slapped him at almost the same moment I knew I was going to. I caught him full across the face, hard enough to pull a string of saliva from the corner of his mouth. My hand stung from the impact.

After a moment, he smiled and wiped his lips with the back of his hand. The slap appeared to have afforded him great satisfaction, to have proven something he'd suspected all along.

"I'm sorry," I said. "I never meant to hit you. I never have before, have I?"

He stood without speaking and walked upstairs, carrying with him that air of satisfied discovery. His boots reported like cannon fire on every tread.

Our old friendship was finished. Jonathan and Bobby spent more and more time out of the house, coming home late and going directly to bed. They did not invite me up to get stoned with them, or to dance. Ned told me they came to the movies fairly often. Sometimes, he said, he sat with them, watching a film he'd seen a half-dozen times already. He said Jonathan was

93

surprisingly astute about movies—perhaps he had the makings of a film critic.

I knew better than to try barring Bobby from the house. Hadn't my own parents forbidden me to see Ned? Hadn't their glacial ultimatums driven me straight into marriage? I couldn't honestly have said whether I worried more about Jonathan's love of boys in general or about his particular devotion to Bobby. Although of course I hoped he would grow into conventional manhood, meet a girl, and have babies, I knew that that decision already lay beyond my powers of intervention. Jonathan was on his own there. But Bobby, a sweet, uncertain boy of no discernible ambitions and questionable intellect . . . If Jonathan remained tied to Bobby he might never know what the larger world had to offer. Bobby was, ineluctably, a Cleveland boy, and I knew the future Cleveland offered. The downtown streets were full of young men who hadn't gotten out: men in bright, cheap neckties, thick-waisted at twenty-five, dawdling in luncheonettes before returning to a job performed under fluorescent lights while the second hand swept the face of the clock.

It was nearly another week before Bobby and I had our encounter.

I had gone down to the kitchen well after midnight, to roll out the crust for a couple of pies. I had not been sleeping well during the past two weeks, and the problem wasn't helped by Ned's asthmatic snoring. Finally, resigned, I'd gone down in my nightgown, hoping that some simple kitchen task would help settle my mind for sleep.

I only turned on the dim light in the hood of the range, and didn't truly need that. I could easily enough have made pies in a coal mine.

I was nearly finished when Bobby appeared, looking sleepily disoriented, though with Bobby it was sometimes difficult to tell. He stood in the kitchen doorway, large and pallidly muscular in boxer shorts.

"Oh, hi," he murmured. "I didn't know you were here. I just, um, came down for a drink of water?"

Water flowed reliably enough from the bathroom taps. I knew

what he had come for: the gin we kept on a kitchen shelf was nearly half water by then. I played along, though.

"I couldn't sleep," I said. "So I decided I might as well do something useful."

"Uh-huh," he said. He remained standing in the doorway, caught between the danger of advance and the embarrassment of retreat. I filled a glass with tap water and held it out to him.

"Thanks," he said. When he stepped forward to take the glass from me he brought his distinctive smell into the kitchen, a young male odor with an underlayer like the smell of metal on a cold day. I could hear the steady gurgle his throat made in swallowing the water.

"Bobby," I said.

"Uh-huh?"

"Bobby, aren't we friends? I thought we were friends, you and I."

He nearly dropped his glass. He smiled in an agony of nervousness, and said, "Well, we are. I mean, I think you're, you know, really cool."

"Thank you. I'm glad you think I'm really cool. But we haven't seen much of one another lately, have we?"

"I guess not," he said. "I've been, you know, pretty busy—"

I couldn't stifle a snort of derisive laughter. "You're not exactly the chairman of the board of General Motors," I said. "Let's not try to fool one another, all right? It's just a waste of time."

His smile wilted, and he shrugged helplessly. "Well," he said. "You know. Jonathan—"

"Jonathan what?"

"Well, he sort of. You know. You're, like, his mother."

"That sounds exactly right," I said. "I'm *like* his mother. I resemble someone who can be fooled with lame excuses."

Bobby offered another Punch-like smile, as if I'd made a joke. I could see that there was no point in pursuing the subject with him. He was only following orders. I stood before him with my arms folded over my breasts. I could easily have said, "Leave this house now and don't come back." I could have confirmed his romantic status.

95

Struggling visibly to change the subject, Bobby asked, "What's that you're making?"

"What? Oh, a pie. I'm making a couple of pecan pies for tomorrow."

"You're a great cook," he said avidly. "I've never tasted food like this that somebody just *made*, I mean it's like a restaurant."

"No big deal," I said. I could tell from his face that this was not a conversational gambit, after all. He was genuinely interested in the fact that I had come downstairs to bake pies at midnight.

"I'd like to open a restaurant one day," he said. "I mean, I think it'd be cool to have a restaurant in a big old house somewhere."

He looked with open fascination at the pie crust, a pale, lucent circle on the pastry board.

"No real trick to it," I said. "I could teach you to cook. It's just a step-by-step process, no magic involved."

"I don't know," he said doubtfully.

"Look here," I said. "I haven't rolled out the second crust yet, why don't you try it?"

"Really?"

"Come here. You'll be amazed at how easy it is, once you've learned a few of the tricks."

He came and stood close to me at the counter. I slipped the rolled crust into one of the tins, refloured the board, and plopped the remaining dough onto it.

"Lesson one," I said. "You want to handle it as little as possible. It's not like bread dough—you *maul* that until it comes to life. Pie crust is just the opposite, it needs kid gloves. Now. Roll away from you, in sort of upward motions. Don't bulldoze it."

He took up the rolling pin and pressed it into the soft bulk of the dough.

"Just coax it," I said. "Good. That's right."

"I've never done this," he said. "My mother never made things like pies."

"You'll be a good student," I said. "I can tell already."

"Do you know how to make those fancy edges?" he asked.

"Sure I do," I said.

*   *   *

During the ensuing year I taught Bobby everything I knew about cooking. We had long sessions in the kitchen together, moving from pies to bread and from bread to puff pastry. When his work came successfully out of the oven, fatly golden and steaming, he contemplated it with frank, unmitigated wonder. I have never seen anyone take so to baking. He seemed to believe that from such humble, inert elements as flour, shortening, and drab little envelopes of yeast, life itself could be produced.

Jonathan sometimes sat in on our baking sessions, but his heart and mind were clearly elsewhere. He lacked the patience for precise measurements and slow risings. Truly, he lacked the fundamental interest in nourishment itself. Even as a baby he'd been indifferent to food.

He would linger a while in the kitchen, then wander up to his room and put a record on. Sometimes he played Jimi Hendrix or the Rolling Stones, sometimes a new record I'd never heard before.

Neither of the boys ever again invited me to listen to music. Now, instead, Bobby would trot into my kitchen, saying, "Look here, I found this recipe for fish that's, like, inside a pastry." Or, "Hey, do you know how to make something called brioche?"

Jonathan applied to several colleges and was accepted at New York University and the University of Oregon. All the schools he'd applied to were at least a thousand miles from Cleveland.

Bobby applied to no colleges—he did not even mention the possibility. He just continued bringing me recipes, and buying ever more elaborate kitchen aids. He bought a Cuisinart, and a set of German knives so thin and sharp they could have sliced away the kitchen wallpaper without disturbing the plaster beneath.

In June, Ned and I attended their graduation ceremonies with Burt Morrow, whom we had not seen in over a year. Burt had exchanged his goatee for muttonchop sideburns since our last meeting. He wore a green sport coat and a turtleneck, with a gold medallion the size of a half dollar hanging from a chain around his neck.

We took seats toward the rear of the high school auditorium, a vast, pale, salmon-colored chamber that smelled, even on this occasion, faintly of damp cement and brown-bag lunches. As the students' names were called and they stepped up onto the stage to receive their diplomas, they were accompanied by the various hoots and catcalls of their peers. You could gauge the popularity of each individual by the uproar his or her name produced. Neither Bobby nor Jonathan inspired any outburst at all—they might have been unknown to their classmates, although Burt did emit a surprisingly shrill whistle at the sound of Bobby's name.

Afterward, Bobby and Jonathan went off to an all-night party at an amusement park on a school bus full of other kids. Ned and I invited Burt out for a drink, since we could not just let him drive home alone.

"A drink?" he said. "Yes, a drink with the adults would be nice. I think we should do that, yes."

His eyes held no light. They might have been made of agate.

We went to a quiet place near the lake, with copper tables and young waitresses dressed as Mother Hubbard. I ordered a vodka gimlet, which was given to me on a doily instead of on a napkin.

Ned lifted his glass and said, "To the new generation. Best of luck."

We all drank to the new generation. Through hidden speakers, a band played "Moon River."

It seemed we were in the least important place on earth.

Burt Morrow said, "Jonathan chose NYU, did he?"

"Yep," Ned answered. "The decision was made strictly on an economic basis. NYU is more expensive than Oregon."

Burt blinked, and lit a cigarette. "Well, I'm sure he'll distinguish himself there," he said. "Bobby doesn't seem to be very much interested in college."

"He's still young," Ned said. "You never know what'll happen in a year or so."

Burt said, "Whatever he chooses is all right with me. I wouldn't interfere in his life. Oh, no. I wouldn't think of it. He's got to do his own thing."

"I guess," Ned said. "They've all got to do their own things, don't they?"

Burt nodded, pulling deeply at his Pall Mall as if sucking up the stuff of life itself. "Certainly," he said sagely. "Certainly they do."

It was his use of the word "certainly" that got to me. It made him sound so like a precocious child left in our care.

"They do not," I said emphatically, "have to *do their own thing*."

"Well," said Burt, "as long as they don't hurt anybody—"

"Burt," I said. "When Jonathan entered into a relationship with your son he was a sweet, open-natured boy, and now three years later he's turned into someone I scarcely recognize. He'd been a straight-A student and by the time Bobby was through with him he was lucky to get into any college at all."

Burt blinked at me through his own smoke. Ned said, "Now, Alice . . ."

"Oh, pipe down," I said to him. "I just want to ask Burt here one question. I want to ask him what I did wrong."

Burt said, "I don't imagine you did anything wrong."

"Then what am I doing here?" I asked. I had begun tapping my glass with my fingernail. I heard the steady rhythmic tapping as if it were an annoying sound being made by someone else. I said, "Why am I living in a city I despise? How did I end up with a son who hates me? I seemed to be doing just one thing and then the next, it all felt logical at the time, but sitting here at this moment, it all seems so impossible."

"Well," said Burt, swallowing smoke. I could still hear my fingernail tapping the glass.

"We just set out to be a family," I told him. "We had every good intention."

"Well," said Burt. "Things will work out. You've got to have faith."

"Faith is something the young can afford. I've read all the great books, and I'm not pretty anymore."

"Whoa there," Ned said. "If you're not pretty I don't know what half the men in the room have been staring at."

"Don't you patronize me," I told him. "Don't you dare. You're welcome to resent me or despise me or feel bored silly by me, but don't patronize me like I was some kind of little *wife*. It's the one thing I won't have. Do you hear me? Do you understand?"

Ned, without speaking, put his hand over mine to silence the tapping of my nail against the glass. I looked at his face.

"Ned."

I said only that, his name.

"It's all right," he said. "We'll pay for the drinks and go home."

"I'm sorry," I said.

"It's nothing," he assured me. "We've had an emotional day. Our only son just graduated from high school."

He kept his hand on mine. I looked across the table at Burt, who had fixed upon me a look of direct, dreadful understanding.

After Jonathan left for New York, Bobby got his own apartment in an austere limestone building across town. He enrolled in culinary school and worked nights as a waiter. He began to talk of our opening a restaurant together.

"A family place," he said. "I think a restaurant would be a good business to go into, don't you? We could all work there."

I allowed as how I might make a passable dishwasher.

"You'll be the head cook," he said. "It'll be, like, the only true Southern-style place in Ohio?"

Soon he was making dinners for Ned and me at our house. He did become a good cook, and seemed to have some cogent ideas about financing a restaurant.

I told him if he wanted to open a place on his own, I'd be his first customer, but to count me out as head cook. He smiled as he had when we first met years before—a smile that implied I had just switched over to a language he didn't speak.

That winter I found a job myself, as a secretary in a real estate office. We needed the money. Ned's theater was faring worse than ever, now that so many malls had established themselves on the outskirts. People avoided downtown after dark. The theater flashed its pink neon on an avenue where streetlights offered only small puddles of illumination; where nude mannequins smiled behind the dark glass of an extinct department store.

Although my secretarial job was nothing exalted or even especially interesting, I enjoyed having a daily destination so much that I began to dread the weekends. In my spare time I started an herb garden in the back yard.

Bobby met me occasionally for lunch downtown, since his cooking school was not far from the office in which I worked. He had grown rather handsome, in a conventional fine-featured way, and I must admit I took pleasure in meeting him at crowded restaurants, where the din of all those hungry wage-earners put an edge on the air.

Over our lunches, Bobby spoke with great animation about the restaurant business. At some undeterminable point he had ceased imitating a clean, personable young man and had actually become one, save for odd moments when his eyes glowed a bit too brightly and his skin took on a sweaty sheen. At those times he put me in mind of a Bible salesman, one of the excruciatingly cordial Southern zealots I knew well enough from my girlhood. In his excitement Bobby could take on that quality but he always caught himself, laughed apologetically, and lowered his voice, actually appeared to retract the sweat back into his pores, so that the effect finally was boyish and charming, a young dangerousness being brought under control.

I confessed my worries to him, and indulged myself every now and then in a complaint or two about my own situation, since I hated to burden Ned. His asthma had grown much worse as business declined, and he had started drinking a bit.

Bobby said numberless times, "I'll find backers and have the restaurant going in another year, two at the most. We can all run it. Everything will turn out all right."

I told him, "That's easy for you to say. You're young."

"You're young, too," he said. "I mean, you're young for your age? You'll love being head chef, wait and see."

"I am not going to be head anything."

"Yes you will. You'll want to when you see the place I'm going to build for you. Come on, Alice? Tell me you're behind me, and I'll build the best restaurant in Ohio."

A man at the next table glanced our way. He was fiftyish, trim and successful-looking in a slate-colored suit. I could see the question in his eyes: older woman, severe of face but not utterly through with her own kind of beauty, lunching with avid, handsome young man. For a moment I followed the thread of his imagination as he saw Bobby and me out of the restaurant and up to a rented room where afternoon light slanted in through the blinds.

Bobby leaned forward, his big hands splayed on the tabletop. I reached out and lightly touched his broad, raw fingers with my own.

"All right," I said. "If you're really all that determined to start a restaurant, count me in. I'll do whatever I can to help you."

"Good," he said, and his eyes actually glowed with the possibility of tears.

He opened his restaurant less than a year later. Perhaps he'd been too much in a rush. If he'd waited until he knew more about the business, he might have done better. But he kept insisting he was ready, and I can only speculate whether Ned's dwindling fortunes had any bearing on Bobby's own sense of urgency. He got backing from a rather dubious-looking character named Beechum, a man with cottony hair brushed forward over his bald spot and several heavy silver-and-turquoise rings on his thin white fingers. This Beechum owned, or claimed to own, a prosperous string of coin laundries, and envisioned, or so Bobby said, similar success in the realm of Southern cooking.

Under Beechum's guidance, Bobby leased space in a small shopping center in the suburbs, between a discount dress store and a bakery that displayed in its window an enormous, slightly dingy wedding cake. I expressed some doubts about the location, but Bobby had compiled a list of virtues that brooked no argument.

"It's near some major retail outlets," he recited gravely. "Penney's is the flagship store, and Sears is practically around the corner. There are other food stores in the area. And it's cheap. I mean, you've got to start somewhere, right?"

I needn't offer much detail about the restaurant's optimistic beginnings and its immediate decline. Suffice to say that Bobby named it Alice's, and did what he could with a fluorescent-lit, acoustic-ceilinged room that had most recently failed as a pizza parlor. He hung framed posters of New Orleans—wrought-iron balconies in the French Quarter, a black man blowing a trumpet —and found old wooden tables and chairs at garage sales. I tested recipes with Bobby, debated over seasonings, though Beechum generally prevailed with admonitions about cost overruns or the timidity of Ohio tastes. The final menu turned out to be a Northerner's version of Southern cooking: gumbo, hush puppies, frozen shrimp fixed every which way. The desserts were remarkable. I made it a point to stop by as often as I could.

Sometimes when I came for lunch I'd find one or two other parties—shoppers with bags from the discount store next door, lone salesclerks on their lunch hours—and sometimes I'd be the sole customer. On those occasions Bobby sat with me while the waitress either wiped the already clean pie case or gave in and read a movie magazine beside the refrigerator.

Through it all, Bobby never lost his Bible-salesman's good cheer.

"Things are always slow at first," he said. "You've got to let word of mouth get around. The people who leave here have all had great meals, they'll tell ten other people. You've got to give it some time."

"The food is fine, Bobby," I said. "I'd like to think people will come to recognize a good thing."

"Sure they will," he said. "If you've got the product, people'll find you. It's a matter of time."

We sat talking together in the empty room, under the fluorescent tubes. People passed by the spotless window and looked in with an expression I recognized: the humorous and rather frightened face one turns toward any ill-fated enterprise. I had looked in just that way through countless windows myself, into the depopulated interiors of fussy little gift shops, understocked delicatessens, boutiques in which every dress was five years out of style. As people rushed past with packages from Sears and Penney's, I understood their feelings; I understood the particular sort of nervous disdain inspired by any singular evidence of mankind's general failure to spin the straw into gold.

* * *

On an unseasonably warm night in November, six months after the restaurant's opening, Burt Morrow burned himself and half his house to ashes by falling asleep with a cigarette. Ned and I were awakened by the sirens, though of course we could not know their destination.

Still, I had a feeling. I just had a nameless edgy feeling and so I stayed awake long after Ned had returned to his noisy, almost painful-sounding slumber. When the phone rang I knew. We drove straight over, with coats pulled on over our bathrobes.

Bobby saw us pull up. He did not move. He stood on the lawn beside a black-coated fireman. As Ned and I ran to him, Bobby watched us with his old numbed, uncomprehending expression; that foreigner's look.

I put my arms around him. He was still as salt. He said in a high, clear voice, "My father died tonight at about twelve-thirty."

Bobby's shirtsleeves were singed, and his hair emitted an awful burnt smell. He must have tried to go into the burning house.

I stroked his ruined hair. He stood unmoving in my embrace. Half the house had burned to rubble; the other half was obscenely unscarred. The front door hung open, offering the blackened floral paper of an interior wall on which a mirror still hung in its ornate frame.

Presently Ned went off to see about Burt. I stayed with Bobby. He soon began to tremble, so I held him the harder, which seemed in turn to inspire more trembling. His spasms frightened me but I did not loosen my hold. I just dug in the way I had with Jonathan, when he was a baby given to mysterious crying fits and I, ignorant even for twenty-two, knew nothing but to hold him tight through my own terror and uncertainty.

Jonathan came home for the funeral. His blond hair still tumbled down past his shoulders, but he had taken to wearing loafers and a tweed jacket with his jeans. Bobby dressed in the style of the working young of Cleveland: sharply creased synthetic slacks, pastel shirts with epaulets.

They went for drives together, watched old movies on television. Bobby was pale and distracted, as if the interior of his own skull was putting out a noise only he could hear. Jonathan watched him carefully, sat close by, touched his shoulder or hand.

They might have been a convalescent and his nurse. There was compassion between them, but no hint of romance. For all their youth, they had taken on an elderly quality; sitting on the sofa together, they made you think of curio cabinets and venetian blinds. Bobby always sat beside Jonathan, childishly close. At any given moment a stranger might not have been able to tell which was the comforter and which the consoled. After a week, Jonathan returned to his new life in New York City.

Bobby soon closed the restaurant, and finally declared bankruptcy as a way of clearing his debts. Now he works in a bakery. He seems to feel more secure amid the floured surfaces, the fresh eggs and pastry tubes.

Because he could no longer pay the rent on his apartment, he has moved in with us. He stays upstairs, in Jonathan's room, sleeping on the narrow bed.

We don't much mind having Bobby. To be honest, we can use even the small amount of rent he pays, what with Jonathan in college and Ned's theater refusing to pull out of its slump. He has started booking foreign films, the kind that don't play in the mall theaters. He mends the lobby carpet with duct tape.

Jonathan calls on Sundays, like a dutiful son. He's moved out of the dormitory into an apartment in Greenwich Village. I try to imagine his life: movies and coffeehouses, music in basement clubs. I need to imagine those details because he relates none of them. What I hear from him is that his classes are going well, and that he requires no bedding, kitchen utensils, or new clothes.

Sometimes I think I'll leave Ned. Sometimes I think I'll just announce the fact and go, like a child of seventeen. But I can't imagine doing it, not really. One of the revelations of my early middle age is the fact that I care for him, right down to the marrow of my bones. He inspires my tenderness, even my pity. If he were more successful, perhaps I could manage it.

Instead, I am making another effort to fit in here. I've rejoined the church guild. I've begun giving a baking class at the YMCA, for wives who want to surprise their families at the holidays. My class has attracted a surprising number of students. Many of them are humorous and good-hearted, and some can probably be coaxed away from their devotion to Jell-O and granulated-pudding mix. When the class ends at Christmastime, three or four of us will probably continue as baking friends.

This is what you do. You make a future for yourself out of the raw material at hand. I sit typing at a desk from Monday to Friday, and twice weekly instruct other women in the art of folding eggs into batter, of rolling dough so thin you could read newsprint through it. I have little time for housework, but Bobby keeps the whole place spotless in my absence. Save for the hours he puts in at the bakery, he is always home. Always. He makes dinner every night. After dinner, Ned returns to the theater and Bobby and I watch television or play cards. I sit with him until it's time for bed. Sometimes I suggest he go out and see what the world is up to. I even offer to slip him some money, but he always says he's exactly where he wants to be. So there we sit, passing the hours. To be perfectly frank, I sometimes wish he'd leave. He's so dogged in his devotions, so endlessly agreeable.

PART II

JONATHAN

W̲E̲ W̲E̲R̲E̲ half-lovers. Together we occupied love's bright upper realm, where people delight in otherness, cherish their mates' oddities, and wish them well. Because we were not lovers in the fleshly sense we had no use for the little murders. Clare and I told our worst secrets and admitted to our most foolish fears. We ate dinner and went shopping together, assessed the qualities of men who passed on the streets. Looking back, I think we were like the sisters in old stories; the stories in which the pretty younger girl can't marry until somebody claims the older, less attractive one. In our case, though, we were both sisters at once. We shared a life of clothes and gossip and self-examination. We waited, with no particular urgency, to see whether someone would claim one of us for the other, more terrifying kind of love.

For three years we'd lived together in a sixth-floor walk-up on East Third Street between Avenues A and B, where Puerto Rican women argued in Spanish and drug dealers moved perpetually in and out of basement apartments. Drugged, heartbreakingly beautiful boys danced to enormous radios on the corner. We lived there because it was cheap, and because—we'd admitted this one drunken night—it struck us as more interesting than the safer parts of the city. I'd further confessed that I considered this neighborhood a source of anecdotes to be told in the better life that was still to come. When I'd said this, Clare had looked at me skeptically and said, "Belief in the future is a disreputable virtue, don't you think? It's sort of like building ships in bottles. You know? Admirable, but in a creepy kind of way."

Clare was thirty-six, eleven years older than I. She lived according to several assumptions, which she held with quiet but unremitting ferocity. She believed that James M. Cain was the greatest American writer, that society had reached its pinnacle in the late nineteen-thirties, and that there were no men left for a woman of her age and peculiarities. When contested on the final point, she replied in a tone of willing but nearly exhausted patience, like a good teacher facing her ten thousandth unpromising student. "Eliminate the following," she said, counting on her fingers. "Gay men. Married men. Men under the age of twenty-five. Men over the age of twenty-five who are only interested in young, beautiful women. Men who are still available because they can't commit to anyone. Men who are just plain assholes. Rapists and psycho killers. All right, now. Who's left?"

She conducted her daily affairs with ironic good cheer, like the second banana in a thirties comedy. Like a survivor of a war, who still wears heels and lipstick to walk among the wreckage.

When she grew depressed, we talked about having a baby together. Clare had already gotten through a marriage, an abortion, dozens of lovers, and three changes of career. I was three years out of college, writing a food column for a weekly newspaper, certain only of my lust for the man I called my lover. At night our street glittered with broken glass. Every morning an enormous Hispanic woman passed under our windows, singing loud sentimental love songs on her way to work.

One morning in early spring, when a single pale ivy leaf had worked its way between the crosspieces of the burglar-proof grate on the kitchen window, Clare sighed into her coffee and said, "Maybe I'll have my hair dyed back to its normal color. Don't you think a woman of a certain age should stop trying to look eccentric?"

She wore a kimono from a thrift store, not a delicate watery silk but a garish, lipstick-red rayon that must have been bought new in Hawaii or Las Vegas five years earlier. Clare was not beautiful, and claimed to be opposed to beauty in general.

"No," I said. "I think a woman of a certain age has all the more right." I stood in the doorway, because our kitchen accommodated only one person at a time.

"The difference between thirty-six and twenty-five," she said, "is that at twenty-five you can't look pathetic. Youth is the one overriding excuse. You can try anything out, do anything at all to your hair, and walk around looking perfectly fine. You're still thinking yourself up, so it's okay. But you get a little older, and you find your illusions starting to show."

"Is this going to be another Black Saturday?" I asked.

"Early to tell."

"Let's not. It's so pretty out. Let's go shopping and see a movie instead of contemplating suicide."

"When we have the baby," she said, "what sort of hair do you think it'll have?"

"What color is yours supposed to be?"

"Lord, I'd have to think way back. A sort of dull dark brown, I think. Salesgirl hair."

"Maybe the kid would get my coloring," I said. "I'll bet it's surprising what weak but determined genes can do."

She sipped her coffee. "To be perfectly frank," she said, "I have a feeling my black Rumanian ancestors would swarm all over your pensive Swedish·ones."

"Is that what you'd want? A miniature version of yourself?"

"Lord, no. Another me? We'd hate each other. I'd want the kid to have your intelligence, for one thing."

"Don't be coy," I said. "You're plenty smart."

"If I were all that smart," she said, "I don't suppose I'd be thirty-six years old, standing in a teensy little kitchen trying to think of the best way to have a baby without falling in love."

We kept talking about the baby. We did not make plans, but we talked a good deal. That was our way together. We'd had other ideas in the past: we'd talked about starting a breakfast-in-bed catering service, and about moving to the coast of Spain. We always discussed the particulars of these actions in such detail that eventually we crossed an invisible line and began to feel as if we had already performed them; our talk ultimately took on an aspect of reverie. We had practiced getting eggs Benedict from Third Street to upper Park Avenue in a steam cabinet (they arrived a congealed mess); we'd bought travel guides and cassettes that taught conversational Spanish. I did not expect the baby to be any different.

"I like the name Ethan for a boy," I said. "Or Trevor."

"Honey, please," she said. "No fancy names. If it's a boy let's call it Jon Junior. If it's a girl, how about Mary or Ann?"

"Why not Clare Junior?"

"I told you. I want her to be different from me."

Clare's rival was her own image, the elaborate personality she'd worked out for herself. She lived at a shifting, troubled distance from her ability to be tough and salty and "interesting." When her gestures were too perfectly executed she could be slightly grotesque—practiced and slick. I saw how it troubled her. Sometimes she embraced her persona with palpable defiance, looking out at the world as if to say *That's right, so what?* Sometimes she frightened herself. She had grown so adept it was hard for her to act out of character.

Still, she'd led what I considered to be a full, interesting life, and I disliked hearing her self-disparagements. She'd been married to a dancer now living in West Berlin whose troupe periodically played New York to extravagant acclaim. She'd been the lover of a semi-famous woman author. She'd taken heroin and opium, and enough Dexedrine to require treatment at a clinic in Baltimore. My own life, compared to hers, seemed timid and cautious. I hated to think that either choice—an oversized, dangerous life or a comfortable wage-earning one—led eventually to the same vague itch; the same conviction that the next generation must improve its lot.

"What do you think about punishment?" I asked.

"Personally? Or for the baby?"

"The baby."

"I wouldn't hit her," she said. "I couldn't. Oh, I don't know. I'd probably be one of those mothers who get huffy and disappointed, and the kid wishes you'd just haul off and smack him and get it over with."

Clare worked for a jeweler on St. Marks Place. She had a genius for putting odd things together—she made earrings and brooches out of rhinestones, broken glass, rusted tin, and tiny plastic figures from dime stores. Her work had a small but loyal following. I had unexpectedly become the restaurant critic for a weekly newspaper that started underground and grew too popular for its own crude facilities and its inexperienced staff. When I took the job, straight out of NYU, I'd thought of it as a first step toward my true career on the staff of a glossy national magazine, but as it happened I'd stumbled unawares—almost against my will—onto the ground floor of a good thing. In three years the paper had moved from dank offices in the garment district to a suite on Union Square. Its staff had tripled. And I'd been promoted from typist and occasional reporter to food columnist.

The joke was this: I knew nothing about food. It had been my mother's obsession, and I'd vehemently denied ingress to every particle of knowledge on the subject. When the editor decided to add a restaurant section, and told me he wanted me to write it, I protested that I didn't even know what quiche Lorraine was made of. He said, "That's the point. A lot of people don't." He offered a raise, and a minimum of twenty-four column inches every week. And so I became Plain John, a character of relatively modest means who appreciated good food but was not transported by the unexpected dash of cardamom in a red-pepper puree; who liked to go out to dinner with friends or lovers once or twice a week and was willing to spring for something fancy when the occasion demanded it. I reviewed Polish and Chinese restaurants, scoured Manhattan for the best hamburgers and pizza and pad Thai. I indicated which trendy restaurants treated even noncelebrities kindly, which served ludicrously small portions, which would be impressive but nonthreatening to parents when they visited from out of town. Both Clare and I subsisted on the meals paid for by the paper, though we repaid the debt through the eccentricities of our diet. One week we ate only burritos, another nothing but Peking duck. Clare speculated over whether our nutritional monism might be doing us some sort of lasting harm. She brought home vitamins, and drinks made with aloe vera, and protein powders supposedly favored by famous bodybuilders, who grinned and flexed on the brightly colored labels.

We told one another that the baby should be read to constantly, even before it was old enough to understand. We agreed that parents should above all be honest with their children, about the darker facts as well as the pleasant ones.

My other half-lover's name was Erich. He and I had sex, though he did not inspire in me the urgency or the sorrowful, exhilarating edge that, combined with desire, must add up to love. I kept my head with Erich. To be honest, since leaving Cleveland I had never loved a man I'd slept with—I hadn't come close to the feeling, though I'd gotten to know dozens of bodies in their every mood and condition. My own capacity for devotion focused actually on Clare and hypothetically on certain men I saw walking the streets of the city: strong-looking men who didn't aspire to conventional fame or happiness, who cleaved the air with definitive thoughtlessness. I looked as unobtrusively as possible at punks in black army boots, sullen Italian boys, and tough long-haired kids from small towns who had come to New York expecting their criminal reputations to hold.

I knew my interests were unrealistic, and probably unhealthy. But they obdurately remained—they were the geography of my desire. A particular boy I saw sometimes at the corner newsstand, with unkempt hair and an irritated expression, could make me tingle by brushing my elbow with his sleeve. The man I slept with seemed sketchy and remote.

Erich and I made love once or twice a week, usually at his apartment in the East Twenties. We'd met two years earlier, in the restaurant where he tended bar. I was reviewing gay restaurants that week—my column would evaluate the various places gay readers could go with their lovers if they wanted to hold hands across the table. I'd eaten alone that night, and I stopped at the bar for a brandy on my way out. Although the bar wasn't crowded, the bartender took nearly five minutes to ask me what I wanted to drink. He was hunched at the bar's opposite end, his forearms folded on the splashboard like a Flemish housewife leaning out her door, nodding with steady emphatic little bobs of his head at a story being told by an elderly man wearing gold jewelry and an emerald-green scarf. While I waited I watched the bartender's ass, which was small and compact, twitching in counterrhythm to his nods.

Finally the old man who was telling the story inclined his head in my direction, saying, "I think you've got a customer." The bartender turned with a startled look. His face was thin, the nose and chin too sharply pointed for ordinary handsomeness, though his color was good and his eyes were as milkily, innocently blue as a child's. His was the sort of face that, given a proneness to vanity, could be agonized over in a mirror—a face that could switch from beauty to plainness and back again. New York is full of faces like that, the not-quite-handsome faces of young men and women who have been fussed over by their mothers and who believe, with rigorous if slightly apologetic hopefulness, that they can make a future with their looks.

"Oops, oh, sorry," he said. "What can I get you?"

I ordered a brandy. "Business a little slow tonight?" I asked.

He nodded, pouring brandy into an oversized snifter. The elderly man in the emerald scarf pulled a cigarette out of the pack he'd set before himself on the bartop and slipped it into a short gold cigarette holder with elaborate concentration.

"It's been, you know, a little slow in general," the bartender said.

I suspected the restaurant wouldn't last much longer. It had an air of decline, and I knew more or less what I would write in my column the next day. A few phrases had already suggested themselves: "A fifties-ish nowhere zone that serves formal, vaguely embarrassing food"; "like a ghostly ocean liner that steams into port at midnight every hundred years." It was the sort of place a rich old aunt might take you, except that the customers were older men and bright-eyed, hungry-looking boys instead of dowagers in furs and brooches.

"Well, to tell you the truth," I said, "this place is a little frightening."

He set the brandy in front of me on a cocktail napkin and glanced at the old man, who was languidly expelling plumes of smoke through his nostrils. "Isn't it just the creepiest?" he said in a low voice. "I've been looking for another job."

"That's probably a good idea," I said.

He glanced again at the smoker, and settled himself at my end of the bar. He folded his arms on the splashboard and nodded his head.

"You'd be surprised how hard it is to get bartending jobs," he said. "I mean in, you know, good places. You haven't been here before, have you?"

"No."

"I didn't think I'd seen you."

A depth of scrutiny passed briefly behind his pallid blue eyes. He was trying, without deep conviction or curiosity, to figure me out. I imagined the bar was frequented by young men looking to meet up with money. I was neither handsome enough to be on the block nor prosperous-looking enough to be a buyer.

"I just wanted to try it," I said. "You can't keep going to the same old places over and over again."

He nodded, unconvinced. It was not a casual restaurant; not the sort of place for people without an ulterior motive.

"Do you, um, work around here?" he asked.

"Downtown," I said. "I was just in the neighborhood. I'm a writer."

"Really? What do you write?"

I told him the name of the newspaper, and he nodded with particular zeal. The paper was hot then. "What do you write?" he asked again.

"Oh, different things. Listen, do you get off soon?"

"Well, we close in another hour."

"You want to meet me for a drink in a less creepy place?" I asked.

"Well, okay," he said. "I mean, yes."

"My name is Jonathan."

"I'm Erich. My name is Erich."

He nodded as he announced his name. His eyes lost their uncertainty. Here was my subvert business—I'd come to pick up the bartender.

* * *

I went for a walk, and met him an hour later at a place in the
Thirties. He'd arrived ahead of me. He stood at the bar with a
bottle of Budweiser, feigning interest in the Esther Williams movie
on the videoscreen. He said hello and nodded slightly, as if agree-
ing with his own salutation.

I ordered a beer, and we worked our way through a conversation. We talked about the usual things, delivered brief accounts
of our origins and ambitions. It was a Wednesday night, the crowd
at the bar was sparse. Technicolor chorus girls splashed in a brilliant aquamarine world on the videoscreen, filling the room with
a colored, shifting dusk. Erich was all edgy inattention, the sort
of person who shreds napkins and taps his feet and fails to hear
fully half of what's said to him. His hair was already thinning on
top—I would be surprised to learn he was three months younger
than I.

After what seemed to both of us a decent interval—two beers
—we went to his apartment on Twenty-fourth Street, where he
introduced his second surprise.

He was great in bed. There is no other way to put it. It seemed
nothing less than transfiguration. Conversing, he was fidgety and
evasive, given to arrhythmic pauses and odd spasms of laughter.
But when he got out of his clothes he took on the fluid self-
assurance of a dancer. His physique was modest and sinewy, with
veined arms and a prominent rib cage. That first night, when we
got to his studio (a single room with a Pullman kitchen and bath),
he was naked so quickly he might have been wearing a breakaway
suit, the kind comedians use. He was dressed one moment and
nude the next, while I was still unfastening the last button of my
shirt.

"Hey," I said, "how did you do that?"

He smiled, and helped me out of my own clothes. His movements were swift and efficient but gentle. He had abruptly traded
his skittish, roving manner for calm focus and suave, unhurried
competence. He unbuttoned my jeans and slid them tenderly down
to my ankles, wrapped his arms around my waist and lifted me,
with only a hint of strain, up onto the bed.

117

I was not excited by him. I was excited by the idea of sex, the ease of it—I had gone out and caught someone, an unacclaimed man who was mine to do with as I liked. I admit it—there was a streak of sadism in my lusts. There was the taint of vanity. I chose ordinary men who would not refuse; who would feel lucky to have me. I did not thrill to the sight of their flesh—which was either bulky or scrawny but always abashed and grateful—so much as I did to the fact of their capture. As Erich set me on his bed I was aroused in the general, unfocused way that had become familiar. I would let him command the sex but I would leave his apartment undefeated. Part of me was already gone, even now, as our chests touched for the first time and our legs fumbled for position. I was more important than this. The excitement I felt was edgy and not entirely pleasant, like a swarm of bees inside my chest.

Erich nuzzled my shoulder, ran his fingers lightly along my ribs. He had a dry, powdery touch. There was something sweet about his earnestness and his balding, elusive beauty. There was something dreadful about it.

He lay for a while on top of me, peppering my chest with kisses. Then he deftly revolved our bodies so that I was on top. I got a thorough look at him, for the first time. He was thin but big-boned, his abdomen more densely furred than his chest. His cock angled off to the right, raggedly skirted by a vein. His gaunt, hairy stomach and skewed cock suddenly repulsed me. Usually with strangers there was a moment of shock like this, when I fully comprehended the privacy of their bodies. Looking at Erich's thin torso, I felt as if I had caught him in some indiscretion. I saw the otherness of him, and it flipped me over from excitement to disgust—my own agitation soured, and I began bluffing my way through, cramming his cock blindly into my mouth. I was already thinking of going home and having a drink with Clare. Even as it happened, this was a story I would tell her. She and I would shake our heads together, and discuss the perplexing scarcity of love.

"Relax," Erich whispered. I didn't answer, because my mouth was full. When he repeated it, I pulled my head up and said, "I'm perfectly relaxed, thank you." I would make him come quickly, come myself, and be back in my own skin, free on the street.

He slipped away, directing me to lie belly-down on the mattress. "You're too tense," he said. I skeptically obeyed, and he began massaging my back, tracing the curves of my shoulders and spine with his fingertips. "You're very tight," he said. "I can feel it all through here."

Against my better judgment, I consigned myself to his hands. I disliked being told I was tense—it seemed he had recognized a flaw in my character. For the occasion of sex I always slipped over into an identity that was not quite my own. When making love I was like my own hypothetical older brother, a strong, slightly cynical man who lived adventurously, without the rabbity qualms that beset my other self. At my desk or on the subway I daydreamed of powerful, angry men who needed me to ease their pain. In bed with meek strangers I thought only of quick orgasm and escape.

Erich worked my back with ardent delicacy, his fingers expertly following the confluence of tendon and bone. When I remarked on his proficiency he said, "I took a course in this." I would learn that he believed in acquiring accreditation. He was a diligent student of the world at large, and liked things broken down into sequences. He had also taken courses in conversational French, creative writing, and quiltmaking.

Under his ministrations, I relaxed almost against my will. Without having decided to, abruptly, I fell asleep. It was utterly unlike me. But I'd been keeping late hours, and working long days. The sensation resembled that of slipping under an anesthetic. One moment I was awake, looking at a framed photograph of two bland-faced strangers propped on the nightstand, and the next I was being roused from slumber by a kiss.

I startled, and nearly jumped off the bed. For a moment I lost track of everything. Where was I, and whose cologned jaw was this? "Shh," he whispered. "It's okay."

"Oh God, did I fall asleep?" I asked. I was groggy and ashamed. Had I snored? Had I drooled?

"Just for a couple of minutes," he said. He kissed my neck and gently but steadily positioned himself between my legs.

"I can't believe this," I said. "I've never, you know."

"Just stay relaxed," he said. "This is a dream you're having."

For some reason, I obeyed. Although my instinct was to return to myself, to quickly polish off the sex and get on about my business, I decided to relax. There was surprising, voluptuous pleasure in it. I let Erich manage things and our lovemaking passed as if in fact I was dreaming. He carried it through the way he pursued all his projects, with a scholar's scrupulous attention. If our coupling lacked the abandon of true passion it had a schooled solidity that was the next best thing. Erich could pour a precise ounce of whiskey without measuring. He could make a double-wedding-ring quilt by hand. And he could tell how far to thrust, when to withdraw, when to throw in an unexpected move. I gave myself up to it. He enjoyed being in command, and I relinquished my own desire to impress.

We made love three times that night. After the first time we did not roll away. I didn't make my escape. He held me, and I stroked his sparsely haired thigh. I could smell his sweat, which was sharp but not unpleasant. We embraced in silence for ten minutes or longer. Then he said, "Are you ready again?"

By the time I got dressed his apartment had lost some of its strangeness. It was not in any way an auspicious or even particularly comfortable home—a viewless room in a white brick building that must have been built, hurriedly, in the early sixties. It contained a platform bed covered with quilts, a stereo and television, and an absurdly large black sofa which, at sunrise, would begin its daily function of sucking up whatever light filtered in through the single window. On the wall was a silver-framed poster depicting a Matisse painting of a gaudy, lavishly draped room empty of life except for three dagger-shaped goldfish suspended in a bright blue bowl. Erich's apartment could have been a doctor's waiting room. It conveyed little about its inhabitant beyond a certain thin sorrow. Still, by the time I'd dressed, and had written down his phone number and left my own on a slip of paper, the apartment had taken on weight. It did not appear to be any less bleak than it had when we first arrived; it had merely begun to reveal itself as a place in which someone did, in fact, live. A red light blinked on the answering machine, signifying unheard messages. I blew Erich a kiss from the door, whispered, "See you later," and walked three flights down to the street.

This was usually my favorite moment, after the sex was finished and I was restored to myself, still young and viable, free to go everywhere. Tonight, though, I felt irritated and weightless; I couldn't quite pick up my sense of myself. Twenty-fourth Street lay quietly in its bath of dark yellow light. A lone hooker strolled in black stockings and a fur jacket, and an all-night produce stand offered displays of oranges, waxy apples, and carnations dyed green for St. Patrick's Day. I was infused with a bodily pleasure that was intricately, brittlely edged in regret. Something had been lost, at least for the moment—some measure of possibility. I walked twenty blocks home, but couldn't shake the feeling. It followed me like a thief.

I didn't get home until after four. Clare was asleep. When I saw her the following evening, I didn't offer to tell her much about Erich. Clare and I based our conversations about men on a shared attitude of ironic disdain, and I wasn't sure how to present a man like Erich. I was not in love, but for once an evening's sex had been something other than clownish comedy, desperation, or boredom.

Clare said, "You're being very quiet about this, Jonathan. What exactly is up?"

"Nothing's up." We were sipping Pernod on the sofa. Pernod was our latest drink. We had a habit of brief but devout loyalties to different exotic liquors.

"You're being circumspect," she said, "and you're not the type. Does this guy seem like he could turn out to be someone special? What exactly are you hiding?"

" 'This guy' is another would-be actor slinging drinks in hell. He happens to be a great fuck."

"Honey, don't toss something like that off lightly," she said. "I met my last great fuck in, what, 1979? Let's have a few details, please. Come on, give. This is your Aunt Clare."

She took a deep swallow of her drink, and I thought I saw under her friendly avidity the plain fear that I would leave her; that I'd disappear into love. It showed in her eyes and along her mouth, which could go stern and disapproving despite her lavish crimson lipstick.

"Honey, there are places even the best of friends can't travel together," I said.

"Oh, that's not true," she said. "You don't mean that, you're just embarrassed by the subject. Right?"

Clare and I kept no secrets—that was the heady, reckless aspect of our friendship. Perhaps it was our substitute for the creaturely knowledge other couples glean from sex. Clare and I confessed everything. We stripped ourselves naked and numbered our faults. We knew one another's most disreputable fantasies; we confessed our deceits and greeds, our self-flattering lies. We described all our sexual entanglements, and we knew the condition of one another's bowels.

And now, for the first time, I wanted to hold something apart. I wasn't sure why. It may have been that very uncertainty I hoped to preserve. Erich had surprised me with his gentle competence. Something about him touched me—his edgy good cheer and slender prospects. Something about him made me angry. I didn't know what I felt and I disliked being asked to give my feelings a name. I may have feared that in describing them so early I'd sap them of their potential for growth or change. I may have been right.

But I chose that night not to cultivate secrets. I, too, feared solitude and abandonment, and I knew I would never make a life with Erich. He would, at best, have been a first step toward something uncertain that lay beyond the circle of domestic warmth I shared with Clare. She was my main love in the world. I had no other attachment half so profound.

So I told her everything. There wasn't, as it turned out, very much to tell. When I had finished, Clare said, "Honey, you've just found yourself a Doctor Feelgood." She sang a couple of lines from Aretha's song. " 'Don't call me no doctor, filling me up with all of them pills, I got me a man named Dr. Feelgood, makes me feel real gooo-oood.' "

That seemed a sufficient accounting, at least for the time being. Erich would be Doctor Feelgood. From that night on, the longer I called him by that name, the more perfectly it came to fit. Clare and I continued our sisterly relations with our loyalties undiluted. I had found myself a nice little thing on the side. Clare counseled me to ride it until it thinned out, as such flings inevitably did. That seemed like sound advice.

And so Erich and I started dating. Since he worked nights, we usually met after eleven. We'd have a drink or two in a bar, and go to his place.

I did not learn many particulars of his life. He had a singular ambition, an ill-defined but persistent one: to be recognized. The means by which he'd achieve recognition were uncertain—he was simply looking for a break, trying to position himself for discovery. He'd audition for anything. He tried out for Broadway musicals though he couldn't sing. He'd work fourteen-hour days as an extra in any movie being shot in New York, and at Christmastime willingly played a life-sized mechanical soldier at F.A.O. Schwarz. He took endless acting classes, spoke convincingly of his ambition to become a better actor, but as I knew him longer, I began to realize that acting wasn't really the point. Acclaim was the point, and his gig at the toy store provided roughly the same mix of satisfaction and anguish he'd have derived from playing the lead in a Broadway show. He enjoyed methodical pursuit and he worshipped attention; he did not dream of accomplishment per se. In his ordinary life he was all but invisible—he wore jeans and polo shirts, stammered his way through the simplest conversations, lived alone in a barren apartment. But at Schwarz during the Christmas season he never fell out of character, never ceased his stiff-limbed robotic movements during the whole of an eight-hour shift. In gym shorts on a 30° day he jogged forty-five times down the same block of Bleecker Street for the sake of being a shadowy, background figure in a movie that would never be released. At night, with the lights off, he was great in bed.

Although I saw him once or twice a week, I didn't get to know him. I suspect he worried that if I—if anyone—came to know him too well, the motion of his life would somehow wind down—his obscure destiny would be confirmed. I myself worried that he lived on the brink of total surrender to another person's will. I thought that when he finally, fully despaired of achieving fame he would make himself into a fan, find a lover and cheerfully relinquish every vestige of his will. Maybe I'd sensed it the first moment I saw him, nodding eagerly at an old man's barroom conversation. He was practicing his powers of attention. I didn't want them focused too ardently on me.

When we were together, we emphasized the local details: anecdotes from our working lives, the movies we'd loved or hated. Finally, on what may have been our tenth or fifteenth date, as we lay quietly sweating onto one another's flesh, he said, "So, um, who are you, anyway?"

"What?"

His ears reddened. I suspected it was a line he'd picked up from a movie.

"What I mean is, I don't really know anything about you," he said.

"I don't know much of anything about you either," I said. "I basically know you're an actor working as a bartender, you want to change jobs but aren't doing anything much about it, and you loved *The Killing Fields.*"

"Well, I grew up in Detroit," he said.

"I'm from the Midwest, too."

"I know. From Cleveland."

After a pause, he said, "Well, this is very interesting. We're both from the Midwest. That really, you know, explains a lot, doesn't it?"

"No, it doesn't explain much of anything," I said. I believed this conversation was the beginning of the end for us, and I didn't entirely mind. Goodbye, Doctor Feelgood. Set me back on the street in my own skin, with my old sense of a limitless future.

After a moment he said, "I used to be a musician. When I was a kid. I was crazy for it. I dreamed about it. I had dreams that were just music, just . . . music."

"Really?" I said. "What did you play?"

"Piano. Cello. Some violin."

"Do you still play?"

"No," he said. "Never. I wasn't, you know, good enough. I was pretty good. But not really good enough."

"I see."

We lay together for a while in uneasy silence, waiting to see what would happen next. We were neither friends nor lovers. We had no natural access to one another outside the realm of sex. I believed I could feel the weight of Erich's unhappiness the way a diver feels the weight of the ocean, but I couldn't help him. This was the price we paid for sleeping together first and getting acquainted later—we shared an intimacy devoid of knowledge or affection. I couldn't listen to Erich's confessions; I didn't know him well enough for that. I remembered Clare's admonition—ride it until it thins out.

"Listen," I said.

He put a finger to my lips. "Shh," he whispered. "Don't talk. This isn't really, you know, a very good time to talk." He started to stroke my hair and nibble his way along my shoulder.

Our relations retained their halting, formal quality. Each time we saw one another, we might have been meeting for the first time. Months later, when I asked Erich about his old love of music, all he would say is "That's over. That's just, you know, ancient history. Have you seen any movies?" Our conversation stalled sometimes, and the ensuing silences refused to take on an aspect of ease. He never came to my apartment, never met Clare or any of my other friends. I left my life to visit him in his. In Erich's company I developed a new persona. I was tough and slightly insensitive; a bit of an object. Our communion took place only at the bodily level, and that came to seem right for us. Anything else would have been sentimental, forced, indiscreet. Our relations were cordial and respectful. We did not infringe. I believe that in some way we despised one another. Because I brought nothing but my nerves and muscles to the affair, I found I could be surprisingly noisy in bed. I could walk unapologetically across the floorboards, my boots ringing like the strokes of an ax. And I could be a little cruel. I could bite Erich's skin hard enough to leave red clamshell marks behind. I could fantasize about him—an unknown man—manacled, humiliated, stripped naked and tied to a Kafkaesque machine that fucked him relentlessly.

In my other life, I went out nightly with Clare for falafel or barbecued chicken or Vietnamese food. We argued over how much television a child should be permitted to watch. We agreed that the sterner reality of public school was an education in itself, and would balance the shoddy educations of the teachers. Sometimes handsome young fathers would stroll by the window of whatever restaurant we sat in, pushing strollers or cradling their sleeping children on their shoulders. I always watched them pass.

That was my life in the dead center of the Reagan years.

Then Bobby came to live in New York.

BOBBY

I STAYED in Ned and Alice's house for almost eight years. The urge to do nothing and not change caught up with me; for eight years I squeezed roses onto birthday cakes and thought of what I'd make for dinner. Each day was an identical package, and the gorgeousness of them was their perfect resemblance, each to the others. Like a drug, repetition changes the size of things. A day when my cinnamon rolls came out just right and the sky clicked over from rain to snow felt full and complete. I thumped melons at the grocery store, dug walnuts from the bins with my hands. I bought new records. I didn't fall in love. I didn't visit my family's graves, three in a row. I waited for asparagus and tomatoes to show up again, and played Dylan's *Blonde on Blonde* album until the grooves flattened out. I'd be living like that today if Ned and Alice hadn't moved to Arizona.

The doctor announced it: Ohio air was too heavy with spoor and lake water for Ned's tired lungs. It was go to the desert or start planning the funeral. That's what he said.

At first I thought I'd go with them. But Alice sat me down. "Bobby," she said, "honey, it's time for you to get out on your own. What would you do in Arizona?"

I told her I'd get a bakery job. I told her I'd do what I was doing now, but I'd do it there instead.

Her eyes shrank, pulled in their light. The singular crease, one deep vertical line, showed up in her forehead. "Bobby, you're twenty-five. Don't you want more of a life than this?"

"I don't know," I told her. "I mean, this is a life, and I like it pretty well."

I knew how I sounded—slow and oafish, like the cousin who gets ditched and goes on playing alone, as if he'd planned it that way. I couldn't quite tell her about the daily beauty, how I didn't tire of seeing 6 a.m. light on the telephone wires. When I was younger, I'd expected to grow out of the gap between the self I knew and what I heard myself say. I'd expected to feel more like one single person.

"Dearie, there's more to it than this," she said. "Trust me."

"You don't want me to go to Arizona," I said in a balky cousin's voice. Still, it was what I had to say.

"No. Frankly, I don't. I'm pushing you out of the nest, like I probably should have some time ago."

I nodded. We were in the kitchen, and I could see myself reflected in the window glass. At that moment I looked gigantic, like a geek from a carnival, with a head the size of a football helmet and arms that hung inches above the floor. It was strange, because I'd always thought of myself as small and boy-like, the next best thing to invisible.

"Do you understand what I'm telling you?" she asked.

"Uh-huh."

I understood that my life would change with or without my agreement. I understood that my supply of this particular drug— these red-checked dish towels and this crock of wooden spoons —was about to run out.

I decided to go to New York. It was the only other logical place. My Cleveland life depended on Alice and Ned—I needed their house to clean, their dinner to cook. I needed them to protect and care for. Otherwise Cleveland was just a place where things failed to happen. The air reeked of disappointment: river water thick as maple syrup, cinder-block shopping centers with three out of five units dark. Working in a bakery, you get to know the local unhappiness. People stuff whole cakes into their sorrow, brownies and cookies and Bismarcks by the dozen. The regularity of my days with Ned and Alice was like a campfire. I'd loved that part of Cleveland. But, without them, there would only be bus stops, and the wind blowing off Lake Erie. I wasn't ready to be a ghost so soon.

I called Jonathan. I did it with true nervousness—by then we were more like relatives than friends. We bought presents, and smoked joints together before Christmas dinners. That was friendly enough. But months went by between holidays, and he wore clothes I would never have thought of on my own. He talked about theater; I went to the movies with Ned or watched TV with Alice. I lay in my room—formerly his room—for hours, just listening to music. Jonathan was quick and bright, going places, and although I loved him his visits always embarrassed me. In his presence I could feel like that gawky cousin or, worse, like a bachelor uncle; a jovial undemanding type who only knew the outer surface of things. Jonathan put my life in a miniaturizing light, and I couldn't help looking forward to the day he got back on the plane because I knew on that day my life would return to its proper size, and I could walk down the Ohio streets with no washed-up, refugee feeling.

Still, when my Cleveland life ran out on me, I called Jonathan. I didn't want an arbitrary new life in Boston or Los Angeles. I couldn't imagine being so alone. And though I was friendly enough with Rose and Sammi and Paul at the bakery, I didn't have what you could truthfully call friends. You don't necessarily meet a lot of people in this world. Not when you let yourself get distracted by music and the passing of hours.

The first few times I called I got Jonathan's answering machine, and couldn't talk to it. Each time the machine answered I hung up with a small criminal pang. Finally, after almost a week of trying, he answered in person.

"Hello," he said.

"Jon? Jonny?"

"Mm-hm."

"Jon. It's Bobby."

129

"Bobby. Hey, this is a surprise. Is everything all right?"

That was where we were together. A phone call from me implied bad news about the family's fortunes.

"Oh yeah," I said. "Everything's fine. Fine and perfect, couldn't be better."

"Good. How are you?"

"I'm good. I'm very, very good. How about you?"

"Oh, all right," he said. "You know. Life goes on."

I sat through my own urge to say, "Well, that's great, goodbye," and hang up the phone. A scene from my possible Cleveland future passed in front of me. On my next birthday, the bakery would have a party for me. Rose, who'd be seventy by then, would kiss a lipstick mark onto my cheek and call me her best beau. There'd be a cake, free to the customers. We'd cut a big slice for George Dubb, a three-hundred-pound bachelor who bought Napoleons and a dozen Linzer cookies every day.

"Listen," I said. "Um. You know how Ned and Alice are going to Arizona?"

"Well, sure. Sure I do. I think it'll be good for them. They've needed a change of scene since about 1953."

"Yeah. Well, you see, now that they're leaving, I've been thinking, like, what am I hanging around here for? They tore down the Moonlight, did you hear about that?"

"No," he said. "God, I haven't thought about that place in ten years. Have you been going there?"

"Well, no. You and I went once. Remember? On acid."

"I'll never forget. I spent the whole night getting my skates on and going once around the rink."

"It's gone now," I said. "It's a Midas Muffler now."

"Huh."

"Jon?"

"Yes?"

"Would it be okay with you if I came to New York? I mean, could I stay with you for a little while? Just until I got, like, a job and an apartment?"

There was a pause. I could hear the buzz of the miles, all those voices cutting the air between Jonathan and me. He said, "Do you really want to come to New York?"

"Yeah. I really do. I think I really do."

"It's a rough place, Bobby. Last week somebody was murdered a few blocks from where I live. They found the body in four different trash cans."

"I know it isn't Cleveland," I said. "I know that. But, Jonny. I'm, like, up to my elbows in frosting here. I mean, I've made a million cupcakes by now."

He let another pause slip through the line. Then he said, "If you honestly think you want to give New York a try, of course you can stay with me. Of course you can. I'll see what I can do to keep you safe here."

I took the train, because it was cheaper and because I wanted to see exactly how much distance I was covering. I looked out the window the whole time, with my full attention, as if I was reading a book.

Jonathan met me at the station in New York. He wore a black T-shirt, black jeans, heavy black shoes with a dull shine like licorice. You could count on him to be wearing something you didn't expect.

We hugged in the station, and Jonathan put a precise little kiss on my cheek. He led me out to the sidewalk. Seeing him hail a cab was my first lesson in how different we'd become. He stepped off the crowded curb and shot one hand straight up, with the calm certainty of a general. It was a small enough act, but the sense of his own entitlement was unmistakable. I myself tended to move like a long apology.

When we were in the back seat of the cab, Jonathan pinched my arm. "I can't believe you're here," he said.

"Me neither. That's why I wanted to see Pennsylvania go by, so I'd believe it. I mean, if I just got off a plane, this'd seem like, you know, some kind of hallucination."

"It is. This city is just a dream you're having," he said. And during the time it took us to reach his apartment, we didn't think of anything else we needed to say.

The cab crept through late-afternoon traffic. I had only been to New York once before, years earlier, when Jonathan was still in school. I'd been interested in it but it wasn't about me; or rather it was only about me in the most indirect way, like a highway or a battleship. I'd done the tourist things. I'd gone to the tops of monuments and walked through Greenwich Village and had a drink with Jonathan and his friends at a bar where a famous poet died. I'd been comfortable in my tourist smallness, pleased with myself for being in an amazing place and for having a snug un-surprising home to return to.

Now I was going to live here. Now it was a different city altogether.

It shimmered. That was the first thing I noticed. Its molecules seemed more excited; things shivered and gleamed in a way that made them hard to see. The buildings and streets put out more light than the sky sent down—it all broke up in front of you, so your vision only caught the fragments. Cleveland offered itself differently, in bigger pieces. There you saw a billboard, a cloud, an elm standing over its own fat shadow. Here, my first ten minutes in New York, I could only be sure of seeing a woman's red straw hat, a flock of pigeons, and a pale neon sign that said LOLA. Everything else was an ongoing explosion, the city blowing itself to bits, over and over again.

When we reached Jonathan's apartment, things settled down and became more visible. He lived in a brown building on a narrow brown street. If Cleveland was mainly a gray city—limestone and granite—New York was brown, all rust and faded chocolate and schoolteacherish yellow-beige.

Jonathan said, "Here it is. The Tarantula Arms."

"This is your building," I said, as if I thought he might not be sure about it.

"This is it. I warned you. Come on, it's better when you get inside."

Inside, the stairwell floated in a green aquarium light. One flu-orescent halo buzzed at each landing. I carried a suitcase and my backpack; Jonathan carried my other suitcase. I hadn't brought much to my new life. Both suitcases were full of records. The backpack held my clothes, which, I could already see, had nothing to do with life in a city like this. I might have been an exchange student.

"We're going up to the sixth floor," Jonathan said. "Be brave."

I followed him. The landings smelled like something fried. Slow Spanish music hung in the swampy light. As we went up I watched my borrowed suitcase, an old blue American Tourister of Alice's, whump against Jonathan's black-jeaned thigh. Even my suitcase looked wrong here—sad and hoarily innocent as an old virgin.

When we got to the sixth floor, Jonathan unlocked three locks and opened the metal door. "Ta-da," he said as the door swung heftily open, squeaking on its hinges.

"Your place," I said. I could not seem to shed the habit of telling him we had reached his apartment.

"And yours, too," he said. He ushered me in with a bow.

The apartment was, in fact, a change from the underwater gloom of the stairs and hall. You stepped straight into the living room, which was painted orange-red, the color of a flowerpot. There was a sofa covered with a leopard-skin sheet, and a huge painting of a naked blue woman twisting ecstatically to reach something that hovered just off the edge of the canvas. The room was full of light. Streams of it tumbled in through the barred windows, which were bracketed by thick fifties curtains crawling with green and red leaves. If you pulled those curtains the sunlight would snap out like electricity. They were as weighty and businesslike as the metal door we had just passed through.

"Yow," I said. And then, without meaning to: "This is your *place*."

"My roommate Clare had a lot to say about decorating," he said. "Come on, let's take your things to my room."

We went down a short hall, past two closed doors, to his room. His room was white, with no pictures on the walls. He had a futon on the bare wooden floor, and a white paper lamp that stood on wire legs thin as pencil lines.

"I got a little carried away with this Zen thing," he said. "I just needed some relief from all that color."

"Uh-huh," I said. "I like white."

We set my bags down, and stood through a moment of difficult silence. Over the years we'd lost our inevitability together; now we were like the relatives of two old friends who had died.

He said, "I've got a sleeping bag you can sleep in. And we'll cram your things in the closet somehow."

"Okay," I said.

"Do you want to unpack now?"

I didn't care about unpacking, but it would have been a logical next step. At that moment I felt I understood about the past. In another century a guest unpacked, and rested, and dressed for dinner, so that everybody had a good long period alone with himself. In the modern age, we have to negotiate vaster expanses of uninterrupted time.

"Okay," I said. "I mean, I mostly brought records."

He laughed. "That's what you'd bring into a bomb shelter, isn't it?" he said.

I opened the American Tourister and took out a short stack. "Have you heard Joni's new one?" I asked.

"No. Is it good?"

"Excellent. Oh, hey, have you got this Van Morrison?"

"No. I don't think I've listened to Van since I was in Cleveland, to tell you the truth."

"Oh, this record'll kill you," I said. "He's still, like, one of the best. I'm going to put it on, okay?"

"We don't have a turntable," he said. "Just a cassette player. Sorry."

"Oh. Well," I said.

He put his hand on my shoulder. "It'll be okay, Bobby," he said. "We have music, too. We don't live in silence. But if Van Morrison is a priority, we can go out right now and get him on tape. The biggest record store you've ever seen is about six blocks from here."

"That's okay," I said. "I mean, you've got stuff of your own I've probably never heard, right?"

"Sure. Of course we do. But look me straight in the eye. We need to go out and buy that Van Morrison tape right this minute, don't we?"

"Naw," I said. "It's okay, really." But Jonathan shook his head.

"Come with me," he said. "We'll take care of the important business first, and then we can unpack."

He took me back out of the apartment, and we walked to a

record store on Broadway. He had not been lying about that store. Nothing shy of the words "dream come true" would do here—it was the cliché made into flesh. This place spanned a city block; it filled three separate floors. In Ohio I had haunted the chain store in the mall, and the dying establishment of an old beatnik whose walls were still covered with pegboard. Here, you passed through a bank of revolving doors into a room tall as a church. The sound of guitars and a woman's voice, clean as a razor, rocked over rows and immaculate rows of albums. Neon arrows flashed, and a black-haired woman who could have been in perfume ads browsed next to a little boy in a Sex Pistols T-shirt. It was an important place —you'd have known that if you were blind and deaf. You'd have smelled it; you'd have felt it tingling on your skin. This was where the molecules were most purely and ecstatically agitated. I believed then it was the heart of New York City. I believe it to this day.

We went downstairs to the cassette section, and found Van Morrison. We also found an old Stones Jonathan didn't have, and *Blonde on Blonde*, and Janis Joplin's greatest hits. Jonathan paid for them all with a credit card. He insisted. "This is your welcome-to-New-York present," he said. "Buy me something when you've got a job."

We walked back with our cassettes in a yellow plastic bag. It was early evening on a day without weather—a warm one with a blank white sky, one of those timeless days that are more like illuminated nights, when only the clock tells you whether it's morning or afternoon. Jonathan and I talked about Ned and Alice as we traveled bright brown streets lined with Spanish grocery stores and warehouses that had already pulled down their metal grates. With those cassettes solidly in the bag and Jonathan talking about his parents I felt an early click of rightness about the place —as of that moment, I had history there. It was my first true experience of being in New York, walking down a street called Great Jones as a Wonder Bread wrapper, stirred by the day's single gust of wind, skittered after us like a crazy pet.

When we got back to the apartment, Jonathan's roommate Clare was home. We walked through the big door and she called, "Hello, dear." Like a wife.

The living room was empty. She had called from offstage.

Jonathan answered, "Honey, we've got company."

"Oh," her voice said. "I forgot. It's today, isn't it?"

Then she came out.

I don't know if I can describe Clare, though I can see her right down to her lazy way of gesturing, loose-wristed, until she gets to the point of the story, when she flicks her wrist with the lethal precision of a fly fisherman. If I close my eyes she's there, and she's there if I open them, too. But what I see is a way of walking and smiling, a way of sitting in a chair. All her moves are particular to her—she has a way of setting a glass on a table, of raising her shoulders when she laughs. Her appearance is harder to nail down. On first sighting, she was like New York made into a woman—she changed and changed. I could tell she was beautiful in a sharp, big-nosed way that had nothing to do with magazines. Her hair was orange then—it bristled as if her brain was on fire. She was several inches taller than I, with dark red lips. She wore tight pants, and a tiger-striped shirt that fell off her shoulders.

"Bobby, this is Clare," Jonathan said.

She tilted her head in a hostess manner, and gave me a hand tipped with long purple fingernails. "Bobby," she said. "I'm glad to meet you."

I would learn later that she was raised by a good Lutheran mother in Providence, Rhode Island, and had never quite overcome her old habit of good manners. I said hello and shook her hand, which was strong and sure as an apple picker's.

"We've been shopping," Jonathan said. "We decided we needed a Van Morrison tape right away."

I was grateful to him for explaining it as something *we* needed. I didn't like to seem so delicate and peculiar, not right up front to a stranger.

"I love Van Morrison," she said. "I used to have all his records. But, you know. You lose things in various divorce settlements."

"Should I put this on?" I asked.

"Honey, absolutely," she said. "Right over there."

I walked across the room to the shelves where the sleek black tape player stood. On the shelf above it a collection of animal skulls silently displayed their empty sockets and their different

136

arrangements of ivory-colored fang and tooth. Jonathan and Clare discussed domestic particulars. I got the cellophane off the cassette, punched Van into the machine, and pushed the *Play* button. After a few moments of soft mechanical whir, Van's voice singing "Tore Down à la Rimbaud" filled the room. I took a breath, and I took another.

"Bobby?" Jonathan said. "Are you hungry?"

"I guess," I said. I was looking at the skulls from a safe distance, surrounded by Van's voice.

"How about if we listen to this for a while, then all go out for dinner?" Jonathan said. "It's on the newspaper. I'm doing meat loaf this week, is that all right with you?"

"Sure," I said. "Perfect." I was lost in the music. I'd have agreed to beaver tail.

We stayed around the apartment through one side of the tape. Jonathan and Clare were being polite—they liked Van's record well enough, but considered it background for a conversation. Clare asked courteous questions about my trip and my past life with Jonathan, which I suspect I must have answered with sweaty, grinning incoherence. I couldn't concentrate with music in the room.

When side one was finished, we went out. Clare put on an old leather jacket with a white peace sign painted on the back. She made an odd kind of sense to me, though she was the least sensible-looking person I'd ever met. She had a gaudy openness—a circus quality, with no hint of a hidden agenda. She made you feel like you could take her hand as you walked down the street.

We went to a restaurant that didn't look like a restaurant. An uninformed pedestrian might have thought it was a cheap insurance agency, with venetian blinds and a few dusty bowling trophies displayed in the windows. But, inside, it was packed with people. Elvis Presley sang through the laughter and the clink of silverware. At a table near the door, a woman in a fur dress said something about gorillas, in an English accent.

I myself had on Calvin Klein jeans and a rugby shirt. It was my most interesting outfit. We sat at a table in a corner, so close to three other tables we had to slide sideways into our chairs. The walls were covered with souvenir plates and old postcards, with

stuffed deer heads and kitchen clocks and faded record albums by
Dusty Springfield and the Kingston Trio. A sign near my head
said "Disregard This Sign."

"This place has a lot of décor," Clare said to me.

"Uh-huh."

"More décor than the entire state of Maine," Jonathan added.

"So, Bobby," Clare said. "What do you think you want to do
here? In New York."

"I'm a pretty good baker," I said. "I guess I'll probably do that.
I mean, that's what I sort of know how to do."

"I thought you came here to get out of the bakery business,"
Jonathan said. "I thought you were drowning in all that fudge."

"I guess so," I said. "I guess I said that, yes. But, well, I don't
really know anything else. I mean, I can't walk into a hospital and
ask if they need any surgeons." My ears burned. I felt like I was
being tested on material I hadn't studied.

"You'd probably be about as qualified as half the doctors there,"
Clare said. "Now, sweetheart, listen to your aunt. One of the
great features of New York is, you can do anything here. This is
the Land of Opportunity, capital L, capital O. Here you can get
paid to do just about anything you can think of."

I nodded, aware that she was tracing little figure eights with a
fingernail on the cloudy Formica. She had green eyes that didn't
waver, didn't seek out the periphery when she talked to you. She
wore one tinkling, complex silver earring that was half a foot
long. Her effect on me resembled the effect of music. I had a hard
time conversing in the face of her.

"It's true, Bobby," Jonathan said. "You don't have to rush right
out and get the first job you can find. You have rich friends."

"Um, what do you do?" I asked Clare.

"Basically, I play," she said. "I run around town finding things
to make jewelry out of."

"Clare's a designer," Jonathan said.

"Hogwash. I'm a junk dealer, is what I am. If women ever stop
wanting to look ridiculous, I'll be out of a job."

I looked at her tangerine hair, and wondered what kind of
women she thought of as ridiculous-looking. What I said was "It
sounds like, you know, fun."

"Oh, it is," she said. "It's a great scam. And when the baby comes, I can just do it at home."

"You're having a baby?"

"Didn't Jonathan tell you? We're expecting."

Jonathan's face darkened. Elvis sang "Jailhouse Rock."

"We're not *expecting*, dear," he said. "We're still in the planning stages."

"Same difference."

I said, "I didn't know you were, um—"

"Lovers?" Jonathan said. "We're not. We're just talking about becoming parents."

"Oh."

"Most parents aren't lovers," Clare said. "Mine weren't. Mine were only married, and they didn't care much for one another. At least Jonathan and I are good friends."

"It's the modern age," Jonathan said, half apologetically.

I nodded. Then the waitress came, and we had to decide on dinner. Jonathan said he was professionally obliged to order meat loaf, but that Clare and I should have whatever we wanted. I had fried chicken with mashed potatoes, and Clare had the special— tuna-fish casserole, with potato chips crumbled on top.

After dinner we went for a walk. We walked down to the Hudson River and stood on a pier looking across the dark agitated water at New Jersey. On the far side a giant neon coffee cup spilled a red drop of coffee, then sucked it back up and spilled it again. Clare and Jonathan were both good talkers. I rode their talk as if it was a hammock stretched between them. Together, they were performers. They seemed happy enough to have an audience—I didn't need to speak much. They talked about babies, about moving to the country, and about how to survive in New York. They traded tips on apartment hunting, and told one another where the bargains were.

"Honey," Clare said to me, "I'm taking you to the Lower East Side on Sunday. That's where you get the best deals."

"It is not," Jonathan said. "Clare has this peculiar devotion to Orchard Street."

"Jonathan buys retail," she said. Her voice implied that it was a slothful, possibly dangerous, practice.

"The Lower East Side," said Jonathan, "is a fine place to shop if you want to look like a disco king, circa 1975."

"Do I look like a disco king?" she said.

"It's different for women. The world doesn't conspire to make them look like assholes in quite the same way."

"Anyone who's spent five minutes in a department store should never make a statement like that. Don't you listen to him, Bobby."

I let myself swing along. I played a sound track, silently, inside my head.

We had cappuccinos in a restaurant with a garden, where Christmas lights blinked in the trees and a small marble boy pissed into a marble clamshell. Then we went home. Clare kissed me on the cheek, said, "Welcome to Perdition," and disappeared into her own room. Jonathan and I spread his fat green sleeping bag out on the floor. He gave me a pillow from his bed.

When we were both settled, when the white paper light was out, he said, "Tomorrow I'll take you up to Central Park. I figure if we do a different part of town every day, you'll have your bearings by next week."

"You know where I'd like to go?" I said. "Um, I'd like to go see Woodstock."

"It's over a hundred miles from here."

"I know. I know that."

"We could probably go sometime," he said. "I've never been. I'm sure it's pretty up there. Full of old hippies, I suppose."

"Uh-huh. Hey, are you and Clare really having a baby?"

"Oh, I don't know. We've been talking about it."

"I like Clare," I said.

"So do I."

A spell of semi-dark silence passed. Noise from the street filtered in through the curtains.

"Bobby?" he said.

"Uh-huh?"

"I don't know. I feel like there are things I need to talk to you about, but I don't really know how. I'm not sure what to say."

"Um, what things?" I asked. He lay on his back, with his head cradled in his hands. Sometimes he fell asleep that way, his waking ideas marching straight into his dreams. He could have trouble separating real memories from dreamed ones. I knew that about him.

"You know," he said. "The things we used to do together. The, well, sexual things. I mean, we never talked about it, and after high school we just stopped. I guess I'm wondering what you thought about all that."

I could hear my own breathing. This was a hard subject. I had realized by then that I didn't feel what others called "desire." Something was missing in me. I felt love—the strain and heat of it, the animal comfort mixed up with human fear. I felt it for all the Glovers, for Sammi at the bakery, for Dylan when he sang "Baby Blue." But nothing built up in my groin. Nothing quickened, or struggled for release. I'd made a kind of love with Jonathan because he'd wanted to, and because I'd loved him. I'd had orgasms that passed through me like the spirits of people more devoted to the body than I was. These spirits were pleasant enough in passing but truly gone when they were gone. After Jonathan left town, I was alone inside myself. This lack was probably what had made it possible for me to live my bakery life in Cleveland; to need no sensations beyond the first feathers of November snow and the living hiss of a needle touching vinyl.

I said, "We were kids, Johnny. That was years ago."

"I know. Are you, I mean, have you been seeing anyone?"

"Not really," I said. "Basically, I've just been working and listening to records. It's pretty strange, isn't it? I mean, at my age."

"Well, there are stranger things."

We left it at that. We lay for a while with the noise washing over us—car horns and shouts. Just before I fell asleep I heard people passing by, laughing, a gigantic group of them—a cathedral choir of laughers.

CLARE

I WANTED a settled life and a shocking one. Think of Van Gogh, cypress trees and church spires under a sky of writhing snakes. I was my father's daughter. I wanted to be loved by someone like my tough judicious mother and I wanted to run screaming through the headlights with a bottle in my hand. That was the family curse. We tended to nurse flocks of undisciplined wishes that collided and canceled each other out. The curse implied that if we didn't learn to train our desires in one direction or another we were likely to end up with nothing. Look at my father and mother today.

I married in my early twenties. When that went to pieces I loved a woman. At both those times and at other times, too, I believed I had focused my impulses and embarked on a long victory over my own confusion. Now, in my late thirties, I knew less than ever about what I wanted. In place of youth's belief in change I had begun to feel a nervous embarrassment that ticked inside me like a clock. I'd never meant to get this far in such an unfastened condition.

I didn't try to sleep with Bobby. He looked too much like a man who'd been in a cartoon accident. He might have had stars and planets fluttering around his head. You got the impression that he was slightly cross-eyed. But still, he touched you. Maybe because you believed that if you took your eyes off him for too long, he'd have another accident. He'd grin rapturously, and fall through an open manhole. He'd get hit by a falling piano, and come up with a mouthful of keys where his teeth should be. I hated to think I was getting protective at the threshold of middle age. I hated to think I was developing a weakness for stunned, inefficient men who'd need looking after, the way my mother looked after my father until her patience failed.

Although I kept my hands off him I couldn't deny Bobby's shaggy, lost-pony appeal. He had big square hands and a face blank and earnest as a shovel. If it weren't for his eyes, his innocence would have been too lunar to touch. It was his eyes that cut through. Imagine a snug little house in the suburbs, with a plaster dwarf on the lawn and petunias in the window boxes. Then imagine someone ancient and howlingly sad looking out through an upstairs window. That was Bobby's face. That's what it was about him.

All I did was notice him, though. Lately I was bothered by desire the way a horse is bothered by flies. It was a minor, if persistent, irritation. It could be flicked away.

Maybe the money was what hampered me. My family had money; my mother's side did. Not the genteel, Old World kind —my mother's father made a killing in costume jewelry. He built the third-biggest house in Providence. He changed his name from Stein to Stone, sent my mother to Wellesley. It's an old story. Rhinestone king shoots for legitimacy through the progress of generations. He bought my mother a Seven Sisters education, set up a trust for me before I was born. According to his timetable the blood would be purified by steady exposure to money, and his great-grandchildren would be true aristocrats, with composure and a serene sense of their own worth. He died when I was ten. But I know the future he had in mind. A cast-iron deer had raised stiff antlers on his front lawn. Gold-plated fish had spit water into the bathroom sinks.

Desire fouled the plan, though. My mother didn't care for the boys she met at Wellesley mixers, or they didn't care for her. She had decisive features and the grim, secretive manners of a jeweler. She didn't flirt. She harbored operatic passions, or believed she did, and had no interest in coy little experiments. A hundred years earlier she'd have been known as a good woman. At Wellesley in the nineteen-forties she could only have been known as a drag. She walked in a disgruntled trance through four years of college and then married my father, who said he was "in sales" and who had enough personality for both of them. He was her one adventure. She never wanted another.

I don't know if he married her for money. I don't think it was as simple as that. My father was a seducer. He bored easily. He must have liked the challenge posed by my mother, a woman who never feigned laughter or any other polite reaction and who'd been accepted by every law school she'd applied to. He was a great, frivolous beauty. Maybe he thought she knew him in some deeper way, and could redeem him through her unamused powers of scrutiny. Maybe he planned on loosening her up.

When I was younger all my lovers had been clenched, possessive people. My husband Denny had danced six hours a day, and still despised himself for dilettantism. My lover Helene had had screaming opinions on every subject from women's rights to washing spinach. I myself had had trouble deciding whether or not to wear a hat. In my twenties I'd suspected that if you peeled away my looks and habits and half-dozen strong ideas you'd have found an empty spot where the self ought to be. It had seemed like my worst secret. I'd offered lovers my willingness and susceptibility—it seemed to be all I had. I'd worked out a general policy of pliable sweetness toward people who eventually changed the locks over some unguessable offense of mine. Who claimed they'd die if I left them but slapped me in a rage when I brought home the wrong brand of beer. After the divorce I'd gone from one lover straight to the next, thinking every time that I'd learned a lesson I wouldn't repeat. This new lover would have a sense of humor, or wouldn't take drugs. This new one would be a woman, or a black man, or a computer magnate whose heart belonged to data.

Since my early thirties I'd been retired from love. I'd been living like a child. Just hour to hour, while other women my age went to their own children's recitals and school plays. Drifting wasn't hard. I had a silly little job, and a big lump of inheritance money waiting for me when I turned forty. There were people to meet for coffee, and movies and clubs to go to. Time had passed pleasantly. And now—it seemed so sudden—salesgirls called me "ma'am." Young men didn't glance up automatically when I passed them in the street. I no longer showed on their radar screens.

In a sense I liked the way I was aging. I'd invented a life of my own. I wasn't a prim careerist living with two cats in a town house full of ancient maps. I wasn't a drunk drifting from binges to purges and back again. I was proud of that. But still, I'd expected by this time of life to have developed a more general sense of pride in my larger self. I'd thought I'd be able to say, if somebody asked me, just exactly what I was doing in the world.

BOBBY

I T WAS the start of my second new life, in a city that had a spin of its own—a wilder orbit inside the earth's calm blue-green whirl. New York wasn't open to the hopelessness and lost purpose that drifted around lesser places. Here, people drove through red lights. They walked cursing in front of cars.

I didn't find a job right away. I admit that I put out a mild-hearted effort. Jonathan went to the office most days. Sometimes he stayed until midnight. He called the paper's fame a natural disaster—a volcano that wouldn't stop erupting long enough for the village to rebuild. The typesetter edited copy, the receptionist did overflow paste-up work with six calls on hold and three advertisers checking their watches in the slick new white-on-white reception room. Along with his weekly column, Jonathan laid out the entertainment pages and wrote reviews of movies he hadn't seen, under an assumed name. Some mornings he mainlined two cups of coffee, steamed out the door, and wasn't back for sixteen hours.

Clare led an easier life. She was one of those people who have more money than they logically should, given what they do. But I wasn't in a questioning mode. I was glad for the company.

I always got up when Jonathan did. I brewed coffee while he showered. We talked and played music as he dressed himself in that day's black. When he was ready he'd kiss me on the cheek.

He'd kiss Clare, too, if she was up by then. He'd say, "Bye, dears," and take off with half a bagel in his hand.

Once he was gone, the morning switched over to its more leisurely pace. Its housewifely, daylight life. Clare and I sat at the dining-room table with second and third cups. We looked through the classifieds. Sometimes she redid her nails in a new color. Sometimes we watched *The Price Is Right*.

She left for work at a quarter to eleven. I straightened up the house, bought groceries for dinner. I went to the record store every day. I didn't buy records. I stood listening to whatever the store had picked as a background for shopping. I watched other people figure out what someone like them would want to listen to.

Clare came home by seven. I always had dinner ready. Jonathan ate out every night so he could write about the food. Clare said she used to meet him wherever, and eat with him, but was happy to have a break from eating the same thing all week. Sometimes after dinner she went places with her friends, and sometimes she stayed home with me, listening to music and watching television. She said going out was starting to seem more like work than her job. On the nights she stayed home we made popcorn and drank Diet Coke. Sometimes she repainted her nails for the second time that day. And on a Wednesday night in June, she took on the long work of redoing me.

She began it with a haircut. Jonathan was at the office, and Clare and I had gone to the movies. She'd taken me to see *All About Eve*, shocked that I'd never heard of it. It turned out to be an old gray-and-white comedy playing at a theater where a mouse ran across our feet, quick and feathery as a bad impulse.

Now we were home again, sitting among the colors of the living room. I started to put Van Morrison on, and she said, "Hey, have you ever heard Steve Reich?"

I told her no. I told her I'd been living outside the music zone, catching whatever happened to blow through. She said, "I'm going to put him on right now." And she did.

Steve Reich's music proved to be a pulse, with tiny variations. It was the kind of electronic music that doesn't come from instruments—that seems made up of freeze-dried interludes of vibrating air. Steve Reich was like someone serenely stuttering, never getting the first word out and not caring if he did. You had to work to get the point of him, but then you got it and saw the simple beauty of what he was doing—the lovely unhurried sameness of it. It reminded me of my adult days in Cleveland, those little variations laid over an ancient luxury of replication.

By then, Clare knew me well enough to let me listen. She didn't talk about unrelated matters during Steve Reich any more than she would have during *All About Eve*. When the record was finished, I said, "Whew."

"I thought you'd like him," she said.

"Oh, yeah. He's great. He's just, you know—"

I tried to finish the sentence by approximating the shape of the music with my hands. I don't know if she understood what I was trying to tell her.

She did shake her head and say, "Bobby."

"Uh-huh?"

"Nothing. You really are a fanatic, aren't you?"

I shrugged. I couldn't tell where my fanaticism placed me in her view of the world. I didn't know whether to claim it or deny it. I looked at the rug pattern between my feet.

"Do you know what I think?" she said. "Can I be absolutely honest with you?"

"Uh-huh," I said, curious about absolute honesty and fearing it with my whole heart.

"I think you need a new haircut, is what I think."

It was only an outer suggestion, a question of cosmetics rather than personal insufficiency. "Really?" I said.

"I'm talking about a little truth-in-packaging here. To be perfectly frank, you don't quite *look* like yourself. And if you walk around looking like someone other than who you are, you could end up getting the wrong job, the wrong friends, who knows what-all. You could end up with somebody else's whole life."

I shrugged again, and smiled. "This is my life," I said. "It doesn't seem like the wrong one."

"But this is just the beginning. You're not going to sit around this apartment cooking and cleaning forever."

148

"Right," I said, though truthfully I had drifted halfway into the conviction that that was exactly what I'd do.

"And, sweetie, that Bee Gees haircut is only going to mislead people. Do you know what I'm saying?"

"Uh-huh. Okay. Maybe tomorrow I'll go to a, you know, haircut place."

My stomach crawled. Would I need clown-colored hair to have a New York life? If I let that happen, I wouldn't fit back into Cleveland, or into Ned and Alice's Arizona house. All my backup options would snap shut.

"I could do it," she said. "Free of charge."

"Really?"

I could tell from her laughter that my every doubt had sounded through that single word.

"I went to hairdressing school, if you can believe that," she said. "I've still got my scissors, I can give you a new look right now. What do you say?"

I paused. Then I decided. It was only hair. I could grow it back to its present state and reapply for my Ohio job; I did not have to lose the thread of my old life.

"Okay," I said. "Sure."

She had me take my shirt off, which was the first embarrassment. I was not in trim or imposing shape. I looked exactly like someone who'd worked in a bakery. But Clare had already switched over to a crisp hairdresser's manner, and did not let her attention stray below my collarbone. She told me in a firmly professional voice to soak my head under the kitchen faucet. Then she put a towel over my shoulders and sat me in a chair in the middle of the living-room floor.

I told her, "The barber at home always just trimmed a little off the sides."

"Well, I'm preparing to do major surgery," she said. "Do you trust me?"

"No," I said, before the instinct to tell cooperative lies could assert itself.

She laughed. "Well, why should you? But just try and relax, okay? Let Momma take care of it."

"Okay," I said. I tried to make myself stop caring about what I looked like. As she started in with the scissors, I reminded myself that our lives are made of changes we can't control. Letting little things happen is good practice. The scissors snipped close to my ear. Wet clumps of my hair, surprisingly dead and separate-looking, fell on the floor around me.

"Just keep going until you're finished, okay?" I said. "I mean, I'm not going to look until you're all through."

"Perfect," she said. She stopped cutting for a minute and put Van Morrison on, to help keep me calm.

She spent almost forty-five minutes on my haircut. I felt the warmth and the faint jasmine smell of her, the quick competent fingers on my scalp. I felt the tickle of her breath. Once it was started I'd have been glad to have the haircut go on all night—to never see my transformed head but just sit shirtless amid a growing pile of my own shed hair, with the crackle of Clare's scented concentration hovering around me.

But then, finally, she was through. With a deep exhalation and a last snip at my temple she said, "*Voilà*. Come into the bathroom and see the result."

I let her lead me, though I knew the way well enough. I wanted to stay a little longer in the cooperative mode, with the state of my hair and my future taken out of my hands. She led me into the bathroom, stood me in front of the mirror, and turned on the overhead fixture.

"Ta-da," she said. And there I was, blinking in the light.

She'd given me a crew cut. The sides were so short my scalp shone through, and the top was a single bristly shelf. Seeing my own face under that haircut, I got my first good look at myself from the outside. I had ears that were small and stingy, curled up on themselves. I had narrow glittering eyes, and a big nose that split at the tip, as if it were meant to be two smaller noses. Those features had always seemed inevitable. Now I saw how particular they were. Seeing my face in the harsh light, backed by white tiles, I might have been a relative called in to identify a body. If we have spirits that fly out when the system shuts down, this may be how we see our own vacated selves—with the same interest and horror we bring to an accident victim.

"Yow," I said.

"You look wonderful," she told me. "Give it a little time. I know it's a shock at first. But trust me. You're going to start turning heads around here."

I just kept staring at the face in the mirror. If this was who I was supposed to be, I didn't know how to do it. Clare might as well have taken me to a pay phone and told me to dial Jupiter.

She said we had to wait up for Jonathan, to show him the new me. I didn't much like the idea of showing myself to Jonathan. I felt too foolish in my exposed vanity, my own willingness to be remade. Still, I agreed. As I've said, Clare had a musical effect on me. She entered my brain. I found myself not only doing what she wanted but losing track of where my desires ended and hers began.

While waiting for Jonathan, we did what had become our usual things. We made popcorn and worked our way through a six-pack of Diet Coke. We listened to Steve Reich again, and watched a rerun of *Mary Tyler Moore*. I found that my revised hair did not affect my way of sitting in a room, or percolate down into my old uncertain thoughts. I was relieved and disappointed.

Jonathan got home after one. When we heard his key, Clare made me hide in the kitchen. "I'm going to sit here very normally," she whispered. "I'll keep him in the living room. After a few minutes, you just walk casually out."

I was reluctant to perform that way. To spotlight my self-concern. But Clare was too big and bright-haired for me. I had a dim recollection of a birthday party at which an old man in a red nose and lettuce-colored wig plucked quarters from my ears and pulled a paper bouquet from inside my shirt. Yes, I'd pretended unhumiliated astonishment and delight.

So I went to the dark kitchen as Jonathan came through the door. I heard the porcine squeak of the hinges, and his simple conversation with Clare. "Hi, honey." "Hello, dear." "How'd it go?" "Cataclysmic. The usual." They could sound more perfectly like a husband and wife than any couple I'd met. I understood how having a baby could come to seem like their logical next step.

I listened to them. Weak air-shaft light floated in through the window like fog. Clare's mason jars full of herbs put out a dull grandmotherly gleam on the sill. They bore their names on paper labels, in her small spiky handwriting: foolscap, star anise, nettle.

I heard Jonathan ask, "Where's Bobby?"

"Oh, he's around somewhere," she answered.

That would have been my cue. It was time to walk out as if nothing unusual had happened. What I did, though, was stay in the kitchen. I got distracted by the pale darkness, the refrigerator's hum and the jars of spices meant to cure headaches, insomnia, and bad luck. I might have been a body buried in a brick wall, eavesdropping on the simple business of the living. It came to me that death itself could be a more distant form of participation in the continuing history of the world. Death could be like this, a simultaneous presence and absence while your friends continued to chat among the lamps and furniture about someone who was no longer you. For the first time in years I felt my brother's presence. I felt it, unmistakably—the purpose and somethingness of him, the Carlton quality that lingered after voice and flesh and all other bodily consequences were gone. I felt him in that kitchen as surely as I'd felt him one cold white afternoon in the graveyard, years ago, when a brilliant future shimmered beyond the headstones, beyond the curve of the earth. He's here, I said to myself, and I knew it was true. I had worked up a habit of not thinking about him; of treating myself as if I'd been born into Ned and Alice's house after our father died. Now I thought of them all, dead in Cleveland. Right now there would be wild daisies on their graves, and dandelions gone to fluff. My harmonica, which I'd tucked into Carlton's breast pocket at the funeral home, would have slipped through his ribs and clunked onto the coffin boards. I was living my own future and my brother's lost one as well. I represented him here just as he represented me there, in some unguessable other place. His move from life to death might resemble my stepping into the kitchen—into its soft nowhere quality and foggy hum. I breathed the dark air. If I had at that moment a sense of calm kindly death while my heart beat and my lungs expanded, he might know a similar sense of life in the middle of his ongoing death. Outside, a line of laundry hung in the air shaft. Empty shirtsleeves dangled. I saw that as myself and my brother combined—in both our names—I could pursue a life and a surprising future. I could feed him in his other world by being both myself and him in this one. I stood in that kitchen while Clare threw me one entrance line after another. I watched a white dress shirt sway gently, six floors above the concrete.

Finally, she came for me. She asked if I was all right, and I told her I was fine. I told her I was wonderful. When she asked what was going on, I gestured helplessly in the direction of the hanging clothes. She made a clucking noise, thinking I'd suffered a simple attack of shyness, and led me out by the hand.

Jonathan shrieked at the sight of my hair. He said I looked dangerous. "A Bobby for the eighties," Clare proudly announced, and I didn't disagree with her. Although Jonathan was exhausted, we took my hair out for a walk in the Village. We had drinks at a gay place on St. Marks and danced together, all three of us. I might have broken through a pane of glass and reached the party, after years of sitting in a graveyard thinking I was alive. When we got tired of dancing I insisted on walking down to the pier on the Hudson, to watch the neon coffee drip from the big neon cup. Then Clare and Jonathan got in a cab for home and I kept walking. I walked all over New York. I went down to Battery Park, where Miss Liberty raised her small light from the harbor, and I walked up to the line of horse carriages waiting hopefully for extravagant drunks and romantics outside the Plaza. I was on Fifth Avenue in the Twenties when the sky started to lighten. A bakery truck rolled by, the driver singing Patsy Cline's "Crazy" in a loud off-key voice, and I sang along with him for half a block. I suppose at heart it was the haircut that did it; that exploded the ordinary order of things and showed me the possibilities that had been there all along, hidden among the patterns in the wallpaper. In a different age, we used to take acid for more or less the same reason.

After that, changes were easy. There was no more need to stay married to the everyday. Clare made a hobby of changing me. She took me shopping for clothes in the thrift stores on First Avenue, where she knew all the salesclerks and half the customers. When shopping, Clare had the concentration of a mother eagle browsing for trout. She could swoop down on a cardboard carton full of bright polyester rags—stained Woolworth's stuff that had been sad and desperate-looking when it was new—and pull out a silk shirt swarming with bright yellow fish. Hers was a garish but scavenging personality; you knew from her eyes that the things she wanted put out a faint glow not visible to other shoppers. I let her make the choices, and after two weeks I had a cheap new wardrobe of old clothes. I had baggy pants from the forties, and loose rayon shirts in putty and tobacco colors. I had old black jeans, and a leather motorcycle jacket, and a box-shouldered black sport coat shot through with random pewter threads. I even had strangers' shoes: brown Oxfords with toes made of brittle leather mosquito net, and black army boots, and a pair of black sneakers spattered with paint.

I had an earring, too. Clare had pulled me into a jewelry store on Eighth Street, and in less time than it takes to say the word "change" a Middle Eastern man had punched a silver post into my left earlobe with a hydraulic gun. It was no more painful than a blackfly's bite. Clare promised she'd make me a perfect earring. The Middle Eastern man smiled. He appeared to have teeth carved from a single piece of wood.

Those days I surprised myself each time I saw my reflection in a store window. I might have been my own rough twin, come from some meaner place to make trouble for ordinary working people. The man whose face I saw floating over shop displays would not have written "Happy Birthday" on ten thousand cakes. He would not have lived contentedly in an upstairs bedroom with a view of the neighbors' jungle gym.

Clare introduced me to her friends: Oshiko the cynical hat designer; Ronnie the high-strung painter who spoke only in full paragraphs; Stephen Cooper who talked about cashing in his marijuana-import business and buying a jewelry store in Provincetown, where he could pay closer attention to his mystical gifts. Those people were like movies playing around me—I watched and listened with the same easy self-relinquishment you'd bring to a seat in the fifth row. They enjoyed being the characters they'd created, and didn't depend on me for input. So we got along. I stood or sat in my clothes, watching things happen. If I developed a local reputation at all, it was for mystery and immovable calm. I learned that New Yorkers—at least the ones Clare knew—value silence in others. Their days and nights are so full of noise. Clare's friends were willing to chalk my silence up to inner knowledge, when in fact I mainly watched, and thought of nothing. Every now and then I asked a question, or answered one. I wore the earring Clare made for me, a wire loop with a silver teardrop-shaped bead, a circle of rusted metal, and a tiny silver-winged horse. Sometimes she asked with a hint of nervousness if I was having a good time, and I always told her yes. It was always the truth. Going to those places—noisy clubs with unmarked entrances, parties in lofts white and spare as the Himalayas—made me simply and purely happy. I had been in a graveyard for years; now I was at the party. In the middle of all that life, I kept quiet as a ghost. A beautiful girl with skin the clear blue-white of skim milk walked serenely among the dancers with a fat, speckled snake coiled around her waist. Two boys in plaid schoolgirlish dresses stood gravely side by side, holding hands as if they were guarding the entrance to a sterner, more difficult world and couldn't imagine that no one would try to get in.

But the best times were the nights Jonathan got off work early enough to go out. Sometimes it would be the two of us, and sometimes Clare came along. On Jonathan's nights we went to movies, then for drinks in one of the bars we liked. Clare's other friends were more intent on giving their lives a fabulous, wind-swept quality. They had dedicated themselves to motion and to knowing the exact right place, the party inside the party. I could understand that urge. But Jonathan, Clare, and I favored elderly bars that had caved in under the weight of dailiness. The Village was full of them then, and is full of them today. They maintain a stale interior dimness the color of dark beer. They sell potato chips and peanuts from a system of wire clips. Regulars—quiet steady drunks who believe things are getting worse and never cause a ruckus—sit on the bar stools as solid as roosting hens. We always took a booth in the rear.

We took to calling ourselves the Hendersons. I don't remember how it started—it was part of a line tossed out by Clare or Jonathan, and it stuck. The Hendersons were a family with modest expectations and simple tastes. They liked going to the movies or watching TV. They liked having a few beers in a cheap little bar. When we went out together, the three of us, we called it "a night with the Hendersons." Clare came to be known as Mom, I was Junior, and Jonathan was Uncle Jonny. The story took on details over time. Mom was the boss. She wanted us to mind our manners and sit up straight, she clicked her tongue if one of us swore. Junior was a well-intentioned, shadowy presence, a dim-witted Boy Scout type who could be talked into anything. Uncle Jonny was the bad influence. He had to be watched. "Junior," Clare would say, "don't sit too close to your Uncle Jonny. And he doesn't need to go into the bathroom with you, you're big enough now to manage just fine on your own."

We came and went in the Henderson mode. It wasn't something we always did. It was the story we drifted into when we lost interest in our truer, more complicated story. Before Jonathan left in the mornings he might say, "I should be through at a decent hour tonight, would the Hendersons like to go see the Fassbinder movie?" Clare and I nearly always said yes, because our lives were freer. We preferred a night with the Hendersons to our other entertainments. Sometimes when Clare and I were alone together she'd say something in her Mom voice, a shrill and vaguely British variation on her actual voice. But without Uncle Jonny, the Hendersons didn't work. Without our bad uncle we were too simple—just bossy Mom and the boy who always obeyed. We needed all three points of the triangle. We needed mild manners, perversity, and a voice of righteousness.

I found work, just a nothing job doing prep at an omelette parlor in SoHo. I told people, and sometimes I told myself, that I was learning the restaurant business from the bottom up, so that someday I could have my own place again. But I didn't believe in that ambition, not really. I could only inhabit it for a few minutes at a time, by concentrating on details: my future self frowningly checking a tray of desserts before they left the kitchen, or running my hand along a mahogany bartop smooth and prosperous as a brood mare's flank. I could want that. It could pull the heat to the surface of my skin. But the moment I lost my concentration I fell right back into my present life, just being in New York with Jonathan and Clare, doing an ordinary job. I was content to spend my days with the Mexican dishwasher in the restaurant's greasy kitchen, chopping mushrooms and shredding Gruyère. That was still my embarrassing secret.

One hot night in August I took a shower and walked naked into Jonathan's bedroom, believing myself to be alone in the apartment. Clare had an old friend in town, who needed to be shown the sights, and Jonathan was supposed to be working. The black sky hung thick and heavy as smoke, and bums left sweat angels behind when they slept on the sidewalks. I walked in singing "Respect," with water beads sizzling off my skin, and found him on the floor, taking off his sneakers.

"Hi," he said.

"Oh, hey. I thought you were, you know, at work."

"The air-conditioning at the office broke down, and we just decided we don't care if the paper doesn't come out this week. There are limits, even in journalism."

"Uh-huh." I stood self-consciously, two steps in from the hall-way. There was the problem of what to do with my hands. In this apartment, we were not casually naked. It wasn't something we did. I felt my own largeness heating up the air. Though Jonathan looked at me with friendly interest, I could only think of how I'd come down, in the fleshly sense. When we were wild young boyfriends, more nervous than ecstatic in one another's hands, I'd been proud of my body. I'd had a flat, square chest. My belly skin had stretched uncushioned over three square plates of muscle. Now I carried an extra fifteen pounds. I'd grown a precocious version of my father's body—a barrel-shaped torso balanced on thin legs. I stood there in my furred, virginal flesh, sending water vapor into the air.

"You just take a shower?" he asked.

"Uh-huh."

"That sounds like it could make the difference between life and death." He peeled off his socks and pulled his black T-shirt over his head. He dropped his black cutoffs, telling me how the staff of the newspaper decided to go home early when the receptionist's desktop rose dropped its head and shed all its petals. "Like a canary in a coal mine," he said.

He took all his clothes off. I hadn't seen Jonathan naked since we were both sixteen, but his body was just as I remembered it. Slim and almost hairless, unmuscled—a boy's body. He had not grown new outposts of hair or fat. He had not taken on the heroic V shape of a more disciplined life. His skin looked fresh and taut as risen bread dough. His pink nipples rode innocently on the pale curve of his chest. The only change was a small red dragon, with a snake's body and a mistrustful look, he'd had tattooed on his shoulder.

He grinned at me, slightly embarrassed but unafraid. I thought of Carlton, boy-naked in the cemetery under a hard blue sky.

"I'm going to turn the cold on full blast," he said. "And I bet it'll still feel tepid."

"Yeah. It will," I said.

He walked naked down the hall to the bathroom. I followed him. I could have stayed in the bedroom and put my clothes on, but I didn't. I sat on the toilet lid and talked to him while he showered.

When he was finished we went into the living room together. Our nudity had clicked over by then, lost its raw foolishness. Our skins had become a kind of clothing. He said, "The trouble with this place is, there's no cross ventilation. Do you think it'd be any cooler on the roof?"

I said yes, maybe it would be. He told me to wait, and ran to the bathroom. He came back with two towels.

"Here," he said, tossing me one. "For decency's sake, in case we run into somebody."

"You mean go up there with nothing but a towel on?"

"People have done worse things in lesser emergencies. Come on."

He got a tray of ice cubes from the refrigerator. We wrapped the towels around our waists, and went barefoot into the hallway. It was mostly quiet. Electric fans whirred behind closed doors, and salsa music drifted up the stairwell. "Shh," he said. He tiptoed in an exaggerated way up the stairs to the roof, holding the dripping blue plastic ice tray. I stuck close behind.

The roof was black and empty, a tarred plateau surrounded by the electric riot of the city. A hot wind blew, carrying the smell of garbage so far gone it was turning sweet. "Better than nothing," Jonathan said. "At least the air's moving."

There was a dreamlike feel, standing all but naked in the middle of everything like that. There was excitement and a tingling, pleasant fear.

"It's nice up here," I said. "It's sort of beautiful."

"Sort of," he said. He took his towel off, and spread it on the tar paper. His skin was ice-gray in the dark.

"People can see you," I said. Two blocks away, a high-rise blazed like a city in itself.

"Not if we lie down," he said. "It's pretty dark up here. And, besides, who cares if they do see us?"

He lay on his towel as if he was at the beach. I took mine off and spread it near his. Moving air from Third Street, full of car horns and Spanish music, touched my exposed parts.

"Here." He cracked the plastic tray. He handed me an ice cube, and kept one for himself. "Just rub yourself with it," he said. "It isn't much, but it's all we've got."

We lay side by side on our towels, running the ice over our sweating skins. After a while he reached over and pressed his own ice cube against the mound of my belly. "As long as Mom's out," he said, "let old Uncle Jonny take care of you."

"Okay," I said, and did the same to him. We didn't talk any more about what we were doing. We talked instead about work and music and Clare. While we talked we ran ice over one another's bellies and chests and faces. There was sex between us but we didn't have sex—we committed no outright acts. It was a sweeter, more brotherly kind of lovemaking. It was devotion to each other's comfort, and deep familiarity with our own imperfect bodies. As one cube melted we took another from the tray. Jonathan swabbed ice over my back, and then I did it to him. I felt each moment break, a new possibility, as we lay using up the last of the ice and talking about whatever passed through our heads. Above us, a few pale stars had scattered themselves across a broiling, bruise-colored sky.

CLARE

I'D BEEN thinking of having a baby since I was twelve. But I didn't start thinking seriously about it until my late thirties. Jonathan and I had joked about parenthood—it was our method of flirtation. We always had a scheme going. That was how we discharged whatever emotional static might otherwise have built up. It's strange for two people to be in love without the possibility of sex. You find yourself planning trips and discussing money-making ventures. You bicker over colors for a house you'll never own together. You debate names for a baby you won't conceive.

Lately, though, I wasn't so sure. I'd get my money in a little over a year, more than half a million, but at thirty-eight you can't think of your life as still beginning. Hope takes on a fragility. Think too hard and it's gone. I was surprised by the inner emptiness I felt, my heart and belly swinging on cords. I'd always been so present in the passing moments. I'd assumed that was enough—to taste the coffee and the wine, to feel the sex along every nerve, to see all the movies. I'd thought the question of accomplishment would seem beside the point if I just paid careful attention to every single thing that happened.

Soon there would be an important addition to the list of things I was too old to do. I could see the danger: aging woman in love with gay man gets pregnant to compensate herself for the connections she failed to make. I couldn't follow that course with a straight face. Still, it gnawed at me. Jonathan had work, and a lover I'd never met. He had the latitude still available to a man of twenty-seven. With my breasts shifting lower on my rib cage, I wanted something permanent. I wanted to do a better job with a child than my parents had done with me. I wanted my money and health and good fortune to be put to better use.

One night Bobby came out of the bathroom in his Jockey shorts, singing "Wild Horses." I was going into my room and we inched past one another in the hall. He smiled. He had a soft, bulky body, muscles vying with incipient fat. My mother would have called him "a big husky fellow," approvingly. Marriage to my father had cured her of her interest in slender, devious men. Bobby was a Midwestern specimen. He was strong and square-boned, untroubled. I said, "Hey, gorgeous."

His face reddened. In the late eighties there was still a man living in New York City who could blush at a compliment. He said, "Um, I'll be ready in a little bit."

We were going out somewhere. I don't remember where. I said, "Take your time, nobody'll be there before midnight anyway."

"Okay." He went into the room he shared with Jonathan. I paused, then walked into the bathroom and rubbed a circle on the steamed mirror. There was my face. Neither pretty nor plain. I'd always been a queasy combination of my mother and father.

Surprisingly, my mother was growing better-looking. At an age when women are considered "handsome" rather than "beautiful," she was in fact quite handsome: slightly mannish, broad-faced, with scrubbed pink skin and hair gone from brown to gunmetal gray. Her inexpressive face hadn't wrinkled, and her abrupt, businesslike manner seemed more attractive as other women her age began appearing in stiff ruffles and too much rouge. My mother had caught up with herself. She'd found her beauty. She was always meant to be sixty, even as a girl.

My father, on the other hand, had withered like a plum. His cheeks had deflated and touched bone. His bristly, blue-black hair had dissolved, and the skin hung loose and leathery on his neck.

As a girl I'd looked hopefully in mirrors for every sign of my father's face remade in mine. Now I checked for signs of his deterioration, and found them. My neck had gone a little slack. The skin around my eyes was darkening. The genes were at work.

Mother, you didn't need to be so jealous of Dad's love for me. You're winning in the end. You're a good-looking attorney untroubled by lusts. Dad and I are fading, and we don't know what to do with ourselves.

I ran my fingers through my hair. Then I went to Bobby and Jonathan's room, and stood in the doorway. Bobby was bent over a dresser drawer, looking for a pair of socks. His ass was larger than the ideal, but shapely. If the word "Rubensesque" applied to men, it would be perfect for Bobby. His flesh was ample but proportionate, like those old pink-and-white beauties cavorting in dusky glades. There was something maidenly about his reticence, though he wasn't feminine in the least. He might have been a stag. A precise tiny-hoofed creature, shy but not delicate.

I said, "Why don't you wear the black gabardine shirt tonight?"

He jumped at the sound of my voice. There was something erotic about surprising him. I felt it like a zipper pulled in my stomach. I was a hunter and he a stout, unsuspecting buck.

"Um, okay," he said.

I went to the closet and took out the shirt. "This is one of my favorites," I said. "We should try and get you another like this."

"Uh-huh."

I held the shirt up to his bare torso. "Beautiful," I said.

Again, the color rose to his face. It wasn't working. Nothing sexual entered the room. I was too motherly in my concern for his appearance. We hadn't worked out a subtext.

Some things couldn't be willed. I'd spent a good deal of time learning even that small lesson.

"Maybe we'll go out for a drink first," I said. "We don't want to get there too early." I laid the shirt on Jonathan's futon. It was black and crisp against the white batting, a snapshot of sexless male beauty. I went to my own room to start putting my face together for another night on the town.

*   *   *

163

A month passed. Winter came early that year. A week before Thanksgiving, snowflakes big as dimes dropped unexpectedly from the sky and eddied around the streetlights. Shop owners on our block frantically swept new snow from their sidewalks as if it was their own youthful mistakes caught up with them. When Bobby came home from work I was sitting on the living-room sofa, doing my toenails and drinking a glass of wine.

"Hey," he said, brushing snow from the shoulders of his coat.

I nodded. I wasn't in a mood for conversation. Winter was back, sooner than expected.

"This is amazing," he said. "I mean, you don't really think of New York as having, like, this much *weather*. You know?"

"Subject to the forces of nature," I said. "Just like anywhere."

I wanted him to choke on his youthful enthusiasm. I was fit company that night only for chain-smoking dowagers or defrocked priests.

"It's really, you know, *beautiful*," he said. "It's so quiet out there. You want to go for a walk in it?"

I offered a look that I hoped summed up my views about frolicking in the snow. But he was rolling now; unstoppable. The weather had him all jacked up. He came and sat on the sofa beside me.

"Watch the nail polish," I said.

"I like that color."

"Bile green. It's what I'm into this season."

"You want to go to a movie later?" he said.

"Nope. I'm getting drunk and wallowing in self-pity tonight."

"Are you okay?"

"I don't know. Don't ask me a question like that right now, unless you really want to hear the answer."

"I do," he said. "I do want to."

"Forget it. It's just wintertime, I don't take well to it. I'll be my old fun-loving self in another six months or so."

"Poor Clare," he said. I defeated the urge to brush nail polish onto his face.

"It's fucking winter a full month ahead of schedule," I said, "and my ex is coming to town in a couple of weeks. Too much in one month."

"You mean your ex-husband?"

"Yep. His troupe is touring again, they're going to be at the Brooklyn Academy."

"Will you see him?"

"He'll probably call. He always does when he comes to New York. He has this idea that we didn't abuse each other enough when we were married."

"You never talk about him," he said. "I sometimes, you know, forget you were married."

"I've been trying to forget it myself."

"Um, where did you meet him?" he asked.

"You want a real laugh? At Woodstock. Yes, the concert. Seven years of torment born from a weekend of peace and love."

"You were at Woodstock?"

"Mm-hm. I'd dropped out of four different colleges and taken up with a group of people who traveled around New England buying old clothes to sell in New York. We heard about a free concert just a little ways from where we were combing people's attics for Hawaiian shirts. This isn't something I tell just anybody."

"You were really there? You went to the concert?"

"Makes me seem like a relic, doesn't it? It's like having been around before there were cars."

"What was it like?"

"Muddy," I said. "You've never seen so much mud. I felt like a pig. I was attracted to Denny because he had a big bar of Lifebuoy soap down at the pond. After we'd washed up together he said, 'You want to get out of here and get a hamburger in town?' And I said yes, absolutely. I'd gotten tired of the used-clothes people. I mean, they thought of themselves as some sort of mystics, but they were paying widows five dollars for old rugs and furs they'd sell for two hundred in town."

"You were there," he said in a tone of hushed amazement. "You went."

"And my life has been one disappointment after another ever since. Bobby, people make way too much of it. It was a concert. It was dirty and crowded. I left before it was half over, and I married a perfect asshole three months later."

I finished brushing green polish onto my big toe. Then I looked over at Bobby, and saw the change. His eyes were bright and a little damp. He sat with his neck craned forward avidly, watching me.

I thought I recognized the expression. It was the way men had sometimes looked at me when I was younger; when I was pretty and exotic instead of just colorful. It was simple, straightforward desire. Right there, on the face of a man not yet thirty.

We didn't sleep together that night. It took us another week. But from that night on, the possibility of sex edged its way onto relations that had been merely cordial and benign. We'd been friends and now we were something else. We bristled a little, grew shyer together. When we ran out of things to say, we seemed to notice the silence.

Still, he wouldn't have initiated anything. He was too uncertain. He was too accustomed to our pattern of sister-instructing-younger-brother. I had never met anyone so unmarked by the world. Men in the Middle Ages might have been like this: intricately considerate, terrified of touching a woman's sleeve. If it was going to happen, I'd have to take charge of it myself.

I did it on a Tuesday night. I hadn't timed it to my cycle. I wasn't as calculating as that. I liked Bobby too much. My attraction to his person was easier to act on than my more complicated interest in his genes. That, I figured, could come later.

We'd been to see *Providence* at the St. Marks, which nearly changed my mind about the whole enterprise. Bobby had talked during the movie. He'd asked me if the wolfman was real. He'd wanted to know if Elaine Stritch was Dirk Bogarde's mother or his girlfriend.

I answered his questions, thinking, Oh, Jonathan. Why aren't you straight?

But once we were outside again, walking home, I regained my interest. Bobby was half child, an innocent. He couldn't really be blamed for what he lacked. New York presented no shortage of people to go to movies with. Other qualities were harder to find.

When we got home I put an old Stones tape on. I lit up a joint, and asked Bobby if he'd care to dance. Jonathan was out with his boyfriend that night.

"Dance?" Bobby said. I passed him the joint. He toked on it, standing in the middle of the living room in jeans and a black T-shirt and a cowboy belt with a steer-head buckle. This was a difficult seduction to accomplish straight-faced. It was hard not to feel like a floozy, in eyeliner and a girdle, playing a scratchy record to try and coax a farm boy out of his overalls.

"Bobby," I said, "I'm going to ask you a direct question. Do you mind?"

"No. I don't mind." He passed the joint back to me.

"Answer truthfully, now. What do you like about me?"

"Huh?"

"Don't make me repeat the question. It's too embarrassing."

"What do I like about you?"

"Are you, well, interested in me?"

"Um, sure. Sure I am." I returned the joint and he took a long, deep hit.

"Bobby, have you ever slept with a woman?"

"Oh. Well, no. Actually, I haven't."

"Do you ever think you might like to?"

He didn't speak. He didn't move. The stones sang "Ruby Tuesday." I said, "Come here. Put that marijuana down now and just dance with me a little, all right?"

Obediently, he took one more hit and put the joint in an ashtray. I opened my arms to him. He walked in. I tried not to feel like a spider; a ravenous old creature who preys on the reluctant flesh of not-quite-bright young men. I skated over the feeling as best I could.

We swayed in a loose circle. He was a fine dancer, which helped. He wasn't awkward or uncertain; his body didn't appeal to mine to show him the rhythm or the next move. Dancing, a little stoned, in one another's arms, we were neither relaxed nor excited. As we danced we could have been a brother and sister practicing for romances of the future but also attracted to one another, attracted and guilt-ridden and slightly mournful over the hopelessness of this ordinary but charged and subtly dangerous contact. Brother and sister, practicing.

167

He smelled clean and woody, like fresh pencil shavings. His back was solid as an opera singer's. He said, "When you went to the concert, did you stay long enough to see Hendrix?"

"Hmm?"

"At Woodstock. Did you see Jimi Hendrix?"

"Sure I saw Jimi. We got to be very good friends. You come here with me, now. I can tell there's not going to be any smooth or sophisticated way to do this."

I stopped dancing and led him to my bedroom. He didn't quite participate but didn't resist either. I left the light off. I closed the door and said, "Are you nervous?"

"Uh-huh."

"Don't be. This is just for fun. This is just because I like you. There's nothing in this world for you to be nervous about." I unbuttoned his shirt, and helped him slide it off his shoulders. His shoulders were damp and ticklish with hair.

"I'm not, you know, in very good shape," he said, though by then I'd seen his bare chest a hundred times.

"I think you're lovely," I said. I took off my blouse and dropped it on the floor. I never wore a bra. I put his hand on my left breast.

"These are below par, to tell you the truth," I said. "You'll be with other women who have a lot more going on here."

"I don't think about other women," he said.

"You're too much, you know that?"

"What's the matter?" he asked.

"Nothing. Not a thing. Come on now, get undressed. Old Clare's going to show you a few tricks."

We took the rest of our clothes off quickly, as if the real tenants might get home at any moment and find us using their apartment. When we were naked I took him in my arms again and kissed him, with more concern than passion. His breath was hot and a little strong but not foul. It was carnivore's breath.

"Don't be afraid," I said. "This is the most natural thing in the world. You might even like it."

"I do like it," he said. "I think I do."

I guided him to the bed, and had him lie down. I'd never before been so completely in charge. If this was part of the aging process,

I didn't mind it. There was something agreeably frightening about running a fuck.

Bobby lay naked across my bed. His cock slumped softly against his thigh—a purplish one, circumcised, large but not enormous. He had a surprisingly sparse little muddle of pubic hair. I could hear the sound of his breathing.

"Everything's okay, sweetheart," I said. "Just relax, I'll take care of everything."

I knelt on the mattress beside him, and massaged his chest and belly. He looked up at me uncertainly. "Shh," I said. "Don't do anything, don't think about anything. Your big sister's gonna manage fine, just close your eyes."

He closed his eyes. I bent over and flicked at his nipples with my tongue. I'd never done anything like this before. He was so big and inert. My sexual career had generally involved forceful people who wanted me, who went after me with obscure imperatives of their own. I did what I could to feign an older woman's serene competence. As subtly as possible, I checked his cock for signs of arousal.

"Clare," he said. "Clare, I don't know if—"

"Shh. Hush. I'll tell you when it's time to speak."

I kissed my way down his stomach, took his limp cock in my hand. It was like a rubber toy. I had to stay mindful of its sensitive humanness. I put it in my mouth and worked it around slowly, lapping the underside with my tongue. I took plenty of time. I tickled and stroked with my fingertips, ran my tongue around his scrotum, and nipped gently at his thighs. I forced myself not to hurry. Other men had had wishes, ways they liked things done. Helene had instructed me on every move. No one had ever abandoned himself to my care like this before. I mouthed his cock and thought of myself as a whore in a movie. A smart triumphant whore who always puts on a good show. I pulled at his pubic hair with my teeth, licked the violet tip of his cock. And finally it began to stiffen.

Then I let myself work harder. I took him into my mouth again and worked him up and down, up and down until my neck started to ache. I played my hands along his rib cage and gently pinched his nipples. I could feel his breathing quicken. I heard him softly moan, a fretful little cry like a dove's. I myself was aroused. Not intensely, but with the ticklish queasiness I remembered as a girl, when I'd first started thinking of large, powerful bodies that wanted control and resisted it.

When I thought he was ready, I got up and straddled him. The look on his face surprised me. He was flushed and panicky, not pleased as I'd expected him to be. Still, I smiled reassuringly. I knew this was no time to lose our momentum. I said, "Ready?" Without waiting for an answer, I worked myself into position and slid his cock in.

Something wasn't right. His face was so raw and terrified. Still, I kept up. There was no backing out now. I didn't think of my own pleasure. I rose and fell, rose and fell. I whispered to him, "Sweetheart, you're doing fine. Oh, yes. You're doing wonderfully." It wasn't exactly what I wanted to say. It was what I heard myself saying. I stroked his chest. His face was shiny with sweat. I reached over and smoothed away a bit of hair that had gotten plastered to his forehead.

And suddenly, unexpectedly, he came. I felt the spasm. When he came he let out a wail of such agony. He might have been stabbed in the gut. It was an awful sound; inconsolable. I forgot what I was supposed to be doing and crouched with my knees pressed in against his rib cage, waiting for the wail to stop. There was a span of thick, echoing silence. Then he started weeping, openly and extravagantly as a baby.

I reached over and touched his face. His cock was still inside me. I knew we were lost to one another in some permanent, irremediable way. Now he was a mystery. I lay down beside him and told him it was all right. I told him everything was all right. He stroked my hair with heavy, flat-handed swipes. He said, "I never. I never thought I would."

"You did," I whispered.

He pressed his chest against mine. I could feel the heat of his tears. He didn't say anything else. He fell asleep in my bed and I let him stay there, though I couldn't get to sleep myself. I lay beside him for quite a while, inhaling his large sweaty essence and asking myself what exactly I had gone and done now.

JONATHAN

THE NIGHT of the day Arthur the theater critic went to the hospital, I traded histories with Erich. We had never talked about our pasts, beyond the broadest details of place and family temperament. When we were together, memory dragged behind consciousness on a shortened rope and any event more than a day or two old fell away into prenatal darkness. We'd spoken to one another from a continual present, in which profundity, despair, and old romantic aspirations did not exist; in which the ordinary vicissitudes of working life took on Wagnerian dimensions, and the periods between a boss's insane demands or a cab driver's hostility were pockets of utter unremarkable calm.

Now we sat in Erich's apartment with a bottle of Merlot, tallying up. He'd put John Coltrane on the stereo.

"I know this is difficult," I said. I was to be the apologist, because I was the one who'd insisted on broaching the subject in the first place.

"A little," Erich said. "It is a little, yes. I'm not very . . . forthcoming about these things. I saw my therapist for over a year before I got around to telling her I was gay."

"You don't have to tell me anything you haven't told your therapist," I said. "I just want us to have, well, an idea about the scope of one another's pasts. To put it delicately."

Erich flushed, and emitted one of the sharp, painful-sounding laughs that social discomfort could produce in him. He was still unformed in some way. The monstrous imitation-leather sofa on which we sat had been a gift from his parents in celebration of his admission into law school in Michigan. His parents had evidently assumed him to be embarking on a twelve-room, wainscoted life, but after less than a year he'd left law school for the hope of an acting career in New York. Now his parents didn't speak to him and the sofa sat wall-to-wall in his apartment, like a cabin cruiser berthed in a swimming pool.

"Just an idea," I added. "No humiliating confessions required."

"I know," he said. "I don't honestly know why I'm so hesitant about things like this. I don't know why. I've always been more the type to, you know, listen to people. I guess it's a habit you get into from tending bar."

"I'll start," I said. And for almost an hour we called in all our old stray business, the affairs both good and bad, which we'd thought had receded too far into the past to impinge in any way on what we were now making of ourselves.

We both fell, it seemed, somewhere toward the middle of the risk spectrum. We had not, either of us, ever been rapacious. We had not worked the back rooms. We'd never made love to ten different strangers in a single bathhouse night, or paid by the hour for tough slim-hipped boys in the West Forties. But between us, we'd gone home with a full platoon of strangers. We'd both met men in bars or at parties; we'd slept with the friends of friends visiting from San Francisco or Vancouver or Laguna Beach. We'd hoped vaguely to fall in love but hadn't worried much about it, because we'd thought we had all the time in the world. Love had seemed so final, and so dull—love was what ruined our parents. Love had delivered them to a life of mortgage payments and household repairs; to unglamorous jobs and the fluorescent aisles of a supermarket at two in the afternoon. We'd hoped for love of a different kind, love that knew and forgave our human frailty but did not miniaturize our grander ideas of ourselves. It sounded possible. If we didn't rush or grab, if we didn't panic, a love both challenging and nurturing might appear. If the person was imaginable, then the person could exist. And in the meantime, we'd had sex. We'd thought we lived at the beginning of an orgiastic new age, in which men and women could answer without hesitation to harmless inclinations of the flesh. It had been with a sense of my own unlimited choices that I'd made love to a simpleminded flute-playing boy I met in Washington Square Park, to an old Frenchman in a purple cashmere jacket I'd met riding the uptown IRT, and to a pair of kindly doctors who sweetened their union by taking on an occasional third party. In my late teens and early twenties I'd seen myself as a Puckish figure, smart and quick-limbed, incorrigible. I'd imagined the prim houses and barren days of Ohio falling farther away with each new adventure.

Erich and I didn't go case by case. We were not so clinical as that. We offered the highlights, but dwelt more explicitly—more happily—on the pleasures we'd denied ourselves. Cupping the bell of his wineglass in his long fingers, Erich frowned and said, "I never cared all that much for totally anonymous sex. That was never for me. I've met sort of a lot of men working in bars, and I, you know, went home with some of them, but I never really did the whole scene. I tried going to the baths, but it just scared me. I just took a sauna and went home." After a pause he added, "To masturbate," and smiled in agony, his forehead turning nearly purple.

Although we sat together on that gargantuan sofa, we did not touch. We occupied different pools of lamplight. This reticence was standard for us, neither more nor less pronounced as we talked about the loves we prayed would not prove fatal. In the conduct of our ordinary affairs, we always maintained a cordial remove. Anyone seeing us in the street together might have assumed we were former college roommates losing our grip on our old intimacy but unwilling to formally declare it dead. Only at home, naked, did we jump out of our separate skins. On the stereo, Coltrane played "A Love Supreme."

"The funny thing is," I said, "I used to feel guilty for not being *more* adventuresome. I'd hear other men talking about how they'd turned four tricks in a night and think, 'I'm the most repressed gay man who ever lived.' I mean, most of the guys I went with, I knew I'd probably never see again. But I always had to feel like maybe I'd *want* to see them again, like in some way it was remotely possible that we might fall in love. Even though we never did."

Erich looked into his wine and said something inaudible.

"Hmm?"

He said, "Well, do you think we're, you know, falling in love?"

I had never seen anyone so embarrassed. His whole head glowed crimson, and the wine in his glass quivered.

I believed I knew what he wanted. He wanted to collapse into love. Life was too frightening. Renown was withheld despite his constant efforts, and the future we'd all counted on could be revoked with a nagging cough, a violet bloom on a shin.

"No," I said. "I care about you. But no."

He nodded. He didn't speak.

"Are you in love with me?" I asked, though I knew the answer. He wanted desperately to be in love with someone. I fulfilled the fundamental age, height, and weight requirements. But his desire didn't attach directly to me. It was not quite personal.

He shook his head. We sat for a while in silence, and then I reached over and took his hand. I had to be tender with him because I hated him; because I had it in me to scream at him for being ordinary, for failing to change my life. I was frightened, too; I, too, wanted to fall in love. I stroked Erich's hand. The turntable, set to repeat, started the Coltrane album again. Erich tried out a laugh, but swallowed it along with a deep draught of wine.

I could have murdered him, though his only crimes were lack of focus and dearth of wit. I could have skewered his heart with a kitchen fork because he was a peripheral character promoted by circumstances to a role he was ill equipped to play. I can't deny this: I thought I deserved better.

Without speaking, we stood up and went to bed. It was our single incidence of psychic accord—ordinarily we explained our simplest acts in lavish detail. But that night we took our wineglasses and went without speaking to his bed, undressed, and lay down in one another's arms.

"These are scary times," I said.

"Yes. Yes, they are."

We lay for a while without discussing the last remaining event in our sensual histories—the fact that we had not exercised bodily precautions together. Now it was too late to protect ourselves from one another. There was no rational accounting, beyond the fact that even four years ago, when we'd met, the disease had still seemed the province of another kind of man. Of course we'd known about it. Of course we'd been scared. But no one we knew personally had gotten sick. We'd believed—with a certain effort of will—that it befell men whose blood was thinned by too many drugs, who had sex with a dozen people every night. Erich had had a good record collection, and framed photographs of skinny brothers and sisters posing by a lake, in a wallpapered living room, and beside a glossy red Camaro. He talked about going to auditions, and about finding a better job. He had seemed too busy to be available to early death. I couldn't say how he'd worked out the equation in his own head, because this did not seem to be a conversation we were capable of holding. We let a lengthy, silent embrace stand in for it. Then, with a new gravity, we made love as the Coltrane record played itself over and over and over again.

Several days later, Bobby told me about himself and Clare. I had been to see Arthur in the hospital. His pneumonia was clearing—he'd expressed optimism about the future, and a conviction that the cessation of alcohol and the adoption of a macrobiotic diet would improve his health a hundred percent. Although there was still important work to do at the office, I hadn't the heart for it. I went home instead, to spend the evening with Bobby and Clare.

When I arrived they were in the kitchen together, making dinner. Our kitchen accommodated two people about as generously as a phone booth would, but they had managed somehow to wedge themselves in. From the living room I heard Clare's laughter. Bobby said, "You've got to, like, move your butt another inch or I can't get this out of the oven."

I called, "Hello, dears."

"Jonathan," Clare said in a high, humorous voice. "Oh my Lord, he's home."

They must have tried to leave the kitchen at the same time, and gotten stuck. I heard more laughter, and a grunt from Bobby.

Clare came into the living room first. She wore a yellow bowling shirt with a strand of red glass beads. Bobby followed, in his T-shirt and black jeans.

"Hi, honey," Clare said. "What a surprise. Did the paper burn down?"

"No, I just missed you both. I'm taking the night off. Want to go bowling or something?"

Clare kissed my cheek, and Bobby did, too. "We were making, like, chicken and biscuits," he said.

"Like none of our mothers actually made," Clare added. "I don't know about you, but where I come from, home cooking was a Hungry Man Salisbury-steak TV dinner. Chicken with cream gravy seems so exotic and foreign."

"Jon's mother was a great cook," Bobby told her. "She never bought anything, you know, frozen. Or canned."

"Right," Clare said. "And she dove for her own pearls and trapped her own minks. Jonathan, dear, would you like a cock-tail?"

"Love one," I said. "What if we made a pitcher of martinis?"

We had taken to drinking martinis. We'd bought three stemmed glasses, and kept jars of green olives in the refrigerator.

"Great," Bobby said. "We can, um, drink a toast."

"You know me. I'll drink to anything. Isn't this Guy Fawkes Day, or something?"

"Well," Bobby said. He grinned with cordial embarrassment.

"Is there something more specific to toast?" I said.

"I'm going to make those martinis," Clare said. "You two wait right here."

She went back to the kitchen. "What's up, sport?" I asked Bobby when we were alone.

He kept on grinning, and looked at the floor as if he saw secrets printed on the carpet. Bobby had no capacity for subterfuge. He could fail to answer a question but could not answer it falsely. Whether it was morality or simple lack of imagination, I couldn't say. Sometimes the two are so closely related as to be indistinguishable.

"Jonny," he said. "Clare and I—"

"Clare and you what?"

"We've started, that is we've fallen. You know."

"No. I don't know."

"Yeah. You do."

"You mean you're sleeping together?" I said.

He lifted his gaze from the floor, but couldn't meet my eyes. He was smiling and wincing at once, with a sense of barely contained hilarity, as if he was waiting for me to realize I'd forgotten to put my pants on.

"Well," he said after a moment. "Aw, Jonny. We're, like, in love. Isn't it amazing?"

"It is. It's truly amazing."

I hadn't expected my own voice to sound so cold and peevish. I had meant to respond in a firm but kindly voice—to cut through the romantic nonsense. At the tone in my voice, Bobby looked uncertainly at me, his smile frozen.

"Jon," he said. "Now we're, like, really a family."

"What?"

"The three of us. Man, don't you see how great it is? I mean, it's like, now all three of us are in love."

Clare came out with martinis on the tray that had become part of our cocktail ritual. The tray was a battered old souvenir of Southern California, featuring oranges the color of manila envelopes and black-lipped, skirted beauties lolling with aloof, disappointed expressions on a pale turquoise beach.

"I told him," Bobby said proudly.

"Just like you said you would." She looked at me with an expression of mingled irony and apology. "Here, Jonathan. Have a drink."

"Is it true?" I asked her.

"About Bobby and me? Yes. I guess we're making our formal announcement."

Bobby took a glass from the tray and raised it. "Here's to the family," he said.

"Oh, really, Bobby," Clare said. "For Christ's sake. You and I are sleeping together." She turned to me and said, "He and I are sleeping together."

I took a swallow of my martini. I knew how I was supposed to feel: gleeful at love's old habit of turning up unexpectedly to

177

throw its transforming light onto the daily business. Instead, I felt dry and empty, like sand falling into a hole of sand. I worked to simulate the required gaiety. I thought I could catch up with it if I performed it convincingly enough.

"It's incredible," I said. "How long has this been going on? That's a song title, right? One of the troubles with love is, you can't talk about it without feeling like you keep cueing old songs."

"Just a few days," Clare said. "We wanted to tell you about it, but it hasn't seemed to come up in the course of regular conversation."

I nodded, and looked hard at her. Neither of us believed what she'd just said. We both knew that she and Bobby, whether consciously or otherwise, had hidden their love from me because they thought there was reason to hide it.

"What if we had a kid now?" Bobby said. "The three of us."

"Bobby," Clare said, "kindly shut up. Please just shut up."

"You two wanted to have a baby, right? You were talking about it. How about if we three had a baby? Or two?"

"Sure," I said. "Let's have six kids. An even half dozen."

"Let's see if we can still stand the sight of each other by Christmas," Clare said.

"Well, here's to the happy couple," I said, lifting my glass.

We drank to the happy couple. I said, "I never expected this. It makes sense now that it's happened. But really, Bobby, when you arrived, it never occurred to me that you and Clare—"

"Never occurred to me either," Clare said.

"Better tell me how it happened," I said. "Every single detail, no matter how intimate."

We had our drinks, and then had another round, as Clare told the story, with Bobby injecting occasional brief clarifications. Unlike Bobby, Clare could exaggerate so artfully she herself sometimes lost track of the line between hyperbole and the undramatic truth. She was not self-serving. If anything, she chose to portray herself in an unflattering light, usually figuring in her own stories as a guileless, slightly ridiculous character, doomed to comeuppance like Lucy Ricardo and prone to hapless, inexplicable devotions like the fool in La Strada. She would always sacrifice veracity for color—her lies were lies of proportion, not content.

She reported on her life in a clownish, surreal world that was convincing to her and yet existed at a deep remove from her inner realm, which was riddled with old batterings and a panicky sense of limited possibilities.

Clare said, "Basically, Mom decided to teach Junior a lesson about life. And, well, I guess Mom got a little carried away. I don't know what the girls in my bowling league are going to say about this."

"They won't like it," I said. "They'll probably make you turn in your shoes."

"Oh, Uncle Jonny. I've been so good for so long. I guess I just couldn't manage it anymore."

"Well, your uncle is speechless. This is such a surprise."

"Sure is," she said.

In a spasm of edgy joy, Bobby reached over to squeeze her bare elbow. His fingertips made pale impressions on the smooth flesh of her arm. I had a vision of them old together: Clare an eccentric, hopped-up old woman in an outlandish hat and too much makeup, telling the well-rehearsed story of her romantic downfall, while Bobby, potbellied and balding, sat blushingly alongside, murmuring, "Aw, Clare." We become the stories we tell about ourselves.

"I guess this is the end of the Hendersons as we know them," she said.

"Yes, I guess it is."

We stood for a moment in an abrupt state of social discomfort, as if we were houseguests left alone together by a mutual friend. Bobby said, "Dinner's just about ready. Do you want to, like, eat something?"

I said I was hungry, because eating would be a next thing to do. My head seemed to be floating somewhere above my body. Numbed by gin, I felt my own emotions like radio transmissions being broadcast by my own disembodied head. I was angry and envious. I wanted Bobby. In another sense, I wanted Clare.

We ate, and talked of other things. After dinner we went to see *Thieves Like Us* at the Thalia. Clare and I had both seen it several times over the years, but she insisted that Bobby had to see it, too. "If we're some sort of item all of a sudden," she said, "I want him to at least have seen a few of the fundamental movies." During the film she whispered to him, and emphasized her points by squeezing his knee. She had painted her fingernails a blazing pink that showed clearly even in the theater's darkness.

I begged off on drinks after the movie, though it had become our habit to finish our evenings together at a bar, no matter how late the hour. Clare put her palm to my forehead and asked, "Honey, are you sick?" I told her no, just exhausted, and claimed to have to be in the office by dawn to make up for what I hadn't done tonight. Bobby and Clare said they'd come home with me, but I told them to go have a drink by themselves. I kissed them both. As I walked home the air was so clear and frozen that the Big Dipper penetrated the lights of Manhattan, angling faintly off the roof of Cooper Union. Frigid air sparkled around the window lights. Even on a night like that, blank-eyed boys walked the streets with black, boxy radios, their music chipping away at the cold.

At home, I rolled up Bobby's sleeping bag and put it in the closet. I knew that, as of tonight, he would be sleeping in Clare's room. I made myself another martini for a nightcap. A light snow began to fall, meandering flakes that seemed little more than the air itself coalesced into hard gray pellets. I drank the martini in my room, and imagined Bobby and Clare embarking on a future together. They were an unlikely couple. They would probably reach the limits of their novelty together, and their affair would wind down into an anecdote. But possibly, just possibly, it would not. If they stayed together, by some combination of attraction, cussedness, and plain good luck, they would have a home of some sort. They would probably have children. They would have unexceptional jobs and find themselves pushing a cart through the fluorescent aisles of a supermarket. They would have all that.

ALICE

Ned and I packed up the home we'd made for ourselves and established a new one in the Arizona desert, under doctor's orders. We bought a condominium less than half the size of our old house, in a complex that had not lived up to its developer's expectations. Nearly half the units stood empty three years after their construction, and strings of multicolored pennants, some of them torn, still festooned the entrance gates. The buildings were done up as pueblos, their concrete walls stained a reddish mud color and the ends of poles protruding above the aluminum-framed windows. We were able to get a good price on a one-bedroom, our means being limited. Neither our house nor the theater had sold for much.

"Hacienda Glover," Ned called it. And, in what passed in him for the darker moods, "Tobacco Road, 1987."

He didn't permit himself much in the way of gloom or pessimism. Perhaps he was incapable. His demonstrated emotions ran the gamut from rueful acceptance to mild disapproval, and as I bid my own farewells to the Cleveland kitchen and the pear tree in the back yard I realized I had always planned, in some uncertain way, on leaving him. Or, rather, I had planned on someday having a life beyond our mild domestic comedy, the cordial good cheer of our evening feedings and our chaste, dreamless sleep. The trouble with an even-tempered union is that it refuses to crack—at no point does injustice or hardheartedness provide an opening through which you could walk blamelessly into another way of being. You live in the details: a kitchen arranged just the way you want it, tomatoes ripening on vines you've staked and tied with your own hands. Now Ned was ill, banished to an unfamiliar place, and I could not summon the anger or self-interest I'd have needed to send him there alone. As I packed my knives into a cardboard carton, I contemplated the rising divorce rate—how did so many manage it? The movies and novels of our childhoods don't adequately prepare some of us for the impression our future homes will make; we are not warned of the seductive powers exerted by our own south-facing living-room windows, or by hollyhocks edging a set of French doors.

And now Ned and I were disassembling it, just like that, because his lungs couldn't negotiate the sodden Ohio air. It was almost shockingly easy. We listed our property with a rouged woman in toreador pants who took less than a month to sell it at a bargain rate to a pair of young computer programmers willing to gamble on a neighborhood that might or might not improve. The theater would be torn down for a parking structure. Less than eight months after the doctor's pronouncement, we lived in a place I had never even imagined visiting.

The desert proved to have its own wild beauty; its odd mix of emptiness and moment and its searing, bottomless sky. Between the time we closed escrow and the day we arrived with our belongings, the cactus in front of our unit had produced a single ivory-colored flower, which it wore like an extravagant hat. Few fates are wholly disagreeable. If they were, we might do a better job of evading them. Ned and I set up housekeeping in those small white-painted rooms, hung curtains and set the copper pans against a new kitchen wall, where they shone just as brightly in the desert light. I realized that in no time this place would take on its own inevitability. Indeed, it was assuming that quality even as we debated the arrangement of chairs and pictures. Ned put a comradely arm around me as we paused in our work, cupping my shoulder in the same firm, gentle manner he'd used as a man of twenty-six, when I'd gotten into a convertible with him and driven into the Louisiana bayous. He said, "This won't be so bad. What do you think, kiddo?"

I told him no, it would be fine, and I did not experience the statement as a lie. We are adaptable creatures. It's the source of our earthly comfort and, I suppose, of our silent rage. Ned held me in what would be our living room. The familiar curtains were parted, and beyond them lay a lovely, desolate landscape in which an unprotected traveler would not last so much as a single day.

JONATHAN

SOMETHING was wrong with me. I lacked some central ability to connect, and I worried that it might be an early indicator of disease. First you felt a floating sensation, as if your hours didn't add up to whole days and your presence—in an airplane, on the streets—didn't affect the landscape as human presences ordinarily do. Then dark sores and fevers, a cough that wouldn't stop. Maybe this was how death announced itself, by breaking up your sense of participation in your own affairs.

The plane taxied, climbed through tumbling whiteness to a blue sky as bright and featureless as the primmest notions of heavenly reward. I sat quietly, flying across the country in a state of dislocation that was almost lulling—almost like going to the movies. I watched myself as a man of twenty-seven, strapped in against the predicted turbulence, pouring Scotch into a clear plastic glass, on his way to visit his parents in a house he'd never seen.

In Arizona, for the first time, my father spoke to me about death. A second doctor had confirmed the diagnosis—emphysema—but insisted that with precautions another thirty years were possible. Still, it was time to talk of certain things.

What my father said was "Son, when it gets down to it, you bury me wherever you want to." He and I were sitting at the dinette table, where we had been playing Yahtzee while my mother made dinner.

"It won't really matter to me," he added. "I'll be dead."

"I don't know," I said. "I don't think I want to decide something like that."

"Well, you should decide," he said. "It's the place you're going to have to visit for the next fifty years. Or the next thousand, if they figure out how to replace your organs with plastic."

My mother could hear us easily from the kitchen, which formed the lesser end of the L-shaped living-room-dining-area-kitchen. "Biological immortality is no longer in fashion," she said. "It went out with monorails and vacations on Mars."

She brought a platter of tortilla chips and salsa to the table. Since she and my father had retired to Arizona she'd stopped styling her hair. She wore it pulled back in a ponytail, and she had a leathery tan. My father, prone to skin cancers, was white as the moon. They looked like a settler and his Indian bride.

"It's not really all that big a deal," my father said. "I'm sorry I brought it up."

I glanced at my mother, who shrugged away any stake in the conversation and returned to her *chilis rellenos*.

"Listen, Jonathan," my father said. "If your mother and I both dropped over right now, if we clutched our hearts and dropped face down in the tortilla chips, what would you do with us?"

"I don't know. I guess I'd have you sent back to Cleveland."

"That's exactly what I don't want you to do," he said. "You'll never move back to Cleveland. What would be the point of having dead parents there?"

"We lived there for years," I said. "I mean, it still seems like home."

"We spent thirty years getting out of Cleveland," he said. "That theater nearly killed me, and the weather just about killed your mother and me both. If you put me back there, I promise to come haunt you. I'll wake you up early every Saturday for the rest of your life and tell you to help me trim the hedge."

"Well, what about here?" I said. "You like it here, don't you?"

"Here I can breathe the air, and your mother's learning to make blue margaritas. That's exactly how much Phoenix means to us."

I could not picture him buried in Arizona. It would be like a joke on him, having a grave in the Western desert, with coyotes howling over his head.

"I don't know if I can talk about this much more," I said. "I don't know what to say."

"Okay," my father said. "How would you like to be trounced again at Yahtzee?"

"I think I'd rather lie down for a while. Do you mind?"

"Of course I don't mind. Are you sick?"

"No," I said. "I just want to close my eyes for a minute." I got up and went to the sofa, which had been newly purchased in Arizona, a copy of the Cleveland sofa, with knobbed maple armrests and a starched colonial skirt. This new one, which folded creakily out into a bed, had been bought especially to accommodate me on my visits, since my parents' condominium had only one bedroom, as did all the others in the complex. It was a neighborhood of widows and widowers.

"Why don't you fold it out and take a nap?" my father said.

"No, I'll just lie on it like a sofa," I said. I lay down, and propped a needlepoint pillow under my head. The sofa upholstery depicted cattails, rust-colored boats, and brown mallard ducks flying away in repeated series of three. A small Christmas tree gleamed on the end table, strung with ornaments I remembered choosing in a dime store as a child. After years of "decorator" trees—with red and silver balls, candy canes, and small white lights—my parents had returned, in miniature, to the gaudy chaotic tree of a household with children.

"I'm glad you came home for a while," my father said. "You're looking a little pale, if you want to know the truth."

"Everybody in New York is pale this time of year," I said. "Maybe I'll move to Arizona."

"Why would you want to move here?" my father said, rattling the Yahtzee dice in their cup. "There's nothing for a young person to do."

"What do *you* do here?"

"Nothing. There's really nothing for anybody to do." He rolled the dice. "Small straight," he said. "Do you want another drink?"

"I don't think so."

As he went to the closet-sized bar to pour another for himself, I could hear the labor of his breathing. The bar, a narrow contrivance between the living room and the dinette, displayed its neat row of bottles on a mirrored shelf. A beige hand towel, never used, sat folded beside the miniature chrome sink.

My parents had brought their Cleveland sense of order to the desert with them. Here, where fine sand blew through the windows at night, where tumbleweed occasionally scratched at the door, the spices on the rack were kept in strict alphabetical order. Each houseplant shone with green, glossy life, and every morning my mother inspected them all, plucking dead leaves and dropping them into a plastic bag.

"As long as you're having another drink, I guess I will, too," I said. I heard the particular gurgle the bourbon made as it flowed out the spout of the quart bottle.

"*Hope and Glory* is showing at the mall," my father said.

"We could go to the matinee tomorrow," I said. "It'd keep us out of the sun."

"Good." He brought me my drink.

"I really don't want to decide about, you know, funeral arrangements for you guys," I said.

"Don't worry about it so much. By the time we're dead you'll probably be settled down somewhere. Just bury us within commuting distance."

"What if I don't settle down, though?"

"You will. Believe me, it gets you sooner or later."

"I think I'll go see if Mom needs help in the kitchen," I said.

"Okay."

"It's just that I have no idea where I'll settle down," I said. "I could end up anywhere. I could go to Sri Lanka."

"Well, that's fine. You should travel while you're young." My father rolled the dice again, and cursed his dearth of luck.

"I'm not that young anymore," I said.

"Ha. That's what you think."

In the kitchen, my mother dried romaine lettuce with weary efficiency. She might have been diapering her tenth baby. I stood beside her at the sink. She had taken on a brittle smell, like dry leaves.

187

"Hey, Mom," I said.

"Will you look at what they call lettuce here?" she said. "I went to three different stores for this, and it still looks like somebody beat it all the way to Phoenix with a stick."

She delivered the complaint in a tone of skittish good cheer. Lately, on my visits home, first to Cleveland and now Phoenix, she alternated between fits of irony and folksy, high-strung friendliness.

"Pretty sad," I said.

We stood quietly as my father lifted himself from his chair and walked upstairs to the bedroom. Once he was out of range my mother said, "So. How's everything? How's Bobby doing?"

"Okay. He's fine. Things are pretty much okay."

"Good," she said, and nodded enthusiastically, as if the answer had been full and sufficient.

"Mom?" I said.

"Mm-hm?"

"To tell you the truth, I've been . . . oh, I don't know. I sometimes feel so alone in New York."

"Well, I can understand that," she said. "It's hard to avoid feeling lonely. Just about anywhere."

She began cutting a cucumber into astonishingly thin, lucent slices. The knife blade seemed to impart illumination to the vegetable with every slice.

"You know what I've been wondering lately?" I said. "I've been wondering why you and Dad don't have more friends. I mean, when I was a kid, I felt like we were marooned on another planet together. Like the family on the old TV show."

"I don't remember any show like that," she said. "If you had a baby of your own, and a house and business to run, you'd know how much energy you've got left over for running around the neighborhood meeting people. And then your kids pack up and go after eighteen years."

"Well, sure they do," I said. "Of course they do. What else would you expect?"

She laughed. "They do if you've raised them right," she said cheerfully. "Sweetheart, nobody wants you to have moved back into your old room after you graduated."

We were not a confrontational family. We did not attempt to draw one another out. As our lives changed, we strove instead to develop new ways of acting normal in one another's company.

"I've just been wondering lately if this is, you know, *it*," I said. "An apartment and a steady job and some people to love. What more could I want?"

"Sounds good to me," she said.

I asked, "Mom, when did you know you wanted to marry Dad?"

She didn't speak for a full minute. She finished with the cucumber, and started in on a tomato.

Finally she said, "Well, I still don't know if I wanted to marry him. I'm still trying to decide."

"Come on. Seriously."

"All right. Let's see. I was barely seventeen, you know, and your father was twenty-six. He asked me on our fourth date. I remember I was wearing white shoes a week after Labor Day, and I felt defiant and sort of foolish at the same time. Your father and I were sitting in his car and I was feigning contemplation when in fact I was still worrying over having worn those damned shoes, and he leaned right over and said to me, 'What if we were to get married?' Just like that."

"And you said?"

She reached for a second tomato. "I didn't say anything. I was so startled. And embarrassed, to have been worrying about my shoes at a moment like that. I remember thinking, 'I am the most trivial person who ever lived.' I told him I'd need time to think about it. And I found I couldn't think of one single reason why we shouldn't get married. So we did."

"You were in love with him?" I asked.

She pressed her lips together, as if the question had been impertinent and slightly irritating. "I was a *girl*," she said. "But yes, sure. I was wild about him. Nobody had ever made me laugh the way he could, do you remember how serious Grandpa always was? And your father had the most beautiful thick chestnut hair then."

"You knew that, of all the people in the world, he was the one you wanted to marry?" I asked. "You never worried that you might be making some sort of extended mistake, like losing track of your real life and going off on, I don't know, a *tangent* you could never return from?"

She waved the question away as if it were a sluggish but persistent fly. Her fingers were bright with tomato pulp. "We didn't ask such big questions then," she said. "Isn't it hard on you, to think and wonder and plan so much?"

From upstairs, I heard the toilet flush. I knew my father would be coming down again, ready for another round of Yahtzee. "How's he doing, really?" I asked my mother.

"Oh, up and down," she said.

"He's looked fine since I got here."

"That's because you're here. But Reuben says emphysema is funny. It can just start getting better. Like that."

"So you think he's getting better?" I asked.

"No. But he could. He could start getting better at any moment."

"And how are you?"

"Me? I'm healthy as a horse," she said. "I'm almost embarrassed by how good I feel."

"I mean otherwise. You said you wanted to get a job here. You were talking about real estate school."

"I should. I keep meaning to go out there and see what's what. But then your father would be alone all day. It's funny. He was always so capable when we lived in Ohio. He was at that theater so much of the time, I suppose I just figured he liked being on his own. But now that we're here, he gets nervous if I'm at the *store* too long."

"Do you think he's getting senile?" I asked.

"No. He's just good and scared, is what he is. Your father was never all that introspective. And now, well, he wants something going on all the time. I'm like the social director on a cruise for one."

She smiled at me, rolling her eyes good-humoredly, but now the irony crackled through like tissue paper folded into silk.

"Two," I said. "There are two of you."

"In a manner of speaking," she said.

* * *

My father and I went the next day to see *Hope and Glory* at the Phoenix Cinema Eight. My mother, who claimed to have seen enough movies that week, stayed home to work on what she called her garden, a small plot of extravagantly watered grass and hardy, thick-stemmed flowers. When we left her she was on her way out into the heat, wearing plaid Bermudas and a faded straw hat and gardening gloves the size of Minnie Mouse's hands.

As we walked out the door my father said, "There goes the last of the gentlemen farmers." She gave him back a look she had developed since they moved to the desert: the patient, clinically affectionate look of a good nurse.

We drove to the movies in my father's Oldsmobile, a big deep blue Cutlass, silent and ponderous as a submarine. He kept his hands on the steering wheel at three and nine o'clock. He wore a pair of clip-on sunglasses over his ordinary glasses. Above us, the sky was a molten, shifting blue. Mountains shimmered in the distance, beyond the housing tracts and shopping centers. When we swerved to avoid a dead armadillo, my father shook his head and said, "Who ever expected to end up living in the desert, anyway?"

I shrugged. "Who ever expects to end up living anywhere?"

"That's too deep for me," he said, and turned into the mall's parking lot, following a line of neon cowboys on horses with flickering legs.

We were two of perhaps a half-dozen people at the movies, it being a weekday matinee. In its emptiness, the theater reminded me of my father's old place. Although it was no more than a medium-sized room surrounded on all sides by a saffron-colored curtain, it had the same depopulated melancholy, and the same smell: mildew and old popcorn. An elderly woman two rows ahead turned to glance at us, because of my father's heavy breathing. Meeting his eyes, she turned back and made a small adjustment to one of her earrings.

I believed I knew what she was thinking: *That one's not long for this world.* She was probably a widow; a frequenter of matinees.

I wanted to tap her fat shoulder and tell her the story of my father's life. I'd have liked for her to know that he was not just an elderly man in a polyester sport shirt, gasping in a remote, sad little theater.

Hope and Glory turned out to be highly satisfying, and afterward my father and I browsed through the mall. It was a big mall, with a central oasis where floodlighted palms dipped their fronds into a fountain. The aged sat on benches, and a smiling man in a white denim suit demonstrated the organ. "Arizona is the state of the living dead," my father told me. He hustled me past the interior grotto and into a Montgomery Ward, to see what was on sale.

We looked at stereos, miniature television sets, and aluminum window frames. We looked at power mowers arrayed on a field of Astroturf. "This is a good machine," he said, trying the hand brakes on a bright red one.

"I'd rather have a Turf Titan," I said, referring to a crimson monster the size of a small tractor. "Look, you can ride on it."

"That's ridiculous for a young person," he said. "This one here is a third the price."

We so vividly impersonated customers that a young salesman with a baldness-concealing haircut strode over and began describing the virtues of a model more expensive than the one my father had picked. As the salesman worked through his spiel, a slender woman walked by, carrying twins in a knapsack-like contraption. She was less than beautiful, with shaggy matte-brown hair and a sharp, shrewd little chin. Her eyes—her whole body—looked tired in a profound, almost permanent way, as if no amount of rest would ever quite restore her. Still, she possessed a sure-footed self-assurance that lent weight to the bright aisle she walked in search of the correct yard tool. Her twins stared with puzzled absorption at the empty air directly in front of them. As she made her way along the aisle I thought of how firmly anchored her life must be, for all its domestic hardship. A year from today, her twins would be walking and speaking. A year from today, she would know exactly how much time had passed.

She turned and disappeared into Lawn Furniture. The salesman pointed out safety features, indicating with his hands the three sensitive spots which rendered the mower incapable of snatching up an arm or a leg and giving it back as a spray of blood and bone chips. His hands were white and thin, the thumbs so curved it seemed they must hurt him.

My father and I listened attentively, promised to think about it. My father, nodding as he received the salesman's card, looked waxily pale under the fluorescence of Montgomery Ward. Hard white light shone through his thin hair onto the scalp beneath. As soon as the salesman had finished I hurried my father out of the store and bought him a drink in the hushed darkness of a steak house. A sign planted in a bucket of plastic tulips said that the "Early Bird Specials" were now in effect. We were the only bar customers at that hour.

"That kid in there was full of beans," my father said over his bourbon. "For an extra hundred dollars all you really get is a bigger grass catcher. You could have a grass catcher custom-made for less than a hundred dollars."

"I haven't got a lawn anyway," I told him.

"Well, when you get one, you should know what lawn mower to buy."

"If I ever have a lawn, then you and I can do some serious mower shopping."

"I may not be around then," he said. "I may as well help you get the information now."

"Listen," I said. "I really don't know if I'm the lawn type. I don't have any plants. I don't even own a car."

"That Olds has less than forty thousand miles on it," he said. "It should still be in good shape when you get it someday."

"I didn't mean I *want* a car. I didn't mean I feel the lack. Nobody in New York has a car. I can afford a cab when I need to get somewhere."

"And you're pretty happy out there?" he asked.

"Yes. I mean, I guess so. Sure."

"That's all I care about. You can turn the Olds into a birdbath if you like. I just want you to be happy."

I drew in a breath, and at that moment, for the first time in months, I felt prodigally—almost obscenely—healthy. I'd been waiting most of my life for him to express desires more detailed and possible than his single overriding wish: that I be completely happy, every minute.

"Excuse me, please," I said. "I've got to go to the men's room."

"I'll be right here," he said.

The bathrooms were at the front of the restaurant, behind the cashier's station. I realized that instead of going to the men's room I could walk out the front door without my father's knowing it, and I did so, with no hesitation and no reason beyond the simple fact that it was possible. I stepped through the smoked-glass door into the even, shadowless light of the mall's main concourse. I stood for a moment, blinking in the sudden brightness, as the door sighed shut behind me. When it had closed, a sensation of wild freedom opened up in me; a giddy vertiginous feeling. I threaded my way among the shoppers to the mall entrance, and passed through the hydraulic doors into daylight proper. The parking lot was filling up with husbands and wives just released from their jobs—golden afternoon sun gilded the windshields and radio antennae of their cars. It was an autumnal light without a hint of autumn's chill. I walked, thinking of nothing in particular, over the parking lot's western range to the line of stunted Joshua trees that separated the mall from the highway. Beyond the highway stood a scattering of mobile homes, and beyond the mobile homes was the desert, an immense cactus-studded flatness rimmed with irregular red mountains. I thought I would cross the highway and walk into the desert. I did not think of motives or consequences. I saw for the first time that one could walk away on little more than a whim. One could elect to leave behind his father's death, his mother's ironic loneliness; his own uncertain future. One could find a job and a room under a new name in a strange city, walk its boulevards without fear or embarrassment. I stood for a while, watching the desert as the cars whizzed by.

It was my father who called me back. Or, rather, it was the thought of his growing agitation as I failed to return. I didn't mind so much the idea of him searching the empty men's room, looking around Ward's or Sears and finally calling the police. I didn't mind thinking of the actions he would take. What I could not abide was the idea of him right at that moment, alone with his drink at the steak house, just beginning to realize something must be wrong.

I jogged across the parking lot, and had to stand for a minute in front of the restaurant, catching my breath.

When I returned to the table, he said, "Are you all right? I was about to go in there after you."

"I'm fine," I said. "A little indigestion."

"You don't look all that well," he said. "Maybe we'd better get you home."

"Nope. I am perfectly, perfectly fine. I guess I'm not really used to drinking in the afternoon."

The waitress, a woman about my age, wearing powder over bad skin, laughed at something the bartender said. They both smoked cigarettes. The bartender was a middle-aged man with the hopped-up, friendly look of a terrier. His own reflection hovered in the smoked mirror behind the bar, dark as a figure suspended in ice. Above the illuminated bottles, a team of small plastic Clydesdales pulled a miniature beer wagon in an eternal circle.

That night after dinner, when my father pulled out the Scrabble set, I asked if he'd like to go for a walk instead. "There's no place to walk to," he said. "It's solid condos for miles around."

"Go on, Ned," my mother said. "Reuben said a little exercise might be good for you."

"Just a short one," I added. "Ten minutes."

He stood with a dry, papery expenditure of breath. "All right," he said. "But don't think you're getting out of Scrabble this way."

"I'm going to hit the bathroom for a minute," I said. "Be right back."

"This kid is in the bathroom more than he's out of it," my father said to my mother.

"I'm twenty-seven," I said. "I'm older than you were when you met Mom."

In the powder room, which was papered in pert orange rosebuds, I splashed cold water over my face. I just stood there for a while, under the low hum of the fluorescent panel. I did not look at myself in the mirror. I looked instead at the wallpaper, its rosebuds arranged in soldierly lines, each suspended over a single olive-drab leaf.

At nineteen, I had worn a strand of pearls around my neck, and gotten a dragon tattooed on my right shoulder. I'd left NYU for a semester, without telling my parents, and used some of my tuition money to enroll in bartending school. I'd thought I could turn into the kind of person who would do a thing like that. And now here I was, standing in a powder room in Phoenix, with no idea what to do with my father, either alive or dead. I'd never expected to find myself in such a usual situation. I stayed in the bathroom as long as I credibly could. I flushed the toilet twice by way of explanation.

When I came out again, my father said, "You sure you're all right?"

"I'm great," I said. "Come on, let's go for that walk."

Outside, it was a clear Arizona night, crazy with stars. When we reached the street my father said, "Which way do you want to go? There's nothing in either direction."

"Left, then."

We went left. On either side of us, windows glowed in the snug parchment-colored houses. My father started softly singing "Give My Regards to Broadway," and I joined in. After we'd gone a couple of blocks I said, "If we cut between two of these buildings, we'd be out in the desert, wouldn't we?"

"Snakes out there," my father said. "Scorpions."

The idea that Ned Glover, former Ohio theater owner, lived in the same place as snakes and scorpions was so impossible that I laughed out loud. My father must have thought I was laughing at his caution. Saying, "Well, I hope you've got good thick shoes on," he headed out between two houses toward the open country.

I hung back, wondering about the snakes. My father walked twenty yards or so, turned and beckoned to me, then walked on. When he passed from the shadow of the buildings into desert starlight the wind blew his hair straight up. It was like seeing him emerge from a tunnel. I trotted after him, checking the ground as I went.

"Are there really snakes?" I asked.

"Yep. Rattlers. Mrs. Cohen two doors down found one drowning in her Jacuzzi."

We walked into the desert together. The ground was level as a movie set, spouting here and there the spiky black starburst of a yucca. Ahead of us stood the flat-topped mountain range, which brightened as it rose toward the sky. In the deep shadows at its base a few pale, watery lights shone, hermits' lanterns or Navajo ghosts or aliens setting up camp.

"Nice night," he said.

"Beautiful. Dad?"

"What?"

"Nothing," I said.

I feared we were running out of time. Although I'd always assumed in an unspoken way that my father would die before me, I'd imagined his demise taking place in some remote future; a future in which I'd be wiser and solider, more present. Suddenly—it seemed literally overnight—his lungs were failing at an unguessable rate and my own blood was possibly under invasion, preparing to manifest the first symptoms. There were things I wanted to ask him, but I couldn't seem to get them phrased in the condo or the Oldsmobile or the shopping mall. I had hoped for more resolve out here under the stars.

"Cat got your tongue?" he said.

"I guess so."

I was still struggling to invent an alternate version of myself, someone proud and unflinching who could gaze levelly at his father and tell him his last secrets. I wanted him to know me; to have *seen* me. I'd been waiting until I was settled and fulfilled, so as to present myself in terms of a happiness he might understand.

My father said, "I've been thinking about that lawn mower."

"What about it?"

"It's such a good deal. Maybe tomorrow we'll go back and get it, and I can keep it here until you need it."

"Would you use it in the meantime?"

"Me?" he said. "What have I got to mow, my rock garden? We've got that big two-car garage, there's plenty of room."

"You mean on the off chance I ever have a lawn, I'm going to come out here and pick up this ten- or twenty-year-old mower?"

"They only make things worse and worse," he said. "Do you

197

know how much your mother would give to have her old Hoover upright back again? You can't buy those anymore for any price, now vacuums are all made out of plastic."

"You're not serious about this," I said.

"Sure I'm serious. You'll inherit everything in that house anyway, why not inherit a good lawn mower at some future time when the only ones you can buy are made of rubber?"

"I don't want a lawn mower," I said. "Really. Thanks for offering."

"Maybe I'll buy it anyway," he said. "Then it'll be there, and if you don't want it, you can give it to the Salvation Army or whatever."

"Dad, I don't want the mower," I said.

"Well, wait and see."

"I don't want a power drill, or a microwave, or a Mercury sedan. I don't want season tickets to the Indians. I don't want a Rototiller, or a rod and reel, or a thermos that keeps coffee hot all day."

"Now, now," he said. "No need to get excited."

"What I'd really like," I said, "is to know what happened to me. Why can't I seem to make a life for myself?"

His face clenched up. It was a familiar expression of his, this gathering of the facial muscles under the skin—it happened when he was confronted by the contrary or the inexplicable. His face actually appeared to pucker and shrink as his features worked their way toward center. He might have been straining to see through a keyhole from a distance of several feet.

"You'll find something," he said. "You're still young, it takes time."

"What *happened*? You were there, you must have seen it. I keep thinking there must be something I don't remember. I've got a decent job, I have lovers and friends. So why do I feel so numb and separate? Why do I feel like a failure? Did you do something to me? I won't hold it against you. I just need to know."

He paused to take in a gulp of air. His face continued to shrink.

"I loved you," he said. "I worked hard, I don't know. I must have made mistakes. Your mother and I took the best care of you we could."

"Well, I know you did," I said. "I know. So how have I turned out to be such a mess?"

"You're not a mess," he said. "I mean, if you're having some problems—"

"Just answer the question."

"I couldn't tell you," he said. His eyes went glassy, and his mouth hung slightly open. What was he remembering? There would of course have been *something*—a spasm of hatred when I would not stop crying, some meanness born from jealousy. Some little act or omission, a brief ordinary failure of love that would not, in the end, explain anything.

We stood for a while in silence, which was rare for us. Ordinarily, my father and I avoided silence. We were both good talkers, and we knew how to keep the air around us thoroughly occupied with talk or games or snatches of song. The sickle shape of a hawk skated over the stars. An empty 7-Up can gleamed in the moonlight like something precious.

"Dad, listen," I said.

He did not reply. It was only then that I realized how he was straining for breath.

"Dad?" I said. "Are you okay?"

His face was dim, his eyes unnaturally large as he concentrated on pulling in air. He had the shocked look of a fish pulled out of the water into a world of piercing, unbreathable light.

"Dad? Can you talk?"

He shook his head. My first thought was of flight. I could still get away; I could deny everything. No one need ever suspect me.

"Dad," I said helplessly. "Oh, Dad, what should I do?"

He gestured me closer. I took hold of his shoulders, inhaling his whiskery, cologned smell, which had not changed since I was a baby. His lungs squeaked like a balloon being vigorously rubbed.

Carefully, as if he were made of porcelain, I helped lower him to a sitting position. I sat beside him, holding him, on the talcumy earth.

So this is it, I thought. This is my father's death. I did not know how to help, what to do; where to bury him. I stroked his wispy hair, which had once been thick and prosperous enough to base a marriage on.

I opened my mouth to speak, and realized I had nothing to tell him. All I could think of were the deathbed clichés, which any stranger might have offered. Still, I offered them. The alternative was to let him die in silence.

"It's all right," I said. "Everything's all right."

He could not speak. His face was darkened and enlarged by the effort of his breathing.

I said, "Don't worry about Mom or me. We'll be fine. Everything's all right, really. Everything's fine."

I couldn't tell if he heard me. He seemed to have gone so far inside himself, to have withdrawn from his own brain and focused his very being on the insufficient action of his lungs. I kept stroking his head and shoulders. I kept telling him everything would be all right.

And, after a while, he recovered. The air started catching in his lungs again and his face, minute by minute, lost its wild, strangled quality. We sat together in the dirt while his lungs, worn thin as cheesecloth, somehow managed once again to negotiate the passage of oxygen.

Finally he was able to say, "Guess I overextended. I got a little carried away there."

"You'd better stay here," I said. "I'll go get help."

He shook his head. "I'll be all right," he said. "We just have to walk back very slowly. Okay?"

"Sure. Of course. Dad, I'm sorry."

"What for?"

I helped him to his feet and we began the long walk home. It would take us over an hour to cover a distance we'd managed in twenty minutes on the way out. Stars fell overhead.

When I was fifteen, my father and I drove to Chicago together on a shopping trip and got caught in a storm on our way back. Rain fell in sheets; the sky deepened to the opaque green-gray that breeds tornadoes. It got so bad we pulled off at a rest area overlooking a muddy lake backed by the vast green of a barley field. Rain hammered on the roof and hood of our car. We sat in silence, occasionally clearing our throats, until a flick of lightning turned the lake's surface a brief livid yellow. Then we both started to laugh. The lightning might have been the punch line of a long, complicated joke. When we were through laughing we talked about my future, about the possibility of getting a new dog, and about our ten favorite movies. After the storm passed we drove home with the radio playing and the windows open. Later we would learn that a tornado had in fact touched down in the vicinity and had flattened a water tower and an Amish cemetery not twenty miles from where we'd been parked.

Now we walked together, very slowly, through the blue-white desert night. "Dad?" I said.

"Yes, son."

"Maybe we can go to another movie tomorrow. I hear *Moonstruck* isn't too bad."

"Fine. You know me, I'm always good for a movie."

Unfamiliar insects produced a soft but insistent chirp; a crisp whir like the sound the earth itself might make rolling through the darkness if we all kept quiet enough to hear it. The lights of the condominium complex shone. They were not far away. Still, they looked almost too real and close to touch. They were like holes punched in the night, leaking light from another, more animated world. For a moment I could imagine what it would be like to be a ghost—to walk forever through a silence deeper than silence, to apprehend but never quite reach the lights of home.

CLARE

ALL HE'D say was "Basic visit to the parents. Guilt and movies. They live in a pueblo now." But Jonathan was quieter after that, more prone to secrecy and half sentences. He kept the door to his room closed. In March, he announced that he was moving out.

I asked him why.

"To get a life," he said.

When I asked what exactly he thought he was living at that moment, he said, "A canceled ticket."

It was morning. One of the pale slushy March mornings that arrive one after another, as if they were raveling off a spool. Jonathan stared out the living-room window. He flicked his hair with his fingertips in a sullen café style when he said the word "ticket."

"Honey," I said, "just tell me what you mean in ordinary English."

He sighed, reluctant to face me on plain terms. Displays of joy, affection, or generosity came easily to him. He could speak decorously in his own voice. But when he was angry or sad, he needed an image to work from. I had seen him get mad in the caustic, eye-popping style of Bette Davis. I'd seen him suffer embarrassment like a street kid, with downcast eyes and hands balled into fists. This hair-flicking, window-gazing thing was new.

"Come on," I said. "Speak."

He turned to face me. "The life I'd been preparing myself for has been called off," he said. "I thought I could stay unattached and love a lot of different people. You and Bobby included."

"You can. You do."

"I can't. It's a new age, everybody's getting married."

"Not me, thank you," I said.

"Yes you are. You're with Bobby now. I've got to find somebody of my own, and I don't feel like I have all the time in the world anymore. I mean, Clare, what if I'm sick?"

I paused. "You're not sick," I said.

"You don't know that. We may not know for years."

"Jonathan, sweetheart, you're being melodramatic."

"Am I?"

"Yes. You're fine, I can just tell. You're perfectly healthy. Now don't move out, you'll break up the family."

"You and Bobby are the family," he said. "Just the two of you." And he turned back to the window, where across the air shaft a young Puerto Rican woman was hanging boys' briefs and men's black socks on a laundry line.

I thought I'd be pregnant soon. I'd stopped taking precautions. But I couldn't seem to tell anyone, not Bobby or Jonathan. I suppose I was ashamed of my own motives. I didn't like the idea of myself as calculating or underhanded. All I wanted, really, was to get pregnant by accident. The unexpected disadvantage of modern life is our victory over our own fates. We're called on to decide so much, almost everything, and we're thoroughly informed about repercussions. In another era I'd have had babies in my twenties, when I was married to Denny. I'd have become a mother without quite deciding to. Without weighing the consequences. But Denny and I had at first been too sensible—we were living on my trust money, and he had big ambitions—and then too furious to let ourselves give birth. I did get pregnant accidentally, by a member of Denny's dance troupe who'd told me he was gay. But I'd had it taken care of. At that age, during that time, you skimmed away the extraneous. You kept yourself lean and unencumbered, ready to travel.

Now I wanted a baby, and I wanted to raise it with Jonathan. We could be a new kind of family. A big disjointed one, with aunts and uncles all over town. But I couldn't bring myself to confess what I was after. I was trying to stage my own accident. I just needed more time.

In an effort to cheer Jonathan up, I got him to bring Erich home for dinner. He didn't want to. He had to be nagged into it. It took more than a week. I wouldn't give in, though, because I believed in what I was doing. My theory of Jonathan's trouble was simple. He had let his life get divided up into too many different compartments. There was his job, and his life with Bobby and me. There were a few friends from college, and a random sexual life with strangers, and an ongoing affair with a man none of us had ever met. I believed he needed more areas of overlap.

"Why don't you want to bring Erich over for dinner?" I asked on a dim morning that would not quite settle into rain. "Are you ashamed of us?"

I had on a pink chenille bathrobe, and had tied my hair up in a zebra-print bandanna. For a moment I could see myself as somebody's shrewish wife, hands fisted on her bony hips. It was far from a flattering image. But I didn't mind it entirely. At least a woman like that knew what she wanted. Ambiguity and indecision didn't swarm around her like flies.

"Of course not," Jonathan said. "I've told you. He and the Hendersons wouldn't get along."

He was trying to leave for work. He had one shoe on. He was sipping at a mug of coffee while Bobby buttered a bagel for him.

"We won't invite the Hendersons," I said. "It can just be the four of us, regular civilians too worried about our own shortcomings to notice anybody else's."

"He and I don't have that kind of relationship," Jonathan said.

"What kind?"

"The 'Come on over and meet the roommates' kind. It'd just be uncomfortable. For everyone."

"How do you know, if you've never done it?" I asked. "Honey, to be perfectly honest with you, I think you set limits on your relationships by deciding in advance and entirely on your own what they can and cannot involve."

Bobby brought Jonathan his bagel, and gave me an affectionate pat on the rump. I thought fearfully of the quiet nights we'd have together. The unvarying domestic routines we'd develop.

"Maybe you're right," Jonathan said. "Got to go now, bye."

I followed him into the hallway. "We wouldn't tell him any of your secrets," I called. "We wouldn't make stupid jokes, or show slides of our trip to a national park."

I finally got my way through ordinary persistence. My persistence, though it worked more often than not, was hard to count as a virtue, since I had no patience to back it up. My own doggish determination had led me, in the face of all reasonable counsel, to marry a Messianic dancer and then fall in love with a renowned woman who said she'd teach me to stop hating myself. It had led me into the used-clothes business, to hairdressing school, to Buddhism and modern dance. Bulldogs must experience a similar kind of trouble. Once they lock their jaws onto a bull's ear or tail they probably believe they've concluded their business with the whole animal.

Erich came to dinner on a Friday night. Bobby and I were making the kind of sparse, crisp dinner that was fashionable then: pasta with fresh herbs, roast chicken, vegetables from three continents. We were looking to impress. As we fixed dinner, we speculated over what Erich might be like.

"Brooding, I think," I said. "One of those silent, temperamental types people say are 'difficult' when what they really mean is 'an asshole.' "

"You think Jonathan would, like, go for somebody like that?" Bobby said.

"I think he could be *attracted* to somebody like that," I said. "Remember, this is somebody he hasn't introduced to any of his friends."

Bobby was dicing a yellow pepper. I stood with my back pressed against his, washing arugula. We had gotten used to working in that minuscule kitchen together. We'd learned to move in concert.

"Uh-huh," he said. "Well, maybe you're right. I picture him more like a criminal type."

"A *criminal*? Really?"

"Not like a murderer. Not a bad criminal. More of a drug-dealer type. You know. Somebody who works scams."

"But he's an actor," I said. "We know that much."

"Oh, I think a lot of those guys deal drugs. Don't you think so? I mean, how else could they support themselves?"

"What do you imagine him looking like?"

"Well, dark," he said. "Not so much handsome as interesting-looking. Sort of hip, in, like, a natty way. I picture him having a little ponytail."

"Hmm. I imagine him very young. You know, one of those squeaky-clean blonds who pour in out of the Midwest and end up in toothpaste commercials."

"Well, we'll see," Bobby said. And half an hour later, we did.

Jonathan and Erich arrived together. They brought yellow hot-house tulips, and a bottle of red wine. Jonathan let Erich in ahead of him. He lingered near the door as if he might slip away and leave the three of us together.

Erich shook my hand, then shook Bobby's. "Pleased to meet you," he said.

He was thin, and balding. He wore jeans and a navy-blue polo shirt with a Ralph Lauren insignia—the polo pony—stitched in red at the breast.

"Erich," I said. "The mystery man."

His high forehead darkened. He had a sharp face, with a small sharp chin and a sharp nose and small bright eyes set close together. It was a squeezed, panicky face. Erich might have been a man with his head caught between a pair of elevator doors. He nodded.

"I'm not really a mystery," he said. "Oh no, not a mystery at all. I'm sorry we haven't met before. I'm, well, just very glad to be here."

He laughed in a way that suggested he had been punched in the stomach.

"How about a drink?" I said. He said a seltzer would be nice, and Jonathan jumped to get the drinks. We sat down in the living room.

"This is a nice apartment," Erich said.

"It's a dump," I answered. "But thank you. You didn't have to step over any dead bodies in the hallway, did you?"

"Oh no," he said. "No. Why? Has that happened here?"

I couldn't tell if he was repelled or excited by the idea of hallway murders. He had one of those enthusiastic, unreadable voices.

"Not lately," I said. "So. You're an actor?"

"Yes. Well, I don't know anymore. Lately I'm just sort of a bartender. What do you do?"

He had seated himself in the armchair I'd found on First Avenue. A fan-backed old monster covered in green brocade. He sat as if he'd been assigned to occupy as little space as possible, with his legs crossed at the knee and his hands folded on his thigh.

"Junk dealer," I said. "I make earrings out of old garbage."

He nodded. "And you can make a living at that?" he said.

"In a fashion," I answered.

I never told strangers about my trust money. I felt too trivial and spoiled, having an unearned income while everyone around me struggled to pay the rent. I always had jobs, but not the awful, unrelenting ones people take when they're paying all their own expenses.

Now I felt, obscurely, that I'd given away something incriminating. Erich could have been a plant from the CIA. An undercover agent so obvious and undisguised that people blurted their petty deceits out of social discomfort.

Jonathan brought our drinks. "Here's to the end of the mystery," I said, and we all drank to that.

"Do you, um, like any special kind of music?" Bobby asked.

Erich blinked in his direction. "I love music," he said. "I love all kinds."

"I'm going to put a record on," Bobby said, standing up. "Is there, like, anything special you'd like to hear?"

"Let me see what you have," Erich said. And with surprising grace he sprang up from the derelict chair and followed Bobby to the cassette player.

Jonathan and I had our first opportunity to make eye contact. He mouthed the words "I told you so."

Bobby squatted before the shelves where the cassettes were kept.

"We've sort of got a little of everything," he said. "We're sort of, you know, all over the map."

"You have Coltrane," Erich said. "Oh, look here, you have the Doors."

"You like the Doors?" Bobby asked.

"When I was younger I wanted to *be* Jim Morrison," Erich said. "I used to practice his moves in the back yard. Every day, I used to practice, and lip-sync. But then I realized I lacked some of the basic equipment." He laughed, that same astonished outrush of air.

"Let's put him on right now," Bobby said, and punched his Doors tape into the player.

"Do you like Bob Dylan?" he asked Erich.

"Oh, sure. I wanted to be him, too."

"I brought some records out from Ohio," Bobby said. "I've got some, you know, pretty rare ones. You like Hendrix?"

"I love Hendrix. He was, you know, the greatest."

"Some of the records I could get cassettes of. But some are just too rare. You want to see them?"

"Okay. Sure. Sure I do."

"We can't listen to them," Bobby said. "We haven't got a turntable yet. We've got to buy one. Even though they're, you know, going out of style."

"I have a turntable," Erich said. "If you want to, you could come over sometime and play your records at my place. If you want to."

"Oh, great. That'd be great. Come here, the records are stored away in Clare's and my room."

Erich said to Jonathan and me, "Would you excuse us for a minute?" And suddenly I could see him as he must have been at the age of eight or nine: polite and overenthusiastic, prone to tears, a mystery to his parents.

"Of course," I said. After they were gone I said to Jonathan in a low voice, "Well, the kids seem to be getting along all right."

He shook his head. "I told you this would be a disaster. You wouldn't listen to me."

"Nonsense. It's not a disaster. Bobby's in love with him."

"And you think he's a twerp and a bore."

"Jonathan. I've known him about five minutes."

"Five minutes is enough. You'd have to sleep with him for him to make any more sense than he does right now."

"I don't know why you've kept seeing him all these years if you dislike him this much," I said.

"Sex," Jonathan said. "And my own craziness. Oh, I guess I'm fond of him in an unromantic way. I just never wanted to mix him in with the rest of my life, and I was right about that."

"You're a very strange man."

"Don't I know it," he said.

When Bobby and Erich came back, I suggested we take our drinks up to the roof to watch the sunset. The important thing was to keep this dinner party moving, physically if necessary. It was a freakishly warm late-March evening. The kind of weather that implies either an early spring or the effects of nuclear testing.

Jonathan agreed enthusiastically, Bobby and Erich less so. I knew what they were thinking. If we went up to the roof, they'd miss the next cut of *Strange Days*.

"Boys, we can start the music again when we come back down," I said, and was surprised at how much like a mother I could sound.

We went up the stairs to the roof, a tarred plateau bound at the edges with patterned concrete pediments. The orange sun hovered over the New Jersey horizon. Television aerials threw intricate, birdlike shadows. The windows of the tall buildings uptown flashed amber and bronze. A fat pink-stained cloud, its every billow and furl distinct as carved ivory, hung soaking up the last light over Brooklyn. Frilled curtains and salsa music blew out of an open window across the alley. We stood facing west, trailing twenty-foot shadows.

"Beautiful," Jonathan said. "Just when you think you're going to move to the country, the city does something like this."

"I adore the roof," I said. I was surprised, again, at the sound of my own voice. When had I turned into such a hostess?

"You don't hear music like this in my neighborhood," Erich said. "Never this kind of Mexican stuff, no."

"I sort of like it," Bobby said.

"So do I," Erich answered.

Bobby swayed his hips in rhythm, and soon began to dance.

Watching him in his cheerful, slightly baffled progress through the day, you could forget what a dancer he was. It was one of his surprises. The moment a note of music sounded he could move with such grace and buoyancy. He appeared to shed some interior weight. A ghost of the flesh, all gristle and bone, that dissolved at a guitar's strum or the first bleat of a horn. On the record, a woman backed by maracas and guitars sang full-throated in Spanish, with shamelessly simple passion. Bobby, who loved all music, good and bad, danced as the last of the sun disappeared.

Erich glanced at Jonathan and me. I knew what he was thinking. I said, "Go ahead." And with a shy smile, he started dancing with Bobby.

He was not nearly the dancer Bobby was, but he moved his feet in time to the music and made little twitching movements with his arms. Bobby turned to him as the sky gave up its last bit of blue and a faint star appeared in the growing violet to the east.

Jonathan and I stood watching, with our drinks in our hands. Jonathan said, "I don't think I want to just be the chaperon at this party. Do you?"

"No," I said. "Not especially."

Jonathan set his drink on the parapet, and started dancing with Bobby and Erich. He was an elegant if contained dancer. He moved within a small column of air, the exact boundaries of which he never overstepped. I watched. For a moment—a moment—I felt the world spinning away from me. I saw myself standing in the last light, aging in a bright purple thrift-store dress as a group of younger men danced together. It was far from an ordinary moment. And yet I felt as if I'd lived it before.

To get myself back into real life, I started dancing. What else could I do? The heels of my shoes stuck in the tar, making soft *pock* sounds until I stepped out of them and danced in my stocking feet.

Jonathan said, "Okay, the rooftop number from *West Side Story*. Are you ready?"

"How does it start?" I asked.

"Let's see. 'I like to be in America.' "

" 'Okay by me in America.' "

" 'Everything free in America.' "

" 'For a small fee in America.' "

We whooped and clapped. When the number was finished I turned three perfect cartwheels in a row. I hadn't done it in at least fifteen years. I felt my legs flashing straight and clean as knives.

"I used to want to be a cheerleader," I told them. "Before I decided to just go to hell."

Something took hold of us up there. I remembered the sensation from childhood, when a game gathered momentum. Bobby unbuttoned his shirt, which bellied in the wind. We all danced exaggeratedly, like members of a Broadway chorus, with leaps and twirls. When the salsa music went off, we started singing. We sang as much as we could remember of the Jets song and "Officer Krupke." We sang every number from *Hair*.

Bobby said, "My brother used to play that record ten times a day. Till our mother threw it out. He just got another one. So then she threw his stereo out."

"One of my cousins was *in Hair*," I said. "A couple of years ago, at a dinner theater in Florida."

We sang a few numbers from *South Pacific*, and all the *My Fair Lady* we could come up with. We danced to the sound of our own voices. When we couldn't dance any longer we sat down on the sun-warmed tar, inhaling its mingled smell of sour earth and chemicals. We kept singing. Once, while we were singing "Get Me to the Church on Time," I glanced at Jonathan and caught him staring at me with an expression I'd never seen before. It was an injured, glowering look, something between anger and sorrow. When our eyes met, he looked quickly back at the sky. We sang "I Heard It Through the Grapevine" and we sang "Norwegian Wood." Bobby and Jonathan sang a couple of Laura Nyro songs together, until I made them switch back to something we all knew. We sat singing on that roof until darkness proper had set in, and the city blazed around us with the light of ten million parties.

BOBBY

THE DAY after we danced on the roof together, Jonathan slipped through the fabric of his life. He left nothing behind but a few words on a piece of notebook paper anchored to the table by the pepper shaker. "Dear B. and C., I wish you great happiness together. That sounds so corny, doesn't it? Anyway, I'm starting again somewhere else, I honestly don't know where. I'll call eventually. Give away whatever of mine you can't use yourselves. Love, J."

Clare and I read those lines over and over, as if they were code for another, more sensible message. She called the newspaper and found he had quit his job that morning, without notice. He had left no forwarding address. His room was as white and uninhabited-looking as it had always been. As far as we could tell, only a few of his clothes were missing.

"Fuck," Clare said. "That motherfucker. How could he do this?"

"I don't know," I said. "I guess he just did it."

Clare was furious and I was stupefied. Departures brought out my blankness—I could feel my brain cloud over. When someone left I lost track of everything. I was filled with a dense, prickly confusion strong as the effect of a drug. It was a kind of retardation, I suppose. A missing neural connection. Somebody who was here isn't here anymore. I couldn't seem to get it.

"Jonathan, you asshole," Clare said. "Just when things were starting to work out." She balled up the note and threw it in the trash, though later she'd retrieve it, as if she thought it might be needed as evidence.

"He'll be back?" I said. I'd thought I was telling her something but it came out as a question.

"What's wrong with men?" Clare said. She stood on the living-room carpet with her arms folded over her breasts and her jaw gone stony. I saw that in another life she could have been a crazy schoolteacher, one of those wild spinsters who strike you as pathetic at first but end up changing your life. I didn't answer. I was sitting on the bald velvet chair, the one we'd dragged home from the corner of Fifth and Eighteenth. My hands were squeezed between my thighs. "Really," she said. "I'd like to know. Do you have any idea? What goes on in their heads? What do they want?"

I shrugged. It was not a question I could answer, though it seemed she expected me to. I might have been the worst student in her class, failing even the easy ones she lobbed in my direction.

"I'm going out," she said. She threw her jacket over her shoulders, the faded leather one with the peace symbol on the back. Her earrings clicked and flashed. She went down the stairs with such heel-clattering determination that I thought she'd be back within an hour, dragging Jonathan by the ear. She'd check the train stations and the airports, stop traffic on the George Washington Bridge. She was too angry and enormous to evade. But less than an hour later she came back alone. I had hardly moved. I'd spent the hour sitting in the living room, watching it go through its own patient history. When Clare returned she stopped for a moment, staring at me in confusion.

"Did you find him?" I asked.

"Of course I didn't find him."

She walked up to me in a blazing, businesslike way. "Do you love me?" she asked.

"I don't know," I said. All I could think of was the truth.

"I don't know if I love you either," she said. She pulled my shirt off hard enough to rip the seams. We made love on the living-room floor. She bit my neck and nipples, pulled at my hair. She left bloodied lines running along my back and over my ass.

* * *

Jonathan had taken all his money out of the bank and bought a ticket somewhere. Clare and I spent a few weeks getting over expecting to hear from him.

"I don't get this," she said. "This doesn't seem real, it's some kind of *gesture*. You know how Jonathan can be."

"I know how he can be," I said. But in fact he had gone. Alice and Ned couldn't tell us anything, and all we knew about Erich was his first name and the fact that he worked in a restaurant somewhere. After dinner that night we'd all congratulated each other for our ability to enjoy ourselves. We'd promised to do something just as riotous again soon. We didn't think we'd need any particulars for getting in touch.

Jonathan might have dropped through a trapdoor. The last time we saw him he'd washed the dishes, downed a final shot of Scotch, and kissed us both good night. He'd left early for work in the morning. And when Clare and I got home that night, there was the note.

"Stupid bastard," Clare said. "What's the matter with him?"

"He's a dramatic kind of person," I said. "He can't help it."

I waited for my true feelings to arrive. I waited for all the proper reactions: rage and disappointment, a sense of betrayal. But weeks passed and the blankness held. Nothing happened; nothing at all. I felt myself slipping back to my old Cleveland mode, living a life made up of details. At work, I shredded mountains of cheese and chopped my weight in mushrooms. At home I watched television, or watched the light change outside the window, or watched time passing as I played my records. I was surprised to learn that New York could be as ordinary and windblown as Cleveland. It could take on that same feeling of disuse. Although we think of the dead inhabiting the past, I now believe they exist in an unending present. There is no hope of better things to come. There is no memory of the human progress that led to each moment.

Without Jonathan, I haunted my own life. I couldn't make contact. I walked through the hours like a shade wandering in helpless astonishment through rooms he'd once danced and wept and made love in; rooms he'd once been alive enough to ignore.

Clare negotiated a more predictable run of feelings, and came out the other end. She taught herself to accept Jonathan's mysteries and his nagging self-involvement. She worked up a story to tell: never trust anyone under the age of thirty. "People can't be held accountable, not even at twenty-eight," she said. "At that age you're still thinking yourself up. I wish Jonathan well, I really do. I hope he gives me a call sometime after he's developed a personality."

For a while she hated me for being twenty-eight. After that one sweaty, clawing session on the living-room floor, she put an end to our lovemaking and sent me to sleep in Jonathan's bed, so she wouldn't feel the lack when I, too, turned up missing one day. Then, after almost a month, she slipped into bed with me at midnight. "I've been a real asshole, haven't I?" she whispered. "Please forgive me, sweetheart. I've got a sort of soft spot about abandonment. What do you think? Do you think we could manage together, just the two of us?"

I told her I thought we probably could. We were in a kind of love, as far as we knew. I liked making love to her; I liked the heat and unexpectedness of her body. I liked the trail of tiny gold hairs scattered from her navel to her crotch, and I liked the creases her ass made when it met her thighs. We made love that night, for the first time in a month, and though all the moves came off, the central point was missing. I'd suspected it would be that way. Now sex was a succession of details, with a sweet implosion at the end. It was another feature of the regular day.

After that, we slept in the same bed again. We made love once or twice a week. But Jonathan took something out of the air when he left—a next thing kept failing to happen. Clare and I got stuck in the present. According to current wisdom, that was the right place to be. But when it happened—when we lost our sense of the past and the future—we started to drift. Clare felt it, too. She called me "sweetheart" and "honey" more often. She looked at me with a certain mild kindliness that was the living opposite of desire. I began to notice how the cords of her neck jumped when she talked. I became more conscious of the way she scratched invisible pictures on a tabletop as she spoke, and of how her mascara sometimes hardened into gluey clumps on her eyelashes.

We did the things we'd always done. We watched television and went to the movies, bought old clothes and took long walks through the changing neighborhoods. We went to clubs and parties sometimes. But our own occasion kept slipping away from us. We didn't find necessary things to say to each other. I was no talker. I took things in, but couldn't give them back again, transformed, as language. Jonathan had had enough voice for both of us. Now there were silences that reached no logical ends. No one but Clare and me was ever coming home. We had no one to gossip about or worry over, except one another.

I thought of my own parents. I thought of Alice and Ned.

This was love between a man and a woman. I'd made that much more progress in my continuing education.

Summer passed, fall came. I didn't see Jonathan until late November, and then only by accident. I had gone to a chiropractor on the Upper West Side, for the damage I did to my back lifting a case of champagne at work. The Upper West Side might have been a different city—we lived a downtown life. Walking along Central Park West to the subway, I gawked tourist-like at the autumn yellows of Central Park and the trim little dogs clipping alongside their masters' glossy shoes. I got so absorbed in the rich otherness of the place I nearly walked past Jonathan.

He was leaning against the brick flank of an apartment building, reading *The Village Voice*. I stared at him as if he was a particularity of the neighborhood. He might have been a photograph come to life, the way the details of Paris must look if you barrel through it on a three-day package tour.

I said, "Jonathan?"

He looked up, and said my name.

"Jonathan, I—this is you, right?"

He nodded. "It's me. I got into town a couple of weeks ago."

"I, wow, man. I don't know what to say. Um, are you all right?"

I was as confused by his reappearance as I'd been by his departure. Once again, my circuits shut down and left me floating in space.

"I'm okay. Bobby, I didn't mean for us to meet like this."

"Uh-huh. I mean, can you tell me what's going on?"

He sighed. "I'm sorry about the way I left. That was sort of ridiculous, wasn't it? I just . . . I knew I wouldn't do it any other way. I'd just stay around being the uncle until you and Clare moved out and left me alone in that awful apartment. How's Clare?"

"She's okay. She's, like, pretty much the same. I guess we're both pretty much the same."

"You make it sound like a terrible fate," he said.

I shrugged, and he nodded again. He was too familiar to see. His face and clothes kept blurring. It seemed possible that I'd crossed a mental line, and was in fact talking to someone who only looked like Jonathan. New York is full of people who've caved in under their particular losses, and decided they have business with everyone on the street.

"You want to go for a drink or something?" he asked.

"Okay," I said. "Sure."

We went to the first place we saw, an Irish bar that sold corned beef from a steam table. It was the uptown version of the Village bars we used to frequent on our nights with the Hendersons. Crepe-paper Christmas decorations had become year-round fixtures there, and the television showed a wavering, too-bright soap opera to the single old woman who sat at the bar waiting to scream at anyone who interfered with her.

Jonathan ordered a Dewar's on the rocks, and I had a beer. He clicked his glass softly against mine. "Did you think you'd ever see me again?" he said.

"I didn't know. How would I have known?"

"Right. How would you?"

"Where did you go?" I asked him. I still lacked any sense of the real. I thought fleetingly of excusing myself, going to the pay phone in back, and calling the police. But what would I tell them?

"Well, I didn't have a whole lot of money in the bank. I mean, if I'd had thousands I'd probably have gone to Florence or Tokyo or someplace. But with what I had, I just went out to California. Remember Donna Lee from college? She lives in San Francisco now, with a woman named Cristina. I went out there and slept on their sofa for a while and just sort of tried to concoct a San Francisco life for myself."

He sipped at his drink, and sucked in an ice cube at exactly the moment I knew he was going to. He still wore the silver Navajo ring he'd bought in Cleveland when we were fifteen. Details whirled and racketed inside my head.

"I don't really, you know, understand all this," I told him. "I haven't understood it since you left that note. We had a great time, the dinner with Erich was fine, and then you just left. That doesn't make sense to me."

"Well, it doesn't exactly make sense to me either. You know, I turned twenty-nine a month ago. I feel like I'll be thirty in about five minutes."

"Um, happy birthday."

"You'll be twenty-nine too, in another few weeks."

"That's right," I said.

"Well. Listen, I've got to go. They're still debating about whether to take me back at the newspaper, I'm supposed to go meet Fred and Georgeanne in half an hour. It seems they haven't decided yet whether I'm a high-strung romantic genius or just plain irresponsible. Drinks are on me."

He tossed a pile of bills onto the table. I reached over and put my hand on top of his.

"Do you want to come over tonight?" I asked. "Clare'll want to see you."

He looked at our two hands. "No, Bobby," he said. "I don't want to come over. This was just an accident. I mean, you never come uptown. I figured I might as well have been in Michigan."

"You don't want to see us?"

Now he looked into my face. He pulled his hand out from under mine.

"Bobby, the fact is, I seem to have fallen in love with both of you. That sounds strange, I know. I never expected anything like this to happen. I mean— Well. It's not what you prepare yourself for. I seem to have fallen in love with you and Clare together. I saw it that night on the roof. I didn't want Erich to be my date, or anybody else. It's just hopeless. As long as I know you, I can't seem to fall in love with anybody else."

218

He stood up. "Wait," I told him. "Just wait a minute."

"Give my love to Clare," he said. "If and when I pull myself together, I'll call you."

He walked out of the bar. In my confusion, I lost track of what would be reasonable to do or say. I let him walk away into the November afternoon, and by the time I got out to the sidewalk he was gone.

He did as he said. He lived a life apart. Although we were in the same city, I never ran into him again, and he didn't call. He let the fall and winter pass. And then in the spring he left a message on our answering machine.

"Hi, Bobby and Clare. This is such a weird thing to say on a tape like this. Bobby. My father died this morning. I thought I should let you know."

His voice was followed by a mechanical click and whir, as the machine moved along to the next message.

CLARE

WE WERE flying two thousand miles to the funeral of a man I'd never met. Through the airplane window I watched fat clouds throw shadows onto Texas. Texas was flat and one-colored as a manila envelope. Down there, in whatever farmhouses had chosen to attach themselves to the endless beige earth, people might be looking up at the airplane. They might be wondering, as I myself sometimes did, what rich interesting lives were being passed along to their next incident.

"Sure you don't want some wine?" Bobby asked. I shook my head.

"I'm going on the wagon for a little while," I said. "Maybe she could bring me a club soda or something."

Bobby leaned over to signal for the stewardess. The stream of cold air blowing from the overhead nozzle disarranged his hair, which he'd taken to wearing longer, slicked back with gel. I smoothed his hair into place. Then I changed my mind and messed it up again.

I was over two months' pregnant. I hadn't told anyone. I wasn't sure what I wanted to do about it.

"I'm really, like, glad you're here," he said.

"Well, I hate to miss a funeral."

"You know what I was thinking?" he said. "I was thinking the three of us could rent a car and drive back. We could, you know, see the country."

"I guess we could," I said.

"We could go to Carlsbad Caverns. We could see the Grand Canyon."

"Mmm, I've always wanted to see the Grand Canyon."

"Sure," he said. "We could probably rent hiking boots and backpacks. We could camp overnight."

"Bobby. They don't *rent* things like that. People own them. Some people have camping lives. You and I are more the nightclub type."

I had only imagined seeing the Grand Canyon. Not hiking in it.

"You don't want to," he said.

"I only brought funeral clothes," I said. "Can you see me tottering along some trail in a black dress and heels?"

Bobby nodded. He smoothed his hair with his fingers. The light over Texas shone silver on his square face and his heavy, intricately veined hands. Despite the glossy Italian hair and the earring, his face was innocent as an empty bowl. It was still the face of a man who believed human differences could be resolved by a pilgrimage to famous geological phenomena.

"Just, you know, an idea," he said.

"I know. Let's leave it for another time."

He nodded again. The baby coalescing inside me was following the dictates of his genes as well as my own. Tiny nails were being driven into the passing moments. Bobby sipped his wine. We stared out the window at the emptiness passing below.

Jonathan met us at the airport. He looked physically diminished, as if some air or vital fluid had leaked out of him. I hadn't seen him in almost a year. Had he always been so small and wan? Sunburned, brightly dressed people crowded around him in the waiting area. He might have been a refugee, in his pallor and his black T-shirt. Someone newly arrived from a grim, impoverished place. When Bobby and I got off the plane he gave us stiff, formal embraces, like the ones French politicians exchange.

221

"How's Alice, Jon?" Bobby asked.

"Made of stern stuff," he said. "Much sterner than me."

"And how are you?" I asked.

"Hysterical," he said calmly. "A mess."

We drove to Jonathan's parents' condominium in Jonathan's father's car, an enormous blue Oldsmobile. I had never seen Jonathan drive before. He looked both childlike and paternal behind the wheel of that big car. He held the wheel with both hands, as if he was steering a ship.

On the way he told us how his father's heart attack had struck him on his way to the mailbox. He explained that fact in particular. His father had had asthma and then emphysema. So his death by heart failure seemed to make everyone feel as cheated as they would have had he been in faultless health. Bobby asked, "On his way back from the *mail*box?" as if that were the most appalling thing about it.

I put on my sunglasses and watched the shopping centers pass. They shimmered in the heat. Between them lay open country, reddish-gray, studded with cacti. Arizona was the first place I had ever been that turned out to look exactly as I'd pictured it. As we drove along the blindingly bright highway I felt powerful and competent. I was an older woman in sunglasses who'd come to help a couple of confused men contend with their grief. I thought at that moment that I would leave Bobby and have the child by myself.

"I'd written him a letter," Jonathan said. "The first one in at least a year. I hadn't gotten around to mailing it, though. It was still in my jacket pocket when I heard."

Jonathan's parents' condominium was part of a sprawling, mud-colored complex several miles from a shopping mall called Teepee Town. A sign beside the entrance said "Choice Units Still Available" in faded blue letters. Jonathan parked. He led us up a crushed-gravel walk to one of the buildings, past the mailbox, a conventional one painted brown to match the adobe-like substance. I suspected the adobe had been sprayed on with a hydraulic gun. I wondered what sort of people would want to live in a place like that.

The inside of the condominium was dark and cool. Instead of Indian rugs and pottery, there were wing chairs, ferns, family photographs in chrome frames. The only evidence of death was the flowers. There were a half-dozen arrangements in vases and foil-wrapped pots. A white porcelain shepherdess stood on a round polished table between two bouquets, serene and alarming as a bone. Before we had had a chance to acclimate ourselves to the interior darkness, a small, deeply tanned woman came out of what must have been the kitchen. She wiped her hands on her jeans.

"The prodigal returns," she said with a hint of a Southern drawl. "Welcome to the reservation."

"Hello, Alice," Bobby said.

She took Bobby's chin in her hand and turned his face one way and another. She examined it as keenly as an anthropologist checking the completeness of a skull. Suddenly I knew where Jonathan had picked up that stiff, politician's embrace.

"Hello, beautiful," she said. She planted a tight little kiss on his lips.

Bobby stood with his arms at his sides, as if struck dumb by her. Jonathan had to introduce me. Alice scanned me with a scientific eye and shook my hand. "Thank you for coming," she said.

"Thank you for having me," I said. It seemed like the stupidest possible thing to say to a woman whose husband had just died.

"I'm so sorry about Ned, Alice," Bobby said. He had put one of his arms uncertainly over Jonathan's shoulders.

"I know," she said. "I am, too."

"Are we the first ones to get here?" I asked.

"Well, we're not making a big party of it," Alice said. "I'm expecting Ned's brother from Muncie, and a few of the people from around here. We decided to keep it intimate."

"Oh," I said. I had blundered again, obscurely, and rather than go on worrying over my behavior, I decided to just give in and dislike Alice. New widow or no.

"How about a drink?" Jonathan said. "Does anybody want a drink?"

Everybody agreed to want a drink. Jonathan made himself busy, getting them. I realized that was probably how he grew up, ushering things along, proposing drinks or Scrabble games or walks in the park. I could picture him at two, frantically interrupting with a new word he'd never spoken before, to draw his mother's attention away from herself. Now, at thirty, he was turning into her. He administered dry kisses in airports. He was cultivating a life as orderly and cut off as his mother's Early American living room.

After we'd had drinks and dinner, Alice announced that she was spending the night in a motel. Bobby and Jonathan objected. But she had made up her mind. "There's not enough room to swing a cat in here," she said. "The last thing anybody needs in quarters this close is to have to try and respect the privacy of an old lady."

Bobby insisted that he and I should be the ones to go to a motel, but Alice wouldn't budge. "My bag is already packed," she said. "I'll be back in the morning, before any of you are up."

"But it isn't right," Bobby said. "We don't want to put you out of your own house."

I gave his knee what I hoped was a discreet squeeze. Couldn't he see how much Alice wanted to spend the night alone? I knew just what she'd do. She'd step into the scoured motel room, turn the air-conditioning on high, and lie down on an impersonal bed. She'd have a few hours outside her life. I'd done that myself, when a romance ended and my own apartment seemed suddenly too personal. Whether or not Bobby caught the meaning of the squeeze, he soon gave up on his protests. Alice got herself out of the house, promising to have Belgian waffles made before anyone stirred in the morning. I said a brisk unapologetic goodbye, which might or might not have telegraphed the fact that I knew Alice wasn't doing anybody any favors. That although I understood the impulse it didn't make me like her any better.

Then she was gone. Then we were alone together, with no idea of what to say or do. Although I'd been through plenty of departures, I hadn't had any direct experience with the death of the body. My parents were still alive. My grandparents had all died discreetly, in other states, when I was very young. Whatever sense of competence I'd felt in the back seat of the Oldsmobile had evaporated. In its place was nothing but a feeling of vague stupidity, and irritation at the prospect of sleeping in an unfamiliar house and going to a stranger's funeral.

"Anybody want another drink?" Jonathan asked.

We had another drink. We arranged ourselves in the wing chairs and on the ugly colonial sofa. If I'd ever imagined the process of mourning I'd pictured it as an untrammeled exchange, flowing freely as tapwater between people who either loved one another without reservation or were so depleted by their loss that the little daily differences and old grudges spiraled down the drain. But here, sipping tonic in a cheaply furnished, formal little parlor, I didn't forget my ordinary meanness and vanity. I couldn't feel the shock of the father's death. I couldn't make the desolate condominium complex seem like anything other than a place where death was logical and somehow appropriate. A mild surprise the residents were only too well prepared for.

Jonathan said, "I'm sorry we have to be seeing each other like this. I suspected I'd see you two again, but I'd imagined different circumstances."

I knew he had to strain to make a direct statement like that without adopting someone else's gestures and inflection. It was Jonathan's overriding instinct to act as if all were well. As if we were having the time of our lives.

"It's not what I pictured either," I said. "To tell you the truth, I wasn't at all sure if I should come. I'm still not sure I should have."

He nodded. He didn't reassure me.

Nearly beside myself with nervousness and bile, I said, "I'm sure your father was a wonderful man."

Bobby said, "Ned was great. He was really, you know, *great*. I'm sorry you never got to meet him, Clare. You'd've liked him a lot."

"Well, I'm sure I would have."

A silence passed. The ice cracked in Jonathan's glass.

I said, "Listen, Jonathan, I don't know why you did what you did. I suppose you needed to. We should probably just try to forget about it as long as we're here."

"I told Bobby," he said. "I tried to tell you, too. I can't seem to have a life around you."

"Do you have a life now?"

225

"A sort of one. They wouldn't take me back at the paper, but they helped me get an editorial thing at *Esquire*. I'm working my way back up. Unexplained disappearances don't go over all that well, even in the magazine business."

"Well, I hope you're happier than you were," I said.

"Not really," he said. "But I could start getting happier at any moment."

"Good."

He looked around the room as if he couldn't imagine how he'd gotten there—as if a moment earlier he'd been in his bed in New York.

He said, "I keep telling myself, 'My father is dead.' I can't seem to make it feel like a fact. It keeps feeling like something that would happen on television. I mean, you'd think it would be so dramatic, but actually I feel sort of minor. Like this makes me less important. More of a bit player. Do you know what I'm talking about?"

Bobby said, "Ned was, you know. A really good man. Clare, you'd have been crazy about him. Really, you would."

I could hear the possibility of tears in his voice.

Jonathan said, "Oh, Bobby, please just shut up."

"That isn't called for," I said. I got up from my chair and went to sit beside Bobby on the sofa. I massaged his neck. It felt as if it had steel cables running through it.

"He was like my father," Bobby said. "I mean, that's what he was like. More than my own father was, I guess."

Jonathan sighed, a thin dry whistling sound that reminded me of his mother. "Bobby, if you want my family, you can have it," he said. "I hereby give you my entire former life. You can decide where to bury my father. You can worry over the fact that, without him, my mother won't know what to do with herself. If you want all that, you're more than welcome to it."

Jonathan sat in his oversized chair like a polite, furious child. His face was pale and his eyes glowed. I had never heard him speak in this voice but I knew somehow that it was his true voice, clear and calm and crackling with anger. It seemed at that moment that his loving, generous side had been another characterization.

It had been his most successful, an elaborate system of kindly gestures that had covered all traces of the coldly raging, dwarfed little boy who faced us now. His head seemed too large for his body. His feet seemed barely to touch the floor.

"Stop it," I said. "This is no time to talk like that."

"Jon," Bobby said. "Jonny, I—"

"Just go on being me," Jonathan said. "I don't know how to, you're better at it than I am. Tomorrow when they put my father's body in the oven you be the son and I'll be the best friend. I'll shed a few tears and feel awful for a while and then go back to my regular life."

"Jon," Bobby said. He was not crying, but his throat was clotted, his voice thick and phlegmy.

"You're a better son, anyway," Jonathan said. "You bring girl-friends home and you'll have babies someday. You wouldn't have just kept turning up alone at the holidays. Some sort of peculiar bachelor character with a job and no other life worthy of mention. You make more sense. It's too late for my father but you can still be my mother's son. You can rustle up some grandchildren for her so she doesn't have to just sit alone in this condominium watching the tumbleweeds blow by."

"You little shit," I said to Jonathan. I was standing, without having decided to. "All he's ever done to you is worship you. And all you've ever done is walk out on him. You have no right to talk to him like that."

"Oh, you're a fine one," he said. "You let me fall in love with you and then you start sleeping with my best friend. You're a fine one to tell me what I've got a right to do."

"Wait a minute. *Let* you fall in love with me? Who ever said you were in love with me?"

"I did. I'm saying it. With both of you. Now I just want you to leave me alone."

"Jon," Bobby said. "Aw, Jon—"

"I've got to go," Jonathan said. "I feel like I'm losing my mind in here. I'll see you later."

"Your mother took the car," I said.

"Then I'll walk."

He got up from his chair and went out the front door. It made a pathetically small sound as it closed behind him—cheap wood clicking into an aluminum doorframe.

"I'm going after him," Bobby said.

"No. Let him go, let him cool off. He'll be back."

"Uh-uh. I've got to talk to him. I've been sitting here not saying anything."

"His father just died," I said. "He's not in his right mind. He needs to be alone."

"No, he's been alone too much," Bobby said. "He needs me to go after him."

Bobby got around me and out the door. I couldn't have held him if I'd wanted to. I should probably have just stayed inside by myself, but I couldn't imagine sitting there with the funeral flowers and the ticking clock. I followed Bobby and Jonathan. Not to intervene, but because I didn't want to wait for them, alone, in that immaculate house.

By the time I got outside, Jonathan was already a block away. He was a ridiculous little figure walking hunched and hurried under a streetlamp. I reached the street in time to hear Bobby call him. At the sound of his name, without looking back, Jonathan started to run. Bobby ran after him. And I, nervous about being left alone in a haunted condominium, ran after Bobby.

He was the fastest of us. I never exercised, I was pregnant, and I had on heels that made me run like the heroine in a thriller. A tiny-footed, curvaceous woman who needs to be rescued over and over again. As I skittered breathlessly down the block I saw Bobby close the distance between himself and Jonathan. Around us the absurd condominiums stood floodlighted behind their white gravel lawns. Some had lighted windows. Most were dark, uncurtained, deserted. Over the sound of my breath I could hear the dry nocturnal rumble of the desert, a racket of dust and wind.

I was almost two full blocks behind when Bobby caught up with Jonathan. I saw him take hold of Jonathan's shirt, pull him up short. I saw Jonathan's legs keep churning for a moment, like a cartoon character's. And then I saw Jonathan rear back and punch Bobby. It was a wild inefficient punch that caught Bobby in the

228

stomach and doubled him over, more from surprise, it seemed, than force. Jonathan turned and ran again but Bobby was on top of him with a howl. Then they fell together, gouging at one another with their fists.

"Stop it," I screamed. "You assholes. Stop, do you hear me?"

When I reached them they were rolling in the street, kicking awkwardly and trying to get a purchase on one another's bodies. A line of blood flashed on Jonathan's cheek. I bent over. After a moment I was able to grab both of them by the hair and pull it hard.

"Stop," I said. "Stop. Right now."

They stopped. I didn't let go of their hair until they had separated and were sitting face to face on the velvety blacktop. Jonathan bled from the gash in his cheek. His shirtsleeve flapped raggedly off the yoke, exposing a crescent of pale shoulder. Bobby, the larger and stronger, had a smudge on his forehead and a rip in the knee of his slacks.

"You motherfuckers," I said. "You really are crazy, aren't you? Both of you."

"Uh-huh," Bobby said. And at the same moment, they both started to laugh.

"Are you all right?" Jonathan asked. "Did I hurt you?"

"No. I'm okay, I mean I'm fine. You?"

"I think so." He dabbed at the cut on his cheek, looked with surprise and satisfaction at his bloodied fingertips. "Oh, look," he said. "Blood."

"It's not bad," Bobby said. "It's just, you know, a little cut."

"I never had a real fight before," Jonathan said. "I never punched anybody in my life."

"I used to when I was a kid," Bobby said. "I used to punch my brother. But he was so much bigger than me. He'd just, like, laugh and push me away."

"I hope you both know what assholes you sound like," I said.

"Well, I guess I know," Jonathan said.

"Yeah. I guess I do, too," Bobby answered.

They stood up and we walked back to the condominium. On the way Jonathan said, "I'm sorry about how I've acted. I mean, tonight and for about the past year."

"It's okay," Bobby said. "I mean, I think I get it. I think I understand."

Jonathan linked his arm in Bobby's. They walked along stolid and pleased with themselves as two burghers strolling through the village they controlled. Jonathan offered his other elbow to me, but I declined. I walked alone, at a distance. I figured I'd get through the funeral, get back on a plane, and never see either of them again.

Ned's funeral took place the next day at four o'clock. His brother, a furniture salesman named Eddie, flew in from Indiana that morning. Eddie's cigarette smoke crept out of his nose and into his watery eyes the same way my father's had. I knew I could never like him. I didn't seem to like anybody at this funeral. Also present were a big, white-haired woman named Mrs. Cohen, and a small white-haired one named Mrs. Black. I felt nothing particular about them but my observations edged over to the unfavorable (a handbag full of wadded Kleenex, pink powder caught flaking in the folds around a mouth) because that was the drift of things.

We all drove out to the crematorium in a short string of cars: the Oldsmobile, a Honda, and a Plymouth. We duplicated the car order when we walked from the parking lot toward the chapel: Jonathan, Alice, and Eddie first, followed by Bobby and me, followed by the two women. On the way I whispered to Bobby, "Why do you think Alice wanted to keep the funeral so small?"

"I think this is just all the people who came," he whispered back. We were moving along a blinding concrete walk bordered by flowering hedges. Pink trumpet-shaped flowers protruded from among waxy green leaves. Bobby sweated in a dark jacket. I had forgotten to bring any sunglasses but the triangular ones with the scarlet frames, which I couldn't very well wear to a funeral.

"He must have known other people," I said. I slipped my hand into the crook of his elbow, so I wouldn't step off the path in the dizzying light. I found I liked holding on to his arm. It had nothing to do with affection for Bobby. Holding somebody's arm made me feel more like a real mourner, less like a funeral-crasher.

"He just ran a theater in Cleveland," Bobby said. "I mean, who's going to come, ushers from ten years ago?"

"Well, *some*one," I said. We had nearly reached the chapel. It was a gabled building that seemed to be made of stained glass and mirrors. The crematorium was in back. When we first pulled up I had checked for chimneys, but all that was visible behind the church was a flat-roofed cement building with grooves running along its sides, as if it had been combed with a giant comb while the cement was still wet. Of course, it would be too technologically advanced to have chimneys sticking up.

We seated ourselves in the front pews, in the air-conditioned hush. Ned's casket, dark wood with a dry sheen, was displayed under a hanging Lucite cross. On the casket was a single wreath of hollyhocks. It reminded me of the lei Donna Reed threw overboard at the end of *From Here to Eternity*. I thought Ned, a former theater-owner, would probably have liked that.

I sat at the far end of the pew, with Bobby on my right and nothing on my left. Jonathan sat on Bobby's other side, and Alice sat next to Jonathan. Jonathan was crying, quietly but without reserve. Today he had quit being dryly courageous. The cut on his cheek bore a brown hairline scab. A single tear, stained by the light from the colored glass, trembled on his chin. I touched my own chin, and tears started to leak out of my eyes as if I'd pushed a button. I thought about my own father. Once, during a drunken argument with my mother, he had dropped me in a snowbank. I believe that was my first memory. My mother had reached for me, and in their jostling I'd fallen into the snow. My father had had a sure grip, even drunk. He wouldn't have dropped me if my mother hadn't grabbed. The snow had been white and cold and silent as death itself. I had sunk down deep. The two of them dug me out, cursing one another. If Ned had been my father, I'd have made sure he didn't end up with a sparse little funeral in the middle of the desert. The tears flowed. Bobby pressed my hand. For a moment I felt as if Jonathan and I were brother and sister, being comforted by a mutual friend. Then I remembered I was crying for myself and my little sorrows, not the big sorrow of someone actually dead. That reminder only seemed to make me cry harder.

After the funeral the casket was wheeled out to be cremated. We mourners got back in our cars and went home. The ashes would be ready the following day. They worked fast. I wondered if they used some new vaporizing process. Once we were out of the chapel I put my sunglasses on, which helped hide my red eyes.

Everyone started back to Alice's house, what was now Alice's house, what had been Alice and Ned's. I thought of how much Alice must hate that house, with the muddy sprayed-on cement walls and air conditioners humming under the little raw poles that stuck out over the windows. I suspected Ned had probably learned to like it. In a humorous sort of way. People who went to a lot of movies were usually able to see the irony in a wider variety of situations.

Bobby didn't speak the whole way back. *He is respecting my grief,* I thought with surprise. My grief over a stranger, over my own memories, while he himself had known the living person. My face burned. I had lost track of things. I reached over and stroked his hair, then let my hand drop down to his chest, the soft squarish mounds of muscle and fat. I suddenly desired him fiercely. I desired his kindliness and self-sacrifice as if they comprised a different person, a handsome capable stranger I'd just met. It wasn't lust for the Bobby I knew. I'd have liked this compassionate stranger to pull out of line and onto a side street where we could make screaming, axle-rocking love. I made up for that ghoulishness by kissing Bobby on the ear and whispering, "It's all right, sweetheart."

He smiled. His own eyes were unreadable as mine behind the smoky oval mirrors of his glasses. He didn't say anything.

Bobby and I and Jonathan and I—our mingled love and friendship, the lopsided family we'd tried to form—had come to seem like just another foolish episode. Another sprayed-concrete house with twigs over the windows. Now, unexpectedly, the weight of the moment filled that rented Honda. Bobby and I were driving on a desert highway, second in a makeshift funeral procession. I was pregnant. He was the baby's father. Jonathan, who'd broken both our hearts in some obscure way I couldn't quite name, sat in the car ahead of us, beside his unflinching mother. The radio, playing an old Fleetwood Mac song, glowed orange in the relentless white light of mid-afternoon.

Back at the house, the two old women went straight to the kitchen to do things to the casseroles and desserts they had brought. That human preoccupation with food in the face of death. I felt a little better about my urge for a wild, hot fuck at about the same time Ned's casket must have been sliding into the oven.

Ned's brother Eddie sat smoking in a wing chair. He smelled of flowery cologne and everything the cologne was intended to cover up. I wondered where his wife was, and if he had children. How could he help but have a wife and children? I was always astonished at how simple and inevitable those facts were for most people.

"It was a nice service," he said.

"I suppose," Alice said. The old women had banished her from her own kitchen. She paced around the room, making minor adjustments. She straightened a picture that had not been crooked. She was wearing a black cocktail dress that must have dated back to Cleveland. She would certainly have had no use for a dress like that in the desert. Years ago, when she packed up and moved, she had probably decided to keep the dress for today.

At that moment I could picture her in an Ohio bedroom, packing to move to a foolish house in the desert. I could see her sorting through her things, making bundles for the Salvation Army. I could see her coming upon this particular dress. She would have known she'd need it one day. She would have sat down on the bed, holding the slick dark fabric with a certain disbelief. A dress she'd bought offhandedly in a mall, not too expensive, no big thing. She would have sat for a while on a white chenille bedspread, in jeans, with the black fabric spread over her lap. Then, in an efficient and scientific manner, she would have folded the dress in tissue and packed it along with her sun suits and Bermuda shorts.

I could see her so perfectly. I gave my head a little shake, to clear it.

"Now there's no one," Eddie said. "Except the people in this room. How did we get to be such a small family, anyway?"

"You don't necessarily meet a lot of people in this world," Alice said. She licked her thumb and rubbed a spot off a philodendron leaf. "You do your work and raise your kids and live in your house and that's that. Neither Ned nor I was ever much of a joiner."

"You always seemed to have friends in Cleveland," Eddie said.

"Neighborhood people," Alice said. "Some of them were very nice. But we moved out of the neighborhood. They all sent flowers."

She crossed the room briskly, and opened the drapes. Light exploded into the room like a flashbulb. Jonathan gasped, then said, "Excuse me," as if he had committed some minor bodily embarrassment. I figured Alice and Ned must have been one of those everybody-loves-him-but-nobody-can-stand-her couples. I thought that if I'd been married to Ned, he'd have had some friends who thought enough of him to buy a plane ticket to Arizona. I felt the tears rising again, and clenched my fists to stop them. I settled in closer to Bobby. *I'm sorry, Ned*, I said silently. For a moment, Bobby and Ned seemed to get confused in my mind. I might have been sixty-five, sitting there with Bobby, my dead husband, who had come back from the grave to point out my inadequacies and mistakes.

The old women kept up a skittish conversation in the kitchen, occasionally striking a series of notes with a spoon against a pot. I questioned Eddie about his life, just to keep things going. His wife was dead. He had two married daughters, who, he explained, could not get away for the funeral. He was the veteran of an orderly life, a sequence of births and deaths in Muncie, Indiana, Memories kept intruding on my attention as I listened to Eddie. My father had stood me on a bartop when I was four years old, to the applause of men. He'd bought frilly dresses my mother didn't want me to wear. "She looks like a hooker," my mother had said, and for years I'd believed a hooker was someone who hooked men's hearts. I'd thought it was a grudging form of flattery. My father was fun and indulgent. My mother believed in a life of work. It was only as I grew older that I began to see her side. My father cursed and wept, fell down the back stairs. He wrecked cars, and began to accuse me of conspiring with my mother. He grew too big and noisy, too dangerous, and if Mother had been any fun at all I'd have joined up with her. My father stumbled naked down the hall. He said something to me I couldn't understand, and soon after that he was gone. Mother repapered her bedroom in bright sexless daisies. She said, "Things will be better now."

Eddie sat smoking, his eyes dim and yellowed from fifty years of absorbing his own smoke. "I never expected to outlive him," he said. "He was the oldest, you know. But still."

"Yes," Alice said softly. "I know."

Mrs. Cohen and Mrs. Black came out of the kitchen. One of them, I couldn't remember which was which, dried her hands with a striped dishrag. "Rest in peace," the other one said.

"He didn't have a bad life, though," Eddie said. "He always loved the movies, and he ended up owning a movie theater. Not bad."

"He was a very kind man," said the old woman with the dish towel, Mrs. Cohen or Mrs. Black. "I always slept better at night, knowing I could call him and he'd come right away. I never did have to call him, thank the Lord, but I always knew I could."

"A very kind man," the other one said.

Jonathan had shuffled over to a chair. Bobby went and sat close to him, with one haunch hung over the chair arm. If they could have fused into one being they'd have done fine in the world.

"Thank you for making dinner," Alice said to the two women. "It must be after five o'clock. Why don't we all have a drink, or two or three?"

"Oh, I never drink," said the woman with the dish towel. "I had a kidney operation. I have only one kidney, and that's my sister's."

"That's right," said the other.

I wondered if the two women were sisters.

After dinner, they went home. Eddie went back to his hotel room "to freshen up," promising to return "for a nightcap."

Alice said, "Maybe you boys should have some time alone together. Why don't you go out for a drink?"

"I don't know," Jonathan said. "Should we?" He checked with Bobby for an answer. Bobby glanced at me. I wondered how the decision could possibly have come around to me. I nodded imperceptibly, yes.

Jonathan asked if he should take a jacket. Bobby told him he probably should. "You two," said Alice, "are a pair." I had never seen anyone as lost as Jonathan, as anxious to be told what to do.

Bobby kissed me on his way out, a moist peck on the cheek. "We won't, you know, be gone too long," he whispered. I swatted him away as if shooing a fly. My sense of the real had evaporated. I was back in an arbitrary place, being left alone with a mean-spirited woman I scarcely knew. This episode would end. It would be just another small story in my life.

Jonathan lingered at the doorway. "Bye," he said. "We'll be back soon."

"Go," I said. If I'd been his sister, I could have kept Alice from drawing the juice out of him. I'd have put Alice in her place, and inspired Jonathan to stand up for himself.

"Goodbye, Mom," he said.

Alice took hold of his chin in her direct, scientific way. She looked straight into his eyes. "Goodbye, son," she said. "I love you."

After they had gone, Alice asked, "Can I get you anything?" in a sunny, hostess's tone, reminding me that I was only a guest.

"Nothing, thanks," I said. "Can I do anything for you?"

"No. I'm going to spruce up the kitchen a bit, I think."

"I'll help."

"No, thank you," she said, with a firm smile. "I'd really rather do it alone. You just make yourself comfortable out here."

That was fine with me. Now neither of us would have to think of things to say. After Alice had gone into the kitchen I turned on the television, with the volume all the way down, so as not to intrude on her thoughts.

I stared at the screen. I didn't recognize the show, and didn't care. If I watched television at all, I only watched it for the feeling of something happening. At home I usually turned the sound down and turned up the stereo, so I didn't have to listen to what one unfamiliar character was saying to another.

Alice stayed in the kitchen for a long time. One show ended, and another. I alternated between watching TV and flipping through magazines. Just killing the time. I figured Bobby and Jonathan were out at some roadhouse, getting drunk and talking about themselves and Alice and me. I felt jealous—not of their devotion to one another so much as their history together. The simple, neurotic fact of their bond. I, a more reasonable and complete person, would fly back to New York and go on to something else. I'd have my baby alone. There was nothing inevitable, no element of fate or doom, about my attachment to anyone here. I leafed through *Arizona Highways* and *National Geographic*.

Then I heard something break in the kitchen. I wasn't sure if I should go in there or not. Maybe Alice was having some kind of temporary breakdown, and would rather not be bothered. I didn't want to butt in. On TV, a thousand children sang soundlessly about Coke. I knew the song. It was an old commercial, being mysteriously revived. I decided on second thought that it would probably be rude not to check on Alice.

In the kitchen, she was holding two halves of a plate. "Dropped it," she said. She said it with a peculiar smile, as if dropping it had been an accomplishment.

"That's too bad," I said.

"It wasn't anything, though," she told me. "They sell for a dollar ninety-eight at the K mart. No trouble at all to replace it."

"That's good," I said.

"Isn't it?" She was still holding the two halves of the plate, which were perfect as two half-moons. After a moment she dropped them again.

"I'm sorry," she said. "I'm truly sorry. You go on in the other room and watch TV. I'll be just fine." She turned and walked out the screen door. It banged behind her, with the flimsy sound of lightweight aluminum.

I bent over and picked up the plate. It had broken into several pieces this time, thick triangular shards. I picked them all up and dropped them carefully into the trash. I was afraid of breaking them any further. I stood for a while in the silent kitchen, wishing Bobby and Jonathan would get home. I almost went back into the living room and sat down as I'd been told, but I just couldn't picture myself doing it. I made up my mind to follow Alice and offer whatever help I could, being careful not to make a pest of myself. I was, after all, only a guest.

I opened the door and stepped out into the rectangle of light it made. Stars were visible even through the brightness of the condominium complex. The back yard wasn't much. Just a plot of spongy grass with a flower bed and two lawn chairs, surrounded by an adobe-like wall. Alice stood in the middle of the grass, facing away from the house. She held her hair with both hands, and rocked from side to side. As I started toward her she let out what began as a moan but collapsed into itself and became a sigh, a long slow hissing exhalation. With one hand she took hold of and tore a piece of hair from her head. I could hear the sound it made, ripping out.

"Alice?" I said.

She turned, holding the hair in her fist. It hung down almost a foot, kinky strands in the electric light. "You shouldn't see this," she said. "This isn't your life. You should go back in the house."

"Can I do anything for you?" I asked.

She laughed. "Yes, dear," she said. "Run down to the K mart for a new plate. And a new husband."

We stood facing one another. I believed she was waiting for me to go back into the house, offended. I didn't go back into the house. Maybe because I *was* offended, and refused to give her the satisfaction.

After a minute she looked down at the handful of hair. "This is all I have," she said.

I didn't say anything. I didn't move.

"I don't want the boys to see me this way," she said. "I don't want Jonathan to. I don't think he could stand it, seeing me like this."

"Don't worry about that," I said.

"I do, though. I suppose you can see me this way. You've never really known me any other. Yes, you can see me like this. It's all right, isn't it?"

"Yes," I said. "Yes, it's all right."

She reached up with her free hand and grabbed at her hair. I took hold of her wrist. "Don't," I said. "You don't have to."

I hadn't expected to touch her.

"Don't I?" she asked. "Don't I have to do something?"

"No," I said. "No, nothing."

She sighed. I kept hold of her wrist. I held on tight. A part of me waited to see what Alice would do next and a part of me thought of my own child, grown up, bound to me by an endless snarl of love and hatred. I could hear the children in the commercial, singing their song to Coke. All those voices. It was like having a loudspeaker in my head.

"You see, I'm more than this," she said. "We all are. No, I don't really mean that. I'm just feeling sorry for myself right now, not for the whole damn race. Not even for Ned. I'm more than this. And what am I going to do with poor Ned? How are we not going to be a joke?"

"You're not a joke," I said.

"Don't patronize me. Do you want to know a secret?"

I kept my mouth shut. I held Alice's thin wrist.

"I was going to leave Ned," she said. "I'd made up my mind. I was thinking about how to tell him, and then he dropped over dead on his way to the mailbox."

"Oh, honey," I said. It was all I could think of to say.

"The funny thing is, I'd been planning on leaving for most of the last thirty years. But I couldn't think of where to go, or what to do. I seemed to have lost track of what it was possible for a woman to do on her own. And our house, the old one in Cleveland, just seemed so permanent."

"You could have kicked him out," I said.

"Oh, but I didn't want to stay in Cleveland on my own. It was a dreadful place. And I kept thinking, 'If I leave, this won't be my kitchen anymore. I won't have my plates stacked in this corner cupboard, or light coming in at just this angle.' I could imagine the larger parts. The lonely nights and working a job. What I couldn't seem to relinquish was those little daily things. And then it would be time to make dinner, and another day would go by."

"Well, I actually admire you for staying," I said. "My father left, and I don't know if I've ever quite gotten over it."

"Really, I think staying is the cowardly thing," she said. "I pressured Jonathan to keep me company, and when I saw that he was falling in love with Bobby, I drove a wedge between them.

239

I packed Ned off to his theater because, well, as you might imagine, nothing much went on between us in bed. And he wasn't the type for affairs. He just got lost in the movies. Now I'm an old woman, and Ned's gone, and poor Jonathan doesn't know what to do with himself."

I noticed a plane flying silently overhead. "I don't know what to say," I said finally.

"There's nothing to say. You could loosen up on my wrist a little. You're cutting off the blood."

"Oh. Sorry." I let go and was surprised when Alice took my hand.

"We're not friends," she said. "We don't even like each other all that much. Maybe it's lucky for me, to have someone here who isn't a friend. I couldn't tell this to anyone but a stranger. Thank you for not running away."

"Keep quiet," I said. I hadn't expected to hear that much vehemence in my own voice. "If you start getting grateful, we won't be able to look at each other after this. I'm not doing anything for you that anybody wouldn't do."

"But you're here," she said. "You came two thousand miles to stand out here with me. That's all I'm grateful for."

"It's damn little," I said.

"It's a great deal," she answered.

"Well," I said, and the two of us stood in silence, holding hands like shy kids on a date.

After a minute Alice said, "I wonder if you could do something for me. It's going to sound very strange."

"What?"

"I wonder if you'd take hold of me and squeeze me, hard. I mean hard."

"Really?"

"Yes," she answered. "Please."

I put my arms awkwardly around her shoulders and gave her a squeeze. I didn't know her well enough to refuse. I inhaled the crisp odor of her hair.

"Harder, please," she said. "Please don't be careful with me. I want to be held one last time by someone who isn't treating me delicately."

I breathed deeply and pressed Alice to my breasts. I could feel her smaller breasts in their brassiere, and her ribs and spine. I could tell she had a skeleton.

"Good," she said. "Even harder."

I held one of my own wrists with the opposite hand, like a wrestler, and squeezed until I heard her gasp for breath. I realized she had taken hold of me, too.

"Oh Lord," she whispered. "Hold me tighter. Don't let go."

I was still holding her when a car pulled up in front. "Bobby and Jonathan are back," I said, relaxing my grip.

"Oh no," she said. "I need a little longer without them."

The car door slammed. "Now, now. It'll be all right," I said helplessly.

"I'm not ready," she said. "I need a little longer."

The front door opened. There was no place to go. The wall ran all around the yard, chest high, and on the other side were more buildings exactly like this one. "Come on," I said. I led her by the hand to the farthest corner of the yard, where the brightness was less intense.

"Just stand here," I said, setting her in the curve of the wall. I could hear Jonathan calling for his mother. A window blazed with light.

"I'm not crying," she said. "Am I?"

"No. Stand right here," I said. I placed myself in front of her, with my back to the house, blocking the light.

Soon Bobby opened the back door and stood in the doorway, a dark shape cut out of the light. "Clare?" he called. "Alice?"

"We're all right, Bobby," I said. "Go back in. We'll be there in a minute."

"What's the matter?" he asked. "Is something the matter?"

"Oh, don't let him come out here," Alice said.

"Nothing, darling," I called. "We're fine. Just go back in, please."

"What's wrong?" He walked out onto the grass and stood several paces away. He planted his fists on his hips, like an angry father. I felt the strongest twist of dislike I'd ever felt for him.

"What?" he said.

Alice had by that time begun to cry, from humiliation as much

241

as grief, long dry sobs that caught in her throat and made a tearing sound. "Is that Alice?" Bobby said.

"Of course it's Alice," I said. "Go inside."

He came and stood next to me. "Alice?" he said, as if he didn't recognize her.

I put my hands on her shoulders. I didn't try to embrace her. I just held on to her, so she wouldn't feel like she was dropping away from everything.

"Oh, Alice, I'm sorry," he said. "Oh God, I'm so, so sorry."

"You didn't do—" was all Alice could get out.

Bobby drew a noisy breath and started to cry, too. I wanted to punch him. How dare he be anything but strong at a moment like this? I actually lifted one hand to do it, to slap him out of himself. I had always wanted to make a gesture like that. But my hand stopped halfway and, following the line of least resistance, settled comfortingly on his back instead. What else could I do with my hand? I wasn't the heroic type. I had no plan of action. Bobby trembled, and as I touched him his trembling went through me like an electric shock. My father popped into my mind. Suddenly he was there, solid as a photograph, handsome and arrogant in his winter coat. I kept one hand on Alice and one on Bobby. I could see my father so clearly, and my mother: outraged, efficient, aging in a square-shouldered red jacket. I saw Ned distinctly as if I had known him, turned away by his discontented wife, watching movies among his dwindling audience, dreaming of Faye Dunaway or Elizabeth Taylor.

I held on to Bobby and Alice. Obeying no one but myself I put my head back and laughed. Not that anything was funny. But I laughed anyway. I knew I ought to feel embarrassed, for laughing at a time like that, but things had gone too far. I decided not to be embarrassed, and wasn't. I kept laughing. The fact that nothing was funny only seemed to make me laugh harder.

Soon a light, questioning touch landed on my shoulder. It was Jonathan, looking timid and hungry, asking by his touch to be let into the circle. I made room for him between myself and Bobby, and laid my arm across his shoulders so I could keep my hold on Bobby, too. I let myself go on laughing. I felt a weight beginning to rise inside me, something big and sodden, like a lump of dough

I'd swallowed so long ago I'd forgotten it was lodged in my gut. I laughed on. I laughed at my father, a drunken boy tortured by his own devotion to sleaze and disorder, and at my tough, vengeful mother. I laughed at Ned, a dreamer reduced to ash and bone; at wimpy Jonathan; at Bobby and at myself, knocked up three months after my fortieth birthday by a man I wasn't sure I liked. I laughed at Alice, stuck in a fake house in the desert because she couldn't imagine a life without a corner cupboard. At every lousy little thing.

JONATHAN

C LARE got sick in seven different states. She was nauseated first at the Grand Canyon, standing wan and erect beside an unused telescope on the South Rim, looking in the direction of the view from behind dark glasses. As Bobby strained against the railing, exclaiming over the profound distances, Clare touched my elbow and said in a low voice, "Sweetheart, I don't think I can manage it."

"Manage what?" I asked.

"This," she said, waving in the direction of the abyss. "All this grandeur and beauty. A great moment like this. It's too much for me."

I stood close to her. Although the morning was calm, I had some idea of shielding her from whatever winds might be stirred up by the canyon's vastness. The sun had just risen. It threw a hammered, golden light onto the cliff faces, which tumbled down into an unsteady, shimmering lake of translucent purple darkness that appeared to be bottomless. Bobby danced ecstatically at the rim, hugging himself and emitting surprised little groans.

"There's nothing to it," I told Clare. "Just stand here and look, and when we're through looking, we'll go have breakfast."

The word "breakfast" made her retch. She caught the telescope for support. It swung creakily up toward a vivid pink gash of cloud. She crouched, gagging, but did not vomit. A thread of saliva dangled from her mouth, shining in the light.

I held her shoulders. "Honey, you're sick," I said.

"Too goddamn beautiful," she said. "Better put me back in that Chevy Nova."

"Wait a minute, I'll go get Bobby."

"Leave him," she said. "Don't interrupt, he's in a trance or something."

She may have been right. Bobby had ceased his hopping, wound-up little dance and was now standing with both hands on the rail, like a captain commanding his ship in a storm. He was more available than Clare or I to outright fits of sentiment—he had no sense of going too far.

I helped Clare into our rented Chevrolet. She and I had agreed, with mingled feelings of irony and plain interest, to drive back to New York from Arizona. This was our first morning—we'd set out at 3 a.m. from my mother's house to make the Grand Canyon by sunrise. In the next five days we would cross the Rockies and the Plains, pay our respects to the Ohio dead, buy Shaker boxes in Pennsylvania. It was Bobby's trip at heart. He would drive most of the time, and insist on stopping in stores that advertised "Homemade Jam" or "Local Handicrafts," which, three times out of four, had been made somewhere in Asia. He would, with my credit card, buy over a hundred dollars' worth of cassette tapes: the Stones, David Bowie, Bruce Springsteen. He would play "Born to Run" over and over, until Clare finally threw it out the window on the road approaching Sandusky.

I settled her into the front seat. The car had an immaculate, rubberized smell and she inhaled deeply, as if the disinfected air could revive her. "Thanks, honey," she said. "Now go. Look at the view."

"No, I'll stay here with you."

"Do you think I want to be the one who made you sit in a subcompact instead of seeing the Grand Canyon? Go. For Christ's sake."

I went. I stood beside Bobby at the railing. At this hour, in the off-season, the observation area was empty. One crushed paper cup sat luminous on the thin lip of red earth beyond the rail. The morning light, brilliant but without warmth, washed our faces and clothes.

"Amazing," I said.

Bobby turned to me. He couldn't speak, and probably wished I wouldn't either. But his politeness never failed him.

"Uh-huh," he said.

"You don't expect this," I said. "I mean, you've seen it so many times on coasters and dish towels and I don't know what-all. I thought maybe it was going to be sort of kitschy."

"Uh-huh."

"It actually knocked Clare out. I had to put her back in the car."

"Hmm." He put his arm over my shoulder, because he loved me and because he ardently wished I would shut up. I slipped my arm around his waist. Here was his smell and his solid, familiar flesh. We watched the sun come up. Bobby was warm and substantial, his brain crawling with thoughts that were at once familiar and utterly strange to me. His wrist still bore the liver-colored mole. Clare waited for us in the car, defeated by the view. I believed, at that moment, that I had never loved anyone but my parents and these two people. Perhaps we don't fully recover from our first loves. Perhaps, in the extravagance of youth, we give away our devotions easily and all but arbitrarily, on the mistaken assumption that we'll always have more to give.

Clare was sick again the following morning, at Pikes Peak. "Maybe I'm allergic to national monuments," she said. We got her to the women's room in a Shell station, and waited for nearly half an hour. She emerged pallid and straight-backed, with her sunglasses on and dark red lipstick newly applied. She might have been an ancient movie star. Behind her, granite peaks stood dusted with snow.

"Honey," I said, "should we drive straight to Denver and put you on a plane?"

"No," she said. "I think I'm all right. I got over it yesterday, didn't I? It's probably just some little bug."

She had, in fact, recovered by ten o'clock. The color returned to her face, and her body gave up its clenched, formal posture. We drove among meadows that were taking on their first green, backed by mountains covered with pine and bare white aspens. It was a verdant, uncomplicated landscape—wide open, with no underlayer of menace. Farther north, I suspected, the terrain was rougher, the peaks more jagged, and if you strayed too far from the road you could be swallowed up by the sheer fathomless distance of the land and sky. Here, in the heart of Colorado, we passed only simple manifestations of broad, unterrifying beauty. There were mountains, and fields of cattle. There were silver streams that clattered alongside the highway, studded with chocolate-colored rocks. The landscape touched you with its fertile kindliness, but didn't change you in any way. It never threatened to break your heart.

We drove all day, and reached Nebraska before dark. Clare read *Vogue* and *Interview* and *Rolling Stone*. "The thing I love best about car trips," she said, "is the way you're entitled to read stupid magazines for hours and hours. I mean, you can look at scenery anytime, scenery's everywhere. But the chance to read an entire *Interview* without guilt? That's rare."

We slept in a motel fifty miles west of Lincoln, and started again just after daybreak. Clare was only slightly ill that morning. We fell into a lulled rhythm of driving, reading, eating, and listening to music, with the farmland of Nebraska and Iowa and Illinois rolling by. You have to travel through the Plains to fully appreciate the emptiness of this country. Its main characteristics are not traffic and abundant store displays but a windswept solitude that lacks the dignity of true remove—no horizon is truly empty. The sun always glints on a remote water tower or silo, a billboard or a tin-roofed, temporary storehouse. Every twenty or thirty miles you pass through a struggling town which continues to exist because at some point in the past it set out to exist. We stopped for meals in some of those towns, hoping for homemade hash browns or pies baked an hour earlier by the owners' wives, but all the food was dead, thawed and microwaved. Fields rolled by, seeded but still bare, hour after hour of blank black earth exposed to the raw sky. Clare read to us from a book of Flannery O'Connor's stories. Our car became more and more disreputable, littered with wrappers and empty bottles. By nightfall, when we stopped at a motel in Indiana, we had all but lost track of our histories and futures—it seemed we had always been driving across a vast table of farmland and would always continue doing so. That is both the horror and the marvel of long travel. You lose track of your life with astonishing speed. An interstellar traveler would be not quite identifiable as an earthling within two weeks; after six months in deep space he or she might as well not return to earth at all.

The next day we drove through Cleveland. Clare was sick in the morning, worse than Nebraska but less severe than Pikes Peak. By the time we reached the Cleveland city limits, just after 11 a.m., she was more or less recovered.

"Cleveland," she said. "Who ever expected to visit such a remote, exotic place?"

Bobby and I were overtaken by giddy nervousness at the town line. We pointed out buildings to one another, joked about their stature. They had seemed so grand. We drove past the limestone clutter of downtown, took the familiar exit. Our itinerary was brief. First we passed the six-story brick-and-concrete parking structure that stood where my father's theater had been. The new building was an arrangement of tiered ramps with an unintentionally beautiful blue neon arrow pointing out the entrance. It was serene and uncomplicated, utterly functional, and it had the look of something that would stand for hundreds of years. My father's old theater, built during the Depression, had been cheaply ornamented, its yellow bricks laid in a herringbone pattern and its aluminum marquee arched and buckling like an ocean wave. Even when it was new, it must have seemed temporary, a small monument to forgetfulness and good cheer thrown up during hard times. The parking structure was more businesslike, hard and smooth as a roach.

"That's that," I said. "Rest in peace, Dad." I managed a brusque, flippant tone because I couldn't bear the idea of myself gone maudlin at such an obvious moment. I didn't mind my own sentimentality but I hated to be a sucker. I was not wholly sorry my father's business was gone. I was vaguely ashamed and lonely, yet pleased with myself simply for being alive; for surviving into the future. Only the most dedicated nostalgist could have argued against the notion that this part of town had been generally improved. New restaurants announced their names in gilt letters, and a famous department-store chain was renovating the defunct family-owned store that had stocked drab outdated clothes and gaudy costume jewelry.

We passed my family's old house, which looked wonderful. The new owners had painted it pine green, and had reshingled the roof. A skylight had been installed over my parents' former bedroom. I could imagine the current state of the rooms: the woodwork would be painted white, and the carpet taken up to expose the oak floors. There would be art, and spare leather furniture.

"Shit," Bobby said. "Look what they did to it."

"It looks great," I told him. "Don't stop. It isn't ours anymore, don't even think about going up to the front door and asking if we can look inside."

"I wouldn't want to," he said, though I knew if he'd been alone he'd have done just that. Bobby had no talent for leaving things alone.

Our last stop was the cemetery. We drove to the tract where Bobby had lived, past the low flagstone wall on which the word "Woodlawn" floated in scrolled wrought-iron letters, the final "n" broken off but its silhouette remaining, a pale shadow on the stone. We followed the serpentine street, past houses that repeated themselves in threes, and parked at the site of Bobby's old home. The house was gone, burned almost twenty years ago and bulldozed away, but no one had built anything in its place. This subdivision was not undergoing renewal. It appeared that the residents had annexed the property without formally purchasing it: a small garden was staked out, ready for spring planting, and a swing set stood rusting among the weeds. It seemed the Morrows' holdings had become a sort of People's Park in the suburbs of Cleveland. The others on the block, those who still lived in the fading jerry-built ranch houses with birdbaths or plaster dwarfs on their lawns, had appropriated it. I could imagine them gathering there at dusk, their children swaying creakily on the swings as the women planted sunflower seeds and murmured over the day's events. It was slightly criminal, an unfounded claim made by people who were not prospering but only getting by, and as such the property had passed beyond reclamation. To own this parcel of land now you would have to wrest it back from those who had learned to care for it. If you leveled their tiny works and put up a new house you would be an invader, not much different from a colonial, and the land would be tainted until your house fell down again. This suburban quarter-acre had returned to its wilder purpose, and could not be redomesticated without a fight that would leave the victor's hands stained.

"This was it," Bobby said. Clare looked around incredulously. She had not expected anything so ordinary, although we'd done our best to prepare her.

We got out of the car and walked onto the patch of bare ground under the singular openmouthed gaze of a red-haired boy who had been digging in the dirt with a tablespoon when we pulled up. As we walked across, Bobby said, "Here's where the front door was. And, like, this right here would have been the living room. That was the kitchen over there."

We stood for a moment in the phantom house, looking around. It was so utterly gone, so evaporated. Sun shone on the bare earth. Clare bent to pick up a little beige plastic man crouched with a bazooka.

"This was the den, I think," Bobby said. "Or maybe it was over there."

We crossed the gully that separated the property from the grave-yard, jumping the trickle of brown water that ran along the bottom. Bobby looked for a moment at a stone angel balanced atop a marker, the tallest monument around. She stood canted forward, on tiptoe, her slender arms raised in an attitude more ecstatic than solemn. I don't imagine the carver intended her look of triumphant sexuality.

"There used to be a fence here," Bobby said in a tone of defensive pride. "Our back yard was, you know, more private than this."

I remembered that the angel had appeared over the top of the Morrows' fence, floating among the branches.

"Mm-hm," Clare said. She had grown quieter since we reached Cleveland. I couldn't tell what was on her mind.

Bobby led us straight to his family's graves. They lay some distance from where the house had been, in a newer section of the cemetery. Rows of markers continued for some fifty feet, and beyond that we could see the line where the advancing tide of graves ended and the unbroken grass lay waiting for those who were, at that moment, still alive.

"This is it," Bobby said. His father, mother, and brother had similar granite stones, shiny and dark gray, wet-looking, carved only with their names and dates. We stood before the graves in silence. Bobby gazed at the stones with a simple and almost impersonal respect, like a tourist visiting a shrine. By now his mourning was over and he'd fallen away from the ongoing process of his family's demise. They had sailed off, all three of them, and left him here. After a while he said, "Sometimes I wonder if there should be, you know, some kind of message on their stones. You can't tell anything about them, except that they were related."

"What kind of message would you want?" I asked.

"I don't know," he said. "Just . . . Aw, man. I don't know."

I looked at Clare, who was looking at Bobby with a mingled expression of wonder and uncertainty. I think until then she had not realized he was fully, independently human, with a history of loss and great expectations. He had presented himself to her as a collection of quirks and untapped potential—she'd all but invented him. Just as the hypnotist must see his subject as a field for planting suggestions in, Clare would have seen Bobby as a project whose success or failure reflected only on her. She was the one woman he'd slept with. She selected his clothes and cut his hair. Arranged marriages might have been like this, the bride arriving so young and unformed that she appears to absorb the union into her skin, her husband's proclivities taken on and made indistinguishable from her own. Clare, the husband, must have seen for the first time that Bobby had had a life outside her sphere. I couldn't tell whether she was pleased or dismayed.

After a while, we left the cemetery again. It seemed there should have been more to say or do, but the dead are difficult subjects. What's most remarkable about them is their constancy. They will be dead in just this way a thousand years from now. I was still getting used to it with my own father. The whole time he lived I had thought in terms of how we might still change in one another's eyes. Now we could not revise ourselves. He'd taken the possibility with him into the crematorium's fire.

We got back into the car. I touched the two silver hoops I wore in my ear, looked down at my own clothes. I was a man in cowboy boots and black jeans. I wore ten black rubber bracelets on one wrist. I could still travel, change jobs, read Turgenev. Any kind of love was possible.

"Next stop, New York City," Bobby said from behind the wheel. If he was not quite somber, he had grown more blank— it was his old response to sorrow. His voice lost its rhythm and lilt, his face slackened. I have never seen this in anyone else. Bobby could withdraw from the surface of his skin, and when he did so you suspected that if you stuck him with a needle the point would penetrate a fraction of an inch before he cried out. In these vacant states he said and did nothing different. His speech and actions continued unimpaired. But something in him departed, the living snap went out, and he took on a slumbering quality that might have been mistaken for stupidity by someone who knew him less.

I asked if he wanted to go by the bakery to see his old boss and he said no. He said it was past time to get back on the road, as if we needed to reach New York by a particular hour. I stroked his shoulder as we pulled onto the highway. I think we both felt defeated by Cleveland, its ordinary aims and modestly rising prospects. Perhaps others have a more agreeably definitive experience when they revisit their hometowns: those who've escaped from industrial slums or declined from pinnacles of great wealth or happiness. Maybe they're better able to say, "Once I was there and now I'm somewhere else."

We were all quiet for the next hour. Clare was so withdrawn I asked her if she was feeling sick again, and she told me no in an irritated tone. Pennsylvania arrived with its long steady roll of white barns and gentle hills. We drove along in a small hothouse of sourceless gloom.

Without preamble, as we approached a sign for Jay-Dee's Cheese Popcorn, Bobby said, "I've been thinking. Would you both ever want to, like, get a place out of the city? Like a house we could all live in?"

"You mean all three of us?" I asked.

"Uh-huh."

Clare said, "Communes are out of style."

"We wouldn't be a commune, exactly. I mean, we're more like a family, don't you think?"

"I suppose so," I said.

"We are nothing like a family," Clare said.

"Like it or not," Bobby told her. "Too late to back out now."

In a low voice, Clare said, "Stop the car."

"What? What is it?"

"Are you sick?"

"Stop. Just stop the car."

Bobby pulled over to the side, assuming she was going to be sick. We were literally nowhere, in a stretch of farmland gone fallow, the fields weedy and strewn with trash. A Texaco sign shimmered at the curve of the road ahead.

"Honey," I said. "Are you all right?"

She had opened the door almost before Bobby came to a full stop. But instead of leaning out to vomit she jumped from the car and began walking, with fierce determination, along the brushy shoulder. Bobby and I hesitated, searching for the proper response.

"What is it?" I asked him.

"I don't know."

"We'd better go after her."

We got out of the car and ran to catch up with her. An eighteen-wheel truck ground past, swirling grit and a windstorm of garbage around our feet.

"Hey," Bobby said. He touched her elbow. "Hey, what's going on?"

"Leave me alone," she said. "Please just go back to the car and leave me alone."

She may have meant, in a disorganized way, to leave us in Pennsylvania. She may have meant to hitchhike back, or to begin a life of drifting around the country, getting waitress jobs and renting rooms in small-town hotels. I had entertained similar impulses myself.

"Clare," I said. "Clare." I thought the sound of my voice would calm her. I was her closest friend, her confidant. She turned. Her face was dark with rage.

"Leave me alone," she said. "Just go. The two of you."

"What is it?" Bobby asked. "Are you, like, really sick?"

"Yes," she said. To escape us she left the roadside and veered across the flat expanse of chalky, untended ground. Shredded tires lay around, and the matted pelt of a raccoon that had been mummified by the passing seasons. We kept up, flanking her.

"Clare," I said, "what is it? Just what in the hell exactly is it?" Her voice hissed. "I'm pregnant. All right?"

"Pregnant?"

"We're having a kid?" Bobby said. "You and me?"

"Shut up," she said. "Please just shut the fuck up. I don't want to have any goddamn baby."

"Yes you do."

"No. Oh, hell. I've let it go over three months now. I've never had morning sickness before. The other time I was pregnant, I had it taken care of before anything like this happened."

"You want to have the baby," Bobby said.

"No. I've just been, I don't know. Lazy and stupid."

"Yes. We can have it. We can all three have it."

"You're crazy. Do you know how crazy you are?"

"A kid," Bobby said to me. "Hey. We're having a kid."

"*We* are not having anything," she said. " *I* may be having a baby. Or I may not."

"Honey, are you sure?" I said.

"Oh, I'm very sure. I'm quite perfectly sure."

We were halfway across the field, headed nowhere. Nothing lay ahead but a line of bare, cement-colored trees bordering a second field. Still, Clare marched forward as if the answers to all her questions waited just past the horizon. Sun shone anemically through a thin gruel of cloud.

"Clare," Bobby said. "Stop."

She stopped. She looked around, and appeared to realize for the first time that she was in the middle of open country, with no reasonable destination at hand.

"I can't do it this way," she said. "I should either be in love with one person, or I should have a baby on my own."

"You're just scared," Bobby said.

"I wish I was. I'd rather be scared than furious. And embarrassed. I feel like such a fool. What would we do, sign up for birthing classes together? All three of us?"

"I guess so," I said. "Why not?"

"I'm not this unusual," she said. "It's just my hair."

She looked at Bobby and she looked at me, with an expression at once disdainful and imploring. She was forty, pregnant, and in love with two men at once. I think what she could not abide was the zaniness of her life. Like many of us, she had grown up expecting romance to bestow dignity and direction.

"Be brave," I told her. Bobby and I stood before her, confused and homeless and lacking a plan, beset by an aching but chaotic love that refused to focus in the conventional way. Traffic roared behind us. A truck honked its hydraulic horn, a monstrous, oceanic sound. Clare shook her head, not in denial but in exasperation. Because she could think of nothing else to do, she began walking again, more slowly, toward the row of trees.

PART III

PART III

BOBBY

THE CITY'S pleasures were too complicated for raising a kid. They were too wound up with rot. I thought so, and Jonathan did, too. Clare was less sure—she worried that the baby might grow up with its imagination damaged by too much ease.

"What if it turns out to be some sort of Heidi?" she said. "I don't want any child of mine growing up *too* good. I couldn't stand it."

I reminded her of what New York has ready for anyone too small or uninformed to do battle for a body-sized patch of air rights. I invented probability numbers about small-town schools and the effects of the color green on psychological development.

"And listen, growing up in the country doesn't doom anybody to good behavior anymore," Jonathan said. "Most of the really interesting murderers come from derelict farms and trailer parks."

"Well, all right," Clare finally said. "I guess everybody needs New York to escape *to*. If we raise the kid here, it'll just move to the country when it grows up."

And so we started making phone calls. We started driving up-state to look at property so strange or desolate we could afford it with Clare's inheritance money. Shopping for cheap real estate, you get an insider's look at daily human defeat. You smell the dank, vegetable smell of the outdoors working its way in through soggy wallboards, see ceilings and floors in a slow-motion state of ongoing collapse. You see how weather and decay win just by continuing, day after day, until the money runs out.

"We can't stop too long to think," Clare kept saying. "We have to keep looking. If we stop and think too long, I'm afraid I'll come to my senses."

After three weeks we found a two-story brown house five miles out of Woodstock, a place with a motherly, slightly insane dignity whose advantages mostly balanced its faults. Its walls stood on a solid foundation. The price was low—a desperation sale. Light from an alfalfa field floated through the rooms as if the passage of time was man's silliest delusion. Well water clear and cold as virtue itself flowed from the taps.

On the debit side, the wiring had disintegrated and the pipes had gone lacy with rust. The old pine floors were alive with dry rot and carpenter ants.

"At least this one has a soul," Jonathan said. "You know what I mean? I feel like it's not too late. This one isn't dead in the water yet."

Clare nodded. She ran her thumb along a doorjamb, and looked with critical uncertainty at her thumb.

"It feels right," I said. "Don't you get a feeling from this place?"

"Mm-hm," Clare said. "Nausea. Vertigo. Panic." She kept looking at her thumb.

We argued for a week, and bought the house. We bought the well and the afternoon light. We bought fifteen oaks, eight pines, a blackberry thicket, and a pair of graves so old the markers had been worn smooth as chalk. As Clare sat pregnant on a green vinyl chair signing the papers she said, "So long, Paris and Istanbul."

Jonathan added, "So long, Armani. So long, crocodile shoes." The two of them shared a sour little laugh. And then the deal was made. Clare had bought us all a fresh start with her dead grandfather's rhinestone fortune. By way of celebration, the real estate agent gave us complimentary white wine in white Styrofoam cups.

When we left our New York apartment we got rid of everything worn out or broken—nearly half our possessions. We put them out on the street as offerings for the people who were just arriving, full of hope, at the place we were about to leave. We watched from the window as passers-by carried things away. A woman took the lava lamp. Two skinheads and a fat tattooed girl took the swaybacked sofa covered in leopard-skin polyester.

"So long, treasures," Clare said. Her breath made a spool-shaped flicker of steam on the glass.

"So long, old garbage from thrift-store bins," Jonathan said. "Honey, there are times when nostalgia is simply not called for."

"I dragged that sofa down here from Sixty-seventh Street," she said. "Years ago, with Stephen Cooper and Little Bill. We'd carry the damn thing a few blocks, stop and sit on it, then walk another few blocks. It took us all night. Sometimes bag people would sit on it with us, and we'd all have a beer. We made a lot of friends that night."

"And now you're a homeowner and a mother-to-be," Jonathan said. "Did you really expect to scavenge around the streets of New York for the rest of your life?"

"Little Bill died," she said. "Did I tell you?"

"No."

"Corinne told me. He died in South Carolina, oh, at least a year ago. We'd all lost track of him."

"I'm sorry. Is Stephen all right?"

"Oh, Stephen's fine. He really did open a jewelry store up on Cape Cod. I suppose he's making a mint selling little gold whales and sea gulls to tourists."

"Well," Jonathan said. "That's good. I mean, at least he's alive."

"Mm-hm."

We watched the sofa travel down East Fourth Street. On the sidewalk below our window, a man and a woman in leather jackets whooped over Clare's old kitchen clock—a yellow plastic boomerang shape covered with pink-and-red electrons.

"I can't believe I let you talk me into throwing out the clock," she said. "I'm going to go down there and tell those people it was a mistake."

"Forget it," Jonathan said. "They'd kill you."

"Jonathan, that clock is a collector's item. It's worth money."

"Sweetie, it doesn't run," he said. "It doesn't tell time anymore. Let them have it."

She nodded, and watched numbly as the couple jogged away

toward First Avenue, passing the clock back and forth like a football. She stroked her pregnant belly. She breathed steam onto the glass.

That was over ten months ago. Now we live in a field facing the mountains. Spiky blue flowers climb through the slats of our fence. Bees drone in their ecstasy of daily work, and a milk-blue sky hangs raggedly behind the trees. These are old mountains. They've been worn down by wind and rain. They are not about anarchy or grandeur, like the more photogenic ranges. These mountains throw a smooth shadow—their crags don't imply the gnash of continental plates. They are evenly bearded with pine trees. They cut modest half-moons out of the sky.

"I hate scenery," Clare says. "It's so obvious." She is standing beside me in the unmowed grass. It's the first April of the new decade and she's a new Clare. She's sharper now, with more true bite under her jokes. You'd expect motherhood to have had a softening effect.

"Aw, come on," I tell her. "Get over it, huh?"

A pair of crows glide over the house. One lets out a raucous cry, like metal twisting on metal.

"Buzzards," Clare says. "Carrion-eaters. Waiting for the first of us to die of boredom."

I sing softly into her ear. I sing, "By the time we got to Woodstock, we were half a million strong, and everywhere there was song and celebration."

"Stop that," she says, batting the song away as if it was a taunting crow. Her silver bracelets click. "If there's one thing I never expected to end up as," she says, "it's an old hippie."

"There are, you know, worse things to end up as," I say.

"It's too late," she says. "The butterflies are turning back into bombers. Haven't you noticed? They're going to build condos on that mountain, take my word for it."

"I don't think they will. I don't think there'd be enough customers."

She looks at the mountains as if the future was written there in small, bright letters. She squints. For a moment she could be a country woman, all sinew and suspicion, and never mind about her lipstick or her chartreuse shirt. She could be my mother's mother, standing on the edge of her Wisconsin holdings and looking out disapprovingly at the vastness of what she doesn't own.

"As long as there are enough customers for the Home Café. Christ, I still can't believe we decided to call it that."

"People'll love it," I say.

"Oh, this is all just so weird. It's so outdated and—weird."

"Well, it sort of is," I say.

"No 'sort of' about it."

She is so bitter and hard, so much like her revised self, that a rogue spasm of happiness rises up in me. She's so real; so *Clare*. I do a quick, spastic dance. It has nothing to do with grace or the tight invisible laws of rhythm—I could be a small wooden man on a string. Clare rolls her eyes in a wifely way. There is room here for the daily peculiarities.

She says, "I'm glad one of us feels good about all this."

"Aw, darling, what's not to feel good about?" I say. "We're *something* now, I mean we won't just blow away if one of us takes a notion."

"It would be nice if that were true," she says.

"You know what I'd like to do someday? I'd like to fix up the shed as a separate little house, so Alice could move up here when she gets tired of the catering business."

"Oh, sure. Let's build a cottage for my old fourth-grade teacher, too."

"Clare?" I say.

"Mm-hm?"

"You really are happy here, aren't you? I mean, this is our life. Right?"

"Oh, sure it is. It's our life. You know me, I think in terms of complaint. It's how my mind works."

"Right," I say.

We stand watching the mountains, then turn to watch the house. This house is so old the spirits themselves have melted into the walls. It feels inhabited not by anyone's private unhappiness but by the collected days of ten generations, their meals and fights, their births and last gasps. Now, right now, it's a disreputable marriage of old and new disappointments. The floorboards are crumbling, and the remodeled kitchen seethes with orange linoleum and Spanish-style wood-like cabinets. We're going to fix it up, slowly, with the money we make from our restaurant. We are forces of order, come from the city with talents and tools and our belief in a generous future. Jonathan and Clare look at the house and see what it can become. They talk antique fixtures, eight-over-eights, a limestone mantel rescued from a house in Hudson and trucked up here. Although I wouldn't fight progress I like the house as it is, with bug-riddled floors and wood-grain chemical paneling that looks like sorrow and laziness made into a domestic fixture. Sitting on its four overgrown acres, the house answers the elderly mountains. It, too, is docile and worn smooth. It has been humbled by time.

"I've been thinking," Clare says. "What if we painted the windowpanes blue? Like a cobalt blue, you know? Do you think that'd look too cutesy?"

"Ask Jonathan," I answer. "He's the one who knows about things like that."

She nods. "Bobby?" she says.

"Uh-huh?"

"Oh, I don't know. I walk around the place and I feel like I'm standing on an airplane wing. At thirty thousand feet. I guess I want you and Jonathan to think this is as strange as I do."

From the house, the baby starts crying. "That's what really does it," Clare says. "I've always just made my own mistakes, I never had to worry about somebody else like this before."

"It's okay," I tell her. "Everything's fine and perfect. Trust me. Okay?"

She nods uncertainly. She keeps losing the battle to decide instead of worry. Worry is part of what makes her short-tempered; she is trying to develop a personality to match her worst expectations.

"Let's go see how Jonathan's doing with her," she says.

"Okay. Sure."

We go into the house together. The door opens straight into the living room, a big shabby rectangle still papered in scowling red eagles and blue drums. At this time of day it's filled with squares of light that slant in from three sides. Jonathan is walking a circle with Rebecca propped on his shoulder. She wails, a series of short piercing cries like mortified hiccups.

"Mystery tantrum," he says. "Her diaper's fine, and she just ate half an hour ago."

"Let me try with her," Clare says.

Jonathan fails to hide his reluctance. He dislikes giving the baby up, even to her own dreams. But when Clare holds out her arms he passes her over.

Clare folds her in, whispers to her. "Hey, sweetheart," she says. "What's the matter? Just a little fit of existential despair?"

Rebecca is a twenty-pound being with feathery hair and dark, furious eyes. Already, at eleven months, she has a nature. She is prone to contemplation. She resists both laughter and sorrow until they overwhelm her, and then she gives herself up completely.

Clare walks the living room with her, whispering. She speaks to the baby the same way she speaks to Jonathan or me, in full sentences, but she speaks to the baby without an undercurrent of rage.

"Now, Miss Rebecca," she says, "you're not being reasonable. But, hey, why should you be? Lord, if I ever start nagging you to be reasonable, will you shoot me, please?"

Jonathan watches in an ecstasy of edgy affection. Parenthood has brought several surprises—the biggest is his tortured devotion. Clare and I are calmer in the face of Rebecca's fragility and her unending needs. Jonathan hasn't rested since she entered the world. He is a living illustration of love's power to unsettle our nerves.

Now he has something vital to lose. Now there is a small victim for every tragic story he can tell himself.

Rebecca won't be quiet, and we take her outside. She is lost in crying the way a motorboat gets lost in sound and spray. We walk the property with her, and let her cries dissipate in the noon air. Jonathan picks a daisy. He twirls it in front of her pinched red face.

"Hey, kid," he says. "Hey. Take a look at this amazing, unprecedented thing here." Of all her qualities, Jonathan is most in love with her capacity for amazement. He almost weeps when she stares goggle-eyed at a yarn ball or a teaspoon cupping the sun. But she keeps crying, right into the daisy.

"Can't be bought with flowers," Clare says. There is true pride in her voice. If Jonathan loves her for being the world's best audience, Clare loves her stubborn insistence on her own mysteries.

We walk into the stand of trees behind the house. Here, in the endless shade, there is no grass to speak of. There is only forest trash—pine cones and shed branches, the droppings of deer. We walk among the silent trees with Rebecca's noise trailing behind us like a glittery scarf.

Clare asks, "Did you boys call the plumber today?"

"Yep," Jonathan says. "He can't fit us in until two weeks from Tuesday. Why don't you let me try with her again?"

"Shit. This house isn't going to be done until the next century. You know that, don't you?"

"No big rush," Jonathan says. "Come here, Rebecca."

He reaches for her, but Clare maintains her hold. "No big rush," she says. "So we'll just keep heating water on the stove for the rest of our lives?"

"We're pioneers," Jonathan says. "Can't expect all the suburban comforts right off the bat."

"I think," she says, "that both of you are some kind of retards. I honestly do."

She holds the baby close and hurries ahead of us, deeper into the woods. Bars of light, fractured by pine boughs, hang stodgily. Jonathan takes off after her, as if he believes she might be planning to take Rebecca and raise her alone in the wild.

Our restaurant will open in less than a week. Jonathan and I work all day, finishing it up. It's nothing grand, just a nine-table restaurant in a former saloon. We've reformed the saloon like a pair of mail-order brides newly arrived on the frontier. We've painted it white, and hung striped curtains. Jonathan has covered the walls with old photos: school pictures of kids in bow ties and pinafores, men and women in plaid Bermuda shorts posing sunburned beside a lake, somebody's grandmother shoveling snow. He's hung a record-breaking salmon caught in 1957 and a shelf full of trophies. On the trophies bright gold men and women, sexlessly naked as angels, act out human excellence in bowling, golf, badminton, and citizenship. This will be a simple place, just breakfast and lunch. We've bought unmatched tables and chairs from the same secondhand stores where we found the trophies and photographs and the lacquered salmon.

"Come on down, everybody," Jonathan says. "The Homo Café is just about open for business." He daubs white paint over a scar on the molding. He is wearing overalls, with his hair tied back in a ponytail.

I'm in the kitchen, loading five-pound jars of preserves and ketchup onto the shelves. "They didn't send strawberry jam," I say. "They sent, like, half boysenberry and half peach."

"I'll call up and yell at them. They probably think they can send us whatever they're trying to get rid of, just because we don't know what we're doing."

When the jars are all stacked on the shelves I stand at the counter, watching Jonathan paint. "Clare thinks we should think what we're doing is strange," I say.

"It *is*," he says. "Who thinks it isn't strange?"

"Well, I guess she thinks we should be more upset about it."

"She's just anxious because she's paying the bills. She's waited all her life to get this money, and now, wham, it's being spent."

"It's being, you know, in*vest*ed," I say.

"Right. She has been sort of a pain in the ass lately, hasn't she?"

"Oh, I don't know if I'd say that."

"I'll say it. Clare has been a bitch for a long time now. Really, since she got pregnant."

"Well, you know," I say. I punch a new cassette into the sound system. Jimi Hendrix sings "Are You Experienced?"

"I guess she'll be okay," Jonathan says. "Motherhood is hard on all of us. I know it's hard on me."

I get a paintbrush and help with the touch-ups. Jimi puts out his velvet growl, a living voice from the world of the dead, as

Jonathan and I cover the last nicks. We sway to the music. There is some kind of small perfection in this, painting a wall together while Jimi sings. There is a knitting of times, the past tumbling into the future. It comes to me suddenly, in the form of a surprise: I've got what I wanted. A brother to work beside. A revised future shining like a light bulb over our heads.

Here is what's unsayable about us: Jonathan and I are members of a team so old nobody else could join even if we wanted them to. We adore Clare but she's not quite on the team. Not really. What binds us is stronger than sex. It is stronger than love. We're related. Each of us is the other born into different flesh. We may love Clare but she is not us. Only we can be ourselves and one another at the same time. I daub paint over an old scar. The tinted faces of grade-school kids, all in their forties or fifties now, look out from the walls with toothy, clear-eyed optimism.

Later we lock up the restaurant and go to our car by way of the main street. I prefer walking through the middle of things—I'm the one who likes town. I've been on my way to Woodstock since I was nine and now, more than twenty years later, I've arrived. My brother was right—there are still people here. The concert, I've learned, happened sixty miles away, in a broad grassy field that is no more or less than that. An empty space ringed by green-black trees. Jonathan and I tried swimming in the chocolate-colored pond while Clare sat with Rebecca in the weeds, but mosquitoes drove us all back to our car. We ended up having lunch at what Clare believed was the same place she went with her husband-to-be when they fled the actual concert. She said the hamburgers would come with three pickles and a sealed ketchup envelope, and they did.

Woodstock is what towns were supposed to become before the old future got sidetracked and a new one took its place. Bearded romantics still strum guitars in the town square, still dreaming of themselves as forest creatures and apprentice magicians. Old ladies with their gray hair frizzy and loose nod in time on the benches. Clare calls it pathetic and Jonathan doesn't pay close attention one way or the other, but I appreciate the kindness of its quiet streets and the people's cheerful determination to live in ways that are mainly beside the point.

Jonathan and I drive home in our used Toyota, up and down the rises, with branch shadows flicking across the windshield. He sits low in the passenger seat, his sneakers propped on the dashboard. "I'll tell you what's really strange about all this," he says. "What's really, truly strange is the fact that we're doing it at all. People say they're going to move to the country and open a little café, but who actually does it?"

"We did," I say. "We are."

When we top the last hill, I hit the brakes. "What is it?" Jonathan asks.

"Nothing," I tell him. "I just want to look for a second."

From where I've stopped we can see our old brown house raising its chimney among a riot of junipers. Three dormered windows catch the light that will soon slip away behind the mountains, and the ivy that has grown unchecked for decades flutters, the leaves showing their silver undersides. The house has stood for more than a century without giving in to the landscape. No vines have snaked their way through the masonry, no underground lake has increased its boundaries by seeping into the foundation. Although I usually sing it to tease Clare, now I sing the Woodstock song to Jonathan, with a half-serious attitude that is all the pleasanter for being only half. "We are stardust, we are golden, and we've got to get ourselves back to the garden." He listens to a few bars, and joins in.

At dinner, we talk about the restaurant and the baby. Lately our lives are devoted to the actual—we worry over Rebecca's cough and the delivery of our used-but-refurbished walk-in refrigerator. I am beginning to understand the true difference between youth and age. Young people have time to make plans and think of new ideas. Older people need their whole energy to keep up with what's already been set in motion.

"I don't like Dr. Glass," Clare says. She is sitting beside Rebecca's high chair, spooning vanilla pudding into Rebecca's mouth. Between each bite Rebecca looks suspiciously at the spoon, double-checking the contents. She has inherited my appetite but has also inherited Clare's skepticism. She is both hungry and watchful.

"Why not?" I ask.

"Well, he's a *hippie*. And he can't be more than thirty-five. I'd just rather take Rebecca to an old fart. You know, somebody in sensible shoes who got your mother and all her sisters and brothers through things like smallpox and polio when they were kids. When Glass tells me not to worry about these coughing fits I keep thinking, 'I'm being told this by a man in Birkenstocks.' "

"I agree," Jonathan says. "Glass does Tai Chi. I'd rather find somebody who plays golf."

"Glass seems okay to me," I say. "I mean, I like him. You can talk to him."

Jonathan says, "I suppose what it really gets down to is, you want your baby's doctor to be some sort of fatherly type. You know? Someone who seems unaffected by trends."

"Amen," Clare says. "Tomorrow I'm going out looking for a new pediatrician."

"I really think Glass is fine," I say.

Clare holds a spoonful of pudding an inch from Rebecca's open mouth. "I want to try someone else," she says. "I'm nervous about Glass, I think he's too easygoing. Okay?"

"Well. Okay," I say.

"Okay." She slips the spoon into Rebecca's mouth with smooth, practiced accuracy. Clare is turning herself into the Mom character from our Henderson days. We don't talk about the Hendersons anymore, maybe because the difference between our actual lives and their hypothetical ones has shrunk below the measuring point.

Later, after we've put Rebecca to bed, we watch television together. It's what there is to do at night, with a baby, in the country. We lie on the queen-size bed, surrounded by corn chips and beer and Diet Coke. The upstairs bedrooms are snug and dark. Their ceilings follow the curve of the roof. The last owners—the ones who did the downstairs in eagle wallpaper and Spanish-style cabinetry—must have run out of money at the stairwell. Up here the shabbiness has more patina. The wallpaper in this room swarms with faded carnivorous-looking flowers, and the venetian blinds dangle from frayed cords the color of strong tea. Clare flips around the channels. We have cable here, a powerful magnet that sucks down each invisible impulse passing overhead. Along with the normal stations we get strip shows from New York, Mexican soap operas, Japanese women gleefully demonstrating inventions so complex that only other inventions can fully appreciate them. Occasionally we tune in a hesitant, snowy channel that is almost frightening—it looks like men and women walking, just walking, through an empty field. It could be a transmission we've picked up by mistake, something from a world we aren't meant to see.

"A hundred and twenty stations and there's still nothing to watch," Clare says.

"Nothing on TV tonight, let's fuck," Jonathan says.

Clare looks at him with her brows arched and her eyes dark. "You two fuck," she says.

Jonathan jumps on her and simulates frantic, rabbit-like copulation. "Oh baby oh baby oh baby," he moans.

"Off," she says. "Get off me. Really. Go jump on Bobby."

"Ooh baby," Jonathan says.

"Bobby, make him stop," she says.

I shrug, powerless. "I'll scream," she says. "I'll call the police."

"And tell them what?" Jonathan asks.

"That I'm being held prisoner in this house by two men. That they lured me here for purposes of breeding, and force me to live in a perpetual 1969."

"You've done the breeding," Jonathan says. "If that were your only purpose here, we'd be through with you by now."

"The baby still needs milk, doesn't she?" Clare says. "And the house needs a momma. Doesn't it?"

Jonathan pauses a moment, considering. "Naw," he says. "You're free to go." He rolls off of her and picks up the remote-control box. "Let's see if there's anything good coming in from Jupiter tonight."

"If I go," Clare says, "I'm taking the kid."

"Oh no you're not," he answers. Then he remembers to adjust his voice. "She's everybody's," he says more gently.

Clare leans back, cocks her head in my direction. "Bobby?"

"Uh-huh?"

"I'd like to know the secret of your imperturbable calm. Here we are in the middle of a highly peculiar and unorthodox arrangement, in a house that could fall down around us at any moment, Jonathan and I are bickering over possession of my child—"

"*Our* child," Jonathan says. "Really, Clare, you've got to stop with this *yours* business."

"Over possession of our baby," she says, "and you just sit here like Dagwood Bumstead. Sometimes I think *you're* what's coming in from Jupiter."

"I guess I am," I say. "I mean, none of this seems all that strange to me."

She looks up at the ceiling, her eyes dilated to black disks. "I should have known," she says. "I should have figured it out the first moment I saw you, with blow-dried hair and Calvin Klein jeans. And then you could switch practically overnight to East Village hip. It's so funny. It turns out Jonathan and I are the conservative ones. We're the ones who need to look in the mirror and know what we're going to see from day to day. You can just do anything, can't you?"

"No," I tell her. "I can't just do anything."

"Name me something. Name something you wouldn't do."

"Um, well, I wouldn't be alone. I haven't been, you know, by myself since I was a kid."

"That's it," she says. "You're a company man, aren't you? You mirror everybody's desires. Oh, why didn't I think of this before? When you lived with Jonathan's parents you were a nice Ohio boy, when you lived in the East Village you were cool, and now that we live in the country you're this sweet sort of hippie-dad figure. You just give people whatever they want. Don't you?"

"I don't know," I say.

There are things I can't tell her, things I wouldn't know how to say. I am part of the living and part of the dead. I am living for more people than just myself.

"Oh, Clare," Jonathan says from the foot of the bed. "What are you all of a sudden, some sort of Nancy Drew of the psyche?

Do you really think you can sum Bobby up in a sentence like that?"

"You go sentence by sentence in this life," she says.

I reach over and stroke Clare's hair. I try to kiss her troubled lips.

"Boys, boys," she says, pulling away from my kiss. "What a perverse crew we are. What a deeply weird bunch."

"We're really, you know, not much weirder than any family," I say. "At least we love each other. Didn't you say that first?"

"Maybe I did. About a thousand years ago."

I look into her scared, aging face. I think I know what frightens Clare—a certain ability to invent our own futures has been lost. Now we are following a plan that got made in a haphazard way along a highway in Pennsylvania. Now the good things are the predictable ones, and surprises mean bad news.

I put my lips on hers again. This time she returns the kiss. Jonathan continues flipping channels, lazily half-watching.

CLARE

I NEVER expected this, a love so ravenous it's barely personal. A love that displaces you, pushes you out of shape. I knew that if I was crossing the street with the baby and a car screamed around the corner, horn blaring, I'd shield her with my body. I'd do it automatically, the way you protect your head or heart by holding up your arms. You defend your vital parts with your tougher, more expendable ones. In that way, motherhood worked as promised. But I found that I loved her without a true sense of charity or goodwill. It was a howling, floodlit love; a frightening thing. I would shield her from a speeding car but I'd curse her as I did it, like a prisoner cursing the executioner.

Rebecca's mouth worked to form the word "Momma." She fretted whenever I left her. Someday she'd pay a fortune to therapists for their help in solving the mystery of my personality. There would be plenty of material—a mother living with two men, intricately in love with both of them. An undecided, disorganized woman who fell out of every conventional arrangement. Who dragged her own childhood along with her into her forties. I'd been just a private, slipshod person going about my business and now I was on my way to becoming the central riddle in another person's life.

Being a mother was the weighted, unsettling thing. Being a

lover—even an unorthodox lover—was tame and ordinary by comparison.

Maybe that was the secret my own mother discovered. She'd thought my wild, undisciplined father would prove to be her life's adventure. And then she'd given birth.

We worked out a variation on the classic arrangement, we three. Bobby and Jonathan went to the café before sunrise every morning, I stayed home with Rebecca. I didn't want a business. Eventually I'd start making jewelry again, or some other little thing. The restaurant was the boys' project, a way for them to support themselves and begin paying me back. They were good, uncomplaining workers. Or, Bobby was a good, uncomplaining worker and Jonathan more or less followed his example. They left the house at five o'clock every morning, just as the darkness was beginning to turn, and didn't come back until four or five in the afternoon, when the dark was already working its way back into the corners of the house. To be honest, I didn't know too much about their work lives. Bobby cooked, Jonathan was the waiter, and a sweet dim-witted boy from town bussed tables and did the dishes. Although I listened to their stories—furious customers, kitchen fixtures that blew up or caught fire in the middle of the lunch rush, wildly improbable thefts (someone stole the stuffed salmon right off the wall, someone else took the seat off the toilet in the women's room)—it all seemed to happen in a remote, slightly unliving realm of anecdote. I felt for the boys. But to me their single, salient characteristic was an eleven- or twelve-hour daily absence. Real life, the heart and heft of it, was what happened during the hours they were gone.

For years, for most of my recollected life, I'd walked carefully over a subterranean well of boredom and hopelessness that lay just beneath the thin outer layer of my imagination. If I'd stood still too long, if I'd given in to repose, I'd have fallen through. So I'd made things, gone to clubs and movies. I'd kept changing my hair.

Now, with Rebecca to care for, each moment had an electrified

275

gravity that was not always pleasant but ran right down to the core. Sometimes I grew bored—babies aren't always interesting —but always, in another minute or hour, she would need something only I could provide. It seemed that every day she developed a new gesture or response that carried her that much closer to her own eventual personality. From hour to hour, she kept turning more fully into somebody. The hours were stitched together, and nothing limp or hopeless ever threatened to unravel the day. I bathed Rebecca, fed her, mopped up her shit. I played with her. I showed her what I could of the world.

All right, I liked it best when the boys were gone. Once they came home, a sense of continuing emergency was lost. Weary as they were, they told me to relax while they attended to Rebecca. They were being good, responsible fathers. I knew I should feel appreciative. But I didn't want to relax. I wanted to be stretched and beset. I wanted to be frantically busy with Rebecca every waking moment, and then fall into a sleep black and shapeless as the unlived future.

Bobby loved our daughter but was not tormented by her vulnerable, noisy existence. In a world with more room in it he might have been a settler, with visions of reinventing society on a patch of ground far from the site of the old mistakes. He had that religious quality. He was soft-hearted and intensely focused. He was not deeply interested in the flesh. Sometimes when he held Rebecca I knew how he saw her—as a citizen in his future world. He respected her for swelling the local population but did not agonize over particulars of her fate. In his eyes, she was part of a movement.

Bobby and I slept together in a new queen-size bed. Rebecca's room was the next down the hall, followed by the bathroom and Jonathan's room. Bobby's days were unrelenting. He flipped eggs and baked pies, fought with suppliers. He came home to Rebecca's cries and dirty diapers. At night he slept the sleep of the exhausted and depleted—a desperate unconsciousness. I was grateful for his waning interest in sex, not only because I was tired also but because my nipples had turned brown from Rebecca's nursing. Three yellow stretch marks stitched their way from my bottom rib to my crotch. I was forty-one. I couldn't feel pretty anymore. If Bobby had been more ardent or high-strung, if he'd shamefacedly confessed that I repelled him now, I'd have had something to work from. I might have started on a new kind of defiant pride. But he was himself, a charitable, hardworking man. We slept peacefully together.

Jonathan generated more static electricity as he ran through his days. If Bobby moved with the methodical, slightly bovine will of a vacuum cleaner, sucking up each errand and task, Jonathan clattered along like an eggbeater. He was manic and flushed, vague-eyed from lack of rest. He and Bobby both told me that, as a waiter, he offered charm in place of competence. Water glasses went unfilled. Eggs ordered scrambled arrived sunnyside up. He said there were moments during the breakfast rush when he actually seemed to fall asleep while moving. One moment he'd be filling a cream pitcher and the next he'd be standing beside a table, in the middle of taking an order, with no recollection of the intervening time. Soon he and Bobby would hire a waitress, and Jonathan would become the host and backup errand boy. "I'll make sure everybody's happy," he said. "I'll pour them more coffee and ask about their hometowns. We'll hire a specialist to see that they actually get what they order."

His true vocation was the baby. Every evening after work he brought her something: a plastic doll from the dime store, a rose from somebody's garden, a pair of miniature white sunglasses. He took her for long walks before dinner and read to her after.

Around four in the morning he'd wake her, change her diaper, and bring her to Bobby's and my bed. He was comically paternal in boxer shorts, carrying our sleepy child. "I know it borders on child abuse, getting her up like this," he said. "But we need to see her before we go off to bake the bread." He'd crawl into bed beside me, holding Rebecca on his lap. Some mornings she whined sleepily in the lamplight. Some mornings she chuckled and mouthed unintelligible words. "Miss Rebecca," Jonathan would whisper. "Oh, you're a fine thing, aren't you? Mm-hm. Oh yes. Look at those hands. You'll be a tennis player, huh? Or a violinist, or a human fly." He kept up a stream of talk, an unwavering flow. Sometimes when she cried, only Jonathan could comfort her. She'd wail in my arms, and buck and shriek in Bobby's. But when Jonathan took her she'd quiet down. She'd stare at him with eyes that were greedy and surprisingly hard. She clung to him because he was elusive and because, during his hours at home, he took the most elaborate, courtly care of her. Even that early, I believe she was falling in love.

Rebecca and I shared a more nervous kind of love. While the boys were away, she and I lived together in a state of constant need. She needed and, with growing vehemence, resented my protection. I only needed her safety but I needed it completely, all the time. I had to know she was all right, every minute. It took its toll on both of us. Sometimes when we were together, when I checked the temperature of her bathwater or snatched a pencil out of her mouth, I could almost feel the question crackling in the air around us—*What if I fail to protect?* We could grow irritable together. I could be short-tempered with her, and bossy; I could deny her too much. She was addicted to my fears. She wept if I watched her too closely, and wept if she realized that for a moment I'd forgotten to watch her at all.

I was beginning to understand something about my mother. She'd made a choice after I was born. There wasn't room in the house or in her parsimonious nature for two difficult children. She'd been forced to choose. Maybe that was how the battle started. My father had had to fight for a share. He'd used his best weapons, his sex and recklessness, but my mother had prevailed with her powers of organization and rectitude. I'd loved my father more. He'd called me Peg and Scarlett O'Hara, said it was all right to buy anything we wanted. But toward the end, when he fell cursing on the front lawn and drunkenly broke furniture, I'd turned away from him. Finally, a child will choose order over passion or charm.

As a grown woman I'd fallen in love with Jonathan's intelligence and humor and, I suppose, with his harmlessness. He was neither frigid nor dangerous. Neither man nor woman. There was no threat of failure through sex. Now I saw how Rebecca, too, would one day fall in love with him. He had a father's allure. He had a mother's warmth without the implied threat—she would not die if Jonathan briefly lost track of her. He worked all day and then came home with a present in his hands, flushed with the sheer excitement of seeing her after so many hours' separation. Bobby was sweetly remote and I was too constant. Jonathan exerted a steady charm made perfect by his daily absence. Rebecca would be his. She'd care for Bobby and me but she'd belong to Jonathan.

There were times—moments—when I believed I had in fact found my reward. I had love, and a place on earth. I was part of something sweetened and buffered. A family. It was what I'd thought I wanted. My own family had crackled with jealousy and rage. Not a single one of my parents' wedding gifts survived. We'd devoured the past. Now nothing was left to inherit but the improvements my mother had made, the gilt fixtures and floral prints, after my father went off to quit drinking and find Christ and then start drinking again.

But at other times I missed the violent wrongheadedness of my own family. We'd been difficult people, known around the neighborhood: Poor Amelia Stuckart and That Man She Married. I'd grown famous in our suburb for being Their Poor Little Girl. I'd based my early self-inventions on the concepts of deprivation and pride. I'd worn the shortest skirts, teased my hair into a brittle storm. I'd fucked my first skinny bass player at fourteen, in the back of a van. The local forces of order made it easy for me by wearing lumpy bras and girlish hairdos, by slathering their jowls with Aqua Velva. They said, "Join us in our world," and I found a drug dealer for a boyfriend. I watched myself shrink in the eyes of the counselors and the pastors—*perhaps, in fact, Mrs. Rollins, this one is beyond our help*. I went to school with a pint of tequila in my purse. I shot through the frozen Rhode Island nights sizzling on speed. I left a vapor trail behind. People who've been well cared for can't imagine the freedom there is in being bad.

Now, late in life, I'd been rescued. The boys came straight home every night, took care of Rebecca, cooked our dinner. Their love wasn't immaculate. They may have loved one another more than they loved me. They may have been using me without quite knowing it. I could live with that. I didn't mind touching the rough bottom of people's good intentions. What I had trouble with sometimes was the simple friendliness of it. We lived in a world of kindness and domestic order. I sometimes thought of myself as Snow White living among the dwarfs. The dwarfs took good care of her. But how long would she have lasted there without the hope of meeting someone life-sized? How long would she have swept and mended before she began to see her life as composed of safe haven and subtle but pervasive lacks?

ALICE

WHEN I summoned Jonathan to Arizona, I didn't mention the parcel I had for him. It wasn't the sort of gift to talk about over the telephone. I simply exercised my motherly prerogative and demanded a visit. I wasn't generally much trouble to him, and he had always suffered from an exaggerated sense of his own culpability. I suspect he wished I would burden him more. I think he'd have found some relief in a beleaguered, badgering mother. Given his nature, he had little choice but to obey when I called and said I wanted to see him. "The desert's lovely this time of year," I said. "Please come out for a few days." And he did.

I met him at the Phoenix airport. Country life hadn't changed him much. Since he'd left for college more than ten years earlier, and I'd grown accustomed to going months without seeing him, I had learned a new objectivity. As a little boy he'd seemed like an invention of mine, and I'd loved him with a stinging, tangled intensity that hurt me at times. It was as if the part of me I felt tenderest toward, the little wounded part that wanted only to cry and be held, had been cut out and now lived separately, beyond my powers of consolation. His existence compelled and distressed me so much that I scarcely knew what he looked like. Now I loved him less dreadfully, from a deeper reserve of calm, and I could see him better in his human particulars. Among the disembarking passengers at the airport he was pale and pretty but unfinished-looking; as he aged I began to see that he stood in danger of growing old without acquiring a visible aspect of repose. Unmarked and boyish, with a boy's equine beauty, he was taking on the perennially fresh, untried quality that can lead an old man to look like a shocked, ancient child. I waved from among those waiting and he made his way toward me, chipper and a little haunted-looking, threading gingerly through the crowd as if he suspected it might be full of enemies in disguise.

"Hi, Mom."

"Hello, my dear."

We embraced, inquired after one another's health and happiness, and started for the car. On the way he asked me, "How's business?"

"Booming," I said. "I'm getting more calls than I can handle, but I hate to turn anybody away at this stage. I've been trying to hire another cook. But it's hard to find anybody who'll do things the way I like them done."

"I'm proud of you," he said. "Who ever expected you to turn into a catering mogul?"

"Watch yourself, now. Don't get patronizing."

"I'm not being patronizing. When did you get so thin-skinned?"

"Oh, don't mind me," I said. "Nerves, I guess. I've never had a business at all, much less a successful one. I keep thinking something will happen and it will all just come apart."

"Don't worry. Or is that being patronizing too? *Do* worry. Awful things happen to the nicest people."

"True," I said. "Entirely true. How's your own business?"

"Insane. It seems like we're always there, and everything is always right on the verge of total madness. But we're breaking even. On our busiest days we even make a little money."

"Good," I said. "It's a tough field. Breaking even your first year means you're succeeding."

"I guess. I keep waking up in the middle of the night, thinking, 'I forgot to take table five their coffee.' "

"Welcome to the front lines," I said.

When we reached the car, we had a small cordial tussle over who would drive. I preferred to, since I knew the way, but a grown son doesn't care to be chauffeured by his mother even on her home ground. I tossed him the keys, for his comfort's sake.

We drove along the flat bright highway, talking of ordinary things. The sun, which was not too merciless at that time of year, shone on the flowering yuccas and the exquisite charcoal-gray tangles of mesquite. I thought without envy of the drizzle and blear that prevailed just then in the East. The desert, I'd found, had a beauty too severe to sink immediately into your skin. Its nearest geographical relative was the glacier—like a glacier it could fool the uninitiated into mistaking its slow turning for stasis. We who lived there loved it for its simplicity and cleanliness, its daily suggestion of the everlasting. A forested landscape came to seem both crowded and ephemeral, sweet enough but far too young, and subject to unpredictable turns of fortune. It is no accident that the first civilizations arose in deserts. It is no accident that the elderly often return there.

"You look great," Jonathan said as he drove. "I like what you did to your hair."

"Well, I have to make an appearance now," I said. "I can't stumble around town like the wild woman of the mountains anymore. To tell you the truth, I've found a barber. A men's barber. Most of the women's salons out here still insist on giving you these poofy lacquered *hairdos*, and I've got no interest in that. I have it cut once every three or four weeks, and don't think about it otherwise."

"I love it," he said. "My mother is a catering mogul with a crew cut. I'm not being patronizing. I'm being appreciative."

He pulled in at the condominium, and carried his bag into the house. "Place hasn't changed," he said.

"It's just lost a little more ground to the forces of entropy," I said. "I meant to get it whipped into slightly better shape before you got here. But a good steady client of mine called with a last-minute dinner party, so I spent yesterday making shrimp with cilantro pesto instead of vacuuming and dusting."

"It's okay. Our house in Cleveland was always a little too orderly, to tell you the truth. I mean, I'm glad to know you're not out here cleaning all the time."

"That's the least of your worries. Believe me."

Because he'd be sleeping on the fold-out couch, there was no unpacking to do. He simply set his suitcase in a corner. As he did so, I was overtaken by nervousness—I'd brought him all the way to Arizona for such a strange purpose. Perhaps I'd pass it off as a simple visit after all. Feed him, buy him a few new articles of clothing over his protests, and send him home again.

"Are you hungry?" I asked.

"A little. I didn't eat the lunch they served on the plane. At a certain point in my flying career I realized I could just refuse the tray when they brought it. I still feel reckless doing it, though. Like I'm throwing away money."

"Why don't we go out for a late lunch?" I said. "I've found a marvelous place about ten miles from here, where they make their tortillas from scratch. I'd love to hire their cook away from them, have somebody who really knows traditional Mexican cooking, but I don't think I could pay her enough."

"Sounds great," he said. "Let's go."

For a moment he was so like his father that I stopped and stared at him, the blood ringing in my head. All mothers must experience such moments, when their grown children—who have seemed to depart irrevocably into their own personalities—suddenly reveal a strain of their father's nature so pure and undiluted they might be the man himself, reborn, right down to the three-note cough that has punctuated the past forty-plus years. What I saw in Jonathan just then was Ned's easy, boneless willingness; his urge to be pleasantly enthusiastic and to keep things rolling along. If I'd been a different sort of person, a braver sort, I'd have taken him by the shoulders and said, "Want whatever you want more fiercely. Be more difficult and demanding. Or you'll never make a life that uses you."

Instead, I took the car keys from him and said, "I'd better drive this time. Even I'm not sure exactly how to get to this place, and I've been a dozen times."

We spent the next two days talking and eating and going to movies. I gave him the tour of my rented kitchen and makeshift office, introduced him to my staff of three. I inquired after his life as well, although I wasn't always sure how to phrase my questions. "How's the baby?" was the most obvious opening.

"She's fine," he said over a margarita. "She's amazing. Sometimes it seems like she's changing a little every day. I'm beginning to understand why people have a half dozen kids—it's hard to realize that now she can crawl, and she'll never be quite so helpless again. It's a relief, too. But I can see how you'd want to have another one just for the sake of seeing somebody else through that incredibly helpless period again."

"And you spend a good deal of time with her?" I asked.

"Of course. Of course I do. I'm her father. I'm one of her fathers."

I shook my head. "Maybe I don't quite get it," I said.

"What's to get? You've been there, you've seen us all together. We're three people who have a baby. What's the big deal?"

"No big deal," I said. "I guess I'm just old-fashioned."

"You're not old-fashioned. Not with a haircut like that."

"Well, all right. I worry that you're being exploited in all this. Bobby and Clare have each other. What have you got?"

This was delicate ground. We'd never formally acknowledged his proclivities—other than Bobby, I'd never met a liaison of his. As far as I knew, he didn't have them. And here's the awful truth: I preferred it that way. If he'd insisted on it, I'd have tried to accommodate a mental image of my son engaged in sexual acts with other men. But he wasn't prone to insistence. He paid his visits in the guise of a chaste bachelor, and his father and I had always been willing to receive him as such. If life was failing to mark him in some way, I suppose we must have played our part.

"We've all got each other," he said. "Mom, you're right. You're not getting it. Maybe we should talk about something else."

"If you like. Just tell me this. You're happy doing what you're doing?"

"Yes. I'm ecstatic. And I'm part of something. I'm part of a family and a business. We're building a home together. You get too caught up in the fact that we don't look exactly like an ordinary family."

"All right. I'll try not to get too caught up in that."

And, after a moment, we moved on to other subjects. I could have responded to confessions of unorthodox love, if he'd chosen to make them. But I could not demand such candor. I simply couldn't. It would be his move to make.

I didn't get around to my own business until the night before his departure. We had eaten in—I'd made a simple avocado vinaigrette and done salmon steaks on the grill. After the plates were cleared away I started coffee and said, "Jonathan, dear, there's a reason I asked you to come this time. There's something I want to give you."

His eyes quickened—he must have thought I had a family treasure put away for him. For a moment I could see him perfectly at the age of four, precociously well mannered but beside himself with greed in a toy store, where no acquisition was too lavish to lie beyond imagining.

"What is it?" he asked, his eagerness politely concealed.

I sighed. If I'd had a quilt or a gold watch I'd have given it to him instead, but neither Ned nor I had ever saved things like that. We both came from families more interested in the future than in the past. I went upstairs to the bedroom without speaking, got the box out of my dresser and brought it down.

He knew what it was. "Oh, Mom," he said.

I set it gently on the table, a smooth wooden rectangle with a brass plaque that bore Ned's full name and his dates. "It's time for you to take charge of this," I said. "That was your father's one request. That you decide about disposal."

He nodded. He looked at the box but did not touch it. "I know," he said. "He told me."

"Have you been thinking about it?" I asked.

"Sure. Sure I have. Mom, that's part of why I'm doing what I'm doing. I'm trying to make some kind of home."

"I see." I sat down beside him. We both watched the box as if we suspected it might move on its own.

"Have you looked inside?" he asked.

"Yes. At first I thought I couldn't stand to. Then as time passed I realized I couldn't stand not to."

"And?"

"It's sooty. Yellowish-gray. There's more than you'd think. I'd imagined just a handful, something talcumy you could toss into the wind with one hand. But it's not like that, there's quite a lot. There are some little slivers of bone, dark, like old ivory. Honey, I can tell you this—it's no more of your father than a pair of his old shoes would be. Do you want to look?"

"No. Not right now."

"All right."

"Why are you giving this to me now?" he asked. "I mean, well, exactly that. Why now?"

I hesitated. Here was the truth: I had started seeing someone. He was younger than I, his name was Paul Martinez, and he'd begun teaching me a range of pleasures I had hardly imagined while married to Ned.

It seemed I was living my life in reverse. With Ned I had had order and sanctuary, the serenity one hopes for in old age. Now, at the onset of my true old age, I seemed to be falling in love with an argumentative dark-skinned man who played the guitar and kissed me in spots Ned had hesitated even to call by their names. I felt wrong about having his ashes in the house now.

But all I said to Jonathan was "I'm afraid I'm turning into Morticia Addams, with my husband's ashes on the mantelpiece. I shouldn't have kept them this long."

There would be time to tell about Paul, if the attraction caught and held. Although his attentions thrilled me, I didn't trust them yet—there were so many reasons for a younger man to fleetingly believe he loved an older woman. Why upset Jonathan needlessly? I'd wait and see whether this affair was serious enough to merit upsetting him.

"I can understand that," he said. "I can't quite believe these are his real ashes here. It seems so . . . It doesn't seem like something that would happen in the twentieth century. For a private citizen to just have his father's ashes in a box."

"Do you want to take them out to the desert together?" I said. "We could go right now."

"Here? You mean take them out and scatter them behind the house?"

"Yes. Now listen. This isn't the life your father and I dreamed about. It wasn't our fantasies come true. Hardly. But it's where we ended up, and we weren't unhappy here. To tell you the truth, I've been very happy."

"He told me not to bury him in the desert. He told me that explicitly. He wanted me to settle down, and bury him wherever I made a home."

"Jonathan, honey. Don't you think there's something a little . . . *kitschy* about all this yearning for a home?"

He fluttered his eyes in mock astonishment. "Mother," he said. "Are you telling me to get hip?"

"I'm telling you to stop worrying so much," I said. "Your father's dead. He was concerned about your rootlessness because he couldn't imagine anyone being happy if he wasn't tied down. That was his nature. But it would be a shame to let your father's lack of imagination curb your own life. Especially from beyond the grave."

He nodded. After a moment's hesitation, he put out his hands and touched the box. He ran his fingertips lightly over the engraved letters on the plaque. Without looking up he said, "Mom, if anything happened to me—"

"Nothing's going to happen to you," I said quickly.

"But if something did."

I sucked in a breath, and looked at him. Here was the real reason I'd lived unquestioningly with my image of Jonathan's simple bachelorhood, his sexual disenfranchisement. I knew I could get a call someday, from Bobby or Clare or from someone I'd never met, giving me the name of a hospital.

"All right," I said. "If something did."

"If something did, if you got stuck with both Dad and me, I don't want you scattering our ashes in this desert. It gives me the creeps. Okay?"

I didn't speak. I got up and poured coffee.

"Do you want to take them back and scatter them in Woodstock?" I asked as I set down the steaming mugs.

"Maybe. I'm not sure."

"It's up to you," I said. "This is strictly your decision."

"I know. I'll find a place. Do you want to go to the movies?"

"How about a game of Scrabble instead?"

"Fine," he said. "Great. You're on."

The following day we drove to the airport with Ned's ashes tucked inside Jonathan's black shoulder bag, swaddled among the socks and underwear. This time I'd claimed the driver's position, and Jonathan didn't protest. It was a rare overcast day, the sky filled with clouds that had bumped their way down from the Rockies, still heavy but depleted of their rain. The air was silvered, imbued with a steady, shadowless, and all but sourceless light that could as easily have emanated from the desert floor as from the atmosphere.

Jonathan was telling me of his growing interest in carpentry when I turned off the highway onto a side road I knew about.

"Hey," he said. "Is this a shortcut?"

"No. It's not."

"Where are we going?"

"Just hang on."

"I'll miss my plane," he said.

"No you won't. If you do, you can get another one."

The road, a thin ribbon of newly laid asphalt, led into the mountains where a scattering of wealthy men and women had built their homes. One of my customers lived out there, in a house so intricately married to the surrounding rocks it was barely distinguishable as a house at all. Before the road reached those elaborate dwellings, though, it dipped through a shallow ravine that held one of the desert's small surprises: a surface manifestation of underground water, not so blatant as to form a pool but moist enough to grow lush grasses and a modest stand of aspen trees, the leaves of which shimmered as if in perpetual surprise.

I stopped the car in that ravine. It looked especially beautiful in the cloudy light. The white trunks and pale green leaves of the aspens were luminous, and a spoke of sunlight, breaking through, set fire to a single facet of the rough red mountainside beyond.

"Jonathan," I said. "Let's scatter the ashes here. Let's be done with it."

"Here?" he asked. "Why here?"

"Why not? It's lovely, don't you think?"

"Well, sure. But—"

He glanced at the back seat, in the direction of his bag.

"Get out the box," I said. "Come on, now. Trust me."

Slowly, with great deliberation, he reached into the back and unzipped his bag. He returned with the box cradled in both hands.

"Are you sure?" he said.

"I'm sure. Come along."

We got out of the car, and walked several paces into the thick dry grass. Jonathan held the box. Flies buzzed lazily around us, and a dust-colored lizard froze atop a waist-high pink rock, staring at us with the whole of its darting, speeded-up life.

"This *is* pretty," Jonathan said.

"I pass by sometimes," I said. "I have customers out here. Whenever you come to visit from now on, we can come out here if you like."

"Should I open the box?" he asked.

"Yes. It isn't hard. Can you see how it works?"

"I think so." He touched the catch. Then he took his hand away, without lifting the lid.

"No," he said. "I can't. It isn't the right place."

"Honey, they're only ashes. Let's scatter them and get on with our lives."

"I promised. This isn't the right place. It isn't what he'd have wanted."

"Forget about what he wanted," I said.

"You could do that. I can't."

He held tightly to the box, his knuckles whitening as if he feared I'd take it away from him. I said, "That isn't fair."

"I don't know if it's fair. It's true. Mom, why did you want to marry Dad?"

"I've told you that story."

"You've told me about wearing white shoes after Labor Day and him having nice thick hair and how you couldn't think of any reason not to, so you did," he said. "But why did you marry him, why did you *stay* married to him, if you weren't any more interested than that? Did our whole family start just because getting married and having a baby was what you thought you were supposed to do?"

"Now watch yourself, young man. I loved your father. You didn't sit it out in that condominium for years. You didn't wake up with him in the night when he couldn't breathe and fell into a panic."

"No. But did you love him? That's all I really want to know. I know you sacrificed for him, and supported him, and all that. But were you in love with him?"

"What a question to ask your mother."

He cradled the box in his arms. "I think maybe I was in love with him," he said softly. "I adored him."

"He was just an ordinary man."

"I know. Don't you think I know that?"

We stood for a while at the edge of the aspen grove. Nothing happened; nothing moved. Jonathan held the box, his face set stubbornly, his eyes squeezed shut. After several minutes I said, "Jonathan, find someone of your own to love."

"I've got someone," he said.

It gave me a kind of vertigo, to hear us both talk like this—a tingling, lightheaded sensation of great height and insufficient protection. We had always been so circumspect with one another. Now, rather late in the game, when I had things to discuss with him, we possessed no easy language.

"You know what I mean," I said.

He looked petulantly away, as if something on the horizon and to my right had captured his attention. There, right there before me, angrily avoiding my eyes, was the four-year-old boy I'd known more intimately than I knew myself. Now he was back in the guise of a man aging in a British, professorial way; taking on a weedy, slightly ravaged, indoor quality.

"You don't know anything about it," he said at length. "Our lives are more different than you can imagine."

"I know well enough about women," I said. "And I can tell you this. That woman is not going to let you have equal rights to her baby."

Now he could look at me. His eyes were hard and brilliant.

"Rebecca isn't *her* baby. Rebecca is *our* baby," he said.

"In a manner of speaking."

"No. Literally. Bobby and Clare and I don't know which of us is the father. That's how we decided to do it."

I didn't believe him. I knew—somehow I knew—that he and that woman had not been lovers. He was telling me a story, as he'd liked to do as a child. Still, I went along with it.

"And that's what Clare wanted, too?"

"Yes. It's what she wanted."

"It may be what she said she wanted," I said. "It may be what she thought she wanted."

"You don't know Clare. You're thinking of a different kind of person."

"No, my darling. You are. I know what it is to believe the people you know are different, that your life is going to be different. And I'm standing here telling you there are universal laws. A woman won't share her baby."

"Mom," he said in an elaborately calm voice. "Mom, you're talking about yourself. It's you who wouldn't give your baby up."

"Listen to me now. Go out and find yourself someone to love. Have a baby of your own, if that's what you want."

"I've already got one," he said. "Rebecca is as much mine as she is anyone's."

"Three is an odd number. When there are three, one usually gets squeezed out."

"Mom, you don't know what you're saying," he said. "You don't have any fucking idea."

"Please don't speak to me that way. I'm still your mother."

"And please don't pull rank on me. You're the one who wants to talk."

He had me there. I was the one who wanted to talk. I was the one who had disappeared into marriage, let myself be carried along by the simple, ceaseless comfort of domestic particulars. And now in a desert grove I wanted to talk.

"All I'm saying," I said, "is that there seem to be certain limits. We have a hard enough time staying together as couples."

"And I," he said, "am seriously considering the possibility that those limits are a self-fulfilling prophecy. Bobby, Clare, and I are happy together. We plan on staying together."

"History teaches differently."

"History changes. Mom, it isn't the same world anymore. The world's going to end any minute, why shouldn't we try to have everything we can?"

"People have believed the world was ending since the day the world began, dear. It hasn't, and it hasn't changed much either."

"How can you say that?" he said. "Look at yourself."

I was aware of the ground under my feet, chalky and red-gray. I was aware of myself in jeans and a suede jacket, under the open sky.

I said, "Do you think that when it comes down to brass tacks, Bobby will chose you? That's it, isn't it? You think Clare will recede, and you and Bobby will raise that child together, with her in the background."

He looked at me, and I saw him. I saw everything: his hunger for men, his guilt and disappointment, his rage. I saw that in ways his anger was a woman's anger. He had a woman's sense of betrayal. He believed he'd been pushed unfairly onto the margins, been loved by the wrong people for the wrong reasons. For a moment I felt afraid of him. I feared my own son, out in that wild place so far from other beings. We had protected ourselves with silence because our only other choice was to howl at one another, to scratch and bite and shriek. We were too ashamed, both of us, for ordinary anger.

"You don't know what you're talking about," he said quietly, and I conceded that I probably didn't. We had lost track of one another; we were strangers in some deep, impenetrable way that ran like a river under our devotion and our cordiality. Perhaps that had always been the case.

"We'd better go try and catch your flight," I said.

"Yes. We'd better."

"About the ashes. It's your choice. Let me know what you decide, whenever you decide."

He nodded. "Maybe I'll give them to Rebecca someday," he said. "Here, kid. Your family heritage."

"She won't know what to do with them either," I said.

"If I have any say in things, she will. I want her to grow up with no question about where to put her grandfather's ashes."

"That would be nice. That would be nice for her."

"Mm-hm."

"Come on, then," I said. "We can just barely make it if we hurry."

We got back into the car, and drove the rest of the way in silence. Jonathan returned the ashes to his bag and closed the zipper. As I drove I tried to phrase some bit of parental advice, but I couldn't think of how to get it said. I'd have liked to tell him something I'd taken almost sixty years to learn: that we owe the dead even less than we owe the living, that our only chance of happiness—a small enough chance—lay in welcoming change. But I couldn't manage it.

Because we'd lost time, he had to jump out at the curb in front of the terminal. "Bye, Mom," he said.

"Goodbye. Take care of yourself."

"Yep. I always do."

"I'm not so sure about that. Go, quick. You'll miss your plane."

He got out of the car and slung his bag over his shoulder. Before sprinting for his plane, he came around to the driver's side. "So long," he said.

Was he ill, or simply aging? Why did he look a little haggard, his eyes slightly too large in his skull?

"Jonathan? Call me when you get in, all right? Just so I know you made it in one piece."

"Okay. Sure."

He bent before the open window and I kissed him, lightly but square on the mouth. I kissed him goodbye. And then, without a wave or a backward glance, he was gone.

JONATHAN

Bobby and I arrived at the station a few minutes before Erich's train was due. At a small-town station like that—which was only a maroon-brick building the size of a toolshed, fronting a concrete platform—you got a true sense of your own remoteness. Here, where the country and the city met, you understood that the important fact about an approaching train was its subsequent departure for other places. Even as we watched the silver line of the train snake around the last green hillside, I could imagine the gritty windstorm it would cause on its way out. Cinders and a stray paper cup would blow briefly around the platform and then settle again into the prevailing hush. A lopsided red vending machine that had once sold newspapers stood gaping among the cattails and nettle across the tracks.

I had called Erich because I was lonely. That's not true: I should call my condition by its proper name. When we moved to Woodstock I'd thought there would be more unattached gay men around; I'd imagined meeting them in bars and yard sales. But, as it turned out, the gay men who lived there had all arrived in pairs. So, eventually, I'd called Dr. Feelgood and invited him up for a weekend.

I patted Bobby's shoulder, because I was nervous. I hadn't seen Erich in over a year. The only other person on the platform was an obese elderly woman searching with mounting irritation for something in a white straw bag. I kept my hand on Bobby's shoulder as the train curved toward us. A figure from my old, more sensible life was about to visit me in my strange and bucolic new one.

The train rumbled in, its doors sighed open. A family disembarked, followed by a bald man in a brown suit, followed by the obese younger woman who was being met by the old woman with the white straw bag. For a moment, it seemed Erich was not on the train after all. And then he appeared, holding a blue canvas suitcase, at the top of the train's three metal steps.

I knew the moment I saw him. On someone as wiry as Erich, the loss of even five pounds would have had a noticeable diminishing effect. He had lost at least ten. His skin was gray and dense-looking.

He smiled. He got down the stairs competently if slowly, moving as if he balanced an invisible jug atop his head. Bobby took his elbow when he stepped from the last tread to the concrete.

"Hi," Erich said. "Here I am."

"Here you are," I said.

After a brief hesitation, we embraced. Through his clothes—black jeans and a blue denim shirt—I could feel the true thinness of him. It was like holding a bundle of sticks. In his embrace I felt a surge of panic. The blood rushed dizzyingly to my head. All I could think of was breaking away, running from the platform into the cattails. As Erich and I held one another the world broke down into bright swimming specks before my eyes, a garish moil of color, and I could for a moment have knocked him down, kicked him under the wheels of the train so he'd be ground to nothing. So he would no longer exist.

Instead, I took his bony shoulders in my hands and said, "It's good to see you." The train started up again, pulling away in a knee-high fury of sparkling dust.

"Thanks," he said, nodding. "Thanks a lot. It's good to be here. I haven't been in the country in a long long time. Hello, Bobby."

He and Bobby shook hands. I couldn't tell from Bobby's face how much he knew. He carried Erich's suitcase to the car with the impassive certainty of an old family retainer. Erich could walk well enough, though there was palpable caution in his step, an elderly deliberateness, as if his bones were soft and brittle as wax.

"Did you have a good trip?" I asked.

"Fine. Oh, yes, fine. The train goes through some beautiful parts, it really is, well, just beautiful up here, isn't it?"

"Yes," I said. "If you like this sort of thing."

He blinked uncertainly. Erich understood formal jokes, but lost track of small ironies.

"We like it here," I said. "It's every bit as restful, satisfying, and dull as you ever imagined the country would be."

"Oh," he said. "Well, good. That's good."

We got into the car and started for home. Bobby drove, and Erich sat in the front seat. I sat in back, the child's place. As we drove over the familiar road, I looked out at the fields of wild grass and could not stop thinking of hiding myself in it; of burrowing deep into a grassy field until I was completely hidden among the yellow-green blades, which were blanching with the coming season. Fourteen months ago, when Erich and I last made love, we'd been careful with one another. But less than a year before that, we had practiced no caution. I ran my fingertips lightly over my chest, and watched the leaves of grass sway under the sky.

Erich said, "Bobby, did you bring your record collection here with you?"

"Oh, sure," Bobby said. "You know me. We got a turntable and everything."

"I brought you some presents from the city," Erich said. "There's a great record store down in the financial district, if you can believe that."

"Oh, I know that one," Bobby said. "Yeah. I used to go there."

We drove home, managing our conversation in spasms. I found, to my surprise, that I felt a distinctly social aversion to asking Erich about his health. It was not horror but embarrassment that prevented me from mentioning it; he might have come back from a war missing his arms or legs. From where I sat, I could see the patch of unprosperous skin that showed through his thin hair— both skin and hair had lost a luster that was perceptible only by its absence. Although Erich had never been robust, his hair now looked as if it would break off in your hands. The scalp underneath was hard and dry; juiceless. What I did, faced with his evident decline, was point out my favorite views, discuss the eccentricities of the local population, and tell of our recent visit to the county fair, where prize cucumbers and 4-H piglets had been proudly displayed. I could not stop stroking my chest. We crossed the Hudson. Beneath us, barges cut through the sparkling brown water. The trees on the far bank were going yellow and red from the first frosty nights. Among the trees, the crumbling mansions of dead millionaires looked blindly out at the cooling, ice-blue sky.

When we reached the gravel drive that led up to the house, Erich gasped and said, "Oh, this is wonderful. I can't believe this is yours."

I had never heard this note of excitement in his voice—this undertone of quivering wonder. I wasn't sure if I believed it. It had a false, gushing quality. He might have been the wife of an ambitious man, taken to the boss's country house.

"Wait till you see the inside," I said. "It's got a long way to go."

"Oh, no, it's perfect. It's just perfect," he said. "Whatever it looks like inside."

"Just you wait," I said.

Clare met us on the porch with the baby. Rebecca, recently bathed, looked at us with buggishly astonished eyes, as if she had never seen anything like us before—three men getting out of a car and mounting the porch stairs. Clare called, "Hello, boys."

"Hello," Erich said. "Oh, it's, well, it's very good to see you again. Oh, look at the baby."

I could tell from Clare's face that she suspected something. I could almost see the interior process she went through, struggling to match this Erich with the Erich she'd met years ago. Had he always been so ashen and thin? Had his skin been so opaque?

"This is her," Clare said after a moment. "You're catching her on a good day, she's been angelic from the moment she opened her eyes this morning. Better admire her quick, because things could change at any moment."

298

Erich, uncertain about small children, stood several feet away and said, "Hi, baby. Hello there." Rebecca gawked at him or at the empty air in his vicinity, a string of saliva dangling voluptuously from her chin. She'd been talking for months by then. In private she could babble for hours, mixing actual words with her own private vocabulary, but when faced with strangers she retreated, staring with unabashed and slightly fearful fascination, committing herself to nothing, waiting to see what would happen next. When she was uncertain she still claimed the infant's privilege, and in her boggled fixations there was a quality of self-abandonment that was almost sexual. I'd already learned one lesson about fatherhood—you love your child, in part, because you see her utterly naked. A baby has no subvert life, and by comparison everyone else you know seems cloaked, muffled, and full of sad little tricks. In a year and a half I'd learned that while I could imagine Rebecca growing up to make me angry, to hurt or disappoint me, I did not see how she could ever make herself strange. Not if she came to weigh three hundred pounds. Not if she preached the ascendancy of an insect god, or committed murder for personal gain. We were connected; we'd established an intimacy that couldn't be undone while we both lived.

"How about giving me a squeeze?" I said. Clare reluctantly passed her over. As I took her in my arms she looked at me with unflinching amazement. I said, "Hey, Miss Rebecca," and she laughed abruptly and ecstatically, as if I had just popped out of a box.

I held her close to my chest. I put my nose to her fat shoulder and inhaled.

Erich said, "This is really interesting. What you all are doing out here. I mean, it's just very very interesting."

"Putting it mildly," Clare said. "Come on inside, I'll show you to your room. Ooh, I've always wanted to say that to somebody."

Clare led Erich into the house, and Bobby followed with the suitcase. I stayed outside with Rebecca for a moment. Afternoon light, which had taken on the golden weight of October, picked out each individual tree on the mountainside. A fat speckled spider sat motionless in the exact middle of a web that described a taut hexagon between two posts and the porch rail. As quickly as we swept the webs away with a broom, these country spiders—some gaily colored, some pale as dust—rebuilt them. Rebecca murmured. She started batting her hands in the frantic, exasperated way that preceded her sourceless fits of crying. I stroked her hair, waiting for the tears to start. I thought of walking away with her, just taking her into the mountains with me.

"There's so much still to do," I whispered. "The floors have still got dry rot. And we haven't even started on the kitchen yet."

We took Erich to see the restaurant, which was doing well enough by then for Bobby and me to have left it for a few hours in the charge of Marlys, our prep cook, and her lover Gert, the new waitress. When we started the restaurant we'd set out to simulate the kind of place we'd hoped to find on the drive back from Arizona—an eccentric little café that served honest food made by human hands. As it turned out, we weren't alone in our desire for that simple, elusive café. Our place was always full, and on weekends the customers lined up halfway down the block. It was gratifying and slightly uncomfortable to see people so avid for such ordinary food: bread and hash browns made from scratch, soups and stews, two different pies every day. I sometimes felt we were deceiving them by pretending to be simple—we'd led convoluted, neurotic lives and now we were earning our living by arranging lattice crusts over apples from an orchard less than ten miles away and contracting with a local grandmother for homemade preserves. Still, half our customers wore country clothes they'd ordered from catalogues and rustic sweaters knitted in Hong Kong or Guatemala. I don't suppose anyone was fooled.

"Oh, this is *wonderful*," Erich cried. The restaurant had closed for the day, although half the tables were still full of customers finishing up. Marlys and Gert greeted us with their particular mix of comradely good cheer and fleeting, untraceable hatred. I found that I was vaguely embarrassed by Erich's pallor and thinness—it seemed I had brought some perversity of mine, some unpleasant secret, into the place where I had effectively simulated innocence.

Marlys took Bobby into the kitchen to show him what needed

reordering, and to point out the leak she had managed, temporarily, to plug in the dishwasher. I'd learned that even a small, successful restaurant operated in a continual state of crisis. The machinery broke down, caught fire, failed when it was needed most. Produce arrived bruised or unripe, mealworms tunneled into the flour. The customers' appetites followed distinct but unpredictable patterns, so that the ingredients we ran out of one week would spoil on our shelves the next. The profits, though steady, were small, and it seemed that literally every hour it was time to bake more pies, cut more potatoes, haggle with the vegetable man about a carton of wilted lettuce. Sometimes I'd walk into the dining room and see, with a certain astonishment, that people sat at every table eating without concern or particular attention, talking to one another about the facts of their lives. They believed this was a restaurant, they found it unextraordinary that we'd fought decay and parasites, the endless petty dishonesty of suppliers, to get this simple food onto these white ceramic plates. On the rare occasions when a customer complained that his eggs were overcooked or his bacon underdone, I had to force myself not to scream, "Don't you realize how lucky you are that we do this at all? Don't you *get* it? Where's your gratitude, for God's sake?" I'd begun to better understand the appeal of the flash-frozen, the freeze-dried or microwavable. *This tastes almost as good, and it's predictable. It's already diced or kneaded, already rolled or chopped. It can't rot. It will keep until the customers decide they want to order it again.* Less than two years ago, the proprietors of all those brightly lit, desolate roadside cafés had seemed like our enemies, selling corrupted food out of greed and laziness. Now I saw them as victims of a more practical, seductive kind of defeat.

Gert asked Erich and me if we'd like anything. The coffee was still on, she said, and when last she checked there were still two pieces of blueberry pie. Did she know Erich was sick? Was that the true cause of her solicitude? I could tell Erich was charmed by Gert, for she was in fact charming, a strong-faced, ruddy woman with long gray hair who had left a good job in publishing to live up here with Marlys. She dressed like a farm wife, in print dresses and cardigan sweaters, but she spoke Russian and had edited the work of a great poet. After we'd said no thank you to coffee and pie and she'd returned to the customers, I had to work to keep from whispering, "We think she's stealing from the register."

Erich said in his new, overanimated voice, "This place looks so sweet."

"Part of the package," I said. "An integral aspect of our appeal to our target audience."

"Who are all these children?" he asked, meaning the photographs on the walls.

"Strangers," I said. "Five for a dollar at a junk store up the Hudson. Half of them are alcoholics or Jesus freaks or inmates at the state penitentiary by now. The other half live in trailer parks with their six kids."

He nodded approvingly, as if those were good ends for grown children. Bobby came out of the kitchen followed by Marlys, a hefty, freckled woman with apricot hair. "I think the dishwasher may be shot," he said. "It looks, you know, pretty bad."

"Great," I said. "It'll take them weeks to get a new dishwasher up here. You know how they are."

Marlys threw me a shadow punch. "Hey, butch," she said.

I threw my hands up over my head. "Ooh, don't hurt me," I answered. This was the method Marlys and I worked out for threading our way through the maze of sexuality and power. She earned good money at our restaurant and was constantly pummeling us, pinching our cheeks too hard or slapping our asses. I was her boss, and I feigned a physical terror not wholly unrelated to my actual feelings. Marlys was broad and calm and competent in worldly matters. She had repaired the dishwasher in the midst of the morning rush. She was an expert sailor and skier, and she knew the names of trees.

"Well, we'll have to manage with this one until it breaks down completely," Bobby said. "You and I may have to be back there washing dishes by hand for a while. And hope the health inspector doesn't stop by."

"The glamorous life of a restaurant owner," I said to Erich, who nodded agreeably.

We had dinner at home, and talked mainly about the baby.

Clare and I used Erich as an audience for our own interest in the minutiae of child-rearing. As we passed around the corn and the hamburgers and the tomato salad we clamored over each other to tell the next story of Rebecca's peculiarities, our own shock at the various moral and bodily issues of parenthood, and our assorted resolutions about how to usher her, relatively undamaged, into a life of love and wages. Erich, whose good manners might have been imprinted on his genes, feigned or actually felt ardent, blinking interest in our talk. There was no telling.

After dinner, we put Rebecca to bed and watched one of the movies Clare had rented. ("We are *not*," she'd said, "relying on conversation alone this weekend. I'm laying in movies, games, whatever. I'd hire a dog act if I knew where to find one around here.") After the movie, we stretched and yawned and talked of how weary we were—a partial truth. Yes, we agreed, it was just about time for bed. Erich sat folded into his chair, with his hands slipped between his knees as if the room was freezing. He was so small, and so determined to be a good, unobtrusive guest—one who agreed to everything, who insisted that his hosts' desires exactly matched his own. Almost before I knew I'd do it, I said, "Erich, how long have you been like this?"

He looked at me with a mingled expression of surprise and disappointment, blinking rapidly. It occurred to me that he might consider me the source of his illness. As in fact I might have been.

"I wasn't sure if it showed," he said. He spoke so softly I could barely hear him. His voice was mild as a radiator's hiss. But he blinked furiously, and pressed his thighs tighter around his hands. "I've been feeling *better*," he said. "I mean, well, I thought I looked all right."

"How long has it been?" Clare asked. Before I'd spoken she had stood, on the pretext of making herb tea, and she remained standing, fixed in place beside the sofa. Bobby, still seated, watched in silence.

Erich hesitated, as if struggling to remember. "Well, I'd been feeling sick for more than a year," he said. "I couldn't believe it, I mean it seemed so strange to have imagined these symptoms so clearly and then start having them. I thought for a while that maybe

I was just being a hypochondriac. But then, well. I got the diagnosis about five months ago."

"And you didn't call me?" I said.

"What good would it have done?" he said. Now his voice cut through the air cleanly as a cable through fog. His voice had lost its polite, enthusiastic tone and taken on a bitterness I'd never heard from him. "It's not like there's a cure," he said. "It's not like you could do anything but worry about it."

"I've seen you when you were sick," I said. "You didn't mention it."

But at the same time I remembered: we have no relationship to speak of. Our exchange is based primarily on sex and shared loneliness.

He looked at me. His eyes were terrible. "To tell you the truth, I was embarrassed," he said. "When I thought about something like this happening, when I thought and, you know, *imagined* it, I knew I'd be afraid and angry. And, well, guilty. None of those things surprises me very much. But I'm surprised to be feeling this embarrassed about it."

"Sweetheart, it's okay," Clare said.

Erich nodded. "Of course it's okay," he said. "What else could it be but okay?"

"Nothing," she said. "Sorry."

"I thought I was working my way toward something like this house," he said. "You know, trying to figure out what to do with my life. I thought I'd make money somehow and end up somewhere like this."

"The nights get long out here," Clare said.

"It's paradise," he said. "Don't try to kid me. It's fucking paradise, and you know it is."

We remained where we were, with the lights on and the clock ticking. All I could think of was Rebecca. Just as I had wanted, earlier, to disappear into the tall grass, now I wanted only to go to her room, wake her up, and comfort her. I thought of her perfect feet, and of the way she clutched at her hair with one hand as she sucked the thumb of the other. I wondered if, at twenty-five, some vestige of the habit would remain. Would she, as a young woman, tend to play with her hair when she grew anxious or tired? Would someone love that about her—the brown hair being twirled and untwirled and twirled again around an unconscious finger? Would someone be irritated by it? Would someone someday look at her in her exhaustion, her fingers working busily, and think, "I've had enough of this"?

I said, "I'm going up to check on the baby."

"She's fine," Clare said. "She hasn't made a sound."

"Still, can't hurt to check."

"Jonathan, she's fine," Clare said. "Really. She is."

Erich slept alone in my bed that night. Although I'd claimed I was going to sleep on the futon downstairs, I ended up with Bobby and Clare in their bed. I lay between them, with my arms folded over my chest.

"What I feel really shitty about," I said, "is how worried I am for myself. Erich is *sick*, and I feel sorry for him, but in this sort of remote way. It's like my self-concern is a Sousa march, and Erich's actual illness is this piccolo playing in the background."

"That's natural enough," she said. "But listen, you're probably fine. You've been healthy for, what, over a year since the last time you and Erich . . ."

"It can incubate for at least five years," I said. "Lately they've been thinking it could be as long as ten."

She nodded. Something was wrong; she wasn't responding the way I'd expected her to, with Clare-like grit and flippancy. She seemed to have fallen out of character.

Bobby lay in silence on my other side. He had barely spoken since dinner. "Bobby?" I said.

"Uh-huh?"

"What's going on over there? You're so damn quiet."

"I'm okay," he said. "I'm just thinking."

Clare squeezed my elbow. I knew what she meant: leave him alone until he's had time to settle into his own reaction. Bobby negotiated the world's surprises with a deliberateness that was almost somnolent. Clare and I had decided privately that if the house caught fire, one of us would take responsibility for helping him decide which window to jump out of.

"I just feel so . . . strange," I said. "How am I going to get through the days from now on without checking myself for symptoms every five minutes?"

"Honey, you're probably fine," Clare said, but her voice lacked conviction. By way of compensation, she patted my chest. Since the baby was born, Clare had become more prone to physical contact, though her caresses were still flighty and vague, as if she suspected the flesh of others might burn her hands.

"What do you think, Bobby?" I asked.

"I think you're okay," he answered.

"Well, that's good. I'm glad you think so."

Clare said, "I wonder how Erich is going to manage this. I have a feeling he hasn't got a lot of friends."

"He has friends," I said. "What do you think, he lives in a vacuum? You think he's just some sort of bit player with no life of his own?"

"How would I know?" Clare said.

I realized, from the sound of her voice, that she blamed me in some way for failing to love Erich. Since the baby was born she'd discarded a measure of her old cynicism, and held the world more accountable to standards of unfaltering affection.

"Please don't get peevish with me," I said. "Not now. You can get doubly peevish with me another time."

"I'm not being peevish," she said. It was a habit of hers to disavow her actions even as she performed them. I believed, at that moment, that by being herself she could do serious harm to the baby. How would it affect Rebecca to grow up with a mother who screamed, "I'm not screaming"?

"Right," I said. "You're not. You always know exactly what's coming out of your own mouth, and whatever anybody else thinks he hears is an illusion."

"We don't need to have a fight right now," she said. "Unless you really want to."

"Maybe I do. You're pissed off at me for not being in love with Erich, aren't you?"

"Of course I'm not. How could I be mad about something like that? Either you're in love with somebody or you're not."

"Oh, we three are more used to ambiguity than that," I said. "Aren't we? Tell me this. Do you think I've fucked up my life? Do you think there's been something wrong about my being in love with you and Bobby and having a strictly sexual relationship with Erich?"

"You're saying that," she said.

"But I want to hear what *you* think. You think there's something unfinished about me. Don't you? You think Bobby and I are each half a man. That's why you ended up with the two of us. Together we add up to one person in your eyes. Right?"

"Stop this. You're just upset, this isn't a good time to try and talk."

"This isn't what I asked for," I said. "It's just what happened. I don't want you turning on me all of a sudden because of it. Clare, for God's sake, I'm too scared."

She started to say, "I'm not—" but caught herself. "Oh, maybe I am," she said. "I'm scared, too."

"I don't have to love Erich just because he's sick," I said. "I don't have to suddenly take responsibility for him."

"No," she said. "No, I don't suppose you do."

"Shit, why did I have to invite him?"

"Jonathan, honey," she said. "Erich's being here doesn't make any difference. You sound as if you think he's brought some sort of germ with him."

"Hasn't he? I could go a full day without thinking about it before. Now I've lost that."

"You're not making sense," she said. "Well, you're making crazy sense. I know what you're saying. But don't blame him. It isn't his fault."

"I know," I said miserably. "I know that."

My limitation was my own rationality. I was too balanced, too well behaved. Had I been a different sort of person I could have stormed through the house, shattering crockery and ripping pictures off the walls. It would not of course have solved anything, but there'd have been a voluptuous release in it—the only pleasure I could imagine just then. The idea of sex revolted me, as did the comfort of friends who knew their blood was sound. My one desire was to run screaming through the house, tearing down the curtains and splintering the furniture, smashing every pane of glass.

"Try to sleep," Clare said. "There's no point in staying up worrying about it."

"I know. I'll try."

"Okay. Good night."

"Good night."

She slipped her arm over my belly, and pulled me closer into her own nimbus of warmth and perfume. Bobby breathed softly on my other side. I knew I should have felt comforted and I almost did, but the actual sensation of comfort trembled just beyond my reach. I was in a remote place with people whose lives would continue unchanged if I died. I lay between Clare and Bobby, listening for Rebecca. If she awoke and cried, I'd go to her room and console her. I'd heat a bottle and hold her while she drank it. I lay listening for the first whimper, but she slept on.

BOBBY

I**T WAS** after midnight. The clouds had rolled past on their long journey to the Atlantic from the heart of the continent. The full moon blared freely through our bedroom window. As I crossed the moon-whitened floorboards I paused to look at Jonathan and Clare, asleep in the shadow of the dormer. She released her low snores, blowing soft, breathy bubbles. He lay with his head canted away from her, as if he was dreaming pure noise and didn't want to disturb her sleep.

I went down the hall and tapped on the door, but I didn't wait for an answer. That room was on the moonless side of the house—it maintained a deeper darkness. I stood for a moment by the door, then whispered, "Erich?"

"Yes?"

"Are you sleeping?"

"No. Well, no. I wasn't, really."

"I just, you know. I wanted to make sure you were comfortable."

"I am," he said. "This is a good bed."

His head was a spot of moving darkness at the edge of the bright quilt. I caught glints of him: his eyes, his domed forehead. The room didn't smell of sickness.

"It was Clare's old bed," I said. "Well, Clare's and mine, for a while. Now it's Jonathan's and we have, you know, this other one."

"It's a good bed. Not too soft. I always think they're going to have soft beds in the country."

"Sometimes a mouse gets in here," I said. "We keep saying we should trap it, but we never do. I'm not sure if we're really, you know, thorough enough to be country people."

"The mice out here are probably cleaner," he said. "They're probably more like real animals."

A silence passed. After a moment, we heard the mouse scrabbling inside the wall. We laughed.

"Do you have, like, people in New York to help take care of you?" I asked.

"Well, there are volunteers," he said. "If I get really really sick I can call one of those agencies."

"What about your family?"

"My family's written me off."

"They won't help you?" I asked.

"They don't *speak* to me. I'm gone. My sister calls, but she wouldn't want to be in a room with me. She thinks her kids could catch it."

"Do you still have your job?" I asked.

"No. No, they laid me off a few weeks ago, after I was in the hospital with pneumonia."

"And your friends?"

"A few of them have died in the last year. They just went like *that*, three people in, like, six months. The guy I've always thought of as my best friend is sicker than I am, he's in the hospital. He doesn't recognize people unless he's having a very very good day."

"Are you scared?" I said.

"What do you think?"

"Yeah. Well, I would be, too."

He sighed. "And then sometimes I'm not," he said. "It sort of comes and goes. But every minute is different now. Even when I'm not afraid, things are different. I feel—oh, I can't explain it. Just different. I used to lose track of myself, you know. Like I didn't have a body, like I was just, I don't know, like I *was* the street I was walking on. Now I never lose track of myself."

"Uh-huh."

"And, you know," he said. "If I ever really thought about it, I pictured myself as being old and having no regrets. You know? I pictured something like a famous old man in bed with people around him, and him saying 'I have no regrets.' That's really pretty silly, isn't it? It's really very silly."

"What do you regret, exactly?" I asked.

"Oh, well. Nothing really, I guess. I mean, I did think I'd do more with my life than this. I just thought I had more time. And like I said, I thought I'd be famous and retire to a place like this."

"Uh-huh. Well, this wouldn't be for everybody," I said. "There's only one movie theater. And no place to hear good music."

He laughed, a low sound with a rasp to it, like scraping a potato. You could hear his illness in his laugh. "I never really did those things in New York," he said. "I just, well, I guess you'd have to say I've been gambling with my life. I guess you'd have to call it that. I was thinking things would somehow work out. I thought I just needed to work hard and have faith."

I walked over to the bed. I stood beside him, as the mouse went about its scratching inside the wall. "Um, hey, how about if I get in bed with you for a while?" I said.

"What?"

"It doesn't seem right for you to be alone here," I said. "How about if I just got in under the covers with you for a little while?"

"I don't have any clothes on," he said.

"That's okay."

"What's the matter with you?" he said. "You want to sleep with me because I'm sick?"

"No," I said.

"Would you have wanted to if I wasn't sick?"

"I don't know."

"Oh, for God's sake. Will you get out of here, please? Will you just get out of here?"

"Look, I'm sorry. I didn't mean to, like, offend you."

"I know you didn't. But go. Please."

"Well. Okay," I said.

I left the room, and closed the door behind me. I felt a weight in my arms and legs, a stodgy sense of disappointment and name-less, floating embarrassment. I hadn't wanted to intrude on his privacy. I'd only wanted to hold him for a while, to guide his head to my chest. I'd only wanted to hold on to him as his body went through the long work of giving itself up to the past.

JONATHAN

E RICH came back the next weekend. I'm not sure why the invitation was issued or why it was accepted—none of us, Erich included, had seemed to have an especially good time. All day Sunday he'd been sulky and withdrawn. Still, when we took him to the train station Bobby asked, "Do you want to come back next weekend?" Erich hesitated, and then said all right. He said it in a flat, determined voice, as if laying claim to that which was rightfully his.

As Bobby and I were driving home I asked, "Do you really want to have Erich back again so soon?"

"Jon," he said, "that guy needs some time in the country. Really, did you *look* at him?"

For a moment it seemed Bobby did not yet understand the nature of Erich's illness; he seemed to believe Erich was only stressed and overtired, in need of a good long rest. "He needs more than that, Bobby," I said.

"Well, a little time in the country is about all we can give him. He's, like, a member of the family now. Whether we like it or not."

"The family," I said. "You know, you're going to drive me crazy with this shit."

He shrugged, and smiled ruefully, as if I was being petulant about a condition that clearly lay beyond anyone's control. Erich was attached to us now, however tenuously, and in Bobby's private economy we were obliged to offer everything we had.

Erich returned the following Friday on the five o'clock train. By then he'd regained his polite, slightly squeaky enthusiasm, though now it was more prone to lapses. Bobby took the main responsibility for seeing to Erich's comfort, and by the end of the second visit the two of them had embarked on a kind of courtship. Bobby was doggedly affectionate, and Erich accepted his ministrations with a wan and slightly irritable greed, like an indignant ghost come back to exact reparations from the living.

Late Sunday afternoon I was in the kitchen with Clare and Rebecca. Clare sliced an avocado. Rebecca sat on the counter top, sorting through a set of plastic animal-shaped cookie cutters, and I stood alongside, to keep her from falling. Outside the window we could see Bobby and Erich sitting in the unruly grass, talking earnestly. Bobby made sweeping motions with his hands, indicating enormity, and Erich nodded without much conviction.

"So, Bobby has a new love," I said.

"Don't be nasty, dear," Clare said. "It isn't becoming in you." She laid avocado slices on a plate, began peeling a Bermuda onion.

"I just don't feel like Erich needs to suddenly become our favorite charity," I said. "He's practically a stranger."

"We have room here for a stranger, don't you think? It's not like we lack for anything ourselves."

"So now you're Mother Teresa?" I said. "This seems a little sudden."

She looked at me with an even-tempered calm that was more cogently accusing than any censure could have been. Something had happened to Clare. I couldn't read her anymore—she'd given up her cynicism and taken on an opaque motherliness. We were still friends and domestic partners but we were no longer intimate.

"I know," I said. "I'm just a rotten person."

She patted my shoulder. "Please don't *pat* me," I said. "You never used to pat me like this."

Rebecca, who had been droolingly contemplating a cookie cut-ter shaped like a moose, started to cry. Discord cut into her skin like a fine cord; she wept whenever anyone in her vicinity spoke in anger.

"Hey, kid," I said. "It's okay, never mind about us."

I tried to take her in my arms but she didn't want to be held by me. She insisted on being picked up by Clare, who walked with her into the living room while I finished slicing the onion.

Eventually, Erich took up residence. He had nowhere else to go except his sparse, comfortless apartment in the East Twenties. He'd have endured his illness in the company of volunteers until he moved to whatever hospital beds were available to the unprosperous and the uninsured. Bobby insisted that he visit us often, and when the trip got to be too much for him he moved in for good. I offered my bedroom, claiming I'd learned to prefer sleeping downstairs. Taking Erich in was not a simple process. I resented him for being sick and at the same time felt compelled to treat him in ways I hoped to be treated if I fell ill myself. I practiced the tenderness I hoped I might inspire in others if my vigor leaked away and my body started to change. Sometimes I caught up with the feeling and experienced it, a flush and flutter of true concern. Sometimes I only manifested it. After a period of resistance Erich agreed to take over my bed, and in doing so almost palpably relinquished a degree of participation in the ongoing, living world. This moment may come to us all, at some point in our eventual move from health into sickness. We abandon our old obligation to consider the needs of others, and give ourselves up to their care. There is a shift in status. We become citizens of a new realm, and although we retain the best and worst of our former selves we are no longer bodily in command of our fates. Erich needed my room for the complex business of his dying. He was a private person and would not suffer well in the midst of our domestic traffic. So with a courteous and slightly aggrieved smile he allowed me to put him into my bed. I turned thirty-two the day after he arrived for the final time.

We took him for walks in the woods, cooked meals that

wouldn't tax his system. He was an elderly spirit in the house, alternately courtly and short-tempered. Our grandfather might have come to live with us.

Winter passed, spring came. The restaurant prospered. Rebecca cut new teeth, and discovered the lush possibility of saying no to whatever was asked of her. Erich declined unpredictably. His energy dwindled and returned, sometimes from hour to hour. He had intestinal trouble, fevers, a cloudiness of vision. His mind drifted occasionally—he could grow vague and forgetful. He made weekly trips to the hospital in Albany. On his best days he could walk into the woods with a basket, hunting mushrooms. On his worst days he lay curled in bed, neither discernibly awake nor asleep.

I lived slightly apart, in the middle of everything. I would not have asked Erich to live with us but I couldn't bring myself to actively wish him gone—I was too nervous about my own status as the house crank. I learned to find a chilly comfort in being good to Erich. It offered some obscure hope of appeasing the fates.

One evening when I came home from the restaurant I found him sitting on the porch, wrapped in a blanket. The sun had fallen behind the mountain. Violet shadows were gathering though the sky was still bright—we would always suffer early dusks in this house. Erich sat on the ancient wicker chair with an old blue blanket of mine pulled up to his neck, looking like a tubercular teenager. As his flesh grew gaunter, his appearance became more and more adolescent. His ribs stuck out, and his ears, hands, and feet came to seem too large for his body.

"Hi," I said. "How are you?"

"Okay," he answered. "Not too bad."

A formality prevailed between us, just as it had when we were sleeping together. We were courteous and remote. We continued to act as if we had recently met.

"Bobby's staying late at work," I said. "Marlys had some kind of women's thing to go to, so Bobby's doing the pies for tomorrow. Are Clare and Rebecca around?"

"They're in the house," he said.

"I'm going to go get Rebecca. Maybe I'll bring her out here for a while, okay?"

"Okay. Jonathan?"

"Mm-hm?"

"This is going to be, you know, hard for me to say. But I've been thinking. Do you ever, well, wonder about us? I mean, about you and me."

"I think about us," I said. "Sure I do."

"I don't mean just *think*. I don't just mean that. I mean, well, do you ever wonder why we always held back? It seems like we could have done so much more to make each other happy."

Even in an extreme condition, such direct talk was hard on him. His fingers kneaded the edge of the blanket, and his foot tapped dryly against the wicker chair leg.

"Well, we had a certain kind of relationship," I said. "It was pretty much what we both wanted, wasn't it?"

"I guess so. I guess it was. But lately I've been wondering, you know. I've been wondering, what were we waiting for?"

"I suppose we were waiting for our real lives to start. I think we probably made a mistake."

He drew a ragged breath. At the exact center of the web that stretched between the newel posts, a pretty yellow spider hung motionless.

"We did make a mistake," he said. "I mean, I think we probably did. I think I was in love with you, and I couldn't admit it. I was, I don't know. Too afraid to admit it. And now it just seems like such a waste."

I stood on the weathered boards atop my own purple shadow. I looked at him. He had an ancient, utterly dignified quality at that moment, an aspect neither old nor young, neither male nor female. His body was invisible under the thick folds of the blanket, and his eyes were brilliant in his colorless face. He could have been a sphinx posing a riddle.

I believed I knew the answer. Erich and I were never in love; we weren't meant to be lovers. We had missed no romantic opportunity. Instead we'd hidden out together, in our good sex and

317

undemanding companionship. We'd kept one another afloat while we waited. We might have been servants, two chaste balding men who'd given up their lives to vague ideals of obedience and order.

But I said, "I think I was probably in love with you, too."

I didn't want him to die untouched. If he died in that condition I might have to, too.

"You're lying," he said.

"I'm not."

I thought of my father in the desert, receiving nothing from me but empty reassurances. He had died on his way back from the mailbox, with a handful of catalogues and flyers. I'd had a letter for him, in my pocket.

"Yes, you are," Erich said.

I hesitated. Then I told him, "No, really. I think I was probably in love with you."

He nodded, in a cold fury. He was not comforted. An early moth, so white it was nearly translucent, more an agitation of air than a physical presence, whirred past.

"We could have done better than this, you and I," he said. "What was the matter with us?"

"I don't know," I said.

We didn't move or speak for at least a minute. We stared at each other in furious disbelief. "We're cowards," I said at last. "This wasn't a dramatic mistake we made. It was just a stupid little one that got out of hand. What do they call them? Sins of omission."

"I think maybe that's what bothers me most."

"Me, too," I said. And then, because there was nothing more to say, I went into the house to find Rebecca.

CLARE

Erich brought something new into the house. Or maybe he conjured up something old. Something that had been there all along. He rattled down the halls, skimmed failing breath from the dusty air. The plain facts of illness and death can seem remote as long as you don't smell the immaculate chalk of the medicines. As long as you don't see skin turning the color of clay.

Being a mother made certain things impossible, things I could have done almost without thinking in my other life. I couldn't deny Erich what he needed and at the same time I couldn't embrace him. I found that more or less against my will I'd become capable only, singularly, of protection. I suppose it was sentimental, though I didn't taste anything like sentiment in my mouth. I felt hard and clinical, glacial. For the first time I didn't think about myself. A district in my brain, that which I'd thought of as *me*, seemed to have been sucked clean. In its place was this steady uninflected drive to do what was needed. I fed Erich while the boys were at work, saw that he took his medicine, helped him to the toilet on the days he needed help. I spoke kindly to him. Nothing could have stopped me from doing that. But I didn't *care* about him. In a sense our relations were strictly business. I cared only, truly, for Rebecca, who was alive and growing. Erich had already passed partway out of the world. While his comfort and safety were vitally important to me his existence was not. Now

I better understand why mothers appear so often in stories as saints or as monsters. We are not human in the ordinary sense, at least not when our children are very small. We become monsters of care, inexorable, and if we occasionally lose track of the finer, imperishable points of the soul while ministering to the fragile body, that can't be helped.

I was alone most days with Rebecca and Erich. Now that the boys had Marlys and Gert they were able to get home more often. But, still, the bulk of my time was spent with a two-year-old and a dying man.

I rented movies and poured juice. I began toilet training Rebecca, and occasionally changed Erich's soiled sheets. He had passable days and worse days. On the bad ones he could be cranky with me. He could suddenly say "I *hate* apple juice, I'm just so sick of it, don't they have any other kind at the market?" He could complain about the movies I brought home. "Mrs. *Miniver*? God, is this all they had left?"

But he never lost patience with Rebecca. Sometimes, on the days he stayed in bed, the two of them watched videos together. I brought home *Dumbo*, *Snow White*, and anything involving the Muppets. Erich liked those movies, too. He didn't charm Rebecca as thoroughly as Jonathan did, but he held her interest. He had a singular ability to focus, and I suspect she felt secure with him. He could so perfectly imitate a man who was good with children. He let her boss him around. He performed, on demand, a particular spastic dance with a stuffed monkey she had mysteriously named Shippo while she turned a doll named Baby Lou upside-down and waggled its stiff plastic legs in the air. He agreed to all the games she invented, many of which involved passing a rubber dinosaur back and forth while reciting a long, ever-changing list of demands. He could do the voice of Kermit the Frog, which she seemed to find hilarious and slightly upsetting.

Sometimes when I brought them a snack I found them sitting together on Erich's bed, watching television, with toys scattered everywhere. Sometimes I had to catch my breath at the sight of them like that, Rebecca chattering and walking one of her mini-

ature farm animals over Erich's skinny knee or Erich absent-mind-
edly stroking her hair as they both watched cartoons. No matter
how he felt on a given day, he was always attentive to my daughter. His powers of concentration were formidable. He seemed to
have taken on a project: never to show this little girl any unpleasant
or mean-spirited behavior, never to be anything but pliant and
companionable in her presence. He was different from Jonathan.
He didn't love her. He liked her well enough. Being good with
her was one of the organizing principles around which he built
his days. He made it his job.

At first I felt it as a vague unrest that fluttered around in my
belly, halfway between nausea and pain. I believed at times that
I was developing an ulcer, or worse, though the doctor told me
it was just anxiety. Finally, after several months, I realized. I was
coming to a decision. Or a decision was coming to me. It was
growing inside me, almost against my conscious will.

It didn't reach its finished state until an afternoon in May, as I
was taking a nap with Rebecca. She'd grown balky about naps,
and would lie down in the afternoons only if I took her into
Bobby's and my bed and read to her from one of her books. She
was almost two and a half then. She'd developed obsessions with
several books, including one about a rabbit saying good night to
every article in his bedroom and another about a pig who finds a
magic bone. We'd read both books twice, and drifted off to sleep
together. I woke twenty minutes later to the sound of Rebecca's
voice. She lay beside me, telling herself a story. This, too, was a
recent habit. She could talk to herself for hours. I lay quietly,
listening.

"I go to the store," she said. "I got a *talking bone*. The girl never
saw it before. She picked up the bone and went to Bunny's house.
And Bunny was there, and Jonathan was there. And they said,
'My, my, my, what a fine little kitty.' And Jonathan took the
bone. He said, 'Now I'm going to make something good with
this.' And he made . . . *porridge*. It was very very good. And
Bunny said, um, and then Mommy and Bobby and Erich said.
And I gave Erich some salad, because he was sick. And Jonathan

had some, too. And then it was night, and Bunny had to go to bed. And then it was the next day, and the kitty is going to town. 'My my my,' the kitty said. Just imagine his surprise."

As I lay listening to her, my chest constricted in panic. I could feel the heat rising to my face. I couldn't tell at first why I was unnerved by what I heard. It was only Rebecca's usual stream of consciousness, the kind of babbling I'd been hearing from her for over a month. But slowly, while lying on the bed with her, I figured it out. She was coming into herself. She was emerging from her foggy self-involvement and beginning to comprehend the independent life of other people. Soon she'd leave her disembodied child-world. She'd remember things. She was a camera getting ready to shoot. *Click* a brown house with a blue door. *Click* her favorite toys. *Click* Jonathan coming to get her in the mornings. She'd carry those images around for the rest of her life.

What if she came into her full consciousness as Erich died and Jonathan started to get sick? What would it do to her if her earliest memories revolved around the decline and eventual disappearance of the people she most adored?

One morning a few weeks later I was in bed with Rebecca, Bobby, and Jonathan. It was an ordinary morning. Rebecca had woken up in a good humor, and was telling herself an elaborate story about Bunny and a flying elephant. In a moment Bobby would shuffle downstairs to start the coffee. Erich was still asleep down the hall and Jonathan sat beside me with the sheet pulled over his chest.

Bobby said, "After work I've got to replace some shingles. Did you see how many have blown off? That roof has about, like, had it."

"We should just get a new one," I said. "Let's start calling roofers."

"When the place is more or less in shape," Jonathan said, "I want to have my mother out again. I figure she'd have an easier time believing in my life if she saw more of it."

"Parents, parents," I said. "You know, I've been thinking. I should really take Miss Rebecca to Washington for a few days, to see my mother."

Bobby got up to make the coffee, a half second before I knew he was going to. "Why not, you know, invite her up here?" he said.

"Because she's sixty-five and not the least bit liberal. Believe me, you don't want Amelia up here, going on about our life-style. That's what she thinks we have. Not a life. A life-style."

"Don't you think she'd better get used to it?" Jonathan said.

"Sweetheart, my mother hasn't gotten used to my having *breasts* yet. The sight of me naked still makes her uneasy. Trust me. It's better to take Rebecca down there for a few days."

"Well, you know, if you need to," Bobby said, and went off on his morning errand.

"Only a few days," Jonathan said. "Right? Like two or three?"

I nodded, and stroked Rebecca's hair. I wondered if she might feel the tension in my hand, and start crying. But she babbled on, undisturbed. Our inner deceits don't create much residue in this world.

I only half knew what I was up to. It didn't become a plan until I found myself doing it, and then it seemed I was following a procedure I'd known about for months or even years. I packed Rebecca's things: her clothes and a few essential toys, her stroller and high chair. As Jonathan helped me load the car he said, "Honey, you're only going for a few days. Not till the millennium."

"I want to be prepared," I said. "It's important to avoid shopping with my mother at all costs. If I run out of diapers, she'll take me to Saks."

"Doesn't sound so bad to me," Jonathan said. He wore a denim jacket with Albert Einstein's gentle white face pinned to the lapel. A swarm of reddish-black tulips had sprouted on the lawn. A crazy meadowlark whose nest was nearby raged at us from the lowest branches of the oak. I lifted the stroller into the trunk, and Jonathan arranged the diaper bag around it.

"Guilt," I said. "Even my guilt over my mother's money feels decadent sometimes. It's better to just avoid it. Not get myself into a position where she can buy me a five-hundred-dollar dress that makes me look like an astronaut's wife. It's better to just lay in supplies and stay home with her."

I wondered if I was explaining too much. I didn't want to sound like a criminal whose alibi is suspiciously perfect, her movements too intricately accounted for.

"Whatever you say," he answered. There was no mistrust in his voice.

He closed the lid of the trunk. "I'll miss you," he said.

In another moment, Bobby would come out of the house with Rebecca. I reached over and took hold of Jonathan's sleeve.

"Listen," I said. "I'm sorry."

"What?"

"Oh, you know. I'm sorry I'm such a coward about my mother. Next time I'll bring her up here. You're right. She's going to have to get used to it."

"Well, parents are tough. Believe me, I know about that," he said.

"I'm just really sorry," I said. I could hear the possibility of tears in my own voice.

"Honey, what's the matter?"

At that moment, I felt sure he knew. I shook my head. "Nothing," I said.

He gave me a reassuring little squeeze. "Silly old Clare," he said. "Good old crazy thing." In fact, he didn't know. He still hadn't developed the habit of loss. He believed his life would get fatter and fatter. Maybe that was the fundamental flaw in his perception. Maybe that's what prevented him from falling in love.

"Oh, quit with that 'good old crazy thing' shit, all right? I'm an adult. I'm not some playmate of yours."

"Oops. Sorry."

"Really, Jonathan, I just wish you'd—"

"What? You wish I'd what?"

"I don't know. How long do you plan on being a boy? All your life?"

"As opposed to becoming a girl?" he said.

"As opposed to . . . oh, never mind. I'm being a bitch today. I could feel it the minute I woke up."

"Listen, will you call me when you get there? So I know you're okay?"

"Sure. Of course I will."

We stood for a moment, looking around at the scenery as if we were new to it. As if we had just stepped out of our Winnebago to stretch our legs and marvel at this particular stretch of a national park.

"Aren't things supposed to be simpler than this?" I asked.

"Bobby says it's a new world. He says we can do anything we can imagine."

"That's because Bobby's a deluded asshole. I mean that only in the most complimentary sense."

I realized I was still holding on to the sleeve of Jonathan's jacket. When I let go, the denim held the shape of my grip.

"I'm going to go see what's keeping him," I said. "If Rebecca and I don't get moving soon, we'll hit the New York traffic."

"Okay."

Jonathan waited by the car, hands deep in the pockets of his khakis, sun glinting on his pale hair. I turned to him when I reached the porch. He gave me an ironic, sisterly smile and I went into the house.

Bobby was coming down the stairs with Rebecca. "I just about gave up on you," I said. "If we're not past Manhattan by one o'clock—"

He put his fingers to his lips. "Erich's sleeping," he said. "He's had a hard morning."

I took Rebecca from him. She was having a bad morning, too. "I don't *want* to," she said.

"You got everything together?" Bobby whispered.

"Mm-hm. Car's all packed. Say goodbye to Erich for me, okay?"

"Okay."

"I *don't want* to," Rebecca said.

Bobby stood on the bottom stair, his paunch slightly straining the fabric of his T-shirt. At that moment he looked so innocent and well-meaning. I could have slugged him for being such a sap; such a guileless optimistic character. I could see him old, shuffling along in bedroom slippers. Claiming that the convalescent home was really fine and perfect. They had chocolate pudding on Fridays, he'd say. The maid's name is Harriet, she brings me pictures of her kids.

"Listen," I said. "I've got a wild idea. Do you want to come with me?"

"Huh?"

"Right now. Just throw a few things in a bag and come along."

"I thought, you know, your mother didn't approve of me. Of us."

"Fuck my mother. Do you want to come?"

"We've got to take care of Erich," he said.

"Jonathan can take care of Erich. It's time he started to take more responsibility, don't you think? The two of them will manage all right together. They'll be fine on their own."

"Clare, what's up? What's got into you?"

I held the baby. I said, "Nothing. Never mind. I'm just a good old crazy thing."

I carried Rebecca out the door, and Bobby followed me to the car. As I strapped Rebecca into her car seat she began fussing and whimpering. Eventually the motion of the car would lull her but for a while she'd be inconsolable. I braced myself for her wails.

"Bye, boys," I said.

"No," Rebecca said from her car seat. "No, no, no, no, no."

They both kissed me, told me to drive carefully. They kissed Rebecca. Their attentions were all it took to push her over the edge. She opened her mouth, nearly gagging on a howl she'd been building up to since breakfast.

"Bye, Miss Rebecca," Jonathan said through the window. "Oh, we love you even if you are sporadically monstrous. Have fun with your horrible grandmother."

"Take care of yourselves," I said. I backed the car out of the drive. I waved, and the boys waved back. They stood close together, in front of the dilapidated house. As I pulled away, Jonathan suddenly came running toward the car. I thought for a moment he had something to tell me, but then I realized he was only going to run alongside for a few yards, foolish and faithful as a dog. I drove on. He caught up and briefly kept pace, blowing kisses. I waved again, one last time. Before I reached the turn I looked in the rearview mirror and saw both of them. Jonathan and Bobby, standing in the middle of the road. They looked like a pair of beatniks, sloppily dressed in a remote, unimportant place. In their sunglasses and T-shirts and unruly hair they looked like they were standing at the brink of the old cycle: the 1960s about to explode around them, a long storm of love and rage and thwarted expectations. Bobby put his arm over Jonathan's shoulder. They both waved.

The road was silver in the morning sun. It was a perfect day for traveling. Rebecca kept up her wails in the back seat. Miles ticked away under the wheels. I knew our lives wouldn't be easy. I pictured us together in San Francisco or Seattle, moving into an apartment where strangers argued on the other side of the wall. I'd push her stroller down unfamiliar streets, looking for the grocery store. She wouldn't think of our lives as odd—not until she got older, and began to realize that other girls lived differently. Then she'd start hating me for being alone, for being old and eccentric, for having failed to raise her with a back yard and a rec room and a father. For a moment, I thought of turning back. The impulse passed through me, and if I'd been able to make a U-turn I might have done it. But we were on a straight stretch of highway. I followed the double yellow line until the impulse was absorbed by gathering distance. I kept my hands on the wheel, and didn't think of anything but the next mile and the next. I glanced back at Rebecca. She was finally calming with the motion of the car. Before she went under, she looked at me balefully, her nose running and her cotton hat askew, and said one word. She said, "Mommy." She pronounced it with a distinct edge of despair.

"Someday you'll thank me, sweetie," I said. "Or maybe you won't."

Now I'm alone with this. This love. The love that cuts like an X-ray, that has no true element of kindness or mercy.

Forgive me, boys. I seem to have gotten what I wanted, after all. A baby of my own, a direction to drive in. The house and restaurant may not be much to offer in trade but that's what I've got to give you.

I turned off the highway and headed west.

BOBBY

THE MOON is following us, a white crescent in a powdery blue sky. We are driving home from the grocery store: Erich, Jonathan, and me. Erich these days is a slippery presence. He comes and goes. If I wasn't driving I might hold him to keep him from floating out of the car. Instead, I say to Jonathan, "How's he doing back there?"

Jonathan looks into the back seat. "You okay, Erich?" he asks.

Erich doesn't answer. He is suffering a fit of absence. Who knows what he hears? "I think he's okay," Jonathan tells me. I nod and drive on. Farms pass on either side of the road. Cows go about their ordinary business, steady as history itself.

At the house we help Erich out of the car, guide him up the porch stairs. He smiles with the confused beatitude of the ancient. He could be pleased that we're home again. He could be remembering a toy given him when he was four. We put the groceries away in the kitchen.

"How about a bath?" I say.

"Do you think he needs one?" Jonathan asks.

"I think he'd like one," I answer.

We guide him upstairs, start the bathwater. Steam puts a sparkle on the chipped white tile. While we wait for the tub to fill we help Erich off with his clothes. He neither resists nor participates. His face takes on its boggled look, something different from expressionless. When he loses track of himself he drifts into this look of mute incomprehension, as if he can't quite believe the emptiness he sees. It is astonishment divorced from dread and wonder. It is nothing like a newborn's face.

When he's naked we sit him down on the toilet lid. The tub fills slowly. Erich sits with quiet obedience, hands hung limp between the stalks of his thighs. Jonathan reaches over and touches his hair.

"I'm going to put some music on," I say.

"Okay." Jonathan stays beside Erich, supporting his shoulder bones with one hand. With the other he keeps administering ginger, comforting little swipes at Erich's hair.

I turn on the radio in the bedroom. It is tuned to an oldies station, the music of our childhood. Right now, Van Morrison sings "Madame George." I turn the volume up so it will carry into the bathroom.

When I get back Jonathan says, "This is a great song. This has always been one of my favorites."

"Care to dance?" I ask him.

He looks at me uncertainly, wondering if I'm making a joke.

"Come on," I say, and I hold my arms out. "Erich won't fall. Will you, Erich?"

Erich stares in the direction of his own bare feet. Cautiously, Jonathan pulls his hands away. Erich does not tip over. After a moment Jonathan walks into my arms and we do a waltz. Our shoes clop on the bare tiles. I can feel the agitation of Jonathan's continuing life. It quivers along his skin like a network of plucked wires. I run my hand up and down the buttons of his spine. Van sings, "Say goodbye to Madame George. Dry your eyes for Madame George."

"Bobby?" Jonathan says.

"Uh-huh?"

"Oh, never mind. I was going to say something stupid like 'I'm scared,' but of course I am. We all are."

"Well, yes. I mean, I guess we are."

We dance to the end of the song. I would like to say that Erich smiles, or nods his head in rhythm. It would be good to think he joins us in that small way. But he is lost in his own mystery,

330

staring into a hole that keeps opening and opening. When we're through dancing we help him up, and lower him into the bath. Together, we scrub his head and his skinny neck. We wash the hollow of his chest, and the deep sockets under his arms. Briefly, he smiles. At the sensation of bathing, or at something more private than that.

After his bath, we put him to bed. It's late afternoon. Jonathan says, "I'll buzz down to the restaurant and do the reordering, all right?" I tell him I'll replace the missing shingles.

We go about our errands. It's a normal afternoon, steaming along toward evening. Jonathan drives to town, I prop the ladder against the house and climb up with an armload of new cedar shingles. They will look raw and yellow against the old coffee-colored ones. The old shingles, strewn with pine needles, are crisp and splintery under my hands and feet.

From the roof I can see a distance. I can see our small holdings, and the fields and mountains beyond. I can see a red convertible gliding past. In the grass near the porch lies a toy of Rebecca's, a doll named Baby Lou. It lies grinning with stony rapture at the sky. I can't believe Clare forgot to pack it.

I pass through a moment of panic. I know Clare and Rebecca aren't coming back. I'd have said something before they left but I couldn't risk it—what if Jonathan had decided to go along? I can't let the house break up. It's taken too long to build. Jonathan and I belong here, together. Clare has taken Rebecca to the world of the living—its noise and surprises, its risk of disappointment. She's probably right to have done that. It's where Rebecca should be. We here are in the other world, a quieter place, more prone to forgiveness. I followed my brother into this world and I've never left it, not really.

I have work to do. I have a roof to fix.

The panic passes.

Rebecca will be back someday, and the house will be waiting for her. It's hers. It isn't much—a termite-gnawed frame building remade in small pieces, with the work of inexperienced hands. It isn't much but it stands now and will still stand when she's twenty. Now, right now, I can see her. It's as clear as a window opened onto the future. What I see is a woman with light brown hair, no

331

beauty by the world's standards but the owner of a sly grace and a steadfast, unapologetic way of filling her skin. I can see her come to stand on the porch of a house she's inherited. A house she never asked for, a house she can't quite think what to do with. I can see her there, standing in a winter coat, breathing bright steam into the brilliant air. That's all I see. It's not a significant vision. But I see her with surprising clarity. I see her boots on the floorboards, and the winter crackle of her hair. I see the way her jaw cleaves the frigid light as she stands before this unwanted gift. I touch my own jaw. I kneel there, on the roof, feeling the plain creaturely jut of my lower skull. Time is passing, and I get to work. The hammer makes a metallic, steady kind of music that shivers up and down the framework of this house. I hammer one shingle into place. I hammer another.

Late that night, Jonathan wakes me by touching my hair. I open my eyes and see his face, bright in the bedroom darkness, so close his breathing tickles my cheek. He puts a finger to his lips, and beckons. I follow him out into the hall. The dots on his boxer shorts swim in the darkness. He is wearing only the shorts; I am in Jockeys and an undershirt. He beckons again and I follow him downstairs. Shadows cling to the complications of his back.

In the living room he says, "Sorry to wake you up like this. But there's a job I need your help with."

I ask what kind of job needs doing at midnight. By way of answering, he picks an object up off the table beside the sofa. I take a moment to focus—it's the box with Ned's ashes in it. Holding the box in both hands, he goes to the front door.

"Come on," he says.

We walk out onto the porch and stop at the rail, looking into the deep black like two passengers on an ocean liner. On moonless nights this house could be afloat; it could be sailing through space. All that offers itself from the surrounding night is a starfield and the restlessness of trees.

Jonathan says, "I've changed my mind about waiting to scatter these. It's suddenly occurred to me that this is as good a place as any."

"You mean you want to drop Ned's ashes now? Right here?"

"Mm-hm. I want us both to do it."

"Um, don't you think Alice would want to be here, too? I mean, shouldn't we have some kind of ceremony?"

"Nope. Mom will be glad to hear I've taken care of it. She's not much for ceremonies these days."

"Well," I say.

"Let's go." He steps down off the porch, and I go with him. Walking onto the grass is like stepping off into space proper. I move with a light-headed, space-walk feeling.

"Jon," I say. "Jonny, maybe we should wait to do this. I mean, don't you think you'll be sorry you didn't plan something?"

"If you don't want to, I'll do it myself," he says. He walks several paces toward the road, which is a dull silver stain on the darkness. Tree frogs put out their clicks and groans. The Seven Sisters pulse overhead in a small clustered storm of stars. I follow him. As we cross the road I am reminded of myself in childhood, following my brother into the cemetery to celebrate our heroic future together. Jonathan moves with a determination that is both ritualistic and slightly crazed. He is wearing only those polka-dot boxers as galaxies explode overhead.

An empty alfalfa field stretches beyond the road. Alfalfa brushes and sighs against our bare legs. Although I know from daylight that this field ends in brush and an abandoned shed, all I can see at this moment is an ocean of alfalfa. As we walk Jonathan says, "I just realized how ludicrous it is to hold on to my father's ashes until I find some sort of perfect home for them. I've decided this is a perfect place. This field right here. I don't even know who owns it, do you?"

"No."

"Oh, Bobby. I wanted to be part of something that wasn't dying."

"You are."

"No I'm not. I thought I was, but really, I'm not."

"Jon," I say. "Jonny."

He waits, but I can't tell him. I can't tell him what I know—we both have devotions outside the world of the living. It's what separates us from Clare, and from other people. It's what's held

333

us together as the ordinary run of circumstance has said we should grow up and part.

After a while he says, "So I think it's time to get rid of these. Right now. Here. This seems like a good enough spot."

We are so far into the field that the darkness has closed behind us, blotting out the road and house. All we can see is alfalfa. Crickets make their racket and mosquitoes swarm around our heads, unable to believe their luck. We stand there in a starry, buzzing darkness complete as the end of the world.

"The lid's a little tricky," he says. "Just a minute. There."

He sets the box on the ground. "This is hard to believe," he says. "My father used to carry me on his shoulders. He once tickled me until I peed in my pants. I still remember how bad he felt. And embarrassed. And a little indignant."

"Do you want to, like, say a few words?" I ask.

"Oh, I guess I've already said them. Listen, will you reach in at the same time I do?"

"Okay. If you want me to."

We both bend over. "I'm going to count to three," he says. "One, two, three."

We reach in. There's a plastic bag inside the box, and we work our hands through the plastic. Ned's ashes have a velvet, suety feel. They are studded with chips of bone. When we touch them, Jonathan draws in a breath.

"Oh," he says. "Okay. I think that was the worst part. Have you got some?"

"Uh-huh."

We stand with handfuls of ash and bone. "She was right," he says. "It really isn't much more of him than a pair of his old shoes. Okay. Here goes."

In silence, we sift the ashes into the field. We walk small circles, distributing. It's too dark to see them fall. They disappear from our hands. If they make any sound it's drowned out by the insects and the rustle of alfalfa.

We go back to the box again and again. We don't speak until the ashes are gone.

"All right," Jonathan says. "Dad, I got this far. This was the best I could do."

334

He picks up the box and we head into the area of darkness where we think the house must lie. We've lost our bearings scattering the ashes, and we miss the house by some distance. We must walk along the road for nearly a quarter mile. We give a passing Volvo something to wonder about—two men walking a country road in their underwear, holding an empty box.

"Bobby?" Jonathan says.

"Yeah?"

"You know why I decided to do this all of a sudden?"

"No."

"After Clare and Rebecca left I started thinking about how I didn't want them to come back to Erich doing so badly upstairs and my father's ashes sitting on a shelf in the living room. It suddenly seemed like too much death in the house. That's when I decided to put the ashes out to pasture. I mean, what was I saving them for?"

"Well, nothing, I guess."

"I want to paint Rebecca's room," he says. "It's too dingy in there. What if we picked up some paint tomorrow, after work? Something gaudy that she'll be nuts about, like bright pink. Nobody told me a baby would have such bad taste."

I can hear his breathing. What there is of starlight shines gray and faltering on his bare skin. We walk for several minutes in silence.

"Listen," he says.

"Uh-huh."

"If something happens to me, this will be an all right place to put my ashes, too. If and when the time comes, I want you to tell my mother that. Tell her I had a last request, and this was it. God, if my father and I both end up strewn around here, where will my mother go when she dies?"

"She could come here, too."

"Well, she's always getting dragged someplace she doesn't want to go. Why should things be any different after she's dead, right?"

"Right. I mean, I guess so. This is where we all belong now."

"What if that were true?" he says. "Wouldn't it be something?"

We don't talk anymore. There is too much to say. We travel the last short distance, invisibly watched by night animals. It is

like a dream, one of those childhood dreams of public embarrassment, to be walking on a public road in my frayed underwear.
But, in this particular dream, I feel no embarrassment. I'm just
here, undressed on a country road, with a dark wind blowing
around me. Ned's ashes are mingling with the ground in a miniature world of ants and armored, lumbering beetles. Erich sleeps
his skimming sleep, intricately lit by dreams. There is a beauty in
the world, though it's harsher than we ever expect it to be. It's as
unlike the autumn farm on my family's dining-room wall as a
bone is unlike a man or a woman. Somewhere on this continent
Clare and Rebecca are sleeping, in a motel or a friend's living
room. As the blue silhouette of the house appears ahead of us I
remember that home is also a place to escape. This is ours; we
have it to run from and we have it to return to.

It's black enough right now to see the future—the cold mornings
and the long nights, the daily music. Jonathan and I are here to
maintain a present, so people can return to it when their futures
thin out on them. We've been on our way here for a long time.
We start up the drive and I see something riffle the curtain in the
bedroom window. For a moment I think Clare has come back. I
grab Jonathan's shoulder.

"What?" he says. "What is it?"

"Nothing. It's nothing. Never mind."

Between the impulse and the touch, I've come to my senses.
Clare isn't back. What I saw was just the wind blowing. It was
either the wind or the spirit of the house itself, briefly unsettled
by our nocturnal absence but too old to be surprised by the errands
born from the gap between what we can imagine and what we in
fact create.

JONATHAN

O NE AFTERNOON in April, several months before Erich died, Bobby and I took him out to a pond we knew of, deep in the woods. We drove ten miles to reach it, a circle of shimmering blue-black water ringed by pines. That early in the year, we had it all to ourselves. "First swim of the season," Bobby said as we got out of the car. "It's a tradition with us."

"Beautiful," Erich said. He was frail by then. His legs hurt him, and he had trouble walking—the disease was racing through him more quickly than it moved in most people. His face had altered during the winter. His eyes seemed subtly enlarged, and his jaw was squarer. I suppose the shape of his skull had started to emerge.

"We haven't been out since last summer," I said. Bobby and I helped Erich negotiate the short path that led down a slope to the crescent of earth and pine needles that served as a beach. The lake was almost unnaturally still—it was too early for bees or dragon-flies or the reflections of leaves. Less than a month ago, scraps of snow had lingered brightly in the shadows. Now the tree trunks were wet and vivid as animals' fur and the sun was warm but winter-white, still shy of the deeper colors it would take on by May. The pond reflected a single cigar-shaped cloud that stretched from bank to bank. We stood on the narrow beach, and Bobby skipped a stone along the water's surface, which was smooth and placid as slate.

"You go swimming here in the summer?" Erich asked.

"Mm-hm," I said. "It gets crowded then, it's the local Coney Island. It's a real sight. There are babies and dogs, and eighty-year-olds swimming naked."

He nodded solemnly. I regretted having referred to a future season, one he might not see. I was still getting used to the particular system of courtesy that prevails among the sick. It was like playing host to an impoverished relation, when your own business is still paying off. Only through his unprosperous presence do you realize how much your own wealth has to do with almost everything you do and say.

"So, are we going to go in?" he asked.

"It's freezing," Bobby said.

"You said first swim of the season. You said it was a tradition."

"Figure of speech," I told him. "We're just here to pay our respects. It needs at least another month to warm up."

Although I'd assumed he was merely playing along, I could tell from his voice how much Erich in fact wanted to go for a swim. He couldn't trust the seasons—by the time it was warmer, he might not be able to walk at all. And even if he could manage it, he was far too inhibited to show his compromised body to the crowds of strangers who'd begin gathering here once swimming weather had arrived.

"Do you really want to?" I asked him.

"Yes," he said, in a tone of childish insistence.

"It'd be a good way to get pneumonia," Bobby said.

"Let's do it," I said. "Come on, the water's okay. There hasn't been ice on it for at least three weeks."

"You're crazy," Bobby said.

"That's a fact. Come on, Erich. Let's go."

"You can't," Bobby said. "It's too goddamn cold."

I started taking off my clothes, and Erich joined in. We were not graceful or smooth in our undressing—there was no hint of sex in it. Or whatever there was of sex was as deeply buried as that which prevails among ballplayers before a game, a love of the physical self generous and unlimited enough to extend to other bodies as well, simply because they are present and more or less alike. As Bobby informed us of our folly we worked our way out

340

of our jackets and boots, tossing them onto the ground. We stripped naked in the warm white light. Finally Bobby gave in and began undressing as well, because he refused to be excluded from a mistake he could not prevent.

While Bobby got his clothes off, Erich and I stood together, nude, facing the water. We were too shy to look directly at one another, though I saw enough of him from my sidelong position. His arms and legs were knobbed at the joints, peppered with small purple splotches. His chest and abdomen also bore the scattering of marks, like old tattoos that had blurred into the skin. I held myself through a wave of revulsion, not only because his body was so changed but because his entwinement with the disease was so apparent. In jeans and sweatshirts he looked sick but ordinary; naked he looked like sickness itself. He looked as if his humanity was being eaten away and replaced by something else.

I reached over and took his hand, to protect both of us. In doing so, I caught up with my own gesture. I felt for him, a frightened soul no better prepared to face his mortality than I would be if the disease started working on me now, this moment. My face burned.

"Ready?" I said.

"Ready."

We stepped into the water together while Bobby was getting out of his jeans. The first impression was of warmth—an inch of temperate water floated on the surface. But when we penetrated that, the water beneath was numbingly cold.

"Oh," Erich exclaimed as it lapped his ankles.

"Maybe this isn't a very good idea after all," I said. "I mean, it can't be good for you."

"No," he said. "Let's just go a little ways in. I want to—well, I just want to."

"All right," I said. I was still holding his hand. For the first time I felt intimate with him, though we had known one another for years and had made love hundreds of times. We shuffled ahead, taking tiny steps on the sandy bottom. Each new quarter-inch of flesh exposed to water was agony. The sand itself felt like granular ice under our feet.

Bobby splashed out to us. "Crazy," he said. "Goddamn crazy. Erich, you got two minutes in here, and then I'm taking you out."

He meant it. He would lift Erich bodily and carry him to shore if necessary. Since he and I were boys together, he had made it his business to rescue fools from icy water.

Still, we had two minutes, and we advanced. The water was clear—nets of light fluttered across our bare feet, and minnows darted away from us, visible only by their shadows skimming along the bottom. I glanced at Bobby, who was grave and steady as a steamship. He was a reverse image of Erich; time had thickened him. His belly was broad and protuberant now, and his little copper-colored medallion of pectoral hair had darkened and spread, sending tendrils up onto his shoulders and down along his back. I myself was losing hair—my hairline was at least two inches higher than it had been ten years ago. I could feel with my fingertips a rough circle at the back of my head where the growth was thinner.

"This is good," Erich said. "I mean, well, it feels very good."

It didn't feel good. It was torture. But I thought I understood —it was a strong sensation, one that came from the outer world rather than the inner. He was saying goodbye to a certain kind of pain.

"You're shivering," Bobby said.

"One more minute. Then we'll go in."

"Right. One more minute, exactly."

We stood in the water together, watching the unbroken line of trees on the opposite bank. That was all that happened. Bobby and I took Erich for what would in fact turn out to be his last swim, and waded in only to our knees. But as I stood in the water, something happened to me. I don't know if I can explain this. Something cracked. I had lived until then for the future, in a state of continuing expectation, and the process came suddenly to a stop while I stood nude with Bobby and Erich in a shallow platter of freezing water. My father was dead and I myself might very well be dying. My mother had a new haircut, a business and a young lover; a new life that suited her better than her old one had. I had not fathered a child but I loved one as if I was her father—I knew what that was like. I wouldn't say I was happy. I was nothing so simple as happy. I was merely present, perhaps for the first time in my adult life. The moment was unextraordinary. But I had the moment, I had it completely. It inhabited me. I realized that if I died soon I would have known this, a connection with my life, its errors and cockeyed successes. The chance to be one of three naked men standing in a small body of clear water. I would not die unfulfilled because I'd been here, right here and nowhere else. I didn't speak. Bobby announced that the minute was up, and we took Erich back to shore.

"The Poem That Took the Place of a Mountain," by Wallace Stevens. Copyright 1952 by Wallace Stevens. Reprinted from *The Collected Poems of Wallace Stevens*, by permission of Faber and Faber Ltd.

"Madam George," written by Van Morrison. Copyright © 1969 Songs of PolyGram International Inc. (3500 West Olive Avenue, Suite 200, Burbank, CA 91505). International copyright secured. All rights reserved. Used by permission.

"Aqualung" by Jennie Andersen and Ian Andersen. Copyright © 1971 Chrysalis Music (ASCAP). All rights in the U.S.A. and Canada administered by Chrysalis Music (ASCAP). Used by permission. International copyright secured. All rights reserved.

"Dr. Feelgood" by Aretha Franklin and Ted White. Copyright © 1967 Pronto Music Inc. and 14th Hour Music, Inc. All rights reserved. Used by permission.

"America" by Stephen Sondheim and Leonard Bernstein. Copyright © 1957 by Amberson, Inc., Copyright renewed. Used by permission of Jalni Publications and Boosey and Hawkes, Inc., sole agent.

"Woodstock" by Joni Mitchell. Copyright © 1969 Siquomb Publishing Co. All rights reserved. Used by permission.